Orientation to the Theatre

THIRD EDITION

Orientation to the Theatre

Theodore W. Hatlen

University of California, Santa Barbara

Prentice-Hall, Inc., *Englewood Cliffs, New Jersey 07632*

Library of Congress Cataloging in Publication Data

Hatlen, Theodore W
    Orientation to the theater.

    Bibliography: p.
    Includes index.
    1. Drama. 2. Theater. I. Title.
PN1655.H3 1981   808.2   80-23214
ISBN 0-13-642108-3 (pbk.)

Printed in the United States of America

10   9   8   7   6   5   4   3   2   1

Editorial/production supervision by Joan Lee and Marina Harrison
Interior design by Judy Winthrop and Joan Lee
Cover design by Jayne Conte
Cover photo by Adam Woolfitt/Woodfin Camp & Associates
Manufacturing buyer: Edmund W. Leone

Text and photo acknowledgments appear on page 353

Prentice-Hall International, Inc., *London*
Prentice-Hall of Australia Pty. Limited, *Sydney*
Prentice-Hall of Canada, Ltd., *Toronto*
Prentice-Hall of India Private Limited, *New Delhi*
Prentice-Hall of Japan, Inc., *Tokyo*
Prentice-Hall of Southeast Asia Pte. Ltd., *Singapore*
Whitehall Books Limited, *Wellington, New Zealand*

**For Dorcas, my wife,
with thanks**

Contents

FOUR

Melodrama   77

FIVE

Comedy   98

SIX

Realism and Its Derivatives   131

SEVEN

Theatricalism and the New Theater 159

EIGHT

The Director 204

NINE

The Actor 231

Frontispieces

Chapter 1: *In* Oedipus Rex *of Sophocles, the King blinds and exiles himself for his crimes against his father and mother. He then finds sanctuary and tranquility in* Oedipus at Colonus. *(D. A. Harissiadis.)*

Chapter 2: *In Pinter's* The Birthday Party, *a pair of strangers bedevil and threaten Stanley, an innocuous appearing young man who has tried to find a quiet sanctuary at a summer resort. University of Missouri, Columbia. Directed by Weldon Durham.*

Chapter 3: *In* King Lear *the protagonist experiences terrible suffering before finding release and reconciliation at the end. The storm on the heath echoes Lear's own disordered nature. Morris Carnovsky as Lear. (Courtesy of American Shakespeare Festival in Connecticut.)*

Chapter 4: *James O'Neill made a fortune playing the hero in* The Count of Monte Cristo *for seventeen years, giving 5,817 performances. Here he appears in the duel scene set in a forest of painted trees. (Harvard Theater Collection.)*

Chapter 5: *Orgon, in Moliere's* Tartuffe, *becomes an object of derision because of his gullibility in accepting the imposter into his home. In this scene, Elmire persuades her husband, Orgon, to hide under the table while she pretends to encourage Tartuffe's advances. University of West Virginia. Directed by John Whitty, designed by Gary Daines. (Courtesy of University of West Virginia.)*

Chapter 6: *The realist brought to the stage the environment of the parlor and the domestic problems of daily life. In Ibsen's* A Doll's House *Nora shocked many theatergoers by walking out on her husband and children. University of Toledo. Directed by George Back and designed by William R. Smith. (Jimmie Robinson, courtesy of University of Toledo.)*

Chapter 7: *Beckett's* Waiting for Godot *was a pivotal play of the post-World War II theater. In this landmark of absurdist drama, Estragon and Vladimir dramatize the act of waiting. University of California, Santa Barbara. Directed by Frederick Thon. (Will Swalling, University of California, Santa Barbara.)*

Chapter 8: *Directing an ancient play in a Greek theater was no simple task, especially in a play like* The Suppliants *by Aeschylus: the director had to organize the singing, dancing, action, and blocking of actors and a chorus of fifty in the enormous acting area, the orchestra. Modern revival directed by A. Solomos at the theater in Epidaurus. (D. A. Harissiadis.)*

Chapter 9: *Sean O'Casey creates marvelous acting roles in his plays, such as these three in* Juno and the Paycock. *Walter Matthau as "Captain" Jack Boyle, Maureen Stapleton as Juno, and Jack Lemmon as "Joxer" Daly. Mark Taper Forum, Los Angeles. (Steven Keull, courtesy of Mark Taper Forum.)*

Chapter 10: *Eugene Lee's enormous setting for Sweeney Todd suggests the interior of a nineteenth century foundry with its complex mechanical equipment that includes movable catwalks, platforms, staircases, and set pieces including a large oven. The demon barber wields his lethal razor in his second level shop equipped with a trick chair and trap door that dispatches his victims to his confederate in the bakery below. (Martha Swope.)*

Chapter 11: *The fourth-century B.C. theater at Epidaurus where the Greek National Theater produces a festival of revival of ancient plays each summer. The photograph shows the enormous theatron (capacity 16,000), the sizable orchestra circle (22 meters across), and the temporary scenic background. The solid bank of spectators is not separated by architectural barriers and attention is focused on the orchestra—the acting area. (D. A. Harissiadis.)*

Chapter 12: *The audience gathers for a performance in the Olivier Theater, a part of the National Theater, London.*

Preface

Theatrical production, like all creative expression, is a reminder that a culture is not to be judged by its material accomplishments alone, but also by the aspirations and ideals that motivate conduct. In dealing with significant choices and actions, dramatists have at their disposal special means of illuminating the human condition. Thus a play is more than an evening's diversion in the theater, more than pages of a text; it is a personal statement of the playwright and a clue to the culture that produced it. The objective of this work is to provide students with the tools of analysis that will give them insight into the total imaginative process that makes up theater.

I wish to express my gratitude to my colleague, William Reardon, and to my students over the years from whom I have learned so much. I am grateful to the following persons and institutions for their cooperation in the preparation of this book: Werner Hecht of the Berliner Ensemble; Dr. Jaromir Svoboda of the Prague National Theater; Dr. Eckehart Nölle of the Munich Theatermuseum; Jerzy Grotowski of the Polish Laboratory Theater; the Victoria and Albert Museum; the New York Public Library; Dimitrios A. Harissiadis; Will Swalling; and to my associates and colleagues in regional and educational theaters for their generosity in supplying photographs of their works.

And for assistance in preparing the manuscript, my thanks to Peggy Mathews, Andree Steele, Hanni Scheib, and Dorcas Hatlen.

Orientation to the Theatre

ONE
The
Background

The time: Sixth century B.C. It is the vintage season.

The place: A circular threshing floor of hard-packed earth just outside the city wall in Icaria, near Marathon.

The cast: A chorus of fifty men and boys performing before their fellow citizens.

The onlookers gather about the circle, some stand at the sides, but most of them sit on the sloping hillside. All eyes are on the chorus singing and dancing in unison—their voices clear and bright in the crisp morning air, their familiar steps performed with an easy grace, the flow of the dance and the rhythm of the music and movement felt by all who watch.

Suddenly, a solitary figure breaks away from the chorus and mounts an altar stone in the center of the circle. The crowd is startled when he begins to speak, his voice cutting off the chant of the chorus. Instead of the cadence of the dancing and singing, he speaks in the accents of a storyteller recalling the adventures of an ancient hero. The sunlight catches the chalky white makeup of his face; his body is animated and his voice is charged with emotion. This is the hero himself brought by the audacious act of impersonation from the distant past into the living present. This is no ordinary storyteller.

The wounded hero is carried by the chorus during the exodus from the playing circle in Hippolytus *as performed by the Greek National Theater at Epidaurus. Directed by Spyros A. Evangelatos.*

The chorus, momentarily transfixed by the miraculous appearance of the hero, now draws toward him as he enacts the ordeal of suffering. He seems to be wounded, he struggles mightily and dies. The chorus responds in mimetic action, sometimes singing and dancing, bodies and voices following the hero. During his suffering the chorus sings a hymn of supplication, and when he dies, they gather about the altar in lamentation, take up his body and move in a solemn recessional circling the ring while the onlookers are involuntarily caught up in the stirring atmosphere of the performance.

So it may have been with Thespis in ancient Greece, who is thought to have been the first actor. After he perfected his art and wrote plays to suit his innovation, he took his show on the road to Athens where he quickly won approval and the flattery of imitation. Others followed his example and the ruler Pisistratus was so impressed by "tragedies," as they now came to be called, that he set up contests in them in 534 B.C., as a part of the City Dionysia, a festival in homage to Dionysus, god of wine, vegetation, and fertility. Most appropriately, Thespis was the first to win the prize.

Move ahead to the tenth century at Winchester, England. It is Easter morning and the cathedral is filled with worshippers. As the Mass begins, the faithful notice that something different has been added. Before the altar steps, a tomb has been placed, but it is open. All at once from the side of the altar, two figures appear—they are angels—so their folded wings seem to say. Now down the aisle, three women enter carrying cloths and ointments. These must be the three Marys. As they come near the tomb, one of the angels steps forward, and puts up a restraining hand and speaks:

First Angel: Whom do you seek in the tomb, worshippers of Christ?
The Women: Jesus of Nazareth who was crucified, O dweller of Heaven.
Angel: He is not here, he has risen as he foretold; go announce that he has risen, saying:
The Women: Hallelujah! The Lord has risen today, a brave lion, Christ the son of God!
First Angel: (*pointing to the tomb*) Come and see the place where the Lord was laid, hallelujah! hallelujah!
Second Angel: Go quickly and tell the disciples that the Lord has risen, hallelujah!
Women: (*Singing in unison with shouts of joy:*) The Lord was hung upon the cross for us, has risen from the tomb, hallelujah!

Now the congregation joins in singing "Hallelujah, hallelujah, He is risen." This little trope known as *Quem Quaeritis* (whom do you seek?), the oldest fragment of liturgical drama, shows how the biblical tale came alive: The word became flesh. Salvation is based on Victory over death, and one of the strongest discoveries of the gospel is the discovery of the empty tomb. So on Easter morning, when the three Marys approach the tomb to anoint the body, their hearts are heavy after the agony of the Crucifixion. At the sight of the angels they might at first be apprehensive, but when they hear the good news and see the evidence, sorrow is turned to joy. The discovery brings a reversal that shows the change of fate for the hero.

In the medieval church, the clergy's objective was to convey to their

C. Walter Hodges shows how the church was used for dramatic
production in this drawing of the "The Three Marys at the Sepulchre."
The action was performed before the altar steps on Easter morning.
From Hodges' Shakespeare's Theater.

flocks the message of salvation, but since most of the people were illiterate
and the services were conducted in Latin, the impact of the worship service
left something to be desired. Attempts were made to present graphic
representations of the gospel in mosaics, sculptures, and stained glass
windows. The introduction of enacted material into the Mass was an
extension of the effort to make the biblical story more compelling.

The dramatic action of the tropes in medieval times led to the evolution of
full-scale theatrical pieces until some cycle plays required three days for
performances and included dozens of incidents and characters. As liturgical
plays grew more complex and secular, medieval drama broke away from the
church and developed a remarkably flexible style of playwriting and staging
which was to profoundly influence the nature of English Renaissance theater.

These two instances illustrate the beginnings of theater in the Western
world. When Thespis made the daring leap from narration to impersonation
he changed the *manner* of presentation from recitation to enactment. Before
Thespis, when Greek rhapsodists recited stories of legendary heroes, primarily

4

from Homer, their performance was description and narration. With Thespis, the performer became the character; he assumed a complete identity. The effect was to create dramatic action that seemed to be happening here and now. Theatrical performance ever since has had the quality of an ongoing experience. Similarly, when the Angels and the three Marys acted out the discovery at the tomb, the incident came to life before the eyes of the worshippers. The event was given immediacy by dramatic action.

Thespis' innovation had a profound influence on the chorus too because when the hero appeared in the flesh, it was compelled to respond to him in a new way. Its lamentation was not for some remote figure in the dim past, but for a living character suffering before its eyes. In essence, the chorus became actors too, and while the members did not become distinct individualized characters, they did assume roles of elders, handmaidens, warriors, suppliants, and so on; and they also responded and reacted as actors involved in the fate of the hero.

After Thespis, Aeschylus in the fifth century B.C. added a second actor, and Sophocles a third. Athenian playwrights developed their mastery of dramatic language and action to produce one of the most prodigious outpourings of creative effort known to the Western world—the rich legacy of Greek tragedy and comedy.

Thus far we have seen elementary examples of dramatic action. Now let us turn to a more complicated situation in which Hamlet tried his hand at playwriting. Hamlet is grieved by the sudden death of his father and the hasty marriage of his mother to his uncle, Claudius. Early in the play, Hamlet confronts his father's ghost who tells him that he has been murdered by Claudius. The dead king lays on Hamlet the burden of avenging his murder. For a time he delays, not altogether sure of the new king's guilt. So when the traveling players arrive to perform at court, Hamlet persuades them to play *The Murder of Gonzago* to which he adds "a dozen or sixteen lines" of his own. This interjection which he calls "The Mousetrap" shows a reenactment of the murder of King Hamlet by pouring poison in his ears. Hamlet devises this scene in order to see whether or not Claudius is actually guilty of murder. "The play's the thing/Wherein I'll catch the conscience of the King."

At the performance before the court, Hamlet stations himself so that he can see Claudius' face. Here, then is a dramatic action, to be performed to produce a very specific effect on one member of the audience.

The play begins with a dumb show in which the poisoning is enacted, but Claudius does not respond. Then Lucianus recites the lines that Hamlet wrote:

Lucianus: Thoughts black, hand apt,
drugs fit, and time agreeing,
Confederate season, else no creative seeing,
Thou mixture of rank, of midnight
weeds collected,
With Hecate's ban thrice blasted, thrice
infected,

Hamlet's "Mousetrap" in a production at the Stratford Shakespeare Festival, Ontario, with Christopher Plummer in the leading role. The player king is about to be poisoned while Hamlet, up center, watches Claudius to see his reaction.

> Thy natural magic and dire property
> On wholesome life usurps immediately.

(Pours the poison in his ears.)

At this action King Claudius blanches, rises, and flees from the room. Hamlet's play has produced the desired effect.

"The Mousetrap" is a major advance over *Quem Quaeritis*. Both are discovery scenes, but the medieval trope is relatively passive for we do not see the climactic moment when Jesus breaks the seal and emerges from the tomb. Instead we are presented with the circumstantial evidence of his departure.

In *Hamlet* the discovery is a double one: Claudius' murder of King Hamlet is apparent from his guilty reaction to the simulated poisoning. He discovers that his crime is known, which means that he must take action against the prince. Hamlet also discovers what he needed to know. The ghost of his father was an honest one; his uncle Claudius did indeed commit murder. The relevation of Claudius' guilt culminates the rising tension that preceded it. The audience, as well as Hamlet, is in on the psychological ambush of Claudius, and once the discovery is made, the emotional momentum surges forward toward the next action.

Hamlet's "Mousetrap" is a good example of the dramatic method. A sequence of words and actions is created to be performed to evoke a response.

In the study of drama it is unfortunate that often our first contact with a play is through the printed page. Understanding theater by reading a play text is like trying to take a journey by looking at a map or to visualize a ball game by looking at the box score. Even though Shakespeare wrote his plays in words, what he really created was dramatic actions. Hamlet gave the players a dozen or sixteen lines of text but his creation was not complete until it was put into action before Claudius and the court.

Response in the theater is *empathic*. Empathy means feeling into. It may be defined as "imitative motor response." Notice the word "motor." An empathic response is not mere sympathy; it involves physical identification and participaton. Watch bystanders trying to help a high jumper over the bar. Or feel the tension in your own body as you attempt to help a tailback cross the goal line. We have had the experience of listening to an unsure soprano trying desperately to hit a high note beyond her own range, and have felt some of her tension in our own throats. The largest crowds are attracted to those sporting events that involve vigorous physical action to which the spectator responds empathically. Similarly, film and television fare that exploits vigorous action, such as in melodramas and farces, is the most popular because the audience is called upon for strong empathic response.

Another way of describing theatrical response is found in Francis Fergusson's term "histrionic sensibility"—the theater-goer's ability to perceive and discriminate actions and visual symbols, just as the trained ear discriminates sounds. It is a learned process that we employ when we judge behavior. For example, up in the stands we may not hear the dialogue between an umpire and an enraged second baseman after a close play, but even at a considerable distance we understand the feelings of the adversaries because of the *way they act*. When we communicate with one another on important issues we prefer face-to-face contact which enables us to make judgments about the speaker and his manner.

Take a familiar episode from life that may have the quality of drama.

You apply for a job. You go through a process of action that generates a certain amount of tension because the outcome is in doubt. The action may be intensified if it is critically important to you to succeed. You may have a rival who is also desperate to land the job.

In any case you are obliged to follow a specific procedure. You fill out a form, perhaps, submit letters of recommendation or your service record elsewhere; you make an appointment for an interview. You are prompt for your appointment and when you meet your prospective employer you make every effort to create a favorable impression so that your words and actions will help you to achieve your objective. The employer consults what you have written on the forms and your other papers, and listens to your answers. With a bit of luck, the job is yours.

Why the interview? Because it gave the employer, and you, an opportunity to size one another up. When you entered the boss's office you got certain impressions from the room, the furniture, the decor, the stuff on his desk. And you made tentative judgments about him based on his appearance, his manner of speaking, the way he looked at you as you replied to his questions.

What you were both doing during this sizing up process was evaluating one another by histrionic sensibility. We have learned to read "body language"; we are responsive to others' "vibrations"; we communicate on a subliminal or visceral level that sometimes can be more intense than the spoken word.

This kind of communication is essential for understanding the impact of the theater. The actor's shrug of a shoulder, the lifting of an eyebrow, the anger which he tries to conceal in his voice, the reaction of a listener—or his lack of response, the pace of the action, the cadence of the sounds, the way in which characters interact constitute an eloquent vocabulary of a universal language even though the signals may be ephemeral and ambiguous, vanishing at the moment of creation.

The experienced playwright is fully aware of these multifaceted forces and he creates his actions so as to make optimum use of them. Here, in the opening scene of Arthur Miller's *Death of a Salesman* you see a dramatist making full use of theatrical materials.

A melody is heard, played upon a flute. It is small and fine, telling of grass and trees and the horizon. The curtain rises.

Before us is the Salesman's house. We are aware of towering angular shapes behind it, surrounding it on all sides. Only the blue light of the sky falls upon the house and forestage; the surrounding area shows an angry glow of orange. As more light appears, we see a solid vault of apartment houses around the small, fragile-seeming home. An air of the dream clings to the place, a dream rising out of reality. The kitchen at center seems actual enough, for there is a kitchen table with three chairs, and a refrigerator. But no other fixtures are seen. At the back of the kitchen there is a draped entrance, which leads to the livingroom. To the right of the kitchen, on a level raised two feet, is a bedroom furnished only with a brass bedstead and a straight chair. On a shelf over the bed a silver athletic trophy stands. A window opens onto the apartment house at the side.

Behind the kitchen, on a level raised six and a half feet, is the boys' bedroom, at present barely visible. Two beds are dimly seen, and at the back of the room a dormer window. (This bedroom is above the unseen living-room.) At the left a stairway curves up to it from the kitchen.

The entire setting is wholly or, in some places, partially transparent. The roof-line of the house is one-dimensional; under and over it we see the apartment buildings. Before the house lies an apron, curving beyond the forestage into the orchestra. This forward area serves as the back yard as well as the locale of all Willy's imaginings and of his city scenes. Whenever the action is in the present the actors observe the imaginary wall-lines, entering the house only through its door

Willie Loman makes his first entrance burdened by his sample cases, while his wife, Linda, awaits his homecoming. (Directed by Sam Smiley, designed by James Hooks at the University of Missouri, Columbia.)

at the left. But in the scenes of the past these boundaries are broken, and characters enter or leave a room by stepping "through" a wall onto the forestage.

From the right, Willy Loman, the Salesman, enters, carrying two large sample cases. The flute plays on. He hears but is not aware of it. He is past sixty years of age, dressed quietly. Even as he crosses the stage to the doorway of the house, his exhaustion is apparent. He unlocks the door, comes into the kitchen, and thankfully lets his burden down, feeling the soreness of his palms. A word-sigh escapes his lips—it might be "Oh, boy, oh boy." He closes the door, then carries his cases out into the living-room, through the draped kitchen doorway. Linda, his wife, has stirred in her bed at the right. She gets out and puts on a robe, listening.

Linda: *(Hearing Willy outside the bedroom, calls with some trepidation)* Willy!
Willy: It's all right. I came back.
Linda: Why? What happened? *(Slight pause)* Did something happen, Willy?
Willy: No, nothing happened.
Linda: You didn't smash the car, did you?
Willy: *(With casual irritation)* I said nothing happened. Didn't you hear me?
Linda: Don't you feel well?
Willy: I'm tired to the death. *(The flute has faded away. He sits on the bed beside her, a little numb)* I couldn't make it. I just couldn't make it, Linda![1]

[1]Arthur Miller, *Death of a Salesman* (New York: Viking Press, 1949).

This short sequence shows how a playwright creates a scene in theatrical terms. It is a complex of multiple sensory stimuli precisely chosen to produce a specific effect. As far as possible Miller attempts to control all of the elements of the opening incident. He specifies the kind and quality of the music; he describes in considerable detail the setting—its practical requirements as a place and its atmospheric qualities as an environment. When Willy appears, the playwright immediately provides specific signs that show his age, his profession, and his condition.

The dialogue that follows establishes the relationship between Willy and Linda, her concern for him and his utter exhaustion. In just eight lines, Miller raises the question about his protagonist: What is wrong with Willy Loman? It will take the entire evening in the theater to answer this question through an organized sequence of dramatic action.

Dramatic Action

In its simple form, *action* refers to the physical movement of the play, the entrances and exits, the stage business of the characters, the larger movements of the ensemble, the quarrels, love scenes, reunions, and partings—all of the overt action essential for the plot. Like every other element of the play, the dramatist includes this kind of action because it is significant and pertinent to his overall effect. Sometimes the playwright uses action to set the environment.

In 1902, on the eve of the Russian revolution, Maxim Gorki wrote a play depicting the grim lives of social outcasts in the Moscow slums. *The Lower Depths* was one of the greatest successes of Stanislavski's Moscow Art Theater. In Berlin Max Reinhardt's production ran over 500 performances. In this play, Gorki uses the pantomimic action of several of the outcasts to establish the atmosphere. Gorki begins *The Lower Depths* with these actions:

> *A basement, resembling a cavern, with a massive stone vaulted ceiling, blackened with smoke, and with plaster crumbling away in places. The light comes from the direction of the spectators and from a square window high up on the right side. The right corner is partitioned off by thin boards, making Peppel's room. Near the door into the room is Bubnov's plank bed. In the left corner is a large Russian stove; in the stone wall on the left is a door into the kitchen, where Kvashnya, the Baron, and Nastya live. Between the stove and the door in the wall is a wide bed, screened off with dirty chintz bed-curtains. Everywhere along the walls are plank beds. Near the left wall, in the foreground, stands a block of wood with a vice and a small anvil fastened to it. Sitting before the anvil on a smaller block of wood is Klestch, trying keys in old locks. At his feet are two large bundles of various keys strung on a ring of wire, a battered tin samovar, a hammer, and some files. In the center of the basement are a large table, two benches, and a square stool. Everything is unpainted and dirty. At the table Kvashnya pours tea, the Baron is*

Meyerhold was noted for his vivid theatricalism, stemming from the way he used his performers. In his famous production of Turandot *in 1925, he brought the entire company into vigorous action.*

chewing on a piece of black bread, and Nastya, seated on the stool, leaning with her elbows on the table, is reading a battered little book. On the bed, hidden by the curtain, Anna is coughing. Sitting on his plank bed, Bubnov the capmaker is fitting an old pair of torn trousers on a hat block which he holds between his knees, considering the best way to cut the cloth. Scattered around him are a torn hat box containing cap visors, pieces of oilcloth and buckram, and rags. Satin, just awakening, lies on his plank bed and makes loud guttural noises. On top of the stove, The Actor, invisible to the audience, moves restlessly and coughs.[2]

The action is often used to indicate character and character relationships. An excellent example occurs in O'Neill's *Desire Under the Elms* (1924). This is a powerful drama showing Ephraim Cabot, a tyrannical old New England farmer locked in a struggle with his sensuous young bride, Abbie, over the possession of his homestead. In her effort to gain possession of the property, Abbie seduces Cabot's young son, Eben, and gives birth to his child. But her passion for Eben is stronger than her desire for the property, so she kills her baby to show her love for Eben. When she is brought to justice, Eben insists on sharing the guilt of murder. The two are led away to prison with an exalted acceptance of their fate. The following scene early in the play shows by action

[2]Maxim Gorki, *The Lower Depths*, trans. Dorcas Hatlen.

their first relationship to one another—Eben's alienation, and Abbie's desire for her son-in-law.

> *The exterior of the farmhouse, as in Part One—a hot Sunday afternoon two months later. Abbie, dressed in her best, is discovered sitting in a rocker at the end of a porch. She rocks listlessly, enervated by the heat, staring in front of her with bored, half-closed eyes.*
>
> *Eben sticks his head out of his bedroom window. He looks around furtively and tries to see—or hear—if anyone is on the porch, but although he has been careful to make no noise Abbie has sensed his movement. She stops rocking, her face grows animated and eager, she waits attentively. Eben seems to feel her presence, he scowls back his thoughts of her and spits with exaggerated disdain—then withdraws back into the room. Abbie waits, holding her breath as she listens with passionate eagerness for every sound within the house.*
>
> *Eben comes out. Their eyes meet. His eyes falter, he is confused, he turns away and slams the door resentfully. At this gesture Abbie laughs tantalizingly, amused but at the same time piqued and irritated. He scowls, strides off the porch to the path and starts to walk past her to the road with a grand swagger of ignoring her existence. He is dressed in his store suit, spruced up, his face shines from soap and water. Abbie leans forward on her chair, her eyes hard and angry now and, as he passes her, gives a sneering, taunting chuckle.*[3]

The playwright employs many kinds of physical action for a variety of purposes. Very often, especially in modern plays, the dramatist uses stage directions to describe in detail not only the actions to be played but also *how* they are to be performed, as in the passage just cited from *Desire Under the Elms*. O'Neill's specific directions were an attempt to control as much as possible the performances of the actors during the play.

Since plays are brought to their completed form by directors, actors, and designers, the playwright is at the mercy of those who interpret his work, and while his text and directions may be faithfully followed to the letter, the playwright cannot possibly control the production of his plays, even if he directs them himself. The actor brings the text to life, and his legitimate contribution to his performance is his way of speaking, moving, and reacting as he (and the director) interpret the play. The actors enter, walk, sit, argue, make love, eat, drink, and exit—and all of these movements reflect the performers' way of responding to the playwright's text. Indeed, the *manner* in which the actors perform is their creative contribution to the production—the legitimate and necessary extension of the playwright's script in theatrical terms. Thus, the physical action of the play is a combination of the dramatist's original creation and the enrichment of the actors' and director's interpretation.

Speech itself is a form of action. It can be a way of doing, of creating tension and momentum to move the play forward. Words are the chief weapons of the playwright to reveal the inner life of the characters. Implicit in most dramatic dialogue is an underlying pattern of action as a character strives for a goal, seeks to influence the behavior of others, searches for the meaning

---

[3]Eugene O'Neill, *Desire Under the Elms* (New York: Random House, 1924).

The contrast in the manner of action is evident in these shots from comedy and tragedy. At the left Francesca Annis and Ian McKellen express their genuine suffering in Romeo and Juliet *in the Royal Shakespeare Company's production at Stratford-upon-Avon. At the right Lillian Evans and Woody Eney engage in farcical horseplay in* The Taming of the Shrew *at the Alley Theater, Houston.*

of his experience, or becomes embroiled in a vigorous clash of wills. Good dramatic dialogue calls out for action.

In *Look Back in Anger*, John Osborne created in Jimmy Porter the epitome of the angry young man as a spokesman for the frustrated, post-World War II generation who lashed out at nearly every aspect of contemporary life. As the play opens, Jimmy and a friend, Cliff, are reading the Sunday paper, while Jimmy's wife Alison is ironing. Jimmy, who castigates everyone and everything, turns his attention to Alison in this verbal assault which nearly has the effect of physical blows:

Alison: Really, Jimmy, you're like a child.
Jimmy: Don't try and patronize me (*Turning to Cliff*) She's so clumsy. I watch for her to do the same things every night. The way she jumps on the bed, as if she were stamping on someone's face, and draws the curtains back with a great clatter, in that casually destructive way of hers. It's like someone launching a battleship. Have you ever noticed how noisy women are? (*Crosses below chairs to L.C.*). Have you? The way they kick the floor about, simply walking over it? Or have you watched them sitting at their dressing tables, dropping their weapons and banging down their bits of boxes and brushes and lipsticks?

Speech as action. Two views of Ekkehard Schall in the Hitlerian role when he inflames the crowd in Brecht's The Resistible Rise of Arturo Ui *at the Berliner Ensemble.*

(He faces her dressing table.)

I've watched her doing it night after night. When you see a women in front of her bedroom mirror, you realise what a refined sort of a butcher she is. *(Turns in)* Did you ever see some dirty old Arab, sticking his fingers into some mess of lamb fat and gristle? Well, she's just like that. Thank God they don't have many women surgeons! Those primitive hands would have your guts out in no time. Flip! Out it comes, like the powder out of its box. Flop! Back it goes, like the powder puff on the table.

Cliff: *(Grimacing cheerfully)* Ugh! Stop it!

Jimmy: *(Moving upstage)* She'd drop your guts like hair clips and fluff all over the floor. You've got to be fundamentally insensitive to be as noisy and as clumsy as that.[4]

Among contemporary playwrights, Harold Pinter's dialogue is particularly distinctive because of the emotional freight it carries. His speeches, often clipped and hackneyed, possess a sinister ambiguity that convey a strong sense of aggression. Beneath the surface of the spoken word are suggested layers of meaning, full of latent menace.

This is evident in Pinter's *The Collection* first presented by the Royal Shakespeare Company in 1962. It is a suspenseful sort of psychological play

[4]John Osborne, *Look Back in Anger* (Chicago: The Dramatic Publishing Company, 1959).

based on the relations between two couples, one heterosexual, the other homosexual. In the following excerpt, the dialogue carries the force of physical aggression. James suspects that his wife has had an affair with Bill and now confronts his rival.

James stands, goes to a fruit bowl, picks up fruit knife. He runs his finger along the blade.

James: This is fairly sharp.

Bill: What do you mean?

James: Come on.

Bill: I beg your pardon?

James: Come on. You've got that one. I've got this one.

Bill: What about it?

James: I get a bit tired of words sometimes, don't you? Let's have a game. For fun.

Bill: What sort of a game?

James: Let's have a mock duel.

Bill: I don't want a mock duel thank you.

James: Of course you do. Come on. First one who's touched is a sissy.

Bill: This is all rather unsubtle, don't you think?

James: Not in the least. Come on, into first position.

Bill: I thought we were friends.

James: Of course we're friends. What on earth's the matter with you? I'm not going to kill you. It's just a game, that's all. We're playing a game. You're not windy, are you?

Bill: I think it's silly.

James: I say, you're a bit of spoilsport, aren't you?

Bill: I'm putting my knife down anyway.

James: Well, I'll pick it up.

James does so and faces him with two knives.

Bill: Now you've got two.

James: I've got another one in my hip pocket.

Pause

Bill: What do you do, swallow them?

James: Do you?

Pause. They stare at each other.
Suddenly

Go on! Swallow it!

James throws the knife at Bill's face. Bill throws up hand to protect his face and catches knife by blade. It cuts his hand.

Bill: Ow!

James: Well caught! What's the matter?[5]

[5]Harold Pinter, *The Collection* in *Three Plays by Harold Pinter* (New York: Grove Press, 1962).

The total play may be regarded as an action. Aristotle described plot as a "system of actions"—an organic whole with nothing missing or irrelevant, all parts interlocked in a credible sequence, a cohesive beginning, middle, and end. Action in this sense is the ordered progression of incidents, usually showing a clash of wills and a change in fortune of the characters.

The action of Gorki's *The Lower Depths* is a graphic and compassionate view of the dregs of the Moscow slums. The emphasis is not on a story line, but on the actions of these outcasts—actions designed to reveal character and motivation through their struggles and suffering. The action in O'Neill's *Desire Under the Elms* is the transition from Eben's bitter struggle with Abbie over the ownership of the farm, to the complete acceptance of one another because of their passion and love. The action of *Look Back in Anger* shows Jimmy Porter's rage at the forces that hem him in, the destructive effects of his wrath, and ultimately through suffering his reconciliation with his wife. The action of *The Collection* demonstrates how the lives of four people are disrupted by sexual jealousy. The action, in this sense, is the total configuration of the plot from the opening incident to the final curtain.

The playwright creates an action through his dynamic use of words and movement. While initially he sets his play down in written terms, what he actually creates is a barrage of sensory stimuli—concrete, objective signals externalizing the inner life of his characters. The audience responds to what it sees and hears on stage. And what it sees and hears are actions.

Take Shakespeare's problem of revealing Claudius' guilt. The inner psychic condition of the king must be conveyed by outward signs. The evidence of his guilt must be triggered by some kind of stimulus that will cause him to respond in an overt fashion. The dramatist's solution was to confront Claudius with a mimetic reenactment of the murder. His guilt is shown in specific, tangible signs. When he witnesses the poisoning, Claudius blanches, rises from his throne, calls out, "Give me some light; away!" and storms out of the room.

The spectator watching the play within the play, Act III, scene 2 of *Hamlet*, is confronted with a very complex set of signals. The traveling players must have a place in the foreground where their actions can be seen by the audience and the court, but the central focus is on Claudius and the effect of the simulated poisoning on him. So the King will probably be in an elevated position facing the audience. Near him are the queen and Polonius, who are deeply concerned about the strange behavior of Hamlet. He must be positioned in a prominent place at the side so he can see the king and in turn be seen by the audience. At the precise moment of discovery, set off by the mock act of poisoning, the spectator sees this action and the consequences simultaneously. He sees the guilty starting of the distraught Claudius, and Hamlet's response to the king's reaction. He is also aware of the players' shock at the sudden disruption of their performance, of Queen Gertrude's anxiety over her husband's condition, of Polonius' fear for the king, of Ophelia's astonishment at the king's action and Hamlet's behavior, of Horatio's reaction as he too sees the evidence of Claudius' guilt. These actions of the performers are enhanced by other theatrical stimuli—the scenery, costumes, color, lighting; the use of tempo, rhythm, sound, and space.

Most plays are not as complex or layered as *Hamlet*, but all drama is created in the form of action, and its full effect is not realized until it is presented as it was intended—in the theater before an audience.

The Appeals of the Theater

Why do people go to the theater?

Why did the citizens of ancient Athens rise up in the cold hours of dawn, scale the steep slope of the Acropolis, sit on the hard seats of the Theater of Dionysus while they watched a trilogy such as Aeschylus' *Oresteia*—three plays of unrelieved suffering and seriousness? Why did a London chimney sweep of Elizabethan times make his way across the Thames to the Globe Theater to stand for hours in the pit to see a play like *Hamlet*—a work so perplexing in language and content that literary scholars still argue about its meaning? Why did our forefathers find the lure of theatrical performance so appealing that they journeyed for several days to see second-rate actors in a makeshift showboat production of *The Rivals*? Why does contemporary man after a hectic day's grind in the office submit himself to the ordeal of fighting his way through snarled traffic, rushing through dinner, and paying for expensive seats to be herded into a dark cavern so he can see the latest Broadway musical hit? What is the secret of theatrical appeal so compelling that we find it necessary to install electronic boxes in nearly every living room so that we can huddle in the dark night after night, giving ourselves to make-believe characters going through make-believe actions?

The sources of the theater's appeal are many, and no doubt the theatrical experience is very often a blend of several satisfactions. Let us suggest four of them.

First, the theater offers an effective means of telling a story. Man has always delighted in sharing tales of adventure and excitement. From very primitive times storytellers have entertained their companions around the fire with vivid accounts of heroes' exploits and warriors' triumphs over adversity. Likewise, in the theater the appeal of a good story has been popular. We enjoy a stirring contest between two well-matched opponents. We become involved vicariously with the participants and we are concerned about the outcome. We are moved by the give-and-take of the struggle, the excitement of the chase, the discovery, the outcome.

Most plays rely heavily on story appeal. This is particularly true of film and television fare which is calculated to attract the widest possible audience response. Hence most drama is journalistic and, like a newspaper, intended for immediate popular consumption. But this does not mean that great dramatists have been unconcerned about shaping a compelling narrative, because one of the distinguishing marks of a fine play is that it provides satisfactions on many levels—one of which may be narrative.

Second, the audience finds pleasure in the skill of execution. A sports

One of the sources of the popularity of musical comedies is the execution of the performers—especially the dancers. A recent hit, Chorus Line, *was based on the experiences of the performers auditioning for a show—an admirable showcase for dancers.*

enthusiast at the Olympic Games may marvel at a pole vaulter as he swings his body up and over the bar more than eighteen feet above the ground. Or he may enjoy the incredible balance and timing of a gymnast working on the parallel bars, or the precision of a diver as she lofts her body into the air, executes a complicated figure, and enters the water with scarcely a splash.

In the arts one derives pleasure from the mastery of materials—the painter's brushwork, the sculptor's ability to shape stone and metal, the musician's control of his voice or instrument, the dancer's use of space. We enjoy the repetition of famliar music, at least in part, because of the skills of those who play it. Certainly one of the chief attractions of musical comedy comes from the excellence of the dancing and singing. In more serious drama, the connoisseur enjoys comparing performances of outstanding actors and actresses such as Laurence Olivier, George C. Scott, Maggie Smith, Jason Robards, Ralph Richardson, and Colleen Dewhurst. In Japan, for example, the spectator of the Kabuki theater may compare an actor's performance in a role with that of his father or grandfather as each generation followed precisely the footsteps of the one before him. As a knowledgeable spectator, you learn to note the effectiveness of the ensemble acting, the director's adroit use of pace and rhythm, the actor's ability to react as well as to speak, the appropriateness of the setting in providing a suitable environment, the expressive use of movement and business, the psychological and emotional content implied by the groupings of characters, and the dramatist's use of symbols and metaphors to communicate ideas and feelings. The enjoyment an informed spectator feels at a performance of a great play stems in part from his recognition of the skills of the cast and production staff in translating into theatrical terms the essential values of the play.

A third satisfaction of the theater is the opportunity it affords us for gaining fresh perceptions. Aristotle suggested that man's greatest pleasure is in learning. The theater is an excellent means of extending ourselves beyond the narrow circle of everyday existence. We become acquainted with people and cultures quite foreign to us. Oedipus, on stage, is no murky, legendary king, but a man of flesh and blood, torn asunder by his guilt and suffering. We gain insight into the lives and motivations of a boy whose psyche has been disturbed by his fixations on horses in *Equus*; the distorted personalities of Tennessee Williams' Blanche du Bois, Ibsen's Hedda Gabler, and Strindberg's Miss Julie. We spend a couple of hours getting acquainted with characters we would probably not meet in real life—kings and beggars, geniuses and outcasts, leprechauns and ghosts. We even get quite a representation from the animal kingdom—horses, lizards, rhinoceroses, wasps, birds, insects, flies, frogs, and roosters! The theater offers extraordinary opportunities for insightful experiences.

Fourth, the dramatic experience can also be a spiritual one. As Aristotle suggested, comedy may show us as worse than we are, but tragedy shows us as better than we are. It is serious, elevated in scale, and of a certain magnitude. At its best, tragedy evokes a catharsis—a purging away, a cleansing of the ignoble, the mean, the base. Great works of drama depict great characters exploring the great issues of life. In them man is tested to the utmost, and while his body may be broken, his spirit triumphs. Through suffering he transcends his physical limitations and affirms the dignity of man and his resilient spirit. Greek tragedy was a declaration of faith; it exalted mankind. "Wonders are many, and none is more wonderful than man," sang Sophocles. The trials and sufferings of Antigone, Oedipus, and Prometheus were positive statements about the Greek view of life and of man's potential grandeur. Man's loftiest ideas and aspirations have been the significant content of drama, and spiritual stimulation one of its enduring achievements. Comic writers like Molière and Shaw have attacked and exposed hypocrisy and chicanery. Likewise, those concerned with man as a social animal, writers like Henrik Ibsen, Arthur Miller, and David Rabe have stripped away the facade of social pretense and forced us to see reality. The theater has often been a salutary social weapon for dealing with the truth.

Theatrical Conventions

Theatrical production, like all other forms of art, is conventionalized. That is to say, there are certain common agreements between spectator and theater worker as to the manner of creation and production—certain "ground rules" which determine how the game is to be played. In painting, there is the convention that pigment is applied to a flat surface within a regular framework.

Conventions of realistic production were followed in this modern production of The Championship Season *at the University of Florida. The actors perform in a realistic manner in a setting that stimulates an authentic interior.*

Music is a conventionalized combination of sounds and rhythms which make almost no pretense of imitating nature. The spectator, as he enters the theater, becomes a partner to conventions governing time, space, and the manner of playing.

The conventions of realistic production that dominated the theater during the latter part of the nineteenth century, and for much of the twentieth, attempted to foster the illusion of actuality through lifelike representation of characters and setting. There was tacit agreement that performer and spectator would remain separate from one another. The separation was facilitated by the darkened auditorium and the lighted stage, and by the architectural features of the raised stage that could be closed off by a curtain and the proscenium arch. There was also a psychological barrier known as the "fourth wall," a convention in which the actors pretended that the audience did not exist and avoided direct communication across the footlights. Dramatic structure was usually linear and tied to a story line. Scenery was designed to give the illusion of a genuine environment with practical doors and windows, and properties and furniture that seemed a part of real life. Actually there was a good deal of license in the arrangement of furniture, and exits and entrances to make the setting "open out" to the audience so that the actors could be readily heard and seen.

Artistic conventions are susceptible to change. Just as we had remarkable innovations in painting and music in the twentieth century, we have had rebellion in theatrical conventions. Many theater workers have rejected the limitations of the proscenium arch and are finding ways, such as the thrust or arena stages, to bring the spectator and the performer into a closer relationship. More recently, performances are given in "found spaces" such as warehouses, garages, store buildings, and street corners, abandoning conventional theaters altogether. Scenery has become frankly theatrical instead of illusionistic. As an example of this tendency, a fragment of a wall or a skeletal framework picked out of the darkness by light serves as a setting which a generation ago would have required a complete interior with three walls, ceiling, and a room full of furniture. Playwrights have rejected the conventions of realism in an effort to gain more freedom. Acting is often quite stylized; the separation between spectator and performer has broken down. Indeed, in some instances the theater worker actively seeks to involve the audience in the action. The modern theater-goer is no longer sure how much of the performance will be on stage or in his lap. Nor does the play necessarily have a well-defined plot or even clear language and sharp delineation of character.

There have always been fashions in theatrical conventions which have differed from time to time, and in order to understand the drama of any period, it is essential to know the conventions which influenced the production. In the Greek theater, for example, there were these conventions: Only three speaking characters appeared at one time; there was little or no violence onstage; actors wore masks, special footgear, and headpieces; and the plays were written in verse, dramatizing ancient legends and myths; and they were presented usually in a single permanent setting with a simple story that occurred in a short space of time. In the Elizabethan theater, like the Greek, all roles were played by male actors in an outdoor theater in the daytime with little or no use of illusionistic scenery. The plays written in verse were quite different in form and content from the Greek drama. The play usually was a complicated one involving several plot lines; comedy matter was mixed with serious, highborn characters with low; and the playwright ransacked history and literature for material that would tell an exciting story. The plays were performed by professional actors in theaters whose dimensions and arrangement placed the actor in close proximity to the spectator and allowed the subtleties of the language to be exploited. The convention of the large

In the Greek theater, actors wore masks, probably as a means of making the characters more projectile in the vast playhouse. Masks were used effectively in this modern production of Prometheus Bound *at the Epidaurus festival.*

unlocalized platform gave the dramatist a great deal of freedom in staging an animated and complicated narrative.

In each age, theater conventions have varied according to the influences of the playwrights, actors, audience, and physical theaters, and in turn, the conventions have affected all elements of the drama. It is essential to recognize these conventions in evaluating any drama because of their pressure in shaping the play and its production.

Bibliography

FERGUSSON, FRANCIS, *The Idea of a Theater.* Princeton: Princeton University Press, 1949.

GASSNER, JOHN, and RALPH G. ALLEN, *Theater and Drama in the Making,* 2 vols. Boston: Houghton Mifflin Company, 1964.

MATTHEWS, BRANDER, *The Principles of Playmaking*. Freeport, N.Y.: Books for Libraries Press, 1970.

NAGLER, ALOIS M., *Source Book in Theatrical History*. New York: Dover Publications, Inc., 1952.

NICOLL, ALLARDYCE, *The Development of the Theater*. New York: Harcourt, Brace Jovanovich, Inc., 1966.

ROWE, KENNETH THORPE, *The Theater in Your Head*. New York: Funk & Wagnalls, Inc., 1960.

WILLIAMS, RAYMOND, *Drama in Performance*. London: F. Muller, 1954.

TWO
The Play and Its Parts

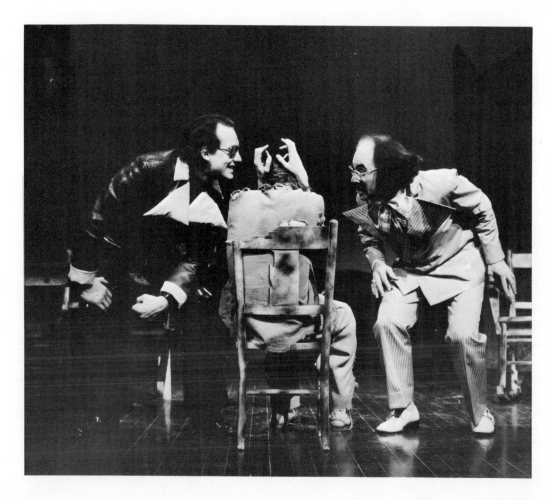

When playwrights create plays, they visualize them in action in the theater before an audience. As they work with the relevant dialogue and movement, they are somewhat like trial lawyers who present evidence, witnesses, and exhibits that will persuade the jury of the validity of their case. Playwrights are not involved so much with the factual aspects of a past action; they are, rather, creating the effect of an ongoing experience happening before the eyes of the spectators, but they too present concrete evidence of human experience in words and actions.

Since most theater begins with the text, let us look first at the play and its parts.

Aristotle, in the fourth century B.C., was the first to write on the theory of dramatic criticism. Although he lived a century after the golden age of Greek drama and some of his views may seem arbitrary, his *Poetics* is the fountainhead of dramatic criticism and one cannot discuss dramatic theory very long without referring to him. We will use some of his ideas and terminology to discuss the elements of drama.

His analysis of tragedy listed these six parts in order of importance:

1. Plot
2. Character
3. Thought
4. Diction
5. Music
6. Spectacle

We will follow this hierarchy as a framework for discussion, bearing in mind that Aristotle's terms have special meanings and that they are subject to endless controversy.

1. Plot

Plot is the structural element of the play that gives the action its form. Plot is to the playwright what composition is to the painter and musician. While most plays tell stories, the plot is not the narrative itself, but the *shape of the story*. The plot is made up of a series of incidents selected and arranged in order to produce an audience response.

Traditionally, a play is structured on a pattern of increasing tension followed by release. In the nineteenth century, the French critic Brunetière offered his celebrated "law of the drama," in which the basic tenet was that the plot showed "the spectacle of a will striving toward a goal." Oedipus strives to learn the cause of the plague; Hamlet's objective is to avenge his father's murder; Romeo's goal is to win Juliet; Estragon and Vladimir wait to meet Godot; in *Equus*, the psychiatrist tries to find the cause of the young boy's disturbed state of mind. The playwright creates a system of actions, showing the protagonists' (leading characters) efforts to attain their goals, despite obstacles. Such a sequence of related events constitutes the plot, though, of course, not all plays follow Brunetière's theory. In many modern works, the characters seem not to have goals. Instead, the play defines a state of being or creates a mood, or reveals character and situation. But the striving of a protagonist toward an objective characterizes most drama and the plot is one of tension and release.

Plots of Western drama have usually followed a linear pattern. The classic view of dramatic structure, as expressed by Aristotle, was for a unified plot of organically related elements in which there was a "beginning, middle, and end" following a "necessary and probable" order with no extraneous material.

By convention, Greek tragedy was simple in structure, consisting of a few episodes involving a small number of characters and usually occurring in a single place over a short space of time.

Golden and Hardison diagram the tragic plots in this way, the one on the left being a "fortunate" plot in which the protagonist reaches his objective, while the one on the right shows the more generally used "fatal" plot representing the protagonist's catastrophic descent.[1]

```
                    6  End   1  Beginning
                  5                2
                4                    3
              3                        4
            2                            5
   Beginning  1                            6  End
```

The ascending or descending line marks the change that occurs as the career of the protagonist moves toward good or bad fortune. The numbered intervals show the steps in his process of change.

Such schematic depiction of plot is helpful only insofar as it projects an awareness of the nature of the play's structure. The importance of plot is that the organization of the material is vital to the effect of a play and for that reason plotting is often considered the most difficult aspect of playwriting.

Medieval plays dramatizing biblical stories or the lives of saints often included dozens of incidents, hundreds of characters, and a variety of locales. This kind of drama was not unified by structure but rather by its theme, or, in the case of the Passion Play, unified by the central figure of Christ. Episodic plotting characterizes the Kabuki plays of Japan, the traditional dramas of China and India, the modern parables of Brecht.

Shakespeare and his contemporaries, and eighteenth-century romanticists were influenced by the loose medieval structure in their attempts to put most

---

[1]Leon Golden and O. B. Hardison, Jr., *Aristotle's Poetics* (Englewood Cliffs, N.J.: Prentice-Hall, Inc., 1968), p. 146.

of the significant action on stage, but their plots were generally more unified around character or story.

The neoclassicists of France attempted to follow their version of the simple, unified structure of the Greeks. The most successful dramatist of this persuasion was Racine. Writers of melodramas in the nineteenth century, in their attempts to involve the audience in violent actions on the stage, structured their plays around exciting episodes; but with the coming of naturalism and realism, the general trend was toward a simple, tight structure in which all the parts fit together as a "well-made play." Contemporary dramatists are not bound by any conventional strictures, but use all manner of plot making; however, the pressures of heavy production and costs—the need to satisfy the box office appeal of a good story—make a strong impact.

The plot of a play is composed of a series of units. Greek tragedies were made up of a sequence of episodes alternating with choric odes. Major divisions from the Renaissance onwards are the acts, which are divided into scenes, and these may be separated still further for rehearsal purposes into "beats," such as the initial appearance of the ghost in *Hamlet* or Willy's first entrance in *Death of a Salesman*.

Another way of looking at plot is to examine its technical machinery, which provides a method of analyzing the content. The basic aspects of plot are:

A. Exposition

B. Discovery

C. Reversal

D. Point of attack

E. Foreshadowing

F. Complication

G. Climax

H. Crisis

I. Denouement

A. Exposition

As the curtain opens, the dramatist faces the problem of capturing the audience's attention and providing the spectators with the necessary background so that they can follow the subsequent action. He must present his characters in such a way that the audience becomes concerned with what happens to them—vicariously sharing their suffering, trials, and triumphs. The function of *exposition* is to acquaint the spectator with the characters, their relationships, background, and present situation. Expository devices vary with theatrical conventions. Very often in classic drama and in the Oriental theater a play begins with a narrator who presents the exposition directly to the audience.

Euripides begins *The Bacchae* with a prologue in which Dionysus informs the theater-goers:

> I am Dionysus, the son of Zeus, come back to Thebes, this land where I was born. My mother was Cadmus' daughter, Semele by name, midwifed by fire, delivered by the lightning's blast. And here I stand, a god incognito, disguised as man, beside the stream of Dirce and the waters of Isemenus. There before the palace I see my lightning-married mother's grave.[2]

Peter Shaffer begins his *Equus* with a theatrically effective scene that serves as exposition. The central action of the play is the psychiatrist's investigation of the boy's disturbed condition, resulting from his fixation for the horse, Nugget. All three appear before the audience at the outset of the play as Dysart, the psychiatrist, defines the problem.

> *Darkness,*
> *Silence.*
>
> Dim light up on the square. In a spotlight stands Alan Strong, a lean boy of seventeen, in sweater and jeans. In front of him the horse Nugget. Alan's pose represents a contour of great tenderness; his head is pressed against the shoulder of the horse, his hands stretching up to fondle its head. The horse in turn nuzzles his neck. The flame of a cigarette lighter jumps in the dark. Lights come up slowly on the circle. On the left bench, downstage, Martin Dysart, smoking. A man in his mid-forties.

Dysart: With one particular horse, called Nugget, he embraces. The animal digs its sweaty brow into his cheek, and they stand in the dark for an hour—like a necking couple. And of all nonsensical things—I keep thinking about the horse! Not the boy: the horse, and what it may be trying to do. I keep seeing that huge head kissing him with its chained mouth. Nudging through the metal some desire absolutely irrelevant to filling its belly or propagating its own kind. What desire could that be? Not to stay a horse any longer? Not to remain reined up forever in those particular genetic strings? Is it possible, at certain moments we cannot imagine, a horse can add its sufferings together—the non-stop jerks and jabs that are its daily life—and turn them into grief? What use is grief to a horse?

> *Alan leads Nugget out of the square and they disappear together up the tunnel, the horse's hooves scraping delicately on the wood.*[3]

Standard expository devices are "feather-duster" scenes of two minor characters bouncing information off each other to the audience, narrators, confidants, choruses, asides, monologues, prologues, and the use of visual aids. The stage setting is, of course, an important means of presenting environmental material.

Exposition is a part of the general discovery process, but it deals primarily with background material, while discovery includes events that may happen in the course of the play onstage—for example, Nora's discovery of the true

---

[2]Euripides, *The Bacchae*, trans. David Grene and Richard Lattimore, *The Complete Greek Tragedies*, Vol. IV, Euripides (Chicago: University of Chicago Press, 1959), p. 543.
[3]Peter Shaffer, *Equus* (New York: Atheneum Publishers, 1975), p. 21.

Equus begins with an expository scene in which the psychiatrist, Dysart, defines the problem of Alan, seen here with the horse, Nugget, for whom he has acquired an attachment. Portland State University production. Directed by Jack Featheringill.

character of her husband, Jason's discovery of Medea's slaughter of their two sons, and the doctor's discovery of Lady Macbeth's madness.

B. Discovery

The playwright reveals a continual stream of information about the characters, their motivations, feelings, and relationships. Discovery is often accompanied by recognition (*anagnorisis*) when a character learns the truth about himself. A skillful playwright possesses the ability to invent a series of compelling discoveries. We saw how the liturgical trope, *Quem Quaeritis*, was built around the significant discovery of the empty tomb, and in Hamlet's "The Mousetrap" the action hinged on the discovery of Claudius' guilt. Shakespeare's play, as a matter of fact, is built on a series of theatrical discoveries—the ghost's revelation of the murder, the madness and death of Ophelia, the pirates' plot to slay Hamlet, the poisoned sword and drink. There is a good deal of self-discovery in the play, too, as when Hamlet examines his doubts and fears.

Many comedies are built around mistakes, pretendings, and misunderstandings, so that the element of discovery is fundamental to the unraveling of the plot. One of the most notable discovery scenes occurs in Molière's *Tartuffe*, in which the title character masquerades as a priest and worms his way into Orgon's household, scheming to steal not only his fortune but also his wife, Elmire. She unmasks the imposter by getting her husband to hide under a table while she pretends to respond to Tartuffe's advances.

Discovery scenes may be those of recognition, as, for example, in Aeschylus' *Libation Bearers*, when Electra recognizes her brother, Orestes, by a lock of his hair and by their matching footprints! In Sophocles' *Electra*, Orestes is recognized by his father's signet ring, and in the Euripidean version, a tutor recognizes Orestes by a scar. Comedy often employs recognition

Elmire feigns an interest in the amorous advances of the imposter, Tartuffe, in order that her husband, Orgon, hiding under the table, can discover how he is being deceived. Tartuffe, *directed by Larry Clark at the University of Missouri.*

Euripides' Bacchae. Agave recognizes her son's head after she has participated in a ritual ecstasy in which he was killed.

scenes between long-lost relatives and lovers by the use of signs and tokens, such as rings, lockets, and distinguishing physical markings.

Discovery in serious drama may often be self-discovery, as in *Antigone*, *Oedipus Rex*, *King Lear*, *Macbeth*, *Hamlet*, and *Othello*. Certainly one of the pleasures of theater-going is from the discoveries we make about others and ourselves, as we are confronted by insightful probing into character motivation and human experience.

C. Reversal

Many plays follow a pattern of *reversal* in which the fortunes of the leading character turn from good to bad, or vice versa. A protagonist apparently enjoying the fruits of power and prosperity plunges into disaster. In *Oedipus Rex*, the Shepherd expects to bring good news, but his message has the opposite effect, resulting in catastrophe. King Lear intends to divide his land equitably; but when his daughter, Cordelia, is unable or unwilling to compete with her sisters in flattering their father, the king, in his anger, initiates a chain of action that reverses his intention and leads to a series of calamities.

In comedy, turning the tables is one of the most common devices, often showing a lower class character attaining upper class status—such as the woodchopper's suddenly becoming the king's physician in *The Doctor in Spite of Himself*, or an outcast's becoming the judge in Brecht's *The Caucasian Chalk Circle*. Other familiar uses of comic reversal occur when the young lovers, who are thwarted by authority figures at the beginning of the play, overcome the opposition and make a new society in which the pattern is repeated. Still another aspect of reversal in comedy transpires when the trickster or pretender is caught in his own trap, as in Jonson's *Volpone*.

D. Point of Attack

In a linear plot, the playwright creates a chain of events that constitutes the main action. The *point of attack* refers to that moment when the mechanism is set in motion—the first pitch is thrown, the football is kicked off, the first blow is landed, the battle is joined. Disequilibrium is created, resulting in a change that continues until a new equilibrium is established, usually at the end of the play.

In *Romeo and Juliet*, the point of attack occurs in the very opening of the play when the quarrelsome servants of the Capulets confront servants of the Montagues and immediately become embroiled in a street brawl. This initial encounter not only reveals the bitter conflict between the two houses, but it also begins the turbulence that spreads from minor characters to engulf entire families in succeeding waves of violence and suffering.

The point of attack sometimes occurs with the return of a long-absent person whose presence disrupts the situation, such as when Sweeney Todd, a barber, comes back to London to avenge the shabby treatment he received years before when a judge sent him to Australia so that he could seduce the barber's wife. In Aeschylus' *Oresteia*, the king's return from the Trojan Wars precipitates a sequence of violence, beginning with the murder of Agamemnon, and leading to the slaying of his queen, Clytemnestra, and her paramour, Aegisthus.

Another way of triggering the point of attack occurs when a character makes an important decision. Antigone is committed to bury the body of her brother, Polynices, in defiance of the king's edict. Oedipus promises the citizens of Thebes to rid the kingdom of the plague. Dr. Treves accepts responsibility for taking care of a repulsive freak in his hospital in Bernard Pomerance's *The Elephant Man*. A paralytic in Brian Clark's *Whose Life Is It Anyway* decides he wants to die. Still another way of upsetting the equilibrium is the making of an important discovery. Horatio encounters Hamlet's father's ghost, the Madwoman of Chaillot learns of a plot to drill for oil near her cafe. In Anthony Shaffer's *Sleuth*, the mystery novelist, Andrew Wyke, discovers that his neighbor, Miles Tindle, wants to marry his wife.

The point of attack relates directly to theatrical conventions. In medieval drama, a flexible stage was needed to accommodate the desire for long and complex plots, such as those showing the life of Christ or those of the saints, or presenting many episodes from Bible stories. Therefore, medieval drama frequently used an early point of attack. Elizabethan practice often followed the medieval practice in order that complex stories could include a good deal of history, as in Shakespeare's *Henry IV*, Parts One and Two, *Richard II*, *Richard III*, and *Julius Caesar*. In contrast, the Greek conventions of the "unities of time, place, and action," and the limitation of actors to a maximum of three speaking characters appearing at once, required a late point of attack, with the play beginning near the major climax and including only a few episodes and a simple plot. French drama and the realistic plays of the late nineteenth and early twentieth centuries tended to follow the classic pattern of a late point of attack and a concise plot; however, the experimental dramas of expressionism, the epic plays of Brecht, and much of modern drama no longer are constrained to an organic structure or to limitations of time and space, and the point of attack is not bound by conventions.

E. Foreshadowing

Foreshadowing is the playwright's method of preparing for the action that is to follow. It serves several purposes. It makes the subsequent action credible, builds suspense and tension, and carries the momentum of the action forward. It may also reveal character, aid in the development of complications and climaxes, prepare for an entrance, and create atmosphere.

Within the first thirty lines of *Hamlet*, the guards speak of the "dreaded sight" that has appeared twice before—which serves as a means of foreshadowing the ghost's entrance, and of providing the appropriate eerie atmosphere. In *Agamemnon*, the watchman during the Prologue sees the signal fires that indicate the return of the king, but his joy is tempered with apprehension because of the hostility of Clytemnestra. In Ibsen's *A Doll's House*, Nora's deception with the macaroons on her first appearance prepares for the discovery of her larger deception of forging her father's signature.

The playwright values tension and suspense more than he does surprise, and the traditional practice has been to establish a background to prepare the audience for the action that follows. But many contemporary writers, who regard life as illogical and incomprehensible, do not feel obligated to give the audience clear clues to their characters or their motivations. Pinter, Frisch, and Duerrenmatt have written striking plays whose plots reflect a nameless dread, an overpowering sense of unidentified evil, using ambiguous language and actions which the spectator is left to sort out for himself.

F. Complications

Most plots are made up of a series of *complications*. A complication is any force that affects the direction of the action. Comedy very often shows a character striving after a goal but thwarted by obstacles. The hero falls in love with a girl, but he is kept from her by a series of complications—parental disapproval, economic or political differences; he is put in jail or sent overseas; she is ill or involved with another suitor, and so on. In tragedy, the hero frequently becomes committed to action that tests him to the utmost. The suffering and hardships of the testing process are the complications.

Usually a play has a pattern of increasing intensification from the first complication (the point of attack) to the major climax, when the fate of the protagonist is settled or the dramatist has given the spectator an insight into the characters and their experience. Complications create a "straining forward

In Duerrenmatt's The Visit, Madame Zachanassian returns to her village and at a banquet announces a gift of a billion marks to the impoverished village—on condition that the man who betrayed her as a girl be killed. This complication sets off a series of actions testing the avarice of the people. (American Conservatory Theater, San Francisco.) Elizabeth Huddle as Madame Zachanassian.

of interest," to use George Pierce Baker's apt phrase. Their purpose is to intensify the emotions, create suspense, provide the building blocks of the play's structure, and illustrate and determine what happens to the characters.

Romeo falls in love with Juliet, but the situation is complicated by the enmity between the two families. This hostility is aggravated when Romeo slays Tybalt, causing a new complication, the banishment of Romeo. Another complication is raised when Juliet's father insists that she marry Paris immediately. In order to avoid the marriage, a plan is devised for Juliet to feign death through the use of a magic potion. But the letter to Rome disclosing the plan is not delivered, further complicating the action. Romeo learns of Juliet's apparent death, goes to her, and takes poison. Juliet awakens to find her lover dead—another complication. She joins him in death. Shakespeare, like most playwrights, begins with a character trying to reach an objective, but complications intervene and require the character to readjust as the play gathers momentum and intensity. It is through complications that the playwright constructs his plot.

G. Climax

The climax culminates the course of action; it is "the maximum disturbance of the equilibrium," "the moment of most intense strain," "the crisis of maximum emotion and tension." In Hamlet's "The Mousetrap," the climax occurs when Claudius rises from his chair at the sight of the simulated murder of King Hamlet. In *Quem Quaeritis*, the climax is the discovery of the empty tomb.

In Peter Shaffer's *Equus*, a brilliant scene occurs when Alan blinds the horses. Alan, an emotionally disturbed boy, has unaccountably blinded six horses. He has been placed under the care of Dysart, a psychiatrist, who probes for the reason for the boy's violent behavior. Gradually, he learns that Alan has had a fixation for the horse, Nugget, and that his unsuccessful attempt to make love to a girl had been witnessed by the horses, so Alan attacked them. This climactic action is recreated by Dysart's questioning:

> *Alan stands alone, and naked.*
> *A faint humming and drumming. The boy looks about him in growing terror.*
>
> **Dysart:** What?
> **Alan:** (*To Dysart*) He was there. Through the door. The door was shut, but he was there! . . . He'd seen everything. I could hear him. He was laughing.
> **Dysart:** Laughing?
> **Alan:** (*To Dysart*) Mocking! . . . Mocking! . . . *Standing downstage he stares up towards the tunnel. A great silence weighs on the square.* (*To the silence: terrified*) Friend . . . Equus the Kind . . . The Merciful! . . . Forgive me! . . .
>
> *Silence.*
>
> It wasn't me not really me. *Me!* . . . Forgive me! . . . Take me back again! Please! . . . PLEASE!
>
> *He kneels on the downstage lip of the square, still facing the door, huddling in fear.*
>
> I'll never do it again. I swear . . . I swear! . . .
>
> *Silence.*
>
> (*In a moan*) Please!!! . . .
> **Dysart:** And He? What does He say?
> **Alan:** (*To Dysart: whispering*) 'Mine! . . . You're mine! . . . I am yours and you are mine!' . . . Then I see his eyes. They are rolling!
>
> *Nugget begins to advance slowly, with relentless hooves, down the central tunnel.*
>
> 'I see you. I see you. Always! Everywhere! Forever!'
> **Dysart:** Kiss anyone and I will see?
> **Alan:** (*To Dysart*) Yes!
> **Dysart:** And you will fail! Forever and ever you will *fail*! You will see ME—and you will FAIL!
>
> *The boy turns round, hugging himself in pain. From the sides two more horses converge with Nugget on the rails. Their hooves stamp angrily. The Equus noise is heard more terribly.*

The Lord thy God is a Jealous God. He sees you. He sees you forever and ever, Alan. He sees you! . . . *He sees you!*

Alan: (*In terror*) Eyes! . . . White eyes—never closed! Eyes like flames—coming—coming! . . . God seest! God seest! . . . NO! . . . *Pause. He steadies himself. The stage begins to blacken.* (*Quieter*) No more. No more, Equus. *He gets up. He goes to the bench. He takes up the invisible pick. He moves slowly upstage towards Nugget, concealing the weapon behind his naked back, in the growing darkness. He stretches out his hand and fondles Nugget's mask.* (*Gently*) Equus . . . Noble Equus . . . Faithful and True . . . Godslave . . . Thou—God—Seest—NOTHING!

He stabs out Nugget's eyes. The horse stamps in agony. A great screaming begins to fill the theater, growing ever louder. Alan dashes at the other two horses and blinds them too, stabbing over the rails. Their metal hooves join in the stamping. Relentlessly, as this happens, three more horses appear in cones of light; not naturalistic animals like the first three, but dreadful creatures out of nightmare. Their eyes flare—their nostrils flare—their mouths flare. They are archetypal images—judging, punishing, pitiless. They do not halt at the rail, but invade the square. As they trample at him, the boy leaps desperately at them, jumping high and naked in the dark, slashing at their heads with arms upraised. The screams increase. The other horses follow into the square. The whole place is filled with cannoning, blinded horses—and the boy dodging among them, avoiding their slashing hooves as best he can. Finally, they plunge off into darkness and away out of sight. The noise dies abruptly, and all we hear is Alan yelling in hysteria as he collapses on the ground—stabbing at his own eyes with the invisible pick.

Alan: Find me! . . . Find me! Find me! . . . KILL ME! . . . KILL ME! . . . [4]

Actually, in many plays there are series of climaxes, with moments of stability and adjustment in between. The action surges forward and upward in mounting tension through minor climaxes until the major climax, when the emotional impact of the play is strongest. The structure, in this respect, resembles a boxing match between two opponents of similar strength and skill. In each round, there are moments of climactic action with first one fighter gaining the advantage and then the other. In between the peaks of action there are relatively quiet moments and rest periods between the rounds. In the frantic last round, the major climax is reached when one boxer succeeds in knocking the other one out. Dramatic climaxes are the result of an arrangement of actions and events of increasing tension, as, for example, the climaxes of Ibsen's *A Doll's House*.

Krogstad threatens to reveal Nora's secret.

Nora pleads unsuccessfully with Helmer to retain Krogstad.

Krogstad writes his damning letter to Helmer.

Nora dances the tarantella to keep Helmer from reading the letter.

Helmer reads the letter and berates Nora.

Krogstad's second letter saves Helmer's reputation.

Nora tells Helmer of her decision to leave him.

[4]Shaffer, *Equus*.

The climax of Duerrenmatt's The Visit *when the townspeople slay Anton Schill in order to obtain one billion marks from Madame Zachanassian. (Designed by N. Vichodyl).*

Climaxes occur at the moments of greatest turbulence, often as the result of significant discoveries, as when Dysart, in the scene above, finds out why Alan is mentally disturbed. In some plays, particularly in melodrama, the climax is the time of maximum violence or jeopardy—hero and villain fight at the edge of a cliff, the "good guy" is before a firing squad, the space ship is out of control. In comedy, the climax frequently occurs when the characters are the most mixed-up, caught in complicated situations.

H. Crisis

Although the terms *crisis* and *climax* are sometimes used interchangeably because they may happen at the same time, we shall consider a crisis to mean a time of decision, a turning point, a crossroads. After an accident (which may be a climax), a patient hovers between life and death. He is at a moment of crisis. A batter steps to the plate with the score tied and the bases loaded. The count reaches three balls and two strikes. The game is at a point of crisis. (It is probably at the climax, too.)

A crisis involves a clash of interests. The protagonist is faced with alternatives that will determine his fate. Hamlet, sword in hand, must decide whether or not to slay the praying Claudius; Juliet must decide whether or not to take the sleeping potion; Nora must decide whether or not to leave her husband.

Sometimes a character makes his own decisions; sometimes they are

The climax in Ansky's The Dybbuk *when a possessed girl goes through the terrifying ordeal of exorcism as a Rabbinical Court looks on in amazement. (Directed by John Hirsch at the Mark Taper Forum, Los Angeles).*

thrust upon him. A crisis may lead to good fortune or catastrophe, depending on the nature of the play and the author's intent.

A dramatist creates situations that dramatize his characters at critical moments of their careers. For a while the outcome is in doubt. The protagonist teeters on the brink of success or failure. A decisive action occurs that settles the fate of the hero. The moments of decision are the crises.

In the traditional drama of the past, characters have some freedom of choice, but many modern playwrights have created characters who have no chance to assert themselves—their wills are paralyzed and their destinies are imposed on them from the outside. They are victims of unseen or external forces, rather than active agents. These plays avoid crises, and instead the characters are acted upon with no compelling sense of choice.

Despite Brecht's rejection of traditional dramatic structure, he has an excellent sense for creating strong crises within the episodes of his plays. For example, *The Caucasian Chalk Circle* is a sequence of critical actions:

> During the palace rebellion, Grusha rescues and escapes with the governor's child.
>
> Grusha saves the child from the Ironshirts.
>
> Grusha escapes from the Ironshirts by crossing the Rotten Bridge.
>
> Grusha marries a peasant who feigns dying.

An outcast, Azdak, becomes the judge.

Azdak's wisdom gives Grusha custody of the child.

I. Denouement

The *denouement* is the final resolution of the plot, the untying of the knot which the complications have formed. Romeo and Juliet are united in death; the blinded Oedipus goes into exile; Hamlet, Laertes, the queen, and Claudius die, and order is restored in Elsinore. In mystery plays, the guilty person is identified and brought to justice; in romantic comedies, the lovers are united and the problems are solved; in old-fashioned melodramas, the good are rewarded and the bad are punished; in tragedies, the protagonist preserves his integrity and achieves his spiritual goal, even though he suffers

The denouement of Brecht's Caucasian Chalk Circle *at critical moment when Judge Azdak must decide who should have custody of the child—the Governor's wife on the left, or the servant girl, Grusha. Lincoln Center Repertory Theater.*

physical catastrophe. The denouement indicates the ultimate disposition of the major characters. The function of the denouement is to restore order and to unify and complete the course of action.

The modern playwright who rejects the traditional format of a clearly defined linear plot may leave the resolution ambiguous or incomplete. In Beckett's *Waiting for Godot*, Vladimir and Estragon look forward to the arrival of Godot from the very beginning, but he does not come. The act of waiting is the force that animates the play and allows the dramatist to reveal the characters and their ideas. Ionesco, in the denouements of *The Chairs* and *The Leader*, tricks expectancy by negative endings. In *The Chairs*, an old couple await the coming of the orator who will deliver a significant message, but when he arrives, he can only babble, and he writes on the blackboard, "Angel-food, adieu." Those who look forward to the appearance of the leader are shocked when he appears—without a head.

Luigi Pirandello, one of the foremost dramatists of the twentieth century, engages his characters in *Right You Are If You Think You Are* in an intellectual chase to learn the true identity of a family who tell conflicting stories. In the denouement, curiosity is not satisfied and the audience leaves the theater without knowing the answers. Harold Pinter's plays are famous for their ambiguity, not only of the dialogue but also of the characters and their actions, since the playwright does not spell out the answers but allows the spectators to find meanings for themselves. Generally, however, the denouement brings about a clear and ordered resolution.

2. Character

Aristotle, in his *Poetics*, regarded character as secondary to plot, thus beginning an argument that continues to this day. Actually, the controversy is a fruitless one, since plot and character are interrelated. Character is defined by what the character says and does. Plot is character in action.

Like other aspects of drama, characterization has varied with fashion. In Greek, Elizabethan, and Japanese drama, the roles of women were played by men. Medieval drama often made use of allegorical figures representing single attributes of character, such as Wisdom, Greed, and Gluttony. High tragedy has dealt primarily with men "as better than we are," and low comedy with men "as worse than we are." Medieval characters ranged from God to the Devil, from purest saint to most abject sinner. Some characters have been drawn on a heroic scale, masters of their fate, working out their destinies by their own resources; other characters have been treated as hapless victims of an unfortunate heredity and environment, incapable of taking action, defeated, frustrated, and resigned. Modern dramatists of realistic and naturalistic persuasions have endeavored to create the illusion of complicated character by piling up a wealth of physical details, by capitalizing on the significant trifle, and by searching for the psychological meaning beneath the act. The expressionists have experimented with split personalities, or have effaced from characters all aspects of individuality, reducing them to X or Mr. Zero. Dramatic literature is filled with a wide variety of portraits.

A novelist can create characters by using a broad range of actions over many years and under many conditions. He can directly express the thoughts coursing through the heads of his creatures, and he has great freedom with time and space. In sharp contrast, the playwright's work is compressed in time and restricted in scope. Generally, he has felt obliged to limit himself to relatively few characters, since he has only a short time to present them to an audience.

He defines and delineates them by their words and actions which reveal their inner lives. If a character is meant to portray a hero, his heroism must be established in word and action before the audience. Concrete signs are essential, if the theater-goer is to believe in or identify with the character. Remember how Arthur Miller, in *Death of a Salesman*, gave us an immediate sense of Willy by his entrance and first few lines. Tennessee Williams, in *A*

The close relationship of Stella and Stanley in A Streetcar Named Desire *is established by their actions and dialogue. (Directed by Bill Ludel at the Playmakers Repertory Company, Chapel Hill, North Carolina).*

Streetcar Named Desire, quickly reveals the characters of Stanley and Stella in their first appearance:

> *(Two men come around the corner, Stanley Kowalski and Mitch. They are about twenty-eight or thirty years old, roughly dressed in blue denim work clothes. Stanley carries his bowling jacket and a red-stained package from the butcher's. They stop at the foot of the steps.)*
>
> **Stanley:** *(bellowing)* Hey there! Stella, baby! *(Stella comes out on the first floor landing, a gentle young woman about twenty-five, and of a background obviously quite different from her husband's.)*
>
> **Stella:** *(mildly)* Don't holler at me like that. Hi Mitch.
>
> **Stanley:** Catch!
>
> **Stella:** What?
>
> **Stanley:** Meat!
>
> *(He heaves the package at her. She cries out in protest but manages to catch it: then she laughs breathlessly . . .)*[5]

[5]Tennessee Williams, *A Streetcar Named Desire* (New York: New Directions Publishing Corporation, 1947).

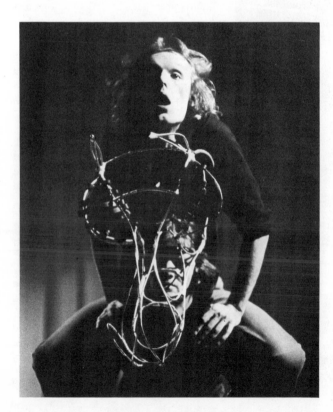

Peter Shaffer's Equus *depends upon the gradual revelation of Alan's fixation for the horse, Nugget, seen here in the University of Houston production.*

During the last quarter of the nineteenth century, developments in scientific method and psychology led playwrights to delineate characters with rich inner lives and complex motivations. Ibsen, Strindberg, and Chekhov were particularly successful in creating figures authentically alive.

Many twentieth-century plays depend for their appeal on solid characters who are psychologically complex. Great stress has been placed not only on revealing the inner life of the individual but also often on exploiting the *interaction* of characters and on exposing the tensions and turbulence that result from interrelationships. Many modern writers and theorists now reject this kind of drama in favor of plays that emphasize philosophical or political content and subordinate the individual identity to the larger social scene. In these instances, character is not defined at all and little attempt is made to create credible people or probe beneath the surface. In expressionistic plays, actors may represent states of mind, or one aspect of character, and not a complete person at all. Pinter's characters, as in his *Old Times*, are ambiguous and blurred figures whose dialogue concerns a stream of incidents simultaneously recalled of the dim past. Or his *No Man's Land*, in which we never know who the people really are, but we get a stirring sense of their situation, which concerns growing old, the need for companionship, and the desperate awareness of instability.

In general, because most traditional drama deals with the fate of individual characters who can be presented with such immediacy by actors before an audience, dramatists have taken great care to create characters whom we recognize as genuine.

Character is delineated in four ways.

First, character may be established by appearance. The performer's physical presence is an immediate stimulus to the audience. The playwright may want to project a very specific image and he describes his characters in detail. For example, Pirandello describes the Father, in his *Six Characters in Search of an Author*, as

> . . . a man of about 50: hair, reddish in color, thin at the temples; he is not bald, however; thick moustache, falling over his still fresh mouth, which often opens in an empty uncertain smile. He is fattish, pale, with an especially wide forehead. He has blue, oval-shaped eyes, very clear and piercing. Wears light trousers and a dark jacket. He is alternately mellifluous and violent in his manner.[6]

The playwright frequently builds a character's entrance in order to place special attention on his initial appearance. Notice the care O'Neill has taken with the first entrance of his major character in *Anna Christie*:

> *There is a ring of the family entrance hall. (Larry [the bartender] comes to the door and opens it a trifle—then with a puzzled expression, pulls it wide. Anna Christopherson enters. She is a tall, blond, fully developed girl of twenty, handsome after a large, Viking-daughter fashion but now run down in health and plainly showing all the outward evidences of belonging to the world's oldest profession. Her youthful face is already hard and cynical beneath its layers of*

[6]Luigi Pirandello, *Six Characters in Search of an Author*, in *Naked Masks*, trans. Edward Stover, ed. Eric Bentley (New York: E. P. Dutton, 1922).

A character's appearance is important in establishing his part in the play. Casting plus costuming and makeup contribute heavily to the visual impact of each role. Note how each performer is individualized in appearance in these characters from Shakespeare's The Tempest. *Stephanie Zimbalist as Miranda, Brent Carver as Ariel, Anthony Hopkins as Prospero, and Michael Bond (below) as Caliban. Mark Taper Forum.*

make-up. Her clothes are the tawdry finery of peasant stock turned prostitute. She comes and sinks wearily in a chair by the table, left front.)

Anna: Gimme a whiskey—ginger ale on the side (*Then, as Larry turns to go, forcing a winning smile at him.*) And don't be stingy, baby.[7]

Hamlet, in Act I, scene 2, describes his own appearance in these lines after Queen Gertrude has chided him for his melancholy:

'Tis not alone my inky cloak, good mother,
Nor customary suits of solemn black,
Nor windy suspiration of forced breath,
No, nor the fruitful river in the eye,
Nor the dejected 'haviour of the visage,
Together with all forms, modes, shows of grief,
That can denote me truly . . .

A character's physical appearance—face, body, voice, carriage, as well as costume and makeup, is an important means of defining character. In some plays the costumes and masks were enough to define the character, as in the commedia dell'arte, or the Noh drama of Japan.

[7]Eugene O'Neill, *Anna Christie* (New York: Random House, Inc., 1922).

Second, character is revealed by speech. The kind of language used by the person, his manner of speaking, his voice quality, his inflection pattern, pitch, rate, and general vitality all say something about the character. Most playwrights take great care to write dialogue that makes an immediate statement about the characters, such as Anna's opening line in the excerpt above.

Except for realistic plays, dramatic convention allowed the use of asides, soliloquies, and monologues for characters to talk directly to the audience about themselves. Contemporary playwrights often use these devices. One of the sources of comedy in *Fiddler on the Roof* is Tevye's asides to God, as he discusses his problems and wishes. Early in Stoppard's *Travesties*, Carr has an extended monologue of five pages, in which he recalls his real and imaginary experiences with Lenin, Joyce, and Tzara during World War I in Zurich. During the speech, the playwright specifies that the actor begins as Old Carr and ends up as a young man, mostly by changes in his voice without the aid of makeup and costuming.

Third, character is established by action. Behavior gives us clues to inner motivations. Roles in the root action of the play are revealed by the culmination of the plot and participation in the incidents, but the small detailed business of characterization helps the audience to build up a composite portrait. Sometimes, the playwright may deliberately give the audience a misleading or ambiguous impression of a character at the beginning of the play and then gradually reveal the truth as the play progresses. In the opening scene of Ibsen's *A Doll's House*, Nora's initial appearance and actions suggest a doll-like character, but our first impression is changed by her subsequent action. In John Osborne's *Look Back in Anger*, the audience is perplexed and even alienated by the protagonist's sadistic behavior, but as they come to know the reason for his suffering, they reach an understanding of his conduct. *The Gin Game* is an engaging comedy about an elderly couple who pass the time away by playing cards, but their actions during the games gradually reveal their irascible inner selves.

Fourth, a character may be revealed by the way others react to him. Sometimes the playwright uses comment about an absent character as a method of revealing the truth. For example, the true character behind the blustering, swaggering barker, Liliom, is indicated by Julie's line: "It is possible, dear, that someone may beat you, and beat you, and beat you— and not hurt you at all." Willy Loman in *Death of a Salesman* is a man who never saw himself or his motivations accurately. His son Biff expresses the truth about Willy when he says, "He had the wrong dreams. All, all wrong. . . . The man didn't know who he was."

The playwright may deliberately mislead or perplex the spectator by having characters say ambiguous or controversial things. Molière begins *Tartuffe* with a domestic quarrel in which he exposes two entirely different points of view about his leading character. Pirandello delighted in making the point time and again in his plays that it is difficult, if not impossible, to really comprehend the character of another. Hence, his plays are filled with

Playwright D.L. Coburn uses a card game in his Gin Game *as a method of gradually revealing the inner lives of the two characters, played here by Jessica Tandy and Hume Cronyn in the New York production.*

conflicting statements about the characters. In his *Right You Are If You Think You Are*, he dramatizes a series of incidents in which the leading characters tell conflicting stories about one another so the audience never knows the truth—thus illustrating the problem of separating illusion from reality.

The sharpness of a character's image is in part dependent on the structure of the drama. Plays written for a theater that permits most of the essential action to appear onstage gives the playwright a greater opportunity to create more vivid and complex characters than plays that are confined to a minimum of action. One reason Hamlet is such a rich and interesting character is the number of views of him we see through his relationship to the Ghost, Horatio, Ophelia, the Players, Gertrude, Polonius, Claudius, Rosencrantz and Guildenstern. When we contrast this variety of character exposure to that of Agamemnon or Orestes or Antigone, we realize how restricted the Greeks were in delineating complex characters. Some playwrights, notably Shakespeare, possess the ability to sketch memorable characters in a very few lines, but most dramatists develop their major characters' roles at length in order to create distinctive and believable personalities.

In most drama the purpose of showing men in action is to enlist our interest and involve our emotions in the fortunes of the characters. To accomplish this purpose, the dramatist creates characters with whom we have some kind of bond, either through temperament, condition, or destiny. If we cannot connect with them, we remain passive and indifferent, and the action does not fulfill its function. Hence, it is important for us to believe in the characters. Sometimes they leave us cold. Their motivations and sense of values seem incredible; they are confused and incomprehensible; they make no effort to decide their fate; they are too self-centered, or too short-sighted. On the other hand, a good playwright can kindle our interest and sympathy for all kinds of characters if he gives us understanding, particularly if these characters are well played by skillful performers.

3. Thought

The third element cited by Aristotle is *thought*, or *dianoia*, by which he meant the intellectual aspect of the play as shown by the characters' speech and actions whenever they argue, plead, or reason. Thought is the rationale for behavior.

One does not go to the theater primarily for information. Plays are not objective debates, nor mere presentations of factual data and logical arguments leading to a clear decision; but like the experiences of life itself, characters make decisions out of a network of feelings and thoughts. Like all forms of literature, good drama usually is meaningful. A play is a unified organization of an imaginative experience and insight, and while it provides emotional outlets, it also engages the mind. We go to the theater for delight and discovery. As Eric Bentley says, the effect of seeing a great play is "of a veil lifted, the scales falling from the eyes, in a word, something momentous exhibited—and said."[8]

A basic ingredient in the theater from the very beginning to the present day has been conflict—the "good guys" against the "bad guys," husband versus wife, children clashing with parents, lovers' quarrels, and rebels against society. In dramatizing such collisions, the playwright has found it necessary to show both sides of the argument. Even in medieval drama, written specifically to show the rewards for following the straight and narrow path to salvation, the clergy were obliged for dramatic reasons to include the Devil as well as God, vices as well as virtues, sinners as well as saints. In most plays, the dramatist presents a variety of thoughts and views. Antigone is in conflict with Creon, and Oedipus with Tiresias. Blanche's sensitivity is opposed by Stanley's brutality; Major Barbara's religious convictions are challenged by her father's capitalistic views as a munitions manufacturer; the El Teatro Campesino of Luis Valdez shows Chicanos against white growers and

[8]Eric Bentley, *The Life of the Drama* (New York: Atheneum Publishers, 1967).

extortionists; the disillusioned war veteran in David Rabe's *Sticks and Bones* is shown in opposition to his family's determined efforts to resist his intrusion into their superficial lives. The rationale for disparate points of view constitutes one aspect of thought in drama.

In addition to the varied views of individual characters, thought concerns a play's theme—a "golden text" that summarizes the moral and indicates the symbolic meaning of the play as a whole, such as "love conquers all," "murder will out," and "niceness pays." But drama does not always lend itself to such neat copybook maxims. A given play may convey a variety of interpretations to an audience. Most of Ibsen's contemporaries were profoundly shocked at Nora's decision in *A Doll's House* to leave her husband and children, although her action is entirely credible to most of us today. Some people regard Antigone as headstrong and foolish in openly defying Creon and thus deliberately choosing to die. In his notes while directing *A Streetcar Named Desire*, Elia Kazan clearly shows that he intended to express Williams' point of view: "If we don't watch out, the apes will take over." But in production, the impression conveyed to many spectators by the actors' performance was that Blanche threatened the Kowalski home, and Stanley's brutal treatment of her was justified. The ideas of great dramas have, of course, been sources of endless academic contention. What is the true interpretation of *Hamlet*? Is Shylock a comic or a tragic figure? Is the tragedy of *Antigone* really the tragedy of Creon? Varied interpretations of a play's meaning indicate that the dramatist has not been explicit in stating a theme. Many great plays have a depth or richness, making them susceptible to all kinds of interpretations. One of the most interesting aspects of the contemporary theater is the astonishing variety of experimental revival productions of plays from the past. Inevitably, the individual reader and spectator is challenged to search his own mind and experience in evaluating a play.

Whatever the purpose of the playwright, the action of significant drama is as meaningful as an experience of life itself. The choices that the characters make, their motivation and behavior, their dialogue and the subtext, and the sequence of action are rewarding subjects for investigation. The content of a play is a valid reflector of the time in which it was written. Current drama very often mirrors the world in a vivid and compelling way, focusing on our life-styles, the shifting sense of values, man's loss of philosophic roots, the plight of minorities, alienation, and the struggles for power, recognition, and security.

4. Diction

The fourth element of drama is diction—the language of the play, the dialogue the actors speak. The diction provides a system of verbal signs that clearly set the characters and their actions before the audience.

Discourse in drama must be clear, since the language must be immediately apprehended by the listener; in the theater, there is no turning back the page, no pausing to weigh and consider a line before continuing to the next. The dialogue must be interesting despite the need for simplicity and economy. It should capture the spirit of life and character. As the Irish playwright J. M. Synge put it: "In a good play, every speech should be as fully flavored as a nut or an apple." The diction must be appropriate for the character and the situation. Lines do not exist in the theater as separate entities. They are always in context, growing out of the emotionally charged incidents of the plot. The language of drama must be dynamic. As we have already suggested, speech is a form of action. Dialogue shows the characters' relationship to others, reflects the progression of the action, indicates what is happening inside the characters, reveals their suffering, growth, or decline. It is a means of articulating the clash of wills and conflicting motivations.

The dramatist needs the poet's feeling for language—a rich imagination; a facility with provocative imagery; and awareness of the weight, texture, and arrangement of words. Dramatic dialogue is not contemplative or static; it is harnessed to action and change. Even in the Japanese Noh dramas, which are often plays of reminiscence, the dialogue pulses with the life of the remembered event. It must be speakable so that it gives the performers sounds and cadences that aid them in projecting the thoughts and feelings of the characters. For the audience the dialogue must have audible intelligibility so that the words are arresting in sound as they stimulate the ear and evoke images that are not only immediately comprehensible but set up emotional reverberations as well.

Much of the serious drama before the nineteenth century was linked to poetry. The Greek and Elizabethan masters of drama were poets as well as playwrights. Their works, therefore, have an added literary value, and their use of verse seems particularly appropriate for their elevated tragedies of high born characters. In modern times poetry has given way to prose as the naturalist and realist bring onstage commonplace figures in everyday pursuits. Many people have lamented the absence of poetry in the modern theater; attempts have been made to recapture some of the enrichment of the poetic speech, notably by Maxwell Anderson, Christopher Fry, Bertolt Brecht, T. S. Eliot, and Federico Garcia Lorca. While modern drama lacks elevated language, it would be a mistake to think that all plays written in the poetic form were notably successful. Indeed, the use of verse in the past was often puerile and ostentatious. Many poets had no sense of dramatic form or theatrical awareness. Oftentimes their plays were not stageworthy; the preoccupation with the language retarded the action, the drama bogged down with linguistic clutter.

Over the years a great variety of dialogue devices has been used. One of the most interesting, devised by the Greeks, is called *stichomythia*, in which short bursts of dialogue are delivered in alternating lines. It was a means of building tension in the way that a motion-picture editor uses rapid intercutting of film clips to intensify the action.

In the seventeenth century, Molière used *stichomythia* in scenes of tension, such as in the clash between Toinette and Argan in *The Imaginary Invalid* (pp. 114–15).

Pinter's language has the capacity for setting up echoes and vibrations far beyond the facade of words. His use of rhythm and silence opens up unexpected associations and a surreal sense of menace. As John Lahr says of Pinter, "The story on stage is deeper than the words that explain it, the language mere signposts for an immense and inaudible despair."[9]

The following passage indicates Pinter's remarkable ability to create theatrical effects with the colloquial idiom. In *The Birthday Party*, Stanley has sought refuge at a seaside resort, but he has been followed by two sinister strangers, McCann and Goldberg, who undermine and destroy him. As they are about to take him away in their long black car, this dialogue occurs (see frontispiece, Chapter Two for illustration):

McCann: He looks better, doesn't he?

Goldberg: Much better.

McCann: A new man.

Goldberg: You know what we'll do?

McCann: What?

Goldberg: We'll buy him another pair. (*They begin to woo him, gently and with relish. During the following sequence,* Stanley *shows no reaction. He remains with no movement, where he sits.*)

McCann: Out of our own pockets.

Goldberg: It goes without saying. Between you and me, Stan, it's about time you had a new pair of glasses.

McCann: You can't see straight.

Goldberg: It's true. You've been cockeyed for years.

McCann: Now you're even more cockeyed.

Goldberg: He's right. You've gone from bad to worse.

McCann: Worse than worse.

Goldberg: You need a long convalescence.

McCann: A change of air.

Goldberg: Somewhere over the rainbow.

McCann: Where angels fear to tread.

Goldberg: Exactly.

McCann: You're in a rut.

Goldberg: You look anaemic.

McCann: Rheumatic.

Goldberg: Myopic.

McCann: Epileptic.

Goldberg: You're on the verge.

McCann: You're a dead duck.

Goldberg: But we can save you.

McCann: From a worse fate.

Goldberg: True.

McCann: Undeniable.

Goldberg: From now on, we'll take the hub of your wheel.

McCann: We'll renew your season ticket.

Goldberg: We'll take twopence off your morning tea.

McCann: We'll give you a discount on all inflammable goods.

Goldberg: We'll watch over you.

[9]John Lahr, *Casebook on Pinter's Homecoming* (New York: Grove Press, Inc., 1971).

McCann: Advise you.

Goldberg: Give you proper care and treatment.[10]

Another contemporary playwright with a special flair for diction is Tom Stoppard, who creates a kind of intellectual vaudeville. In his *Rosencrantz and Guildenstern Are Dead, Jumpers,* and *Travesties* he puts together dazzling pastiches of puns, double entendres, alliterations, and quotations (see pp. 127–28).

As we shall see in Chapter Seven, the new theatricalism often regards language as a subordinate element in production. Following Artaud's edict, "no more masterpieces," a revolt began not only against "great plays" but against language. Innovators have worked with improvised dialogue, invented languages, and nonverbal communication.

Extended soliloquies and monologues, which were a part of drama until the advent of realism, are again a part of the playwright's techniques.

In Stoppard's *Travesties,* Carr launches into a long narration of his World War I years in Zurich. Stoppard's *Dirty Linen* and *New-Found-Land* includes a ten-minute digression describing his view of the American scene. Peter Handke's *A Sorrow Beyond Dreams* is an hour-long account of his mother's life and suicide that is read to the audience. An ingenious use of the single

[10]Harold Pinter, *The Birthday Party* (New York: Grove Press, Inc., 1959).

Stoppard brings to the contemporary theater a special flair for word play, as for example in Rosencrantz and Guildenstern Are Dead, *a plot that develops the story of two minor characters from* Hamlet, *caught up in a political intrigue. (Wayne State University Theater. Directed by Richard Spear; designed by Russell Smith).*

character speaking is found in Samuel Beckett's one-act *Krapp's Last Tape*, in which an old man contrasts his present life with his youthful memories by listening to and commenting on a tape recording of his voice made thirty years ago.

The use of prose in the modern theater has often resulted in stage speech that is flat, pedestrian, and vulgar, filled with clichés of commonplace conversation. As Elder Olson has said, "The drama has increasingly sought to be articulate in the language of the inarticulate."[11] He goes on to lament the loss of subtle expression and profound thoughts available when poetic diction was more flexible.

On the other hand, the current emphasis on functional speech has brought gains in eliminating "purple passages" and pretentious rhetoric. With the poet's feeling for language, some contemporary playwrights have created diction that is vivid and evocative. Among these are Samuel Beckett in *Waiting for Godot* and *Endgame*; Harold Pinter in *Birthday Party*, *The Homecoming*, *No Man's Land*; and David Storey in *Home*.

5. Music

The fifth element mentioned by Aristotle is *music*, which refers to all of the auditory material, including sound effects. It encompasses all aspects of sound—pitch, rate, quality, duration, volume, and rhythm.

We remember that the Greek drama, in its early association with dithyrambs, made full use of the musical potential in the singing and dancing of the chorus. Sound patterns were also important in the acting of the major characters who sang, chanted, danced, and spoke with great variety in cadence, texture, and tempo. In the Oriental theater music has always played an important part. In the Noh and Kabuki theaters of Japan and the traditional as well as modern plays of China, an orchestra is an essential aspect of the performance and music an integral part of the show. Elizabethan drama was rich in lyricism that broke into song. Later English drama continued the use of music and in burlettas the entire performance might have been sung or chanted. Melodrama was originally linked to music, and even though the spoken word came to dominate the genre, musical backgrounds were used to accompany exits and entrances of major characters and to reinforce the mood of emotionally loaded scenes, such as chases, fights, escapes, love scenes, and deaths.

America's major theatrical invention, musical comedy, grew out of popular entertainment of the nineteenth century. The minstrel show appealed to a wide audience from 1840 onwards; its male ensembles usually played in blackface in a melange of comedy, singing, and dancing. The first musical comedy to become a hit was *The Black Crook* (1866), an extravaganza that featured spectacle and scantily clad chorus girls. Other early influences were

[11]Elder Olson, *Tragedy and the Theory of Drama* (Detroit: Wayne State University Press, 1961).

the operettas by European composers that were built around sentimental stories about charming people in make-believe places that provided opportunities for picturesque scenery and tuneful music—for instance, Lehar's *The Merry Widow* (1907) and Oscar Strauss' *The Chocolate Soldier* (1910). From France came the influence of "leg" shows like the Folies-Bergère that combined vaudeville, comedy, and beautiful women in lavish costumes and scenery. Florenz Ziegfeld set the fashion for such display in America.

George M. Cohan added the patriotic note in his bright, energetic musicals such as *Forty-Five Minutes from Broadway*. In 1927 a major change occurred when Jerome Kern and Edna Ferber produced her book *Showboat*, linking literary material with music. George and Ira Gershwin introduced sophisticated musical forms in early works like *Lady, Be Good* (1924), but their landmark was *Porgy & Bess* (1935), a play about the Southern black that created the first successful native folk opera. In 1931, the Gershwins with Morrie Ryskind produced the political satire *Of Thee I Sing*, the first musical to win the Pulitzer Prize. In 1943 Rodgers and Hammerstein made another significant change in the musical with their *Oklahoma*, based on Lynn Riggs' folk play, *Green Grow the Lilacs*. The dancing of chorus girls was replaced by Agnes de Mille's ballet, and the story and music were melded organically in a plot that dealt with simple, lively country folk instead of dramatizing frivolous, upper class love affairs of big city dwellers. Other memorable musicals produced by Rodgers and Hammerstein were *South Pacific* (1949) and *The*

Annie, based on the popular comic strip, "Little Orphan Annie," was a box office hit with its engaging old-fashioned story told in a lively way.

Sound of Music (1959). Leonard Bernstein and Stephen Sondheim combined serious subject matter with sophisticated music in *West Side Story* (1957). In the late sixties the "American Tribal Love-Rock Musical" *Hair*, a brash, formless protest against the established culture, created a new style of show. In 1964 *Fiddler on the Roof* became a phenomenal hit with its warm-hearted treatment of the stories of Shalom Aleichem.

Musical comedies have always been the biggest drawing card at the box office. More than two dozen musicals have enjoyed runs of over a thousand performances on Broadway. The conventional formula of popular music, spectacular scenery and costuming, and excellent choreography will no doubt continue as standard fare in the commercial theater.

Although the motion picture has always exploited the evocative power of music to heighten its effects, naturalistic and realistic drama has usually rejected music as an artificial intrusion. But even in realistic drama, playwrights have used sound to enhance the mood of their plays. For example, Chekhov was very conscious of the use of sounds in *Uncle Vanya*. In the final act of the play a melancholy atmosphere is reinforced by the click of the counting beads, the scratch of the pen, the churring of a cricket, the tapping of the night watchman's cane, the soft strumming of a guitar, and the bells of the carriage when Dr. Astrov departs.

As the theater has become freer in recent years, music and sound have often played an increasingly important part in performance. In Jack Gelber's *The Connection* a jazz orchestra is a part of the acting company and actually plays approximately thirty minutes of music in each act. Brecht, with his lyrical gifts, uses music as an important part of his epic theater—for example, in *The Caucasian Chalk Circle*, which follows the Oriental practice of having an orchestra on stage and injecting songs freely into the dialogue. Similarly Kopit's *Indians*, an epic-style exposé of the myths of the old West, makes effective use of music and dance. In *House of Blue Leaves*, John Guare uses Artie, the piano player, to frame the action with his playing and singing beginning and ending the play. In *The Elephant Man* a cellist in evening clothes sits at the side of the stage and occasionally plays music from Elgar and Bach. The cellist is not a character in the play nor is he related to the plot, but the quality of his appearance and music is aesthetically right.

Among present-day playwrights with a keen ear for sound and music as an element of theatricalism is Peter Shaffer. A brilliant example occurs in *Equus*, for which the playwright made this production note on the "Equus Noise": "I have in mind a choric effect made up of all the actors sitting around upstage and composed of humming, thumping, and stamping—though never of neighing and whinnying." The sound was especially striking during the climax (see pp. 00–00).

Sam Shepard, in working on the production of *INACOMA* in San Francisco (1977), attempted to find new ways to integrate music and theater since he felt that through music one could reach an audience more immediately and deeply than through gesture and language. *INACOMA* was a group collaboration in dramatizing the experience of Amy Renfrow who is in a coma as the result of an accident. Her parents and doctors attempt to reach her, but in vain. In the end the plug is pulled and Amy dies. From the very first rehearsal Shepard insisted on using a jazz group to lead, stimulate, and supplement the work of the actors.

In the experimental work of the new theater (Chapter Seven) many innovators make a sharp break from traditional dramatic practice in placing most of their emphasis on music, sound, and spectacle. Oftentimes conventional dialogue is replaced by disparate fragments, some of which may be recorded. Very often a complex sound track accompanies a series of striking images and actions that do not follow a plot line, but serve to evoke moods and feelings through their sensuous appeal.

6. Spectacle

The sixth dramatic element, *spectacle*, includes all visual aspects of the production—scenery, lighting, costuming, makeup, and the stage business of the performers. It also includes the environment of the action whether it be in an actual playhouse or an adapted site such as a Greek hillside, a Japanese shrine in a dry river bed, an opulent hall in a Renaissance palace, an open marketplace, an inn-yard, a factory warehouse, or street. The audience is also a part of the celebration we call theater because spectators often come to be seen as well as to see, and the communal experience of being eyewitnesses to a stirring event has its effect. Because drama is often thought of as *dialogue*, the word threatens to dominate the audience experience. But there is rebellion against this dominance and today we are more than ever conscious of the need to make a theater of images—even at the expense of subordinating the diction and rejecting the conventional playhouse and scenery. By its very nature dramatic action results in compelling visual experiences. Think of the images called to mind in Chapter One, even without the benefit of performance when the Three Marys see the miracle of the empty tomb; or imagine the manner in which Hamlet's "Mousetrap" reveals Claudius' crime; or call to mind Willy Loman's first entrance when he staggers through the gloom, bone-weary and defeated, carrying his heavy sample cases. The theater has a marvelous facility for filling our heads with rich visual experiences.

Throughout history, as we shall see in Chapter Ten on Stage Design, theaters have appealed to the eye as well as the ear whether or not actual scenery was used. In the production of Greek, Elizabethan, and Japanese Noh plays virtually no representation of locale was required except that supplied by the architecture, and, of course, the performers themselves. In the Greek and Noh theaters the use of masks and striking costumes, and the dancing of the chorus and actors enriched the spectacle.

During the Renaissance the proscenium arch was introduced into the theater, separating audience and performers by placing the acting area behind an architectural framework so that the spectators looked through the opening to the stage. This innovation was quickly exploited as theatrical production

Engraving showing the lavish use of spectacle in an eighteenth-century theater in Naples.

was dominated by spectacular changeable scenery which often ran away with the show. Scenic artists vied with one another in creating lavish settings and spectacular effects. The impulse for display often spilled over into the auditorium and theatrical architecture reflected a taste for opulence.

The proscenium arch with its use of pictorial scenery dominates the theater even to the present day although its style and function have changed a good deal, as we shall see.

During the nineteenth century melodrama gained a wide following in the theater; part of its popularity depended upon spectacular scenic effects coupled with vigorous action. As realism and naturalism made their impact on the late nineteenth-century audiences, scenery took on a new importance in production because of the scientifically inspired concern with environment as a conditioning force in determining behavior. Hence spectacle assumed an organic, psychological role in the performance, as reinforcement of the meaning of the action and as a device relating character to the social milieu.

Tastes have changed considerably in modern times and while many plays still require a semblance of representational setting, many innovators not only reject scenery but the theater as well. But even in experimental productions, the visual aspects of drama are important in the environment of the performance and the action. Visual stimuli of lights and color are fundamental in creating states of mind and atmosphere.

The taste for spectacle is not gone, it has merely changed directions—and theater will continue to be a place for show.

Spectacular scenery, costume and action were fully realized in the Wayne State University production of The Royal Hunt of the Sun *by Peter Shaffer. (Directed by Don Blakely; designed by Russell Smith).*

Bibliography

BECKERMAN, BERNARD, *Dynamics of Drama: Theory and Method of Analysis.* New York: Alfred A. Knopf, Inc., 1970.

BENTLEY, ERIC, *The Life of the Drama.* New York: Atheneum Publishers, 1967.

ESSLIN, MARTIN, *An Anatomy of Drama.* New York: Hill & Wang, 1976.

NICOLL, ALLARDYCE, *The Theater and Dramatic Theory.* New York: Barnes & Noble Books, 1962.

WEALES, GERALD, *The Play and Its Parts.* New York: Basic Books, Inc., Publishers, 1964.

THREE
Tragedy

You go to the theater to share an experience that will give you some kind of satisfaction—amusement, relaxation, escape, excitement, stimulation, learning, edification. Apparently most people go to be entertained, judging by the preponderance of musicals and comedies having long runs on Broadway. And yet, there is a kind of drama that is somber in mood, serious in purpose, and filled with suffering and travail, that has a remarkably pervasive and enduring appeal. One of the most perplexing human phenomena is the paradox of deriving pleasure through pain. What satisfaction can we obtain from watching the undeserved punishment of a well-intentioned heroine like Antigone? What is the aesthetic justification for involving ourselves in Hamlet's ordeal in an alien world? How can we find enjoyment in the decline and fall of a powerful king like Oedipus? To answer these questions we need to consider the nature of tragedy.

The idea of tragedy is man-made. There is no ideal tragedy—only a small collection of plays that (with more or less agreement) we refer to when we talk about them. For the moment, we will confine ourselves to classic tragedy which includes the Greeks, the works of Shakespeare and some of his contemporaries, and the French neoclassicists, Racine and Corneille. We will deal with modern attempts at tragedy a bit later.

Although it does not bulk large in the history of the theater, tragedy is the most discussed genre—and the one which has inspired the greatest diversity of opinion. Of the original Greek tragedies fewer than ten percent are extant, so we have only very small sampling. Even among the Greeks, there was no one typical tragedy. Moreover, tragedies from other periods, such as the Elizabethan and the French neoclassic times, differ markedly from those of the Greeks.

In addition to the plays, we have a body of critical theory that is even more diverse and contradictory than the plays themselves.

Since the Greeks invented tragedy as a literary form, let us go back to them for their perspective. Plato in his *Republic* took a dim view of tragic poetry, for while it might be "charming" it was for him an artificial imitation of life removed from the reality of eternal ideas and therefore a distortion of "truth." Ethically, tragedy was suspect to Plato because it stimulated dangerous passions that might get out of control. To him it dealt with unwholesome doubts about the gods and the nature of the moral universe. Plato concluded that it would be folly to give the tragic poet free license in the state. He challenged writers to make literature an edifying force. "The poet shall compose nothing contrary to the ideas of the lawful or just, or beautiful or good, which are allowed in the state."

Plato's premise that the obligation of the writer is to foster morality was widely accepted by later critics such as Sir Philip Sidney in Elizabethan England, who in defending tragic drama argued that it "maketh kings fear to be tyrants." Boileau in France cited the neoclassic dictum to the poet:

Let all your thoughts to virtue be confined,
Still offering nobler figures to our mind.

And Samuel Johnson in eighteenth-century England asserted that "it is always a writer's duty to make the world better."

The Platonic notion that the arts should serve morality and the state is a pervasive one that supports most censorship today.

Aristotle seems to have been answering Plato in his *Poetics*, the seminal work on tragedy and the source of endless conjecture and controversy. It is well to remember that *Poetics* was written a century after the golden age of classic drama, and that it was limited to Greek tragedy. Aristotle based most of his theory on Sophocles; although he refers to Euripides as "the most tragic of poets" he devotes little attention to him or to the other great writer of Greek tragedy, Aeschylus.

During the Renaissance, Italian and French critics leaned heavily on Aristotle but they often distorted his ideas to fit their concept of teaching moral philosophy, or to fit the plays of their time. The Elizabethans, Shakespeare and his contemporaries, except for Ben Jonson, paid scant attention to theory.

Realizing, then, that Aristotle's *Poetics* offers a restricted view of tragedy, we can read it with profit if we remember that he was not the universal law-giver, but only a very sound observer. Most of the plays of his own time did not fit his specifications, not to mention those of the Elizabethans, neoclassic France, or the remarkable variation of forms and styles of the Western drama since Aristotle.

Any consideration of tragedy, however, must take Aristotle into account because of the groundwork he laid—the nature and function of tragedy, the qualifications of the tragic hero, and the structure of the tragic form.

Let us turn our attention to the basic Aristotelian concepts, beginning with his definition of tragedy.

> Tragedy, then, is an imitation of an action that is serious, complete, and of a certain magnitude; in language embellished with each kind of artistic ornament, the several kinds being found in separate parts of the play; in the form of action, not of narrative; through pity and fear effecting the proper purgation of these emotions.[1]

By *imitation*, Aristotle meant an artistic representation, rather than an exact copy of reality. An *action*, as used here, refers to the play as a dynamic organized process. Tragedy is *serious* in nature, not trivial or frivolous. It deals with the most profound problems of humanity—identity and destiny, the nature of good and evil, the mysterious forces of the universe, and the consequences of individual responsibilities. Its purpose is not mere diversion or amusement but an investigation of ethical and spiritual values.

Tragedy attains *magnitude* in the heroic stature of its characters, in the use of poetry, in the universality of its meaning, and in the loftiness of its ideas. Tragedies are elevated; they possess scale and scope beyond the petty vicissitudes of daily existence. Magnitude of character is realized in tragedy through the use of highborn characters, persons of nobility and prominence

---

[1]Ingram Bywater, trans., *Aristotle on the Art of Poetry* (Oxford: Clarendon, 1920).

who occupy "exposed positions"; people who as Aristotle said "are better than we are," or those who achieve greatness.

A tragedy is *complete*; it has a beginning, a middle, and an end—and according to Aristotle each of these parts is a well-articulated structure without extraneous material. The course of action is a "necessary and probable" linking of antecedents and consequents. Such unity and wholeness are fundamental to the Greek aesthetic view of life.

By *language embellished with each kind of artistic ornament*, Aristotle explains, "I mean that with rhythm and harmony or song superadded; and by *the kinds separately*, I mean that some portions are worked out with verse only, and others in turn with song."

The chief difference between the *dramatic* and *narrative form* is a result of the *manner* of presentation. A narrative may be written or told; drama must be presented with impersonation and action—it is "a thing done."

Pity, fear, and *catharsis* are terms that have perplexed and intrigued generations of scholars and critics. This special effect which tragedy aims to produce will be discussed at length later in the chapter. For now, let us recognize that pity goes beyond mere pathos to include the compassion that accompanies shared grief, and that fear transcends sheer fright to convey a sense of anxious concern and profound reverence. Catharsis suggests purgation and purification—a release of emotional tension that results in tranquility.

Plot

Are there aspects of plot that apply exclusively to tragedy? Aristotle felt that the tragic effect was achieved through structure, and he specified the arrangement of the incidents; his preference for various kinds of recognitions, reversals, denouements, and tragic deeds, as well as a tightly knit, unified plot. But tragedy does not depend on the Aristotelian form. It may be achieved by any means that succeeds in creating the emotional effects of tragedy.

There are certain generalizations about the characteristics of tragedy, however, that apply to the treatment of dramatic materials. Tragedy usually deals with positive, active characters caught in sharp conflict with opposing forces. In the ensuing struggle they suffer greatly and generally go to disaster. Although the protagonists may die, their integrity is intact. The dramatist does not contrive a denouement to avert catastrophe; indeed, suffering is essential in tragedy as a means of testing the hero or heroine.

Scenes of discovery or recognition are very important to the tragic plot. Aristotle admired discoveries that resulted in reversals such as in *Oedipus Rex* when the king discovers his identity, and realizes that he has murdered his father and is married to his mother in an incestuous relationship. Tragedy often has scenes of self-discovery in which characters examine their actions and motives in the light of their moral codes. These "moments of truth" are singularly characteristic of great tragedy. One thinks of Phaedra's and

The fate of the Thebans is in the hero's hands. King Oedipus promises the people to rid his kingdom of the plague. Oedipus Rex at the National Theater, Prague. Designed by Josef Svoboda, directed by M. Machacek.

Macbeth's horror when they realize the full import of their actions; of Hamlet's agonizing self-analysis when he tries to square appearance with reality; of Creon's and Othello's bitter suffering when their worlds tumble about them; of the self-torture of Oedipus when his crimes are known.

Suzanne K. Langer in her perceptive book, *Feeling and Form*, sees tragedy shaped by a "tragic rhythm,"—a pattern transferred from nature, of growth, maturation and decline. The action of the play shows the hero's "self-realization" as, under increasing pressure, he reaches his highest potential in "the vision of life as accomplished . . . the sense of fulfillment that lifts him above defeat."[2]

This basic rhythm determines the form of the action:

Dramatic acts are analogously connected with each other so that one directly or indirectly motivates what follows it. In this way a genuine rhythm of action is set

[2]Suzanne K. Langer, *Feeling and Form* (New York: Charles Scribner's Sons, 1953).

Creon's harsh edict forbidding the burial of the rebel Polynices results in the death of Antigone and of Creon's son, Haemon. Here he grieves over his son's corpse, condemning himself for his rash judgment. Antigone *at the Epidaurus festival.*

up. . . . That rhythm is the "commanding form" of the play; it springs from the poet's original conception of the "fable," and dictates the major divisions of the work, the light or heavy style of its presentation, the intensity of the highest feeling and most violent act, the great or small number of characters, and the degrees of their development. The total action is a cumulative form and because it is constructed by a rhythmic treatment of its elements, it appears to *grow* from its beginnings.[3]

The Tragic Hero

One of the most discussed aspects of Aristotelian thought is his concept of the tragic hero. It describes him as a good man, but not free from blemish—"an intermediate kind of personage" who, while not preeminently virtuous, is not depraved. His flaw (*hamartia*, which means missing the mark) is a term that caused endless argument since it is not uniformly applicable to all tragedies, nor does it appear to be consistent in the variety of characters involved in catastrophes.

How does one equate the suffering of Prometheus with that of Oedipus? Antigone or Hippolytus with Medea? Hamlet with Macbeth, Lear with Romeo and Juliet? The degree of guilt seems to have little or nothing to do with justice. All tragic figures suffer, regardless of their degree of guilt or responsibility. Sometimes their fall seems to be a matter of cause and effect rather than

[3]Langer, *Feeling and Form.*

crime and punishment. Pity is not related to vengeance, but to "undeserved misfortune." Our attention then as we look at the hero is not on his guilt or innocence, but on the quality of his spirit. How does he respond to these "boundary situations" when he is tested to the limit? What is the effect on him of evil and injustice?

Northrop Frye gives us the image of the tragic hero at the top of the wheel of fortune, above humanity and below something greater in the sky, who acts as a "conductor" of power from above. "Tragic heroes are wrapped in the mystery of their communion with that something beyond which we can see only through them and which is the source of their strength and their fate alike."[4]

Implicit in the Aristotelian concept of the tragic hero is that he must be a character of some magnitude—one who occupies an important position in his society so that he falls from a high place. One of the basic arguments against the possibility of tragedy in the modern world is the absence of men of great stature. However, Arthur Miller argues that "The commonest of men may take on that stature to the extent of his willingness to throw all he has into the contest, the battle to secure his rightful place in his world. . . . It is time, I think, that we who are without kings took up this bright thread of our history and followed it to the only place it can possibly lead in our time—the heart and spirit of the average man."[5]

Tragedy Deals with Significant Content

Tragedy achieves significance because it is concerned with the deep and abiding questions and problems that have perplexed man throughout the ages. As Allardyce Nicoll says, tragedy puts us in "contact with infinity. If we are religious, we shall say it is in contact with forces divine; if we are aesthetic, we shall say it is in contact with the vast illimitable forces of the universe. Everywhere in tragedy there is this sense of being raised to loftier heights."[6]

Henry Alonzo Myers asserts that "tragedy best expresses its conceptions of the orderly and absolute nature of values";[7] and Francis Fergusson observes that tragedy "celebrates the mystery of human nature and destiny with the health of the soul in view."[8] Tragedy confronts suffering and evil with honesty in such a way as to reveal both the weakness and nobility of human beings, their strength of will, and their capacity for suffering without breaking in the face of inevitable doom. Tragedy is not the drama of small souls bedeviled by the minor irritations of humdrum life. It does not concentrate on

[4]Northrop Frye, *The Anatomy of Criticism* (Princeton: Princeton University Press, 1957).

[5]Arthur Miller, "Tragedy of the Common Man," *New York Times*, February 27, 1949.

[6]Allardyce Nicoll, *The Theory of Drama* (New York: Thomas Y. Crowell Company, Inc., 1931).

[7]Henry Alonzo Myers, *Tragedy: A View of Life* (Ithaca: Cornell University Press, 1956).

[8]Francis Fergusson, *The Idea of a Theater* (Princeton: Princeton University Press, 1949).

man's physical environment or welfare, nor with his getting and spending, his thing-collecting. On the contrary, tragedy lifts our vision beyond petty cares and mundane anxieties by focusing our attention on the great issues that affect our spiritual welfare. Clytemnestra is caught between avenging the death of her daughter and her duty to her husband; Antigone between her sacred obligation to the dead and obedience to the king; Hamlet between the necessity of avenging the death of his father and his moral sensibilities; Lear between sympathy and pride; Macbeth between ambition and conscience. Tragedy deals with matters of great consequence.

The significant content of tragedy gives this form of drama a sense of universality. The effect of the play goes beyond the particular characters and the immediate circumstances to achieve an atmosphere of broad application. If even kings may suffer, how vulnerable are we? To the Greeks and Elizabethans the fate of the rulers was connected directly with that of their subjects. There is implicit in genuine tragedy not only an elevation of life, but also an acute awareness of our common frailty and humanity. Thus the suffering and struggles of the tragic hero become a part of the universal experience of those who share the play.

Tragedy Produces a Catharsis

The most significant element that distinguishes tragedy from other forms of drama is the tragic effect. Just what it is in tragedy that gives pleasure through pain is difficult to determine. Schlegel felt that the tragic tone was one of "irrepressible melancholy" when the audience is consoled and elevated through witnessing human weakness exposed to the vagaries of fate and natural forces. Schopenhauer saw the meaning of tragedy as resignation and renunciation in the face of a miserable and desolate existence. On the other hand, Myers sees evidence of a just order in tragedy:

> Since it is positive and affirmative, great tragic poetry satisfies our deepest rational and moral inclinations. As rational beings, we are always looking for patterns, for order, for meaning in experience; as moral beings, we can be satisfied only by discovering in the realm of good and evil the special kind of pattern or order which we call justice. Tragedy reconciles us to evil by showing us that it is not a single, separate phenomenon but one side of change of fortune, and makes us feel that the change of fortune of a representative man is just.[9]

From these opposing statements, it is clear that what constitutes the tragic effect is capable of many interpretations. The effect is complex and highly personalized, arrived at through one's own contacts with life.

In any discussion of the tragic effect we must keep Aristotle's words "fear and pity" before us. What did he mean by them? Pity is not simply pathos, a soft sentiment of sorrow for one who is weak or unworthy, even though he says it comes from "undeserved misfortune." Pity is not contemptuous or patronizing. Tragic pity implies a sharing of grief. We enter into the experience

[9]Myers, *Tragedy.*

Tragedy often ends in catastrophe. Here Antigone, in The Phoenecian Women, *grieves over the deaths of her brothers. Her suffering engenders our pity for her undeserved misfortune. Greek National Theater festival at Epidaurus.*

of another through our sympathy and our fellow-feeling. Our pity for the tragic hero is an act of compassion.

Aristotle's concept of fear extends beyond sheer fright or terror to include anxious concern, solicitude, awe, reverence, and apprehension. In tragedy, fear is not merely a hair-raising, spine-tingling reaction of the nervous system; it is an emotion that warms the heart and illuminates the mind. Fear carries a sense of wonder that may include admiration for an individual whose spirit remains intact despite all that the world can do to it. The purging of fear and pity, then, in tragedy must be universalized into a general concern for others, rather than a private and personal identification with disaster.

The catharsis is not the automatic result of following a dramatic formula. We have the capacity for compassion for many kinds of people, good and bad, in many kinds of situations, provided that we have understanding. Our sympathies can go out to foolish and evil characters like Lear and Macbeth. What really counts is our ability to enter into the suffering of the characters as they are tested, and to find within ourselves an echo of their frailty and their flaws.

This emotional response to tragedy is a complex one. It must be broad enough to encompass a variety of experiences and extensive enough to

Mother Courage, directed by Bertolt Bretcht at the Munich Kammerspiele, 1950. Setting designed by Teo Otto.

67

include shades of feeling such as the heartbreak at the end of *King Lear*, *Phèdre*, *Romeo and Juliet*, and *Oedipus Rex*; the sense of triumph at the end of *Hamlet*, *The Crucible*, and *Antigone*; and the appalling sense of waste at the end of *The Trojan Women*, *Ghosts*, and *Othello*. Catharsis is a purging of the spectator's fear and pity, resulting in a sense of release and tranquility. We are cleansed and exhilarated when we are liberated from our own emotional entanglements, our disturbing passions. Fear gives way to certainty, even though that certainty is death. Pity goes beyond feeling and becomes understanding. The spectator leaves the theater "in calm of mind, all passion spent." The end result is, as Northrop Frye suggests, that the audience experiences a "kind of buoyancy." Or again, in Edith Hamilton's words, "the great soul in pain and death transforms and exalts pain and death." Myers universalizes the meaning more explicitly:

> These are the main features of the tragic spirit. It lifts us above self-pity and reconciles us to suffering by showing that evil is a necessary part of the intelligible and just order of our experience. It lifts us above the divisive spirit of melodrama by showing that men are neither naturally good nor inherently evil. It saves us all from the pitfalls of utopianism and fatalism. It teaches moderation by showing that the way of the extremist is short, but at the same time it shows the man of principle that an uncompromising stand is not without its just compensations. And most important, it teaches us that all men are united in the kinship of a common fate, that all are destined to suffer and enjoy, each according to his capacity.[10]

[10]Myers, *Tragedy*.

Euripides' The Trojan Women dramatizes the sorrow and suffering that followed after the fall of Troy. The devastation of Queen Hecuba and the other grieving women elicit a feeling of pity and fear. Aleka Katseli as Hecuba, Epidaurus festival.

When Romeo slays Tybalt in a street brawl, a series of catastrophic actions follow, culminating in the deaths of Romeo and Juliet. The play reminds us of Bradley's observation that tragedy carries with it a terrible sense of waste—as when the star-crossed lovers' lives are snuffed out just as they have found one another. Royal Shakespeare Company production.

The eminent Shakespearean scholar A. C. Bradley makes an interesting and valid contribution to the idea of tragedy by suggesting that catharsis results when pity and fear unite with a profound sense of mystery and sadness due to the impression of waste.[11] In the catastrophe, something of value is destroyed. Important and worthwhile connections are broken. This is perhaps one of the reasons the layman speaks of the "tragedy" that occurs through some accident to a person of promise who had a potential, a future before him.

Tragedy is Positive

Although tragedy involves suffering, evil, and death, many critics feel it is a positive statement about life. As Nicoll says, "Death never really matters in tragedy. . . . Tragedy assumes that death is inevitable and that its time of coming is of no importance compared with what a man does before his death."[12]

[11]A. C. Bradley, *Shakespearean Tragedy* (London: Macmillan, 1957).
[12]Nicoll, *Theory of Drama*.

Death may overtake the protagonist, but he is spiritually victorious. He is not an abject, craven victim of fate who goes cowering to his doom. The principles for which he lived and died survive his passing. The hero dies; heroism lives on. We admire the audacity of those who disregard human frailty, revealing an astonishing capacity for suffering in matters of the spirit. Their action is an affirmation of life. They sustain our faith in humanity.

Tragedy is Honest

The writers of tragedy are unflinchingly honest. They show life as it is, not as one wishes it might be. They have the courage to confront the terrors and perplexities of life; they acknowledge human frailty. Their plots are not manipulated to spare the protagonist; the hero or heroine goes relentlessly to catastrophe. Nor does tragedy demonstrate poetic justice in which the virtuous are rewarded and the wicked punished. Instead, the dramatist shows the clash between our desire for justice and what really happens. He presents the evil along with the good. In the treatment of character, the protagonists are not the idealized heroes of romanticism or the unmitigated villains of melodrama. They are a mixture of clay and stardust, they are admirable characters, but they usually possess a flaw, and their imperfection links them to us. Tragedy rests on a solid basis of integrity, making no concessions to the wish fulfillment of the audience. In Anouilh's modern version of *Antigone* the chorus makes this cogent statement about tragedy.

> Tragedy is clean, it is firm, it is flawless. It has nothing to do with melodrama—with wicked villains, persecuted maidens, avengers, gleams of hope and eleventh-hour repentances. Death, in melodrama, is really horrible because it is never inevitable. The dear old father might so easily have been saved; the honest young man might so easily have brought in the police five minutes earlier. In a tragedy, nothing is in doubt and everyone's destiny is known. That makes for tranquility. Tragedy is restful; and the reason is that *hope*, that foul, deceitful thing, has no part in it. There isn't any hope. You're trapped. The whole sky has fallen on you, and all you can do about it is to shout. Now don't mistake me: I said "shout": I did not say groan, whimper, complain. *That*, you cannot do. But you can *shout* aloud; you can get all those things said that you never thought you'd be able to say—or never knew you had it in you to say. And you don't say these things because it will do any good to say them: you know better than that. You say them for their own sake; you say them because you learn a lot from them. In melo-drama, you argue and struggle in the hope of escape. That is vulgar; it's practical. But in tragedy, where there is no temptation to try to escape, argument is gratuitous: it's kingly.[13]

[13]Jean Anouilh, *Antigone*, trans. Lewis Galantière (London: Van Loewen, 1946).

Diction

The elevated style of classic and Elizabethan tragedy, with its characters and themes of great magnitude, required poetic language, and tragedy is characterized by the grandeur of the diction. But like all good language for the stage, it is functional—as an appropriate level of speech for the dramatic situation, not as a separate element of the play. In general, tragedy has been written by dramatists with the poetic gifts to combine dignity with clarity, who speak with an eloquence that is free from bombast or self-conscious display. Their verse gives a lift to the drama through the use of images and rhythms that have the essential quality of being eminently speakable. The language is a form of dramatic action and has a special evocative power to suggest a meaning beyond the sound and image. Like tragedy itself, it has the quality of universality. Note the full range of one of Sophocles' choral odes from *Antigone*.

> The world is full of wonderful things,
> But none more so than man,
> This prodigy who sails before the storm-winds,
> Cutting a path across the sea's gray face
> Beneath the towering menace of the waves.
> And Earth, the oldest, the primeval god,
> Immortal, inexhaustible Earth,
> She too has felt the weight of his hand
> As year after year the mules are harnessed
> And plows go back and forwards in the fields.
> Merry birds and forest beasts,
> Fish that swim in the deep waters,
> Are gathered into the woven nets,
> Of man the crafty hunter.
> He conquers with his arts
> The beasts that roam in the wild-hill country;
> He tames the horses with their shaggy manes
> Throwing a harness about their necks,
> And the tireless mountain bull.
> Speech he has made his own, and thought
> That travels swift as the wind,
> And how to live in harmony with others
> In cities, and how to shelter himself
> From the piercing frost, cold rain, when the open
> Fields can offer but a poor night's lodging,
> He is ever resourceful; nothing that comes
> Will find him unready, save Death alone.
> Then will he call for help and call in vain,
> Though often, where cure was despaired of, he has
> found one.
> The wit of man surpasses belief,

It works for good and evil too;
When he honors his country's laws, and the right
He is pledged to uphold, then city
Hold up your head; but the man
Who yields to temptation and brings evil home
Is a man without a city; he has
No place in the circle of my hearth,
Nor any part in my counsels.[14]

Tragedy Gives Aesthetic Pleasure

The learning pleasure that tragedy affords is not moral but aesthetic. We admire the grandeur of conception, the ability of the dramatists to create significant action around great themes. And we also enjoy "insight experiences" showing us that despite injustice and evil, excessive pride and passion, violence and tyranny, the human spirit has the capacity to endure. As Kenneth Burke puts it, the experience is one of "purpose, passion, and perception." The tragic hero's purpose is defeated, his passion is agonizing, but he comes to terms with his fate through perception. And from that imitation we learn—we attain a clearer awareness of the mystery of our own nature. As Langer suggests, there is aesthetic pleasure in seeing the tragic rhythm completed, the expectation fulfilled, and, within the tragic rhythm, human dignity retained.

There are those who see the universality of tragedy as a way of connecting us to the latent experiences of myth and ritual that have absorbed the attention of Jung and his followers in archetypal patterns of thought and behavior—patterns and experiences that Jung said are "deeply implanted in the memory of the race." Gilbert Murray describes the phenomenon in these terms:

> In plays like *Hamlet* or the *Agamemnon* or the *Electra* we have certainly fine and flexible character-study, a varied and well-wrought story, a full command of the technical instruments of the poet and the dramatist; but we have also, I suspect, an undercurrent of desires and fears and passions, long slumbering yet eternally familiar, which have for thousands of years lain near the root of our most intimate emotions and have been wrought into the fabric of our most magical dreams. How far into the past ages this stream may reach back, I dare not even surmise; but it seems to me as if the power of stirring it or moving with it were one of the last secrets of genius.[15]

[14]*Oedipus the King* and *Antigone* by Sophocles, trans. Peter D. Arnott (New York: Appleton-Century-Crofts, 1960).

[15]Gilbert Murray, "Hamlet and Orestes," in *The Classical Tradition in Poetry* (Cambridge, Mass.: Harvard University Press, 1927).

Modern Tragedy

Our modern temper, with its anxieties and doubts, is often regarded as inhospitable ground for the nurture of the tragic spirit. The political practice of raising the proletariat to a dominant position has changed our fashion in heroes from high born and romantic characters to common, contemporary individuals, certainly not those of magnitude and grandeur. But even more importantly, it is alleged, our cultural condition resulting from a shifting sense of values, and our exaggerated concern with the material world, has crippled our spiritual vision and we now find ourselves in a world of despair, anguish, and absurdity. In place of the "eternal verities" we have situational morality adapting our ethics to the needs of the moment. Without a firm foundation to stand on, the modern playwright shows us the individual's desperate need for illusion—and what happens when illusions disappear.

As a result of the contemporary climate, tragedy is difficult or impossible to write, some critics claim, because the genre depends upon characters of a heroic mold who spiritually transcend their sufferings to attain nobility, giving the spectator a sense of exaltation. But this view no longer holds.

Joseph Wood Krutch laments the "enfeeblement of the spirit" in our society and indicates why he thinks Ibsen could not write dramas of the heroic stature of Shakespeare:

> The materials out of which the latter created his works—his conception of human dignity, his sense of the importance of human passions, his vision of the amplitude of human life—simply did not and could not exist for Ibsen, as they did not and could not exist for his contemporaries. God and Man and Nature had all somehow dwindled in the course of the intervening centuries, not because the realistic creed of modern art led us to seek out mean people, but because this meanness of human life was somehow thrust upon us.[16]

George Lukács, another critic, in his analysis of modern drama, supports Krutch's view:

> The thematic material of bourgeois drama is trivial, because it is all too near us; the natural pathos of its living men is undramatic and its most subtle values are lost when heightened into drama; the fable is wilfully invented and so cannot retain the natural and poetic resonance of an ancient tradition.[17]

On the other hand, it is argued that expecting the modern playwright to imitate antiquity is a mistaken notion. John Gassner voices this point of view:

> A fundamental premise has been the opinion that a great deal of the tragic art of the past, while excellent as far as it went, belongs to the past. The pagan beliefs that served Attic tragedy twenty-five centuries ago are no longer acceptable to

[16]Joseph Wood Krutch, *"Modernism" in Modern Drama* (Ithaca: Cornell University Press, 1953).

[17]George Lukács, "The Sociology of Modern Drama," trans. Lee Baxandall, *Tulane Drama Review*, 9 (Summer 1965).

modern man. Neither are the beliefs of the Elizabethan period and the age of Louis XIV. There is simply no single time philosophy of tragedy any more than there is a single inviolable tragic form. Tragic art is subject to the evolutionary processes, and tragedy created in modern times must be modern. The fact that it will be different from tragedy written three, five or twenty-five centuries ago does not mean that it will no longer be tragedy; it will merely be different. . . . We may also arrive at the conclusion that there is really no compelling reason for the modern stage to *strain* toward tragedy. There are other ways of responding to the human condition. . . . The creative spirit of an age should be allowed, and indeed expected, to engender its own dramatic forms or to modify existent ones. [18]

Gassner's point is well taken. After all, great tragedy is rare in theater history and we should not castigate modern dramatists because they do not recapture the ancient grandeur. Since we are so much a product of the conditioning forces of our times, it is legitimate that the theater should express the concerns of our society—the identity crisis, the clash between generations

[18]John Gassner, "The Possibilities and Perils of Modern Tragedy," *Tulane Drama Review*, I, no. 3 (June 1957).

Eugene O'Neill, one of the few American writers to aspire to tragedy, provided a work of tragic perspective in his treatment of the sufferings of the Tyrone family in Long Day's Journey Into Night. *Indiana University. Directed by Howard Jensen.*

and cultures, the loss of freedom, faith and security, the disparity between illusion and reality, the cost of integrity, and the difficulty of finding meaning in a bewildering universe.

Responding to these themes, the serious playwrights have created a rich harvest of notable theater in the works of Ibsen, Strindberg, Chekhov, O'Neill, O'Casey, Miller, Shaw, Williams, Pirandello, Albee, Pinter, Osborne, David Rabe, Peter Shaffer, and Brian Clark. While the characters in their plays are often victims, rather than active agents who scale the heights, and the plays usually depict the shattering of illusions rather than affirmations of faith, the playwrights' incisive probing into the human condition generates another form of catharsis, not of elevation but of enlightenment—if not in the characters, in the spectator. The questions are not answered, but they are sharply defined. The theater-goer is confronted with a fresh perception. You will recall A. C. Bradley's view of tragedy which includes the sense of waste. This feeling is aroused by contemporary playwrights who so often dramatize characters and conditions in which something of great value is lost—a potential is not realized, a promising life is destroyed, a dream unfulfilled. And while the fall is not from a high place, there is a stark urgency and immediacy in our

Arthur Miller, in his Death of a Salesman, *created a moving portrait of the common man as a tragic protagonist in Willy Loman, who unfortunately "didn't know who he was." (Wayne State University. Directed by Don Blakely; designed by Enoch Morris).*

response because these people are familiar, and their actions close to our own experience.

Arthur Miller may not be far from the mark when he says:

> The tragic right is a condition of life, a condition in which the human personality is able to flower and realize itself. The wrong is the condition which suppresses man, perverts the flowing out of his love and creative instinct. Tragedy enlightens— and it must, in that it points the heroic finger at the enemy of man's freedom.[19]

Bibliography

BRADLEY, A. C., *Shakespearean Tragedy*. London: Macmillan, 1957.

FRYE, NORTHROP, *The Anatomy of Criticism*. Princeton: Princeton University Press, 1957.

HEILMAN, ROBERT BECHTOLD, *The Iceman, the Arsonist, and the Troubled Agent: Tragedy and Melodrama on the Modern Stage*. Seattle: University of Washington Press, 1973.

KERR, WALTER, *Tragedy and Comedy*. New York: Simon & Schuster, 1967.

KITTO, H. D. F., *Greek Tragedy*. London: Methuen & Company, Ltd., 1950.

LANGER, SUZANNE, *Feeling and Form*. New York: Charles Scribner's Sons, 1953.

MULLER, HERBERT, *The Spirit of Tragedy*. New York: Alfred A. Knopf, Inc., 1976.

MYERS, HENRY ALONZO, *Tragedy: A View of Life*. Ithaca: Cornell University Press, 1956.

OLSON, ELDER, *Tragedy and the Theory of Drama*. Detroit: Wayne State University Press, 1961.

[19]Miller, "Tragedy and the Common Man."

FOUR
Melodrama

When we hear the word *melodrama* we are apt to think of the old cliffhangers in which damsels in distress were rescued by stalwart heroes from the clutches of wicked villains. We associate the term with such bygone hits as *East Lynne, Under the Gaslight, Ten Nights in a Bar Room,* and *The Drunkard.* While it is true that such fare dominated the stage in the nineteenth century, the spirit of melodrama is also very much alive and flourishing now. The external trappings have changed and the exaggerations have been toned down, but the basic melodramatic appeals that brought our forefathers to the theater are the same as those that appear tonight on our television and motion-picture screens.

The reason for the enormous popularity of melodrama is that in it we may be sure that something happens. People don't just sit around and talk—they act. The characters are not resigned to meek acceptance of their fate, incapacitated by despair or fear—they cope.

Eric Bentley describes melodrama in these words:

> It is the spontaneous, uninhibited way of seeing things. . . . The dramatic sense is the melodramatic sense, as one can see from the play acting of any child. Melodrama is not a special and marginal kind of drama, let alone an eccentric or decadent one, it is drama in its elemental form; it is the quintessence of drama.[1]

Melodrama aims at maximum involvement so that the spectator identifies with the hero and participates vicariously in the action. Bentley suggests that in its response to melodrama the audience may have "a good cry—the poor man's catharsis." The pity is self-pity. Thus melodrama becomes a means of release of frustration and aggression—a way of achieving wish fulfillment.

Outwardly melodrama tries to create the illusion of real people in genuine jeopardy, but actually it manipulates the plot toward reprieve, rescue, or reform. It exploits physical and material difficulties, and escape from danger is a typical plot line. Melodrama generates excitement, suspense, and thrills for their own sake. Like a game, melodrama builds tension and exhilaration but it is transitory and without substantial significance. One leaves the theater with a sense of relief at the outcome but untroubled by the conditions which caused the suffering and conflicts.

In the previous chapter we considered tragedy, the loftiest and rarest form of drama. How does it differ from melodrama which on the surface seems to deal, like tragedy, with characters involved in serious and critical situations? Fundamentally, the distinction lies in the difference in point of view. Tragedy confronts good and evil with unblinking honesty; melodrama escapes from life. Tragedy considers eternal spiritual problems; melodrama deals with the transitory, the material, the physical. Tragedy evokes fear and pity; melodrama arouses suspense, pathos, terror, and sometimes hate. However, melodrama is not mere ineffectual tragedy. As a matter of fact, a well-written melodrama may be superior to an inept tragedy. The point is that the two forms of drama are different. They are similar only in that they both *seem* serious, but in melodrama the seriousness is only a pretense for the sake of the theatrical game.

[1]Eric Bentley, *The Life of the Drama* (New York: Atheneum Publishers, 1964), p. 216.

Melodramatic scenes and situations have been a part of the history of the theater almost from the beginning. Euripides in striving for effect was sometimes very close to melodrama, and Seneca exploited sensational and horrible material to the hilt. The Elizabethan "tragedies of blood" employed much of the machinery of melodrama with scenes of horror and violence. Jacobean playwrights delighted in grisly scenes of exciting action. The early eighteenth-century "she-tragedies" of Nicholas Rowe, with their sentimentalism and overwrought emotions, were in the melodramatic vein. Schiller's *The Robbers* capitalized on the fugitive situation so dear to writers of melodrama.

The term *melodrama* combines two Greek words meaning music and drama. At one time the word was literally synonymous with opera. Melodrama was first allied with music in Italy and France. In Germany it referred to dialogue passages spoken to orchestral accompaniment. The modern connotation of the word, however, stems from the late eighteenth-century French theater and its subsequent development, especially in England and America. Up until 1791, the Comédie Française and the Italian Comedians enjoyed monopolistic control over the legitimate theaters of Paris. Ingenious managers circumvented governmental restrictions by contriving a kind of entertainment based on pantomime accompanied by dance, song, and dialogue, which elicited a popular following due to its sensational qualities. When freedom of production was granted to all theaters, the word *melodrama* was attached to the pantomime with dialogue and music.

Frank Rahill, in his study of melodrama, with emphasis on the nineteenth century, defines the genre in these terms:

> Melodrama is a form of dramatic composition in prose partaking of the nature of tragedy, comedy, pantomime and spectacle, and intended for a popular audience. Primarily concerned with situation and plot, it calls upon mimed action extensively and employs a more or less fixed complement of stock characters, the most important of which are a suffering heroine, or hero, a persecuting villain and a benevolent comic. It is conventionally moral and humanitarian in point of view and sentimental and optimistic in temper, concluding its fable happily with virtue rewarded after many trials and vice punished. Characteristically it offers elaborate scenic accessories and miscellaneous divertissements and introduces music freely, typically to underscore dramatic effect.[2]

The French playwright Pixérécourt at the beginning of the nineteenth century became the foremost playwright of the new form, which exactly fit the taste of the lower classes. He made a careful study of his audiences until he perfected the machinery that was to dominate melodrama from that time to this and to make him one of the most popular playwrights who ever lived. He wrote nearly 60 melodramas, which played more than 30,000 performances in France alone. His plots were based on exciting action, surprise, and suspense, the sharp contrasts of vice against virtue, the comic and the pathetic, and he thrilled his audiences with spectacular scenes such as fires, floods, and collisions. Although he wrote his plays rapidly, he worked with them in the theater personally, taking great pains to produce them exactly as

[2]Frank Rahill, *The World of Melodrama* (University Park: The Pennsylvania State University Press, 1967).

he intended. The success of his efforts caused him to be known as "the Napoleon of the Boulevard."

Before Thomas Holcroft returned to London from France with his popular melodrama, *A Tale of Mystery* (1802), the taste for its mood and action had been set in the gothic novels' sentimentalized, long-suffering heroines, and in the theater's spectacular scenery. "Monk" Lewis' *Castle Spectre* (1797) employed much of the machinery of melodrama in the dramatization of an orphan girl, Lady Angela, ensnared by the wicked Lord Osmond, who has slain her father and taken over his property. The setting is a castle haunted by the ghost of the girl's mother. Thanks to the efforts of Earl Percy, disguised as a farmer, the villain is foiled and a happy ending ensues. *Castle Spectre* was a smashing success and its basic ingredients were endlessly copied.

In the late eighteenth century in Germany, August von Kotzebue wrote more than 200 plays combining sensational scenes with heavy sentimentality. He was not only commercially successful, but also very influential on playwriting for years to come. In England Sheridan translated and presented Kotzebue's *The Spaniard in Peru*, as *Pizarro* in 1799; and in 1798 William Dunlap adapted Kotzebue's *The Stranger*, one of the first melodramas to be given in America in the nineteenth century, although most plays were imported from France and England rather than from Germany. Later American playwrights learned to exploit the native scene for plays of big city life, rural stories with local color, firemen plays, and dramas of the wild West.

At first melodrama owed its popularity to its story appeal. Its pattern was a series of strong actions performed by clear-cut characters demonstrating the triumph of simple virtues and the ultimate defeat of villainy. To satisfy the tremendous demand for new material, playwrights ground out new plays like our television writers, and like their modern counterparts, most writers followed well-established formulas.

As the nineteenth century progressed, efforts were made to create more realistic melodramas. The easiest way to suggest reality was through the external aspects of production—especially the stage scenery. Toward the end of the century, the theater technician ran away with the show. New and spectacular effects became a primary source of audience appeal. The stage mechanic was called upon not only to represent on stage accurate replicas of familiar landscapes, buildings, and monuments, but also to reproduce all manner of sensational effects. Melodrama tended to become simply a scenario for exciting action. As a result of its elaboration of the visual aspects of production and its demand for strong stories and movement, nineteenth-century melodrama played directly into the hands of the development of the motion-picture industry.

By the end of the nineteenth century the stage melodrama had run its course with the increasing sophistication of the audience and the changes in the world outside. As drama moved toward realism, the old formulas and characters of melodrama gave way. Even when the theater aimed at the popular audience it was necessary to make plots more credible, to include

Action in an early nineteenth-century melodrama, Pocock's The Miller and His Men.

Melodrama thrives on sensational effects and exciting action. One of the most durable melodramas in the American theater is William Gillette's Sherlock Holmes (1899) which has recently been a popular revival. John Wood as Holmes.

more kinds of characters on stage and to give them more depth, to capture the impression of more normal speech. As for one of the major appeals of melodrama—the sensation scenes—the new medium of the film offered potentialities for spectacle far beyond the capacities of the limited stage. Today our films and television plays still use many of the techniques and appeals of the old-time melodrama in horse operas and tales of adventure, crime, and warfare.

Plot

Melodrama in the nineteenth century relied heavily on stories that had colorful characters and opportunities for strong "sensation" scenes and outlets for powerful emotions. Audiences preferred those dramatic situations that showed characters struggling against fearful odds, trapped or marooned, holding out until help comes—the last bullet—the last drop of water—the last bite of food—the last cent. The art of playwriting, therefore, became the art of devising scenes of excitement. Melodrama exaggerated climaxes and crises so

Scene from a Drury Lane production of The Whip, 1909. One of the main appeals of melodrama was in staging such scenes.

83

Boucicault's melodrama The Colleen Bawn, *when the villain Danny tries to drown the heroine, Eily. The scene was staged with every effort to make it as realistic and exciting as possible.*

that the structure of the play was a series of peaks of action rather than a well-knit steady progression of logically related events. A typical scene of climax from Boucicault's great favorite, *The Colleen Bawn* (1860), illustrates not only the kind of situation, but also the emphasis on action:

> *Music, low storm music . . . Myles sings without then appears U.E.R. on rock. . . . Swings across stage by rope. Exit U.E.I.H. Music, boat floats on R.H. with Eily and Danny. Eily steps on to Rock C. (Danny) stepping onto the rock the boat floats away unseen. . . . Music. Throws her into water, L.C. She disappears for an instant then reappears clinging to Rock C. . . . Thrusts her down. She disappears. . . . Shot heard U.E.L.H. Danny falls into water behind C. Rock. Myles sings without. . . . Swings across by rope to R.H., fastens it up, then fishes up Double of Eily—lets her fall. Strips, then dives after her. Eily appears for an instant in front. Then double for Myles appears at back and dives over drum. Myles and Eily appear in front of Center Rock. Tableau. Curtain.*

This kind of physical action is, of course, the standard material of melodrama, made appealing to nineteenth-century audiences by novel effects. It is interesting to note the use of character "doubles" in order to keep

84

the scene moving. Other elements of special interest in this scene are the music for reinforcing the atmosphere and the tableau at the end of the act. The writer of melodrama depended on all kinds of *coups de théâtre* for releasing strong feelings, often utilizing climactic curtains such as in the scene above, literally as "clap traps."

In order to create continuity of the narrative, the dramatist tied the scenes together by a variety of techniques. Changes of scenery were covered by music or special lighting effects. Often, the scenes were changed in view of the audience. Sets were devised for the use of simultaneous or parallel action. Still another practice was that of shifting the locale from one place to another while the action continued. The following example from *A Race for Life* indicates this device, which anticipates cinematic practice:

> *Officers fire. Convicts rush on, struggle with officers. Shots outside; Gaspard seizes Jacques—is thrown off. Officer seizes Jacques, he throws him off when Holmes struggles off with Brady R.H. Men and officers struggle off R. and L. when all clear. Sound Change Bell.*
>
> *Rocks drawn off R. and L. Prison double set center revolves to old Light House and comes down stage. Jacques and Brady come on in boat, Men work sea cloth. Patty throws rope from light house window. Brady catches it. Picture. Slow curtain.*

Good writers of melodrama were skilled craftsmen with a shrewd sense of pace, rhythm, and a feeling for climactic action. They were adept storytellers and showmen. They not only knew the possibilities of the stage, but also understood their audience. Logic did not interest them so long as their plays gave the impression of credibility which they achieved by keeping the narratives moving, and by creating the illusion of actuality through the use of realistic backgrounds, appropriate costuming, and good casting.

Character

Robert B. Heilman suggests that the contrast between melodrama and tragedy is a matter of character treatment:

> The identifying mark of the melodramatic structure is not the particular outcome of the plot, but the conception of character and the alignment of forces. . . . In melodrama, man is seen in his strength or in his weakness; in tragedy in both his strength and weakness at once. In melodrama, he is victorious or he is defeated; in tragedy, he experiences defeat in victory, or victory in defeat. In melodrama, man is simply guilty or simply innocent; in tragedy, his guilt and his innocence coexist. In melodrama, man's will is broken, or it conquers; in tragedy, it is tempered in the suffering that comes with, or brings about, new knowledge.[3]

Heilman's concept, then, of the melodramatic hero is of a whole character, not one torn by internal stress, while the tragic hero is a divided

[3]Robert B. Heilman, "Tragedy and Melodrama," *The Texas Quarterly*, Summer 1960.

human being confronted by basic conflicts, perhaps not soluble, of obligations and passions.

Nineteenth-century melodrama and our motion-picture and television fare testify to the validity of Heilman's observation. Characters are generally good or bad one-dimensional figures who pursue their objectives in a straight line. The opposition comes from without rather than from within. Characters do not think, they act, and as a result they often become involved in entanglements a judicious person might avoid, such as being caught on a train trestle at midnight without a lantern, lost in the snowstorm without food or shelter, or duped by the villain's traps and schemes because of gullibility and ignorance. The writer of melodrama was not concerned with delineating characters as complex individuals who were conditioned by their backgrounds. They were people who were simple in heart and mind. As nineteenth-century melodrama developed, however, some playwrights made efforts to create more credible characters with more complex motivations. Indeed, the waywardness of the villain might be explained at some length as the result of an unfortunate conditioning experience in early life when he was abused or unjustly treated, and as a result he might make some claim on the audience's sympathy and understanding.

Most characters in melodrama were types. This was important in performance so that the spectator could readily recognize them, and it was also essential for the acting company in the distribution of the roles. Owen Davis, one of the most successful writers of melodrama in the early part of the twentieth century, used stock characters in such hits as *The Lighthouse by the Sea* and *The Chinatown Trunk Mystery*. He describes the typical personnel required for his plays:

> There were eight essential characters: the hero, who can be either very poor, which is preferable, or else very young and very drunk (if sober and wealthy he becomes automatically a villain); the heroine, by preference a working girl (cloak model, "typewriter," factory girl, shopgirl, etc.) and practically indestructible; the comic—Irish, Jewish, or German—played usually by the highest paid member of the company; the soubrette, "a working girl with bad manners and a good heart"; devoted to the heroine; the heavy man, identified by a moustache, silk hat, and white gloves; the heavy woman, a haughty society dame or an "unfortunate"; the light comedy boy; and the second heavy, "just a bum," a tool of the villain—it was usual to kill him along toward the middle of the second act.[4]

The pivotal character of old-time melodrama was the villain, who was the motivating force of much of the plot. Just as it was essential to show the goodness of the hero and heroine in order to enlist the sympathy of the audience, likewise it was mandatory to demonstrate the wickedness of the villain in order to generate hostility toward him. One of the pleasures of melodrama was loathing the evil-doers and seeing them get the punishment they so richly deserved. Hence the playwright was careful to build up the iniquitous villains with their sinful desires, their smoldering grudges and passions, and their inexhaustible supply of devilish schemes.

[4]Owen Davis, *I'd Like to Do It Again* (New York, 1931).

Melodrama was the entertainment of the masses, and since maximum identification was the playwright's aim, he often used characters from the ordinary walks of life. Heroes were not the elevated figures of the past; they were firemen, cowboys, soldiers, sailors, farm hands. Although they were stock types, the bare outlines of the text were fleshed out by the imaginations and personalities of the actors who brought them to life. Leading roles in melodrama provided exceptional opportunities for some actors who spent most of their careers identified with a single part. James O'Neill played in *Monte Cristo* for 5817 performances, and Denman Thompson appeared in *The Old Homestead* more than 7000 times.

Thought

Most writers of melodrama were primarily concerned with entertaining an audience rather than delivering a message. But because of the genre's broad appeal, melodrama often reflected a vague humanitarianism in its sympathetic treatment of the downtrodden and its condemnation of arrogant authority, the overprivileged, and the avaricious manipulators in big business. Although there was frequently an implied suggestion to take action and throw off the tormentors so everyone could be free, the implication was not a direct call for rebellion. Instead, melodrama commonly expressed a staunch loyalty to orthodox morality, backed by an optimistic faith in the future. The root of the social evils that oppressed those who suffered was generally lodged in the evil nature of the villains, rather than traced to the political or economic system.

Most melodramas end with arbitrary scenes of poetic justice in which couples are paired off, and rewards and punishments are parceled out according to the actions of the characters in the play. As the final curtain descends, the audience is reassured that virtue will triumph, murder will out, and the wages of sin is death. But melodrama with its sharp conflicts between good and evil did not altogether neglect the opportunity for propaganda. The evils of drink were a favorite target, as were usury, heavy taxes, and the sinful nature of the big city. One of the most popular hits of all time was George L. Aiken's dramatization of Harriet Beecher Stowe's novel *Uncle Tom's Cabin* (1852) which held the stage for 80 years. Its depiction of slavery was one of the strongest pieces of propaganda of the nineteenth century.

Duty and self-sacrifice were pictured as the ennobling virtues of the lower classes. Whatever misfortunes befell, the honorable person performed his duty, confident that in the end justice would be meted out, in the next world, if not here and now. Dozens of heroines declaimed such sentiments, as the following passages from Daly's highly successful *Under the Gaslight*:

Laura: Let the woman you look upon be wise or vain, beautiful, or homely, rich or poor, she has but one thing she can really give or refuse—her heart! Her beauty, her wit, her accomplishments, she may sell to you—but her love is the treasure without money and without price. She only asks in return, that when you look upon her, your eyes shall speak a mute devotion; that when you address her,

A climactic moment when Laura succeeds in breaking out of the tool shed, just in time to rescue Snorky from the onrushing locomotive.

your voice shall be gentle, loving and kind. That you shall not despise her because she cannot understand all at once, your vigorous thoughts, and ambitious designs: for when misfortune and evil have defeated your greatest purposes—her love remains to console you. You look to the trees for strength and grandeur—do not despise the flowers, because their fragrance is all they have to give. Remember—love is all a woman has to give; but it is the only earthly thing which God permits us to carry beyond the grave.[5]

Diction

The language of melodrama was often singularly undistinguished. Since common characters carried the burden of the plot, playwrights attempted to suggest onstage the everyday idiom. This effort performed some service in undermining the bombast and extravagance of romantic diction, although the writer of melodrama was not entirely immune from flowery language. In moments of strong emotion, characters spouted such purple passages as that cited from *Under the Gaslight*. But by and large, the playwright's emphasis on

88

[5]Augustan Daly, *Under the Gaslight* (New York: Samuel French, Inc., n.d.).

common characters involved in scenes of violent action led toward dialogue that suggested the texture of ordinary speech. As a result of this attempt to imitate the language of life, some playwrights endeavored to copy the dialects and provincialism of specific locales, which was a move toward increased realism.

The writer of melodrama made free use of such technical devices as asides and soliloquies, which not only aided him in the difficult problems of exposition imposed by episodic structure, but also gave him the opportunity to reveal character and motivation.

Music

Melodrama, originally linked with music, continued that association. As the excerpt from *The Colleen Bawn* indicated, music was an important accompaniment to the action. When the motion pictures took over melodrama, music was soon found to be extremely useful for eliciting emotional response. Silent films were accompanied by appropriate scores for piano or pipe organ. For more ambitious productions such as *The Birth of a Nation*, a complete orchestral accompaniment was written and played for the showing of the picture. In our present films and television dramas, music continues as an indispensable element of production to establish atmosphere, bridge the action, or generate excitement.

Nineteenth-century melodrama made another interesting use of music. The entrances and exits of leading characters were accompanied by special musical themes suitable for their roles. Actors often performed to music that not only assisted them in establishing the emotional atmosphere of the scene, but also influenced their timing and movement.

Sound effects were sometimes an important adjunct of productions, especially in such climactic scenes as in "turf" dramas when the horses thundered down the straightaway toward the finish line; or when in *Under the Gaslight* the rumbling, whistling train approached with its headlights picking up Snorky tied to the tracks while the heroine, Laura, frantically attempted to shatter the walls of the tool shed in time to save her friend; or when in the firemen plays the firefighters raced onto the scene of a spectacular blaze amid the crackle of flames, the cries for help, and the sound of the equipment.

Spectacle

In the first half of the century almost all theaters made use of two-dimensional stock pieces consisting of backdrops and wings, on which were painted a variety of backgrounds such as a kitchen, a palace, a prison, a grotto, a woodland glade. This system possessed two virtues—it was economical and it made shifting rapid and easy. To change to a new setting, the backdrop was raised to reveal another one behind it, while wings slid along the grooves to

Sweeney Todd is a musical based on the fascinating career of a nineteenth century character known as "the demon barber of Fleet Street." His objective is to gain vengeance on the judge who sent him to prison. At last Sweeney has the Judge in his barber chair. Despite such sensational scenes, Sweeney Todd *escapes melodrama by virtue of Stephen Sondheim's music.*

uncover the new ones for the following scene. Throughout the country, theaters were equipped with stock sets so that a touring company needed to bring only its special effects and costumes along. But as the taste for sensational novelties grew, productions became increasingly elaborate and expensive. Metropolitan stages became more complicated with bridges, traps, elevators, moving platforms, and paraphernalia for producing fires, floods, explosions, and all manner of astounding displays. The two-dimensional scenery was replaced by built-up solid pieces making the sets substantial, and difficult to move. Playwrights built their plays around sensational scenic displays. The following scene from *Pauvrette: or, Under the Snow* shows the kind of effects required.

The summit of the Alps. Rocks and precipices occupy the stage. A rude hut on one side in front. A bridge formed by a felled tree across the chasm at the back. The stone-clad peaks stretch away in the distance. Night. . . . Storm, wind. She (Pauvrette) throws her scarf around her, and hastily ascends the rock—utters a

Cut No. 2040—PAUVRETTE, or UNDER THE SNOW.—For printing in Programmes or Cards.   Electrotypes of this Cut, $5.00 each.]

In such plays as Boucicault's Pauvrette *the stage effects were often more interesting than the characters. Staging a credible avalanche challenged the theater technician's skill to the utmost.*

long wailing cry—listens. . . . Descends to her hut. Maurice cries for help. Takes her alpenstock and a coil of rope, and reascends the rock. The wind increases— the snow begins to fall. She crosses the bridge and disappears off left. Bernard appears below on the rocks, L. He climbs up the path. . . . Pauvrette appears on the bridge, leading Maurice. . . . They cross the bridge. . . . They descend and enter the hut. . . . Large blocks of hardened snow and masses of rock fall, rolling into the abyss. Pauvrette falls on her knees. . . . Pauvrette enters the hut. The avalanche begins to fall—the bridge is broken and hurled into the abyss—the paths have been filled with snow—and now an immense sheet rushing down from the R. entirely buries the whole scene to the height of twelve or fifteen feet swallowing up the cabin and leaving above a clear level of snow—the storm passes away—silence and peace return—the figure of the virgin (in window) is unharmed—the light before it still burns.[6]

[6]Dion Boucicault, *Pauvrette* (New York: Samuel French, Inc., n.d.).

During the third quarter of the nineteenth century Dion Boucicault was the acknowledged master of melodrama both in writing and in staging his plays. He catered to the taste of the public with his sensational scenes to which he gave the utmost care. In *The Octaroon* (1859) he featured a fire aboard a river boat; in *Arrah-na-Pogue* Shaun's prison escape begins inside the cell, then turns inside out to reveal him coming out the window and over the wall.

At the turn of the century "Drury Lane melodramas" were famous for their stage effects. *The Prince of Peace* (1900) presented Parliament in session, a wedding in Westminster Abbey, and a collision at sea in which a yacht is smashed by a steamer. *The Sins of Society* (1907) thrilled the spectators with a huge transport ship that slowly sank beneath the waves on a fog-shrouded stage while a wireless crackled and sparked and a steam siren sounded the alarm.

David Belasco set a new standard for Broadway with ultra-realistic staging of his melodramas celebrating the American heritage, in *The Heart of Maryland* (1895), *Under Two Flags* (1901), and *The Girl of the Golden West* (1905). He toned down much of the violence and blatant sentimentality and made the plot and dialogue more credible, even though he depended a great deal on startling scenes carefully produced. He also had the advantage of working with electricity, which he used with imagination and taste. Typical of Belasco's theatricality was the staging of the prologue to *The Girl of the Golden West*. Rahill describes it in some detail.

> . . . a painted canvas scene, rolled vertically on drums, presented a moving, map-like panorama of the whole picturesque area where the action unfolds; first, the heights of cloudy mountain in the moonlight, then the girl's cabin perched aloft and a steep footpath winding down the walls of the canyon to the settlement below; and next, the little camp itself, shown at the foot of the path, the miners' cabins huddled about the Polka Saloon, through the windows of which drifts the muted din of rough revelry—the rattle of poker chips, the strains of banjo, and concertina, and masculine voices raised in a chorus of "Camptown Races." This is erased suddenly in a blackout, and a moment later the lights come on full to reveal the interior of the saloon, where a shindig is in full swing—the music continuing meanwhile and serving to bind the two scenes together.[7]

It should be kept in mind that while sensational scenery called attention to itself, it was also used for more than pictorial representation. The setting was functional in that it served the actor's needs in a particular scene. A waterfall was not simply shown as an enlarged calendar picture for its visual appeal. It became a factor in the action when the hero struggled to save the heroine from plunging to her death. A railroad trestle was set on stage not merely for the novelty of showing a train, but also as a weapon of the villain who tied the hero to the tracks while the train's light and whistle approached. The setting was an essential part of the action. Hence, a considerable amount of ingenuity was required by the stage mechanic to devise effects which were not only visually credible, but also utilitarian enough to be used in chases, fights, and escapes. Incidentally, the actor had to be something of an athlete to dive from

[7]Rahill, *The World of Melodrama.*

burning buildings, scale steep cliffs, and chase or be chased through a canvas jungle, and then recite lines. (It is no wonder that doubles were often used to keep the action continuous.)

One device by which melodrama sought to create an illusion of reality was through the use of actual and authentic properties. Belasco actually bought pieces of buildings and moved them on stage. Some playwrights and producers cluttered their sets with endless detail to make the stage picture seem real. Often a real property, such as a rowboat, made an incongruous contrast with the obviously painted backdrop of the sea. On the other hand, the use of genuine and homely objects on stage enhanced the realism of the acting by giving the actors an opportunity to create business and pantomime. James A. Herne, a successful writer of melodrama who attempted to emulate the new realism, was very fond of filling his scenes with the everyday objects and actions of life. In some of his plays he brought on dogs, chickens, a horse, geese, and live babies. He showed a shipyard in operation during which a boat was painted each evening.

As the elaboration of scenery progressed, it became increasingly difficult for a road company to tour since many of the outlying theaters could not accommodate the special scenery because of the lack of size or equipment, not to mention the increased cost of the touring production. The solidity and complexity of scenery also affected playwriting. Scenes could not be shifted as rapidly as previously and the cost of production mounted. The result was to reduce the number of scenes so that there were fewer locales and episodes. Under these conditions, the dramatist was forced to use less physical action, the narrative lost some of its fluency, and there was a tendency toward fuller development of character and dialogue.

Realism ultimately made its impact on melodrama, although up until 1900 most American plays were written for the exploitation of a star or for the spectacular effects of the staging. Early in the twentieth century the circuit

Another popular revival is Braham Stoker's Dracula, *a melodrama that exploits two standard ingredients—a maiden in jeopardy and a terrifying villain. (University of Minnesota. Directed by Charles Nolte).*

theaters that catered to the lower classes lost some of their audiences to the film. Porter's *The Life of an American Fireman* and *The Great Train Robbery* taught movie makers that their medium was ideally suited for narratives with vigorous action. In popular melodramas they found stories and situations which became the basic ingredients for film. Stage hits like *Oliver Twist, Under Two Flags,* and *Lady of Lyons* were put on the screen where they attracted large audiences to the new kind of theater.

By and large film has taken over melodrama that is based on action and spectacular effects. It may have changed its external appearance but the fundamental appeal of exciting action is very much in evidence. A glance at the newspaper advertisements for current films carries such blurbs as: "Desires at fever pitch under a blazing sun," "If this one doesn't scare you . . . you're already dead!" "Dramatic dynamite!" and "gripping and totally fascinating."

In the current theater melodrama is largely confined to murder mysteries and psychological thrillers. The external aspects of the old plot mechanics are refined so that dialogue, action, and scenery *seem* real but the old melodramatic mechanisms and situations persist. Sympathetic heroes and heroines are caught in physical jeopardy, good characters are pitted against bad ones, the action generates strong climaxes, and evil is undone. Spectacular staging still has a strong appeal, as, for example, in the revivals of *Sherlock Holmes* and *Dracula.* One of the big hits of the 1979 London season was *The Crucifer*

Sherlock Holmes as a melodramatic hero was also featured in The Crucifer of Blood, *by Paul Giovanni, but the chief attractions were the sensational stage effects, such as this scene in which two boats emerge out of a dense fog and a gunfight ensues.*

of *Blood*, a Sherlock Holmes yarn that featured a terrifying electrical storm and a gun duel fought by adversaries on two boats moving in a thick fog. Another popular melodrama during the 1979 season in London and New York was Ira Levin's *Deathtrap*, an ingenious play about a writer of thrillers who becomes involved himself in a series of crimes. Although the action is mostly psychological, the climax occurs during a raging storm. Because most melodrama depends heavily on spectacle and violent action it is more suitable for film rather than the theater, but when a playwright is able to confine exciting action to a limited space in a short period of time, with scenes that arouse terror, suspense, thrills, and laughter, the public will find its way to the box office.

Drame

Most serious modern dramatists have not aspired to scale the heights of tragedy nor have they been content to confine themselves to melodrama. They have tended to write middle-class plays for a middle class audience dealing with contemporary man in commonplace circumstances. The dramas

The Basic Training of Pavlo Hummel *is replete with violent action but is a* drame *rather than a melodrama by virtue of its emphasis on theme and character. (Wayne State University. Directed by N. Joseph Calarco; designed by Norman Hamlin).*

that emerge from their objective of telling the truth about life are remarkably varied in style and content; but they do have a common denominator in attempting to say something serious about the individual in the present society. This vast body of dramatic literature defies definition because of its great diversity, its technical experimentation in dramaturgy and production, and its mixtures of several forms of writing at once. Some critics simply use the general term *drama*, but we prefer, as a lesser evil, the French term *drame*, by which is meant those plays of serious intent usually dealing with contemporary life. Just as realism has been the dominant mode of modern drama, so the drame has been the preponderant form.

Drame is allied to melodrama in that the playwright often attempts to involve the spectator in the action by identification with familiar characters and by creating suspense and tension. Drame differs from melodrama in that it may be interested in the realm of ideas, with sociological and philosophical issues at stake. Characters may participate in genuinely significant action that provokes thought and discussion after the curtain has gone down.

Drame is allied to tragedy in its seriousness of purpose, in its relentless honesty of treatment, in its concern with the meaning of human conduct. Drame differs from tragedy in its narrowness of vision—with its emphasis often on material, temporary, or local conditions that deny it universality; with its mechanistic or nihilistic sense of values; and with its general lack of

Although Zoot Suit *by Luis Valdez contains a good deal of violence, it is not melodrama but drame, because of its seriousness of purpose as a sociological study of Chicano Culture. Mark Taper Forum.*

Chekhov's plays are serious studies, lightened by comic touches, and may be considered drame. The Cherry Orchard *was one of the Moscow Art Theater's outstanding productions. This shot is from a University of Illinois performance directed by Burnet M. Hobgood; designed by John T. Piper.*

elevation. Frequently, the writer of drames is fascinated by the psychological complexities of character. His dramatis personae are not the stock characters of melodrama; they are individuals with subtle and complicated motivations. They are not the tragic heroes of great stature who fall from high places, but ordinary people painfully searching for meaning and security in a baffling world of shifting values.

Bibliography

BENTLEY, ERIC, *The Life of the Drama.* New York: Atheneum Publishers, 1964.

BOOTH, MICHAEL, *English Melodrama.* London: Herbert Jenkins, 1965.

DISHER, MAURICE, *Blood and Thunder: Mid-Victorian Melodrama and Its Origin.* London: Muller, 1949.

LACEY, ALEXANDER, *Pixérécourt and the French Romantic Drama.* Toronto: University of Toronto Press, 1928.

MOSES, MONTROSE JONES, *American Dramatist.* New York: Benjamin Blom, Inc., 1964.

NICOLL, ALLARDYCE, *A History of the Late Nineteenth Century Drama, 1850–1900.* Cambridge: Cambridge University Press, 1946.

RAHILL, FRANK, *The World of Melodrama.* University Park: The Pennsylvania State University Press, 1967.

VARDAC, NICHOLAS, *Stage to Screen.* Cambridge, Mass.: Harvard University Press, 1949.

FIVE
Comedy

One of the most popular pleasures of life is the enjoyment of laughter, and we seek its solace and release in all manner of activities. Not content with laughter arising spontaneously out of personal experience, we become avid customers of comedy in the theater and on the screen. Making laughter is big business and there is an eager audience waiting for the skilled comedian and the hit play or musical.

To define comedy is first to acknowledge the difficulties of definition. What makes one person laugh may make another grieve. Perhaps it is sufficient to say that comedy has as its purpose to delight, entertain, or regale an audience through the presentation of characters, situations, and ideas in the spirit of fun. As tragedy achieves its catharsis through fear and pity, so comedy aims in its special catharsis through laughter and amusement to keep man close to sanity and balance, and to remind us of our human frailties.

Kinds of Comedy

Comedy wears many masks and appears in many guises—the ill-fitting tattered rags of the drunken hobo, the elegant evening clothes of the most sophisticated aristocrat, the overdressed finery of the fop. Comedy evokes many responses—a belly laugh, warm and sympathetic general laughter, a well-concealed smile. Its armor includes such a variety of weapons as the rapier, the slapstick, the barbed shaft, and the custard pie. Comedy speaks many languages—epigrams, conceits, puns, obscenities, bon mots, wisecracks, insults, double entendres, hard and ruthless derision. The field of comedy is broad enough to encompass many variations.

Alan Thompson, in an effort to regularize the concept of different kinds of comedy, devised a comic ladder which takes this form:[1]

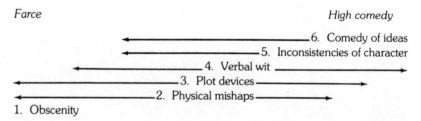

Farce   High comedy

——————————————————————6. Comedy of ideas
——————————————————5. Inconsistencies of character
——————————4. Verbal wit ————————————→
——————————3. Plot devices————————————
——————————2. Physical mishaps————————→
1. Obscenity

Allardyce Nicoll, in a similar effort, suggests five categories of comedy:[2]

In general, there are five main types of comic productivity which we may broadly classify. Farce stands by itself as marked out by certain definite characteristics. The comedy of humours is the second of decided qualities. Shakespeare's comedy of romance is the third, with possibly the romantic tragicomedy of his later

---

[1]Alan Reynolds Thompson, *The Anatomy of Drama* (Berkeley: University of California Press, 1942).

[2]Allardyce Nicoll, *The Theory of Drama* (New York: Thomas Y. Crowell Company, Inc., 1931).

years as a separate subdivision. The comedy of intrigue is the fourth. The comedy of manners is the fifth, again with a subdivision in the genteel comedy.

Both Thompson and Nicoll place low or physical comedy at one end of the scale and the comedy of manners or ideas at the other end—and this seems a logical arrangement, but the problem with the gradations in between, as well as with the two extremes, is that they are not mutually exclusive. The safest conclusion seems to be that comedy ranges between high and low, between physical and intellectual, and that it differs in kind according to the playwright's purposes from play to play.

High comedy, social comedy, or the comedy of manners, is intellectual in appeal, catering to the tastes of a sophisticated audience with a commonly accepted code of behavior that is a matter of manners, not morals. The Restoration period in the late seventeenth century in England is generally acknowledged to be the apex of high comedy. Congreve, Wycherly, Etherege and Vanbrugh ridiculed the gauche, the outsiders, the pretenders whose awkward conduct caused them to lose their sense of balance. In other periods of theater history, writers have used the wit of high comedy to direct criticism at more universal targets. Aristophanes scorned the militarists, sophists, and politicians; Molière attacked hypocrisy and pretense; Shaw delighted in exposing the sham behind the sentimental and rigid precepts of Victorian society. High comedy is therefore a social weapon armed with critical laughter.

At the other end of the comic scale is farce, or low comedy, whose main purpose is to entertain. It demands no intellectual insight, no awareness of a social norm, no linguistic sensitivity in finding nuances of meaning. The response to farce is immediate and direct. The language barriers are apt to be

A scene of violence is made comic by spoofing Shakespeare in the revue, Beyond the Fringe. (University of California, Santa Barbara. Directed by the author).

slight, since the performers express themselves in the universal vocabulary of action. Along with melodrama, farce is our most popular kind of drama on the commercial stage and in film and television.

Farce may involve a complete play, such as *The Taming of the Shrew* or *Bedroom Farce*, or its techniques may be injected piecemeal into other kinds of comedy, such as Dionysus' trip to Hades in *The Frogs* or the rustics' antics in *A Midsummer Night's Dream*.

In between the extremes of high comedy and low is a vast area which, for want of a better term, we simply refer to as "comedy" to distinguish plays that rely heavily on neither intellectual appeal nor exaggerated physicality. These plays attend more to character and the significance of the action. Molière's farces, such as *Sgnarelle* and *The Doctor in Spite of Himself*, are based on extravagant situations calculated to elicit easy laughter, but when more concerned with character and ideas, as in *Tartuffe* and *The Miser*, Molière wrote plays in the general area of comedy.

The Comic Attitude

The question of pain and pleasure arises in comedy as well as in tragedy, for laughter and ridicule can be dangerous weapons. Molière, who was frequently in hot water for satirizing the law, medicine, and the church, observed that people do not mind being wicked, but "they object to being made ridiculous." And Ludovici tells us that "a laugh is a man's way of showing his fangs." Comedy becomes aggressive and easily leads to abuse and to the destruction of its essential lightness of spirit. Teasing turns into torment, mischief into vandalism. The trick is to create and retain the comic atmosphere.

In tragedy there is a good deal of suffering when the integrity of the characters is tested. In comedy there is apt to be discomfiture. The butts of the jokes, usually the unsympathetic characters who arouse our hostility because of their antisocial behavior or self-ignorance, are put in situations in which our aggression or sense of superiority is released. The objects of our derision are embarrassed, rejected, defeated, deflated, unmasked, or deprived of their status or possessions. Even sympathetic characters may be discomfited, especially if they deserve it. In any case, the discomfiture must not become genuinely painful or the comic atmosphere is destroyed.

Most comic playwrights are aware of the need to establish a light atmosphere at the outset as preparation for laughter. Notice how quickly Oscar Wilde creates an attitude of comic expectancy in the first lines of *The Importance of Being Earnest*.

[SCENE—*Morning-room in Algernon's flat in Half-Moon Street. The room is luxuriously and artistically furnished. The sound of a piano is heard in the adjoining room.*] [*Lane is arranging afternoon tea on the table, and after the music has ceased, Algernon enters.*]

Algernon: Did you hear what I was playing, Lane?
Lane: I didn't think it polite to listen, sir.
Alger: I'm sorry for that, for your sake. I don't play accurately—any one can play

Aristophanes enjoyed satirizing Euripides by burlesquing his dramatic practices. Here in Thesmophoriazusae, Mnesilochus disguises himself to spy on the women's assembly. When he is caught and held hostage, he tries to gain his freedom by threatening to kill one of the women's babies. The action becomes comic by exaggerating the tragic style. Greek National Theater. Directed by A. Solomos.

accurately—but I play with wonderful expression. As far as the piano is concerned, sentiment is my forte. I keep science for Life.

Lane: Yes, sir.

Alger: And, speaking of the science of Life, have you got the cucumber sandwiches cut for Lady Bracknell?

Lane: Yes, sir. [*Hands them on a salver.*]

Alger: [*Inspects them, takes two, and sits down on the sofa.*] Oh! . . . by the way, Lane, I see from your book that on Thursday night, when Lord Shoreman and Mr. Worthing were dining with me, eight bottles of champagne are entered as having been consumed.

Lane: Yes sir; eight bottles and a pint.

Alger: Why is it that at a bachelor's establishment the servants invariably drink the champagne? I ask merely for information.

Lane: I attribute it to superior quality of the wine sir. I have often observed that in married households the champagne is rarely of a first-rate brand.

Alger: Good heavens! Is marriage so demoralizing as that?

Lane: I believe it *is* a very pleasant state, sir. I have had very little experience of it myself up to the present. I have only been married once. That was in consequence of a misunderstanding between myself and a young person.

Alger: [*Languidly.*] I don't know that I am much interested in your family life, Lane.

Lane: No sir; it is not a very interesting subject. I never think of it myself.

Alger: Very natural, I am sure. That will do, Lane, thank you.

Lane: Thank you, sir.

[*Lane goes out.*]

Alger: Lane's views on marriage seem somewhat lax. Really, if the lower orders don't set us a good example, what on earth is the use of them? They seem, as a class, to have absolutely no sense of moral responsibility.[3]

[3]Oscar Wilde, *The Importance of Being Earnest* (New York: Samuel French, Inc., 1895).

Wilde carefully creates an elegant atmosphere by the visual aspects of the setting with piano music in the background. In the opening lines we are taken into an artificial world of bright talk filled with comic inversions of the expected norm. He immediately establishes a contagious sense of fun that invites the spectator to join in a game of following the nimble repartee. This is the "general elation" that Bentley describes as "more important than any punch line."

Max Eastman analyzed the conditions essential for the "enjoyment of laughter" in his book of the same title. He observed that humor depends on the existence of a favorable circumstance, and he concludes that "the condition in which joyful laughter most continually occurs is that of play." Laughter is not aroused by those situations where feelings run violent or deep. As a part of his evidence, Eastman cites the native response of a child who may welcome shock and disappointment as a pleasurable experience providing that an atmosphere of play has been established. If the child is teased, however, when he is tired or hungry, the fun is over; the spirit of play has been destroyed.[4] Eastman's point of view is pertinent to our understanding of the comic attitude. How much emotional involvement should the audience be made to feel during a comedy? What is the basis for the comic attitude?

In Shakespeare's romantic comedies, the plays of Sheridan and Goldsmith in the eighteenth century, and in many of our contemporary works, the spectator is invited to enter into the emotions of the characters. We become concerned about the fortunes of the protagonist, our sympathies and hostilities are aroused by the playwright's treatment of his characters, so that we take pleasure in seeing the hero and heroine achieve their objectives, usually accompanied by the jingle of money and ringing of wedding bells. The characters may be laughable, may at times appear foolish and weak, but the playwright treats them with tolerance and indulgence. Examples of comedies that involve our sympathies are *As You Like It, The Rivals, She Stoops to Conquer, Born Yesterday, Juno and the Paycock, The Odd Couple, The Last of the Red Hot Lovers, Fiddler on the Roof, My Fair Lady, The Norman Conquests, Da,* and *One Flew Over the Cuckoo's Nest.*

We usually laugh with the characters, rather than at them; there is no malice in our laughter.

On the other hand, Henri Bergson argues that "laughter has no greater foe than emotion. . . . Its appeal is to the intelligence, pure and simple." Alonzo Myers supports Bergson in this view, saying: "Without detachment, we cannot realize the effect of comedy, which transforms the frustrations of reason into laughter." This point of view is well taken, especially at the extremes of the comic scale—low comedy and high. In most farce, enjoyment stems from the action itself, the momentary laugh, the sudden release. We recognize that it is a form of playing; we do not take the characters' sufferings seriously. No one experiences genuine pain; the feelings do not penetrate the grease paint. Thus the spectators are detached from reality and they are conscious of the artificial world before them.

---

[4]Max Eastman, *Enjoyment of Laughter* (New York: Simon & Schuster, Inc., 1942).

Harry Brock, a gross and violent "operator" is in Washington, D.C., to manipulate some politicians so that he can reap a profit on scrap iron. His girl friend, Billie Dawn, gets acquainted with a reporter who educates Billie and awakens her social conscience so that together they stop Harry Brock's machinations. Her learning process makes it possible for her to turn the tables on Harry and she is an engaging and sympathetic character. (Indiana University. Directed by Gary W. Gaiser).

The comic attitude requires a just sense of proportion so that the essential lightness of spirit is achieved, as Eastman suggested in play with the child. The audience of comedy cannot be pushed too hard in any direction. Excessive sentimentality, bitterness, depravity, exaggeration—any conspicuous straining for effect, any flat-footedness or heavy plodding upsets the niceness of balance so necessary for comedy, making it the most difficult of all the forms of drama to perform. The comic attitude is described effectively by Hegel in these words:

Inseparable from the comic is an infinite geniality and confidence, capable of rising superior to its own contradiction, and experiencing therein no taint of bitterness nor sense of misfortune whatever. It is the happy frame of mind, a hale condition of the soul, which, fully aware of itself, can suffer the dissolution of its aims.[5]

Black Comedy

There is, however, a kind of drama, called black comedy, in which a "gallows humor" is used as a means of twisting the knife in the wound and creating an emotional dissonance. Ridiculous and serious materials are combined to generate an uneasy laughter that is apt to be sardonic or even savage.

The practice of introducing comic relief into a serious situation for heightening the effect by contrast is an old one. We think of the porter in *Macbeth* and the grave diggers in *Hamlet*. With the coming of realism and its emphasis on objective observation, it was apparent to some playwrights that in life the incongruous was often side by side with the beautiful, the comic with

[5]G. W. F. Hegel, *The Philosophy of Fine Art,* trans. F. P. B. Osmaston (London: G. Bell & Sons, Ltd., n.d.).

Joe Orton's amoral black comedies are characterized by his wildly inventive flair for burlesque and bizarre situations. What the Butler Saw revolves around complex sexual relationships after the manner of French bedroom farce, as is evident in this discovery scene. (University of Missouri, Columbia. Directed by David Shelton).

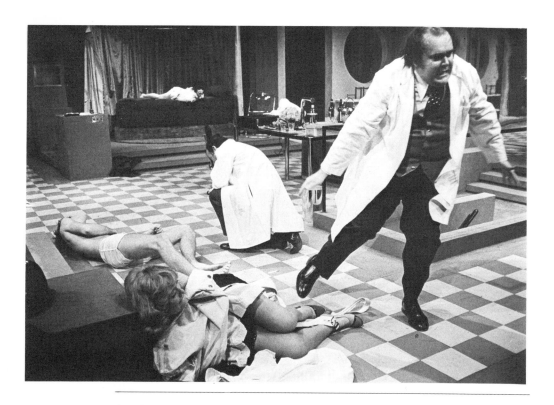

Another scene from What the Butler Saw *captures the wild, zany atmosphere of Orton's black comedy. Cincinnati Playhouse in the Park.*

the tragic. Accordingly they joined the light and the dark in such plays as Chekhov's *Cherry Orchard* and *The Three Sisters*, Pirandello's *Right You Are If You Think You Are*, and O'Casey's *The Plough and the Stars* and *Juno and the Paycock*.

Following World War II, the absurdists, among them Samuel Beckett and Eugène Ionesco, expressed their feelings of alienation and spiritual dislocation in plays filled with bizarre lunacy and bleak humor in *Waiting for Godot* and *Rhinoceros*.

In postwar England black comedy, with its bitterly satiric overtones, made an enormous impact on the theater. Simon Gray in *Butley* mocks the academic world through the protagonist, a university professor who is transformed from a promising scholar into a detestable bureaucrat. Joe Orton's wildly imaginative dark farces, such as *Loot* and *What the Butler Saw* are scathing satirical assaults on the establishment, particularly the police, the Roman Catholic Church, and psychiatry. Peter Barnes' *The Ruling Class* is an attack on religious hypocrisy. The protagonist, a demented aristocrat, imagines himself to be Jesus Christ. He seeks therapy from the Church of England, which convinces him that goodness is irrelevant in a sinful world, so he becomes Jack the Ripper. Peter Nichols in *A Day in the Death of Joe Egg*

In A Day in the Death of Joe Egg, *by Peter Nichols, the parents of a spastic child try to lighten their somber situation by forcing themselves to play games. The resultant laughter has the bitter edge of black comedy. Asolo State Theater, Sarasota, Florida.*

shows how a couple attempts to keep their sanity and preserve their marriage, while caring for their retarded child, by jocular banter and improvised games. In *The National Health*, Nichols introduces black comedy through parodies of soap operas and musical hall sketches to underscore a grim situation.

Tom Stoppard is the most successful writer using black comedy in the recent English theater, although his *Travesties* has a jaunty air and the gloomy environment is never as dark or pervasive as in the works of his colleagues.

Inevitably, black comedy made its impact on the American theater—and on playwrights such as Sam Shepard, Christopher Durang, and Albert Innaurato. Coming out of the protests of the sixties, they found in the grim humor an effective way of making their own statements.

In black comedy, the discomfiture of foolish comic characters is often transferred to the audience, who may feel embarrassed, insulted, or bewildered.

Sources of Laughter

The sources of comic effect have given scholar, critic, philosopher, and psychologist endless stimulation for speculation, and although their efforts have resulted in no universally agreed upon conclusions, we may find some sustenance in their ideas. Let us briefly examine three theories which Allardyce Nicoll cites in his *The Theory of Drama* as the most prominent, realizing that a good deal of their validity depends on personal interpretation and careful selection of examples. The three theories are *derision, incongruity,* and *automatism*. You will recognize immediately the tendency of the theories to overlap because of the mercurial nature of comedy.

Derision

Aristotle's observation that comedy deals with men as "worse than they are" implies a comic theory of derision or degradation. Derision is ordinarily used as a form of criticism to combat pretentiousness or ignorance. Its objective is to keep man humble, balanced, and human. The legitimate targets of derision are stupidity, hypocrisy, and sanctimoniousness. As in life, laughter is used to keep people in line, to insure conformity to a socially acceptable code of behavior. Certainly Aristophanes was fully aware of the possibilities of derision when he ranged far and wide in his jibes against his contemporaries. Not even the audience was safe from his wit. In Aristophanes' *Peace* (421 B.C.) the protagonist, Trygaeus, rears a huge dung-beetle which he attempts to fly to Olympus to beg peace of Zeus. As he flies aloft on the back of the beetle, Trygaeus looks down at the spectators and jeers at them:

> Ah! it's a rough job getting to the gods! My legs are as good as broken through it. (*to the audience*) How small you were to be sure, when seen from heaven! You all had the appearance too of being great rascals, but seen close, you look even worse.

Greek comedy ridiculed physical deformities as well as those of conduct. Comic characters were intentionally distorted and misshapen in appearance through the use of masks, phallic symbols, and padded costumes. A man's attempts to rise above himself were often counteracted by the reminder of his biological needs. Aristophanes delighted in mocking men and gods by exhibiting them in all kinds of embarrassing physical situations. He was ruthless in aiming his shafts of wit at all levels of life. The satirist exploits situations in which characters are debased and reduced to objects of scorn by such formula devices as physical beatings, bodily functions—situations in which an individual is caught off balance, red-handed, under the bed, in the closet, in underwear—in any of the circumstances of life in which people are exposed, their dignity punctured, their flaws revealed, reminding everyone of their kinship with the animal world. Even the most serious moments of life are not safe from the threat of derision. For example, the sacred liturgy of the church was burlesqued by medieval performers in their *Feast of the Asses*. In his film, *Mr. Hulot's Holiday*, Jacques Tati reduces the solemnity of a funeral to a shambles when a floral wreath turns out to be a leaking inner tube, hissing and writhing during the somber ceremony.

Degradation of character often involves a reversal of status. The deviates from normal social behavior, or inflated persons are brought down off their pedestals. Such stock offenders against common sense and decent humanity as fools, fops, hypocrites, bumpkins, louts, misers, philanderers, braggarts, bores, and battle-axes are ridiculed into limbo because of their deformed behavior, their lack of wit or excess of ambition, greed, lust, or stupidity. The

*One of the oldest gags in the world, men disguising themselves as
women, was used by Aristophanes in the 5th century* B.C. *Mnesilochus
dressed up in feminine attire so as to spy on the women's assembly in*
Thesmophoriazusae. *Epidaurus Festival.*

satirist uses barbs of derisive laughter to prick the inflated reputation of
entrenched authority, often a popular form of comic appeal, since the
common people find release and enjoyment in the discomfiture of those
above them.

The comic theory of derision is especially effective when the dramatist is
treating ideas and characters critically. Although physical degradation and
insulting language are confined mostly to farce, the satirist bent on attacking
ideas also makes use of ridicule. Ben Jonson used his wit as an instrument of
mockery against his fellow Elizabethans, as he indicated when he stated the
purpose of his comedy: "to strip the ragged follies of the time." Molière
likewise brought low those who were guilty of excess, deriding those who
were too ambitious in *Le Bourgeois Gentilhomme*, those who were too clever
in *Les Precieuses Ridicules*, too exacting in *Le Misanthrope*, and too gullible
in *Tartuffe*. As we noted earlier, comedy since World War II has been notable

for its vigorous aggression, directed primarily at the establishment and its values. Derision is an effective weapon of criticism in the theater and a suitable source of laughter, but because it is critical with overtones of contempt, it often ruffles those who are laughed at, and may beget bitterness and retaliation unless confined to those without power or status.

Incongruity

Perhaps because it is the most elastic and extensive theory of comedy, the idea of incongruity has the widest application. Incongruity is the result of the tension or dissonance set up by the juxaposition of two objects or people that creates a laughable contrast, such as a large, fat woman matched with a small, skinny man, or a person out of place in his surroundings—in a bathing suit at the opera or in formal clothes at the beach. The contrast usually depends on the establishment of some kind of norm so that the discrepancy is

A delightful incongruity occurs in Aristophanes' The Frogs when Dionysus stops a funeral procession, kneels on the corpse and haggles with him on the price of taking some of his baggage to Hades. Greek National Theater.

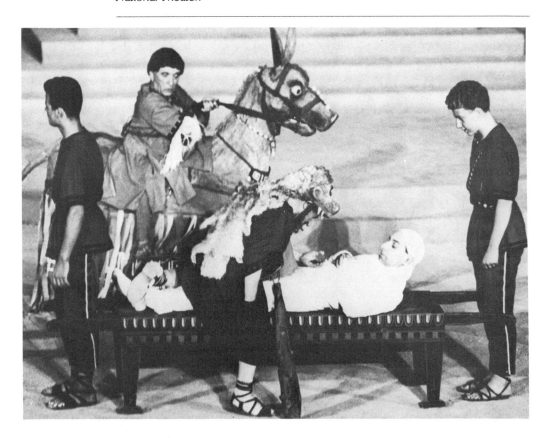

emphasized. The gap between the expected and the unexpected, between the intention and the realization, between the normal and the abnormal results in comic discord.

Incongruity may take several forms—situation, character, and dialogue. The comic situation based on incongruity presents a contrast between the usual or accepted behavior and the unusual or unacceptable. A typical pattern is to place a character in an environment that reveals his social incongruity, such as a country bumpkin in polite society, the socially elite in bucolic surroundings, an intellectual among barbarians, a clown or an inebriate in a dignified gathering, a sailor in a harem, a tramp in the mayor's bed.

Incongruity of character involves a constrast between the ideal and the real, or between appearance and actuality. This may be seen in such situations as Parolles' professed bravery and his actual cowardice when confronted with danger in *All's Well That Ends Well*, Malvolio's grotesque costuming and simpering when he attempts to create a favorable impression on Olivia in *Twelfth Night*, and the depiction of Dionysus, the revered Greek god, as a cringing weakling in *The Frogs*. An aspect of incongruity of character is the inflexible person whose one-track mind separates him from the norm— for instance, Molière's Alceste, whose exaggerated desire for frankness makes him socially bizarre.

Incongruity of language occurs when the dialogue is in sharp contrast to the social context, such as the sudden interjection of vulgarity into a polite conversation, or language having the opposite effect of that intended by the speaker. Mrs. Malaprop in Sheridan's *The Rivals* gave her name to this kind of incongruity, such as when she spoke of "the allegories on the banks of the Nile." In our time, Archie Bunker has exploited the comedic potential of distorted language.

Incongruity in its various forms suggests imbalance and disproportion; there is the implication of an upset equilibrium, of a dissonance caused by a comic contrast.

Automatism

One of the most imaginative and provocative theories of comedy was that advanced by Henri Bergson in his book *Laughter*, in which he contends that the essence of the laughable is automatism—"something mechanical is encrusted on the living."[6] Man becomes an object of laughter whenever he becomes rigid and machinelike, or whenever he loses control of himself or breaks contact with humanity.

Automatism of character occurs when an individual loses his human flexibility, and his behavior becomes mechanical in its repetition, or when a man becomes a puppet, no longer in control of his actions. The gist of Bergson's thinking is indicated by these representative statements about comedy and character: "We laugh *every* time a person gives us the

[6]Henri Bergson, *Laughter*, trans. Cloudesley Brereton and Frank Rothwell (London: Macmillan, 1917).

impression of being a thing." "Any individual is comic who automatically goes his own way without troubling himself about getting in touch with the rest of his fellow beings." "Rigidity, automatism, absentmindedness, and unsociability are all inextricably entwined, and all serve as ingredients to the making up of the comic in character." Bergson's point of view on one-sided characters is similar to that of Ben Jonson's comedy of "humours" in which he ridiculed those characters who were guilty of some imbalance, some excess:

> As when some one peculiar quality
> Doth so possess a man, that it doth draw
> All his effects, his spirits, and his powers
> In their confluctions, all to run one way
> This may be truly said to be a humour.

In such plays as *Epicene, Volpone,* and *The Alchemist,* Jonson makes comic figures of those who have lost control and succumbed to some individual trait of character causing eccentric and antisocial behavior. Such characters fit neatly in Bergson's theory of automatism.

Automatism of situation is often based on repetition. Characters are caught in the grip of circumstances and subjected to mechanical domination. Chaplin made use of this device in his famous mechanized corn-on-the-cob eating sequence, and his hilarious shaving pantomime to the accompaniment of a Brahms Hungarian Dance. Repeated patterns of behavior have been used very often as the framework for comedy, as in D. L. Coburn's *Gin Game*, in which the central action of the play is a series of gin rummy games played by two senior citizens. Fonsia, an apparently prim woman, is inexperienced in card playing, but she wins every hand against Weller, who considers himself an expert. Coburn skillfully devises ways to use repetition not only for comic effect but also to reveal the meanness of the characters. Neil Simon's *The Last of the Red Hot Lovers* exploits repetition in the story of Barney Cashman, a middle-aged proprietor of a fish restaurant, who makes three unsuccessful attempts at seduction. Meyerhold, in directing his interpretation of Chekhov's farce *The Proposal* found thirty-eight references to fainting, which he exploited as a recurrent leitmotif in production. In musical revues, repeated variations of a comic piece of business are called a "running gag." A typical example used by Olsen and Johnson was that of an "escape artist" who, bound hand and foot, is given half a minute to free himself, but at the end of the allotted time is still securely tied. Every now and then he is shown as he continues his unsuccessful struggle. At the end of the performance, when the audience leaves through the lobby, the hapless escape artist is on the floor continuing his efforts.

Automatism of dialogue takes several forms. For example, Bergson says, "Inadvertently to say or do what we have no intention of saying or doing, as a result of inelasticity or momentum is, as we are aware, one of the sources of the comic." Inelasticity, of course, implies repetition, a standard form of comedy, as for example Slender's expression of his love in *The Merry Wives of Windsor* when he sighs every now and then, "Oh, sweet Ann Page." To mock the monotonous dullness of ordinary social conversation, Ionesco in *The Bald Soprano* uses the phrases "That is curious, how bizarre, what a coincidence," in various forms more than two dozen times in four pages of dialogue. One of the most successful uses of automatism of language occurs in Molière's *The Imaginary Invalid* when Toinette, a pert maid-servant, is pretending to be a physician examining her hypochondriac master, Argan:

Toinette: Let me feel your pulse. Come, come, beat properly, please. Ah! I will soon make you beat as you should. This pulse is trifling with me. I see that it does not know me yet. Who is your doctor?

Argan: Mr. Purgon.

Toinette: That man is not noted in my books among the great doctors. What does he say you are ill of?

Argan: He says it is the liver, and others say it is the spleen.

Toinette: They are a pack of ignorant blockheads; you are suffering from the lungs.

Argan: The lungs?

Toinette: Yes; what do you feel?

Argan: From time to time great pains in my head.

Toinette: Just so; the lungs.

Argan: At times it seems as if I had a mist before my eyes.

Toinette: The lungs.

Argan: I feel sick now and then.

Toinette: The lungs.

Argan: And I feel sometimes a weariness in all my limbs.

Toinette pretends to be a doctor and makes a diagnosis of her Master's imaginary ills. The Imaginary Invalid. (Wayne State University. Directed by Robert T. Hazzard).

Toinette: The lungs.
Argan: And sometimes I have sharp pains in the stomach, as if I had the colic.
Toinette: The lungs. Do you eat your food with appetite?
Argan: Yes, Sir.
Toinette: The lungs. Do you like to drink a little wine?
Argan: Yes, Sir.
Toinette: The lungs. You feel sleepy after your meals, and willingly enjoy a nap?
Argan: Yes, Sir.
Toinette: The lungs, the lungs, I tell you. What does your doctor order you for food?
Argan: He orders me soup.
Toinette: Ignoramus!
Argan: Fowl.
Toinette: Ignoramus!
Argan: Veal.
Toinette: Ignoramus!
Argan: Broth.
Toinette: Ignoramus!
Argan: New-laid eggs.
Toinette: Ignoramus!
Argan: And at night a few prunes to relax the bowels.
Toinette: Ignoramus!
Argan: And, above all, to drink my wine well diluted with water.
Toinette: Ignorantus, ignoranta, ignorantum. [7]

It is apparent that Bergson's theory is an interesting extension of the idea of incongruity, the jostling together of the human and the mechanical. By his ingenuity and persuasiveness, Bergson makes quite a plausible argument for automatism, especially for the comedies of Molière, but like other comic theories, automatism does not explain all of the sources of laughter, nor is it appropriate to all kinds of comic effect. Nevertheless, automatism must be recognized as one of the explanations for the phenomenon of laughter, and we are indebted to Bergson for his stimulating analysis.

From the preceding discussion of representative theories of comedy, it is apparent that a case can be made for derision, incongruity, and automatism. It should also be obvious that it is impossible to fix comedy in a single rigid mold, although recurrent patterns and mechanisms show through the diverse forms. This will be increasingly evident as we consider the structure and content of comedy.

Plot

Comedy requires skillful plotting. A comedy is not simply a loosely knit accumulation of gags. Laughs must be carefully timed and built, in context with the complete structure of the play. The jokes are important as they relate to the total effect, not as isolated laughs.

[7]Molière, *The Imaginary Invalid*, in *The Dramatic Works of Molière*, trans. C. H. Wall (London: George Bell & Sons, 1900).

Laughter is the result of the mechanism of tension and release. On the printed page, a joke takes this form:

She: --
He: --
She: --   *Preparation*
He: --
She: --! *Release*

A comic strip often assumes this pattern:

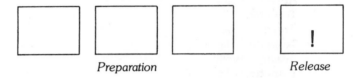

Preparation   *Release*

The mechanism for inducing laughter has this structure:

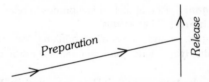

The punch line releases the tension. A surprise occurs. Expectancy is tricked. There is a sudden change in direction. The light bulb goes on.

In making or telling a joke, the structure is important. It cannot be too long or wordy, the punch line must be concise and on cue. The preparation must build expectancy. No tension, no release. Laughter depends on the plot or structure as well as on the idea or the language.

A comedy playscript is a score for playing, and just as the composer must be cognizant of the possibilities of his music in the hands of musicians, the writer of comedy must be fully aware of the techniques and resources of the actor that will animate the material. The comic writer is acutely concerned with the individual in a social environment. Basic patterns of comedy depict a character who deviates from the norm or who is out of place with the surroundings. The implicit contrasts and conflicts require adroit delineation of the social milieu in order to expose the laughable elements of conduct. Tragic writers may concentrate on heroic figures, isolated from other characters and unaffected by their behavior, but comedy exploits the interaction of characters, the human scene, the group situation, the juxtaposition of characters. Comedy is more involved with the particular than with the universal. Its emphasis is on the here and now, not the long perspective. The playwright frequently develops timely allusions, local references, and contemporaneous characters. Comic material must have a sense of crispness and spontaneity. It must not smell of the museum or the dead past. Hence, it is difficult for comedy to survive its time and place of origin because many of its most telling referents are gone.

The earliest extant comedies are those of Aristophanes—"old comedy" from the fifth century B.C. His typical plots were based on "a happy idea." The women in *Lysistrata* hope to bring about peace by a sex strike; in *The Acharnians* a private citizen negotiates his own personal peace treaty with Sparta. In *The Frogs*, Dionysus decides to take a trip to Hades to visit the tragic poets Aeschylus and Euripides. In each play the merits of the idea are debated, and despite opposition, the happy idea is put into practice and the results demonstrated. The plays end in revelry.

In the subsequent development of comedy, the original pattern persists. Characters strive for objectives and are thwarted by obstacles and opposition, but their problems are solved when misunderstandings are cleared up and the truth emerges or the opponents are reconciled. The play ends happily, often with the lovers united in an embrace, a reminder of the orgiastic celebration of the end of most old comedies.

Jan Kott sees the basic comic plot in these terms: "The oldest and most enduring kind of comic action, from ancient comedy to commedia dell'arte, from popular farce to Molière, is a clash between two houses."[8] One house represents authority and appearances; in the second house are bachelors, easy girls, thieves, and crooks. Kott suggests that the fundamental plot is the aggression on the house of virtue by the house of ill repute.

Although Kott's theory is not universally applicable, his analysis is basically sound in that the comic plot usually involves an imbalance caused by the presence of some ridiculous element through error, ignorance, or ambition. The resultant conflicts and contrasts create comic tension which is released in laughter.

The plots of most comedies are made up of sharp complications which require careful craftsmanship in the use of exposition, climaxes, crises, discoveries, and the denouement. The tangled threads of action must remain clear to the audience, which is tricky business in plays of rapid action, mishaps, and misunderstandings. The climaxes and crises of comedy demand technical mastery because the high points of the action often involve a social situation in which a number of people are caught in the same net, obliging the playwright to deal with complex materials. Frequently, the emotional peaks are those of action and discovery, which require that the playwright have a strong sense of visual humor. Climaxes must be built and sustained without prolonging them beyond the limits of the material. The playwright's touch must be deft and sure to keep the pace rapid and to create the special climate of comedy which will insure laughter.

Farce is usually the comedy of situation. The structure of farce is a framework for vigorous, rapid, and exaggerated action in which the characters move, rather than think, and where evoking laughter justifies nearly any means. Once the engine has been cranked up and set in motion, the speed is accelerated, and by unexpected blowouts, backfirings and explosions, the

---

[8]Jan Kott, "The Eating of 'The Government Inspector,' " *Theatre Quarterly*, 5, no. 17 (1975).

Georges Feydeau is noted for his complicated farces filled with frantic action played at breakneck speed. A typical scene from Hotel Paradiso *directed by Tom Moore. American Conservatory Theater, San Francisco.*

mechanism careens crazily, gathering momentum until it finally lurches to an awkward but happy end in a cloud of steam with all of the parts still spinning; and while there has been a whirlwind of activity, the machine has not really moved an inch in any direction.

The skill of plotting farce is determined by the dramatist's ingenuity in inventing a variety of entanglements that will give the comedian a chance to play for laughs. The playwright usually exploits a basic situation which is highly improbable and atypical: A woodcutter reluctantly consents to become a court physician to cure the king's daughter of a feigned illness; two long-lost twin brothers, whose servants are another pair of twins, strive for reunion; two young communists sharing a one-room apartment fall in love with each other's newlywed wives; a shy greeting card writer becomes involved with a gang of racetrack touts because of his skill in predicting the winners; two mismatched divorced men try to live together despite their contrasting life-

In The Norman Conquests, *Alan Ayckbourn exploits the amorous adventures of Norman over a week-end in an ingenious trilogy that relies heavily on mismatching and mixups, some of which end up in surprise discoveries. (Indiana University. Directed by Richard L. Scammon).*

styles; a genial husband undertakes the precarious responsibility of simultaneously maintaining two separate wives and families in Wilmington and Philadelphia.

Low comedy exploits the physical aspects of humanity. The body, its desires, and functions are a primary source of comic material. To a large extent, farcical situations depend on visual humor. Not only sex, but any drive or appetite that causes one to lose his balance or control is a target for ridicule. Farcical characters move in an active physical world; they are out of place in an intellectual atmosphere.

In the days of the silent motion picture, farce was exceedingly popular in the slapstick comedies created by Mack Sennett, Charlie Chaplin, and Buster Keaton. The basic requirement for silent pictures was action—hence, it was a medium ideally suited for farce. Comedians tumbled their way through crazy situations, full of violence set off by the slightest provocation, and usually ending in a chase that annihilated all the restrictions of time and space. Some examples of typical farcical business: Harold Lloyd, playing a book salesman, approaches a tough customer and is thrown out. He returns a dozen times, accelerating the pace. On another occasion he serves as a practice tackling-dummy for a football squad. He makes a speech at a dance with a kitten crawling inside his sweater. Buster Keaton chases butterflies in the countryside, completely oblivious to a band of wild Indians who pursue him. In another picture he sits on a hot stove, then sits on a cake of ice which melts rapidly. Ben Turpin, a cross-eyed explorer, surrenders to a stuffed lion.

These familiar farcical patterns are still in use today; consult the television program log and you will find such comic situations as these:

> Nervous about adopting a child, Woody has a few too many before a crucial interview with the agency.
>
> Oscar loses Leonard's entry in the frog-jumping finals.
>
> Thanks to a "Fight the Flab" radio program, one of the Goodies slims down with only one side effect: he becomes a woman.
>
> An eloping couple seek refuge at Gull Cottage—but the ghost of the house objects.
>
> The girls' apartment catches fire. It's quickly doused, but sparks another flame: a fireman gets a crush on Laverne.
>
> Ricky and the Mertzes frantically rehearse for pregnant Lucy's trip to the hospital.
>
> The unconscious takes over when Oscar becomes a violent sleepwalker bent on braining Felix.

The materials from which comedies are made are venerable ones, as old as the theater itself. The sources of comic effect, which the ancient playwrights Aristophanes, Plautus, and Terence used to delight the audiences of Athens and Rome, are still the stock in trade which you can see on your television or motion-picture screen tonight. Someone has suggested that, after all, there are only seven jokes: (1) the insult, (2) the pun, (3) sex, (4) family life, (5) reversal, (6) odd combinations, and (7) news. This may not be all-inclusive but the list is surprisingly universal.

Similarly, the *devices* of comedy that the playwright uses are well established. Let us consider three as representative examples common mechanisms for evoking laughter.

Comic Devices

One of the most reliable comic devices is that of teasing, which may take a variety of forms, such as the delay of news which Shakespeare employs when the Nurse withholds Romeo's message from Juliet. In *Lysistrata*, Myrrhina, having joined the women in a sex strike in order to make peace, teases her amorous husband Cinesias by a series of delaying tactics. Another version of the teasing device occurs in the opera *The Night Bell*, when the elderly groom who has married a young bride is interrupted frequently on his wedding night by the untimely entrances of his young rival who appears in a variety of disguises. Another form of teasing occurs when characters are intentionally placed in embarrassing or awkward situations. Tony Lumpkin in *She Stoops to Conquer* teases his mother by driving her around her own garden in a carriage at night pretending that they are beset by robbers. In *The Taming of the Shrew*, Petruchio exposes Katherine to a series of teasings before she is finally tamed. He tests her in the following scene when he and Kate, accompanied by Hortensio, are on the road toward home:

Petruchio: Come on, i' God's name; once more toward our father's—Good Lord, how brightly and goodly shines the moon!
Katherine: The moon! the sun: it is not moonlight now.
Petruchio: I say it is the moon that shines so bright.
Katherine: I know it is the sun that shines so bright.

The Taming of the Shrew *is one of the classic battles of the sexes that includes a good deal of teasing, as Petruchio attempts to bring his willful bride under control. (American Conservatory Theater, San Francisco. Directed by William Ball).*

Petruchio: Now, by my mother's son, and that's myself,
It shall be moon, or star, or what I list
Or ere I journey to your father's house.
Go on, and fetch our horses back again.
Evermore cross'd and cross'd; nothing but cross'd!

Hortensio: Say as he says, or we shall never go.

Katherine: Forward, I pray since we have come so far,
And be it moon, or sun, or what you please:
An if you please to call it a rush-candle,
Henceforth, I vow it shall be so for me.

Petruchio: I say it is the moon.

Katherine: I know it is the moon.

Petruchio: Nay, then you lie: it is the blessed sun.

Katherine: Then, God be blessed, it is the blessed sun:
But sun it is not, when you say it is not;
And the moon changes even as your mind.
What you will have it named, even that it is;
And so it shall be so for Katherine.

Another familiar plot mechanism of comedy is reversal or inversion. The entire play may be based on the turnabout of a downtrodden character who ultimately achieves a dominant position, as in such plays as *How to Succeed in Business*, and *Born Yesterday*. The reversal may be one in which the character is temporarily thrown out of his usual milieu, only to return to his customary status, as in *Jeppe of the Hills*, when the drunken ne'er-do-well is placed in the mayor's bed, pampered for a day, and then returned insensible to the gutter where he was found. Similarly, in *The Admirable Crichton*, a butler assumes control of a household when the family is marooned on an island, but at the conclusion of the play he resumes his former servile position. In Brecht's *Caucasian Chalk Circle*, an outcast suddenly becomes a judge and rules over the district. Gogol's *The Government Inspector* tells the story of a disreputable down-and-out clerk who, being mistaken for the Inspector General, makes use of the opportunity and is entertained. The musical *My Fair Lady* based on Shaw's *Pygmalion* shows the process of transforming a cockney flower girl into a lady, sufficiently schooled in social graces to pass for a duchess. The reversal device may involve the plot of the play, or characters' actions, or the dialogue. Note how in the opening lines of *The Importance of Being Earnest* (pp. 102–3), Wilde inverts the expected response and achieves comic surprise.

Another well-worn comic device which frequently includes inversion is the use of the unfamiliar. A character or group of characters is placed in new surroundings, or they are engaged in unaccustomed activities. One form of this device is the process of teaching an inexperienced and often inept person, such as the English lesson in *Henry V*, the fencing lesson in *Everyman in His Humour*, and the dancing lesson in *Le Bourgeois Gentilhomme*. The humor may be heightened by the additional twist of having the instructor as ignorant as his pupil. The awkward, embarrassed, or shy person making an adjustment to a new experience or surroundings is used again and again for comic effect,

The imbecile suitor, Thomas, makes an inept, hilarious proposal of marriage to Angelique in The Imaginary Invalid. *(Miami University, Ohio. Directed by Barry Witham).*

such as the scenes in *The Last of the Red Hot Lovers*, when Barney Cashman makes three unsuccessful attempts at romantic adventures. In *Plaza Suite*, on her wedding day, the bride decides she can't go through with the marriage and locks herself in the bathroom. Two naive Ohio girls in *My Sister Eileen* move into a basement flat in Greenwich Village and find it difficult to adjust. Much of the fun of *Born Yesterday* comes from the tutoring of Billie Dawn as she is changed from an empty-headed chorus girl to a person with a developing social conscience.

These three devices indicate some of the venerable mechanisms of comedy that are endlessly repeated. Other familiar comic mechanisms are mistaken identity, violence, pretending or deception, fancy footwork or skillful recovery, jeopardy, exaggeration, grilling, and exposure or discovery. This is not an exhaustive list nor do the devices usually occur separately, but they mix freely with one another or overlap. It is interesting to note that the use of the device will not in itself create a comic effect, because many of these patterns of action also appear in tragedy. For example, the reversal formula of comedy is likewise utilized in tragedy: a highborn character in an elevated position at the beginning of the play falls to his catastrophe, as in *Hamlet, Agamemnon,* and *Antigone.* In comedy, the reversal often goes in the other direction. The little person, ignored and beaten down, emerges at the end of the play in a dominant position, as in *Three Men on a Horse* and *Beggar on Horseback.* The complications of mistaken identity used for comic purposes by Shakespeare in *A Midsummer Night's Dream, Twelfth Night,* and *Comedy of Errors* are utilized for tragic effect by Sophocles in *Oedipus Rex.* The nature of the mechanism does not determine the response, but more significant is the manner in which the playwright uses it, the spirit of the play. This point is brought forcibly home by comparing the plot mechanisms of *Romeo and Juliet* and the Pyramus and Thisbe episode in *A Midsummer Night's Dream.* The plots are strikingly similar, but one is used for comedy, the other for tragedy.

Character

Because comedy wears many guises, there is great variation in character. Not only is there a difference in kind, but there is also a difference in treatment. A comic character may be the unconscious butt of the joke, such as Hodge in *Poetaster* or Orgon in *Tartuffe.* Sometimes, a character may be conscious of his plight or absurdities, and share his discomfiture with the audience as Falstaff does in *Henry IV.* Again, a comic character may, through his wit and insight, direct the laughter toward an idea or situation as Mirabell does in *The Way of the World* or as many Shavian characters do in mocking contemporary ideas and institutions. Characters may be comical because of their eccentric behavior, their lack of wit or judgment, their delightful facility with language, their engaging animal spirits, their charming manner, or their buoyant attitude toward life.

Comic characters tend to be stock types. Playwrights frequently are more concerned about developing the intricacies of plot than about revealing depth of character. Hence they sketch their figures lightly or else resort to readily recognizable types. Comic dramatists may deliberately create one-sided roles to suit the comic purpose as a means of showing their inhumanity in their fixations and inflexibility. Again, they may purposely keep their characters in the simple mold of stock figures in order to prevent excessive emotional attachment that might destroy the light atmosphere of comedy. As character becomes more genuine and complex, drama moves away from comedy. As an example of how a type character may evolve into a sympathetic and complex human being, thus altering the flavor of the play, we may consider the case of the braggart soldier. As Lamachus in Aristophanes' *Acharnians,* Miles Gloriosus in Plautine comedy, and the Capitano in commedia dell'arte, he is an elementary source of comic effect because of the disparity between his pretended bravery and his cowardice in the face of danger. As Shakespeare's Falstaff, the character is vastly enriched as he rollicks his way through

The Merry Wives of Windsor, and then is developed into such a complete personality in *Henry IV* that Hardin Craig referred to Falstaff as "the first great synthetic character in modern drama."

Characters in high comedies are usually from the upper echelons of society—urbane, sophisticated people who live in a special kind of environment with their own code of behavior. In contrast farcical characters are from the humble walks of life. Their speech and behavior is simplified as they race through the complicated machinery of the plot.

Thought

Most comedy does not bear a heavy burden of thought. The playwright is much more concerned with satisfying the needs of those spectators who come to the theater for diversion—who wish to avoid facing someone else's problems, and who have no immediate interest in intellectual stimulation in the theater. They want to have a good time—to laugh and forget themselves. Because this is the dominant attitude among those who come to see a comedy, the comic writer concentrates on interesting the audience in lighthearted actions and sympathetic characters whose involvements are not taken seriously. While such comedy may imply an accepted code of behavior and a system of values, the emphasis is not on weighing the merits of conventional morality, except insofar as it serves as a frame of reference for displaying incongruity. In most comedy, the playwright is not questioning values but exposing ridiculous behavior. For the writers' purposes, the comic action, rather than the meaning of the action, is important.

If writers of farce do have a message, it is ordinarily incidental to their main purpose which is to amuse. Such plays are not without social significance, however, in that farce releases a great deal of aggression by permitting us to gratify our repressed tendencies through laughter. In the theater we feel free to laugh at authority and conventional restrictions of speech and behavior. For the moment we achieve a sense of superiority over the characters ridiculed on the stage. In the farces of Molière, Labiche, and Feydeau, there is implicit criticism of society and its mores—particularly of hypocrisy and pretension—but this is a by-product of farce, not its main reason for existence. Yet some of the black farces of Joe Orton and Peter Nichols, are directly aimed at social commentary.

Diction

Comedy employs a wide variety of language devices for its effect, from cleverly turned conceits and one-liners to crude puns, insults, vulgarisms, and deformed words. We have already observed some of comedy's comic uses in derision, automatism, and incongruity. Most successful comic writers have excellent ears for dialogue and they take apparent delight in their verbal skill. The Elizabethans were especially fond of exploiting language for comic effect.

We remember the rich texture of the rustics' speech in *A Midsummer Night's Dream*, the lively verbal skirmishes between Beatrice and Benedick in *Much Ado About Nothing* and Rosalind and Orlando in *As You Like It*. Ben Jonson similarly took pains to delight the ear with vivid and lively dialogue.

The writer of high comedy, of course, is especially concerned with dialogue, since wit and repartee are the drama's chief appeal, the animated language and nimbleness of playing with ideas replacing physical action. The English Restoration playwrights of the late seventeenth century, such as Congreve, Wycherly, Vanbrugh, and Etherege, wrote for a select, sophisticated audience comedies mostly about amorous adventuring—depicting truewits in contrast to the unconscious incongruities of the inept witwords. The polished dialogue of this comedy of manners appeared again briefly in the late eighteenth century in the dramas of Goldsmith and Sheridan.

Among modern playwrights no one was more skilled in making his characters articulate than George Bernard Shaw. In *Major Barbara* he contrasts Barbara, who is devoted to the Salvation Army, with her father, Undershaft, a munitions manufacturer who considers poverty the greatest evil.

Undershaft: I save their souls just as I saved yours.

Barbara: (*revolted*) You saved my soul! What do you mean?

Undershaft: I fed you and clothed you and housed you. I took care that you should have money enough to live handsomely—more than enough; so that you could be wasteful, careless, generous. That saved your soul from the seven deadly sins.

Barbara: (*bewildered*) The seven deadly sins!

Undershaft: Yes, the deadly seven. (*counting on his fingers*) Food, clothing, firing, rent, taxes, respectability and children. Nothing can lift those seven millstones from Man's neck but money; and the spirit cannot soar until the millstones are lifted. I lifted them from your spirit. I enabled Barbara to become Major Barbara; and I saved her from the crime of poverty.

Cusins: Do you call poverty a crime?

Undershaft: The worst of crimes. All the other crimes are virtues beside it: all the other dishonors are chivalry itself by comparison. Poverty blights whole cities; spreads horrible pestilences; strikes dead the very souls of all who come within sight, sound, or smell of it. What you call crime is nothing: a murder here and a theft there, a blow now and a curse then: what do they matter? they are only the accidents and illnesses of life: there are not fifty genuine professional criminals in London. But there are millions of poor people, abject people, dirty people, ill fed, ill clothed people. They poison us morally and physically: they kill the happiness of society: they force us to do away with our own liberties and to organize unnatural cruelties for fear they should rise against us and drag us down into their abyss. Only fools fear crime: we all fear poverty.[9]

Among present comic playwrights, Tom Stoppard is noted for his flair with comic language. In *Travesties* (pp. 127–28) he shows off his verbal dexterity with parodies, puns, alliterations, double entendres, literary allusions, and music hall patter. In this play, Stoppard brings together in Zurich in 1919 a marvelous assortment of characters—Lenin, James Joyce, Tzara (one of the

[9]George Bernard Shaw, *Major Barbara* (New York: Dodd, Mead & Company, 1941).

The actors' ability to speak well is essential to performing Bernard Shaw, since his plays are full of witty discussion and wordplay. Major Barbara, directed by Richard Spear at Wayne State University. Designed by Russell Smith.

founders of dadaism), and Carr, a minor official in the English ministry who remembers imperfectly the events that transpired. The odd combination of characters gives Stoppard the chance to play with words and ideas in a dazzling manner. When James Joyce enters he speaks in limericks! Carr and Tzara engage in a delightful verbal exchange.

Carr: Well, let us resume. *Zurich By One Who Was There.* (*Normal light.*)
Bennett (*entering*): Mr. Tzara.
Carr: How are you, my dear Tristan? What brings you here?
Tzara: Oh, pleasure, pleasure! What else should bring anyone anywhere?

(Tzara, *no less than* Carr, *is straight out of The Importance of Being Earnest.*)

Carr: I don't know that I approve of these Benthamite ideas, Tristan. I realise they are all the rage in Zurich—even in the most respectable salon, to remark that one was brought there by a sense of duty, leads to terrible scenes but if society is going to ape the fashions of philosophy, the end can only be ruin and decay.
Tzara: Eating and drinking, as usual, I see, Henry? I have often observed that Stoical principles are more easily borne by those of Epicurean habits.

127

Carr: (*stiffly*): I believe it is done to drink a glass of hock and seltzer before luncheon, and it is well done to drink it well before luncheon. I took to drinking hock and seltzer for my nerves at a time when nerves were fashionable in good society. This season it is trenchfoot, but I drink it regardless because I feel much better after it.

Tzara: You might have felt much better anyway.

Carr: No, no—post hock, propter hock.

Tzara: But, my dear Henry, causality is no longer fashionable owing to the war.

Carr: How illogical, since the war itself had causes. I forget what they were, but it was all in the papers at the time. Something about brave little Belgium, wasn't it?

Tzara: Was it? I thought it was Serbia . . .

Carr: Brave little Serbia . . . ? No, I don't think so. The newspapers would never have risked calling the British public at arms without a proper regard for succinct alliteration.

Tzara: Oh, what nonsense you talk!

Carr: It may be nonsense, but at least it is clever nonsense.

Tzara: I am sick of cleverness. The clever people try to impose a design on the world and when it goes calamitously wrong they call it fate. In point of fact, everything is Chance, including design.

Carr: That sounds awfully clever. What does it mean? Not that it has to mean anything, of course.

Tzara: It means, my dear Henry, that the causes we know everything about depend on causes we known very little about, which depend on causes we know absolutely nothing about. And it is the duty of the artist to jeer and howl and belch at the delusion that infinite generations of real effects can be inferred from the gross expression of apparent cause.

Carr: It is the duty of the artist to beautify existence.

Tzara: (*articulately*) Dada dada dada dada dada dada dada dada dada dada dada dada dada dada dada dada dada dada dada dada dada dada dada dada dada dada dada dada dada dada dada dada dada dada.

Carr: (*slight pause*): Oh, what nonsense you talk!

Tzara: It may be nonsense, but at least it's not clever nonsense. Cleverness has been exploded, along with so much else, by the war.

Carr: You forget that I was there, in the mud and blood of a foreign field, unmatched by anything in the whole history of human carnage. Ruined several pairs of trousers. Nobody who has not been in the trenches can have the faintest conception of the horror of it. I had hardly set foot in France before I sank in up to the knees in a pair of twill jodphurs with pigskin straps handstitched by Ramidge and Hawkes. And so it went on—the sixteen ounce serge, the heavy worsteds, the silk flannel mixture—until I was invalidated out with a bullet through the calf of an irreplaceable lambswool dyed khaki in the yarn to my own specification. I tell you, there is nothing in Switzerland to compare with it.[10]

Diction in farce, on the other hand, is not distinguished by literary pretensions. Only in rare instances has a playwright like Oscar Wilde combined the framework of farce and the repartee of social comedy, because wit depends on an intellectual frame of reference. A critical ear is incompatible with farce. The linguistic devices of low comedy are puns, repetitions, "tag

---

[10]Tom Stoppard, *Travesties* (London: Fraser and Dunlop, 1975).

lines,'' wisecracks, insults, vulgarisms, and deformed language. Although the language of farce is commonplace, writing it requires a special talent. The actor's speech must accompany or thrust the action forward, rather than impede it. Laugh lines demand a feeling for the flavor and cadence of real language, and the ability to make dialogue crackle and snap. The playwright must have an excellent sense of theater so as to pace his dialogue, build for laughs, make effective use of repetition, and realize the comic possibilities in the juxtaposition of words and phrases—the incongruities of human speech.

Comedy in Performance

More than other forms of drama, comedy depends upon performance for its full effect. The timing of the actors, their ability to play pieces of business, to project laugh lines, to bring out the ridiculous in situation and character without destroying the light atmosphere—these are special requisites for the complete realization of comedy.

In performance many comedies are made stageworthy by use of "sight gags"—visual humor often based on exposing characters in embarassing circumstances, such as in this modern dress version of The Taming of the Shrew. *(Directed by Robert C. Burroughs, University of Arizona).*

Comedy often makes considerable appeal to the eye so that scenery, properties, and costuming are essential. An interesting case in point is Peter Shaffer's *Black Comedy*, in which the audience is asked to accept the convention that most of the action takes place in the dark, with the resultant mix-ups in which the performers exploit the visual humor in groping for one another, crawling under rugs, falling down the staircase, and tripping over the furniture.

Since disguises, concealments, discoveries, fights, chases, and entrapments are standard comic fare, the physical aspects of production are apt to be very important in devising "sight gags." In high comedy, in which much of the laughter stems from the wit or awkward social behavior, less emphasis is placed on visual humor, but farce is apt to tax the physical facilities of production to the utmost.

Bibliography

BENTLEY, ERIC, *Let's Get a Divorce and Other Plays.* New York: Hill & Wang, 1958.

BERGSON, HENRI, *Laughter,* trans. Cloudesley Brereton and Frank Rothwell. London: Macmillan, 1917.

EASTMAN, MAX, *Enjoyment of Laughter.* New York: Simon & Schuster, Inc., 1942.

ENCK, JOHN J., ELIZABETH T. FOSTER, and ALVIN WHITLEY, *The Comic in Theory and Practice.* New York: Appleton-Century-Crofts, Inc., 1960.

FELHEIM, MARVIN, *Comedy, Plays, Theory and Criticism.* New York: Harcourt Brace Jovanovich, Inc., 1962.

KERR, WALTER, *Tragedy and Comedy.* New York: Simon & Schuster, 1967.

LAUTER, PAUL, *Theories of Comedy.* New York: Doubleday & Co., Inc., 1964.

OLSON, ELDER, *The Theory of Comedy.* Bloomington: Indiana University Press, 1968.

SEYLER, ATHENE, and STEPHEN HAGGARD, *The Craft of Comedy.* New York: Theatre Arts Books, 1946.

STYAN, J. L., *The Dark Comedy: The Development of Modern Comic Tragedy.* Cambridge: Cambridge University Press, 1962.

SIX

Realism
and Its
Derivatives

In the previous chapters we have been considering *types* or *forms* of drama. Now we turn our attention to dramatic *modes*—realism and two of its derivatives, naturalism and expressionism. *Type* or *form* refers to a particular kind of dramatic composition, just as in painting we speak of a still life or a portrait painting, and in music we talk about a sonata or a symphony. By *mode* we mean the temper or spirit that affects the creator's point of view. The mode reflects the cultural climate in which a work of art was created. The classicism of fifth-century B.C. Greece grew out of the ideal of the golden mean and the emphasis on reason, so that classicism is characterized by beauty of form, proportion, balance, symmetry, and control. When the neoclassicists in Renaissance Italy and France sought to create their own society of enlightenment celebrating the age of reason, they attempted to transplant the Greek ideas, with mixed results. In drama strict application of misinterpretations of Aristotle made it exceedingly difficult to write a playable work and resulted in a rigid theatrical style that emphasized form and rhetoric. It was an elevated drama in its use of verse, highborn characters, and themes of love, honor, and loyalty testing the wills of exemplary individuals.

From the end of the eighteenth century until the middle of the nineteenth, the new audience of the middle classes stemming from the scientific and industrial revolution found its heartfelt desires reflected in Romantic drama—with a capital R. The spirit that animated romanticism was the faith in "the natural man"—an individual unfettered by the artificial strictures of organized society and whose conduct and character were guided intuitively by his heart. Its major representatives in Germany were Goethe and Schiller, who created "Storm and Stress drama." In France, Victor Hugo led the revolt with his preface to *Cromwell* (1827), in which he rejected the rules of the past and called for a new free spirit in the theater. Three years later the tumultuous reception of his production of *Hernani* at the Comédie Française signaled the overthrow of neoclassicism. In England romanticism was more closely associated with poetry and the novel but its effect was clearly marked in the melodramas of the nineteenth century. Romanticism as a literary movement originated as a revolt against the strictures of classicism and it emphasized the subjective and imaginative aspects of nature and man.

The romanticists in the theater rejected the suppression of emotion and they discarded the rigid form of the old classics. They insisted on freedom for a wide scope of action celebrating the individual as a child of nature, and they combined beauty with the grotesque, the lowly with the elevated, the humble with the sublime. Their protagonists were picaresque figures—rebels and outcasts, men of action with uncomplicated motivations. The plays sought to express the sense of wonder and mystery of life; the action often led to the picturesque, the remote, and the exotic. In their language playwrights attempted to use elevated verse, or a colorful rhetoric that would imaginatively express their natural exuberance.

While romanticism was significant for clearing the stage of the austere rigidity of the past, its built-in tendency for excess made it susceptible to such abuses as too much straining for effect, superficiality in character, emotion, and situation. As the basic function of theater became escape, romanticism offered too little contact with the real world and everyday life. Nevertheless, the spirit of romanticism was an appealing one; it easily made its way into popular melodrama. Today not only do we find echoes of romanticism in motion pictures and television, musical comedies and opera, but nearly all of us wistfully compare our present regimented, mechanized, crowded world with the dream of the natural man.

As the intellectual climate of the nineteenth century was profoundly changed by science and technology, a new kind of drama was required—this was realism. In general, we may say that modern dramatic literature has centered around the form of *drame* and the mode of realism. Although in the last few years it has been under attack, realism has been surprisingly persistent and durable. Since most of our serious plays of the last century follow this mode, and since the current rebellion is antirealistic, we need to understand the background and rationale of this mode. In evaluating realism it is important to keep in mind the kind of artificial drama it was rebelling against, and the new thought the realist was seeking to express. Those who led the way were serious individuals, genuinely dedicated to presenting the truth. Their dramatic practice, like that of all playwrights, was to seek the most effective means for touching the minds and hearts of their audiences.

To set down a clear-cut definition of realism is a precarious task since realism varies with the attitudes of writers, critics, and literary historians. Furthermore, the dramatic writer has very little interest in creating a work that will neatly fit into a pigeon hole. The problem of definition is further complicated by the fact that the term *realism* has been used to refer to both a literary technique and a literary theory. In spite of the divergent meanings, there is fairly common agreement that realism relies on sense impressions; that it deals with the here and now; that it is "concerned essentially with detail"; that it is a "copying of actual facts"; that it is a "deliberate choice of the commonplace"; that it is a "factual interpretation of life"; that it is, in short, "truth." Since man expresses himself in art forms, which by their very nature are conventionalized and artificial, complete reality is impossible in art. The term "illusion of reality" is in itself an anachronism. What the realistic dramatist and actor strive to achieve is to "suggest actuality," and to give "the impression of truth" by employing symbols that communicate the effect of reality to an audience.

Any method of communication must necessarily rely on a set of symbols that have mutual acceptance and meaning to the artist and the person for whom the work is intended. The function of the artist is to create symbols and organize them in such a fashion as to elicit a desired, appropriate response. In the theater, the playwright uses all aspects of production as symbols—characters, setting, dialogue, light, sound, movement, and properties, which are arranged into a unified projection of the play, which is itself a symbol. The realist uses symbols that have a direct and immediate reference to life.

Symbols are dynamic. They vary as the artist responds to the environment and influences that press in upon him. Thus, every work of art is an expression not only of the individual who created it, but also of the social forces that shaped the artist and his attitudes toward life. A Raphael Madonna, a Bach chorale, a Louis Sullivan skyscraper, a Restoration comedy are more than works of individual men; they are also social documents of the age that produced them. The dynamic nature of symbolic expression is due not only to the artist's personality, but also to the philosophic outlook he shares with his contemporaries. A society which has a philosophic outlook in which reality is considered to have an existence and validity independent of the psychic processes does not demand of its artists the representation of actuality of objects and actions. Conversely, when a society becomes concerned primarily with the physical and material aspects of living based on sense knowledge, then the artist looks to real life for his means of expression. Throughout the history of Western civilization, there has been an ebb and flow of philosophic thought, now emphasizing an idealistic view of life, now stressing materialism. A complete aesthetic theory of realism could not evolve until the intellectual revolution of the nineteenth century, when the advance of science, materialism, and industrialism made such a theory not only possible, but inevitable.

The Realistic Movement

From the change in speculative thought arising from the works of such men as Darwin, Freud, and Marx, three implications are of particular significance to drama and the theater. The first of these was the dynamic notion of change. In place of the older, static concept of a perfect creation a few thousand years ago, the scientist presented the idea that all life is in a constant process of alteration, and, as a creature of nature, man too is subject to change.

A second implication was that man is a "biochemical entity." Said the biologist: There seems to be nothing about human life or behavior that is not susceptible to explanation according to naturalistic laws and principles. The individual is a product of a callous nature, rather than a child of special providence whose life is subject to divine intervention and revelation. We act mechanistically. Physiology is as important as intellect in determining our conduct. The human being is merely the leading member of the simian group, and for the time being, the dominant species of the animal kingdom on this planet.

A third implication of the new thought was that humanity is subject to scientific inquiry. A person can be a case study, capable of being examined and investigated.

These changes in speculative thought were variously interpreted. At one extreme the nineteenth-century French firebrand, Zola, and his fellow naturalists emphasized the sordid and mechanistic aspects of life to the exclusion of all else. Their thinking was shadowed by a somber view of life which threw a blighting chill of determinism on all human conduct. At the opposite extreme, many realists saw in science a buoyantly optimistic assurance of the ultimate perfectibility of humanity. They extended the doctrine of evolution to a view of the entire universe fulfilling the promise of one glorious purpose—the elevation of mankind. Clarence Darrow revealed this interpretation in his article "Realism in Literature and Art."

> Realism worships at the shrine of nature. It does not say that there may not be spheres in which beings higher than man can live or that some time an eye may not rest upon a fairer sunset than was ever born behind the clouds and sea; but it knows that through the countless ages nature has slowly fitted the brain and eye of man to the earth on which we live and the objects which we see, and the perfectly earthly eye must harmonize with the perfect earthly scene. To say that realism is coarse and vulgar is to declare against nature and her work.[1]

In between the optimistic realist and the pessimistic naturalist was a variety of interpretations, but each stressed the importance of the individual and the significance of the environment as a formative influence on behavior. In addition, most realists were conscious of the humanitarian implications of the new way of looking at life. The artist plays a part in the elevation of mankind by insisting on the necessity of a congenial social atmosphere. The realist deals with the ugly and untrue because they are forces inimical to personal fulfillment. This point of view did not cause the realist to become a professed propagandist; his desire to be objective ruled against this. Nevertheless, humanitarian concern colors the selection of material, the delineation and motivation of character, and the nature of the dramatic conflicts.

The realistic movement had its origin in nineteenth-century French fiction. Balzac, Flaubert, and the brothers Goncourt created conspicuous examples of the new attitude at work. The nature of that realism and its guiding principles is summed up by Bernard Weinberg.

> Realism stating its case in "la bataille realiste," states it in approximately these terms: Romanticism and classicism, striving for an ideal beauty and seeking it mainly in the historical subjects, arrives only at affectation and falseness. Realism, on the contrary, aims to attain truth. Now truth is attainable only by the observation (scientific and impersonal) of reality—and hence of contemporary life—and by the unadulterated representation of that reality in the work of art. Therefore, in his observations, the artist must be sincere, unprejudiced, encyclopedic. Whatever is real, whatever exists is a proper subject for art; this means that the beautiful and ugly, the physical and spiritual, are susceptible of artistic treatment; it does not imply that the artist refrains from choosing his subject and his detail, for choice is fundamental in art. The principal object of imitation is always man; description of the material world, construction of plot, are thus subsidiary and contributory to character portrayal. In setting down his observations, the artist must of course arrange and dispose his materials; but he avoids all possible falsification of them by practicing the utmost simplicity of style and form. The product of this method is moral in the highest sense—truth being the highest morality—and is eminently adapted to the needs of a materialistic, "realistic" society.[2]

[1]Clarence Darrow, "Realism in Literature and Art," *Arena*, 9 (1893).
[2]Bernard Weinberg, *French Realism: The Critical Reaction, 1830–1870* (New York: Oxford University Press, 1937).

In French drama, the theory of realism was rooted in the teaching of Diderot, who in the eighteenth century called for "middle-class tragedy." In the early nineteenth century when Pixérécourt popularized romantic melodrama, he required realistic scenery employing practical steps, bridges, and boats for the exciting action of his bourgeois plays. When Eugène Scribe came to the theater, his technical dexterity in manipulating plots and his portrayal of types found in contemporary society gave his plays an air of superficial probability. His skill as a craftsman resulted in the writing of what became known as "well-made plays," whose techniques were so popular in the theater that his structural pattern was widely imitated. In a well-made play the author attempts to deal naturally with current society and constructs a play with careful craftsmanship so that all parts are connected together in a plausible way. Climaxes are carefully built up by cause and effect progression. The well-crafted play was a controlled environment influencing the characters which inhabit it. Scribe was followed by Émile Augier, an enormously successful playwright whose impartiality of treatment, careful depiction of background based on minute observation of objects and incidents, and his competence in characterization took drama a step nearer to realism. Dumas *fils* continued the advance by his concern with the decadence of the social scene in such plays as *Le Demi-Monde* (1855) and *La Question d'argent* (1857). His treatment of men and women who were not heroic, but weak, sensuous, and selfish added new roles to the theater. Together with Augier, Dumas made a critical assault on the corruption of middle and upper class society.

Elsewhere in Europe, the intellectual revolution taking place found expression in the new playwrights—Henrik Ibsen, Leo Tolstoi, Anton Chekhov, August Strindberg, and Gerhart Hauptmann. These men were interested in telling the truth about the common man in everyday circumstances, but because their dramas were so outspoken and their subject matter so bold, they found it difficult to get a hearing until the Independent Theater movement, a group of subscription theaters, was organized for the specific purpose of opening up the theater to the new drama. Under the leadership of André Antoine in Paris, Otto Brahm in Berlin, Constantin Stanislavski in Moscow, and John Grein in London, this movement broke the shackles of tradition and introduced a new exuberant spirit into the drama, linking the stage once more with literature and life. Ibsen's *Ghosts* was an especially important play because of its sensational impact wherever it was produced. In the play, Oswald Alving has inherited syphilis from his dissolute father. Because Oswald knows he is on the verge of losing his mind, he begs his mother to give him morphine as a merciful escape. As the final curtain falls, Mrs. Alving waivers above her babbling son, holding in her hand the poison which will end his suffering. Because of its bold subject matter *Ghosts* was a highly controversial play, stirring up some of the most vituperative critical abuse in the history of the theater. In Berlin (1889) when the censor banned the play in the public theaters, it was played to a subscription audience at the Freie Bühne. English reaction to *Ghosts* (1891) was especially virulent. One

In plotting, Chekhov did not follow the pattern of other realists, but he achieved an authentic sense of life from his shrewd observation of characters such as these in his The Cherry Orchard. *Asolo State Theater, Florida.*

London critic, Clement Scott, compared Ibsen's play to "an open drain, a loathsome sore unbandaged, a dirty act done publicly, a lazar house with all its doors and windows open."

In America in the 1890s, James A. Herne and a number of disciples of the new realism in fiction attempted to introduce the new spirit into the drama through productions of Herne's *Margaret Fleming* in Boston and New York. This play, the first sociological play in the American theater, recalled Ibsen's boldness in its theme of a wayward husband whose affair with a maid results in her death and the birth of an illegitimate child. But the play ends on an upbeat note as Margaret Fleming forgives her husband and accepts the child as her own. Herne's effort appealed to a limited audience; American theatergoers were not hospitable to such advanced subjects.

In addition to the development of realism as literary theory during the latter part of the nineteenth century, there was also considerable change taking place in the techniques of writing and producing farces and melodramas which made up most of the popular stage fare. Characters of humble origin became more and more prominent; local color was exploited; native speech and costuming were more accurately reproduced; and the stage scenery and effects became increasingly substantial and convincing. Although much of the plot material and character motivation was patently artificial, realism made its influence felt, especially in the external aspects of production.

The ultimate result of the revolution in the late nineteenth-century theater was to win the twentieth century over to realism. While realism as a complete aesthetic theory soon lost its impetus, the techniques and attitudes of the realist have nevertheless continued to dominate our modern stage, even in the face of a great deal of experimentation with new forms, and despite a rather general dissatisfaction with its restrictive outlook.

Observation and Objectivity

Having received their inspiration from the scientists, the realists turned to science for their techniques as well, attempting to follow basic concepts drawn from the scientific method. The first of these was dependence on observation. If the artist is to select symbols which will approximate a one-to-one relationship between symbol and referent, it is imperative that the object be known as completely as possible. The realist, therefore, came to rely on meticulous and precise observation, analysis and recording of specific details. Minutiae that previous writers passed by were accumulated a bit at a time to build up character or locale in much the same manner that Seurat used to apply his paint in tiny spots of broken color. And like Courbet and Manet, who took their easels out of their studio to paint commonplace subject matter from direct observation, rather than saints and miracles from their inspiration and imagination, realistic writers looked hard at life at first hand and jotted down in their notebooks the texture of their responses. The realist was devoted to the sanctity of facts and the deduction of truth based on the evidence of collected data. It was one's mission to see, hear, and report everything. Such an emphasis on observation affected not only the realist's choice of subject matter, but also the method of handling it. The plot must be allowed to develop where an honest treatment of the characters takes it; the environment and its atmosphere must be depicted with scrupulous fidelity; emotion must be employed without artificiality or sentimentalism; the writer must be faithful to the facts as observed.

A second technique of the realists was to maintain an attitude of objectivity toward their work, just as the scientist conducts experiments, examines the data, and draws impersonal conclusions. As the realists avoid idealism and romanticism, they are equally opposed to cynicism and pessimism. As impartial observers they attempt to escape personal bias and report on life as it is.

Against this general background of a literary theory stemming from the intellectual revolution of the nineteenth century, and noting especially the impact of science, let us now consider the application of realism to specific dramatic problems.

Plot

The dramatic structure of the realist resembles classical drama in its unity of action, time, and place, and in its concentration on characters caught in moments of crisis. Thus the realist generally uses a late point of attack, employs a few incidents, and ordinarily deals with a small group of characters over a short space of time. The result of this dramaturgy is a gain in intensity and dramatic tension because the action is continuous and concentrated, free from the extraneous diversions of constantly changing locales and complicated plots and subplots. The writer of popular nineteenth-century melodrama dramatized simple people in a complicated plot based on a pattern of physical conflicts. The realist reversed this approach by showing complex characters in a simple plot involving psychological action. The result was realistic *drame*.

Realistic plays are not full of arbitrary climaxes, building up to "big scenes" of violent action. Even in moments of great stress, the emotional expression is often deliberately restrained, underplayed, suggested rather than exploited. The playwright learned that the most telling moments of his plays might be the quiet closing of a door, the distant sound of an axe on a tree. There is an absence of sensational and "stagey" devices, but not an absence of emotional effect.

To secure the semblance of reality, the realists were obligated to make their work seem logical and plausible, with no clanking machinery or whirr of motors. They avoided all manner of contrivances that might destroy illusion. They did not interrupt the action to make explanations, preferring to integrate exposition of antecedent action by gradual revelation throughout the course of the play.

The realist's method of handling plot was responsible for clearing away much of the trickery of popular drama. Plays became much more credible, closer to actual experience and the observed facts of life. Because they based their dramas on ideas, rather than on external action, and because they were concerned with character revelation, the realists achieved an intensity of effect. On the other hand, their method of working narrowed the scope of action, slowed down the pace, and sometimes became downright sedentary. Critics were quick to point out that in their attempts to condense the action and frame it in a solid mold, amid a welter of concrete details, the realists sacrificed the chance to stimulate the imagination, and to give free play to fancy. They had trapped themselves in the stuffy atmosphere of a middle class living room. As realism has developed in the past half century, the validity of this criticism has been acknowledged, and the contemporary playwright increasingly seeks ways to break through the confining walls to find a freer use of the theater. This has meant increasing flexibility so that the action moves around in time and space without the compulsion of strict conformance to reality. Episodes may flash back or overlap, disembodied voices may comment or intercede, and images and sounds are used to expand the play beyond its setting.

Character

The realists' interest in characterization was centered in problems of psychological motivation. They discarded the stock silhouette figures of the popular theater so obviously manipulated by the playwright to suit the needs of the plot—figures which reacted from conscious intent based on contemporary morality. Such flimsy characterization did not jibe with the realists' concept of behavior rooted in the conditioning pressures of environment, the dynamics of childhood and heredity, and the interaction of desires and inhibitions.

Dramatists became concerned with the psychological forces that conditioned behavior, and they brought into the theater characters whose pathology was explained in terms of repression, subconscious desire, and early childhood frustration. A cause and effect pattern was set up, as Taine, the nineteenth century French critic, observed:

> Whether phenomena are physical or moral does not matter; they can always be traced back to causes. There are causes for ambition, for courage, or for truth-

One of the most beguiling comic pairs in realistic drama is found in O'Casey's Juno and the Paycock. *Jack Lemmon, on the left, plays Joxer; his companion, played by Walter Matthau, is "Captain" Jack Boyle. Mark Taper Forum, Los Angeles.*

fulness as there are for muscular contraction and for bodily temperature. Vice and virtue are products just as are vitriol and sugar. . . . Let us then seek out the simpler data of moral qualities as scientists those of physical properties.

The realists' attempt to achieve objectivity and their reliance on observation led them to bring into the theater an entirely new gallery of characters who were delineated in a new way. In the past, playwrights had used people of the lower classes mostly for minor or comic roles. Now the humble, the downtrodden, and the ordinary people took center stage. They were revealed as complex individuals with conflicting psychological drives, products of heredity and environment. The playwright dramatized these people at critical moments of their lives, not those of violent physical action so much as inner crises, thus penetrating the surface and giving insight into their desires, aspirations, and frustrations. The realist seemed especially concerned with presenting women on the stage and created such memorable feminine characters as Strindberg's Laura and Julie, Chekhov's Madame Ranevsky and Nina, Shaw's Candida and Eliza, and Ibsen's Nora, Hedda, Rebecca West, and Mrs. Alving.

In placing contemporary man in the spotlight on the stage, the dramatists

The realist's concern with environment and the interest in ordinary people was demonstrated in The Effect of Gamma Rays on Man-in-the-Moon Marigolds, *which told the story of Beatrice and her two daughters. Asolo Theater, Florida.*

O'Neill's The Iceman Cometh *at the Circle-in-the-Square Theater in New York. This design by Ming Cho Lee with a few simple elements creates the environment and atmosphere of the play.*

lost the elevation and magnitude of classic tragedy with its heroic figures. The naturalists, as we shall see later in the chapter, carried the mechanistic and bestial aspects of man to an extreme in their over-emphasis of the sordid and the bizarre. The realists, however, found it possible to show both sides of men and dealt with many characters who had redeeming qualities—characters who were close to the norm in behavior and outlook.

Significant contributions to drama were made by the realists in the integrity of their characterization, their concern with sound psychological motivation, their cumulative technique of character revelation, and their treatment of protagonists drawn from the common walks of life. While many playwrights today remain deeply concerned with the problems stressed by early realists, they now have greater flexibility in treating characters. Because of a freer approach to playwriting and staging, characters can be revealed more deeply by more exposure. Flashbacks, monologues, and direct communication with the audience provide for more extensive commentary than the simulated conversation of many parlor-talk plays. Characters now may begin a speech as a young man and shift to old age within a few lines simply by modifying the voice. People mix with animals that may be shown as complex creatures with human traits—without destroying theatrical credulity. While realism gave up much of the grandeur associated with classic drama and the dynamic, imaginative protagonists of romanticism, the playwrights of realism peopled the stage with a remarkable gathering of fascinating creatures who we come to know as authentic human beings.

Thought

The realists dealt boldly with new themes, many of them growing out of their awakened interest in the social sciences—economic conflicts, sex, domestic difficulties, and social strife. Emulating the ways of science, playwrights attempted to record life objectively, so they pulled no punches, honored no taboos, found no material too commonplace or sordid for their probing. They became absorbed in the facts of human existence here and now—commonplace facts about contemporary commonplace people. They tried to discard everything that smacked of the theatrical, the artificial, the contrived, the sentimental. Like the late nineteenth-century painters who drew directly from life, the dramatists recorded what they saw, rather than what they imagined or wished to see.

The result was to open the doors of the theater to the dramatization of day-to-day struggles. In insisting on the right to select dramatic materials from all walks of life, the realists brought about a franker, freer stage. Dramatic literature had found a connection with the intellectual life of the time. Melodrama became *drame*.

An upsurge in black theatrical activity has resulted in a number of compelling plays. One of the most durable is Lorraine Hansberry's A Raisin in the Sun (1959), a compassionate, realistic treatment of a hardworking Chicago black family caught in a domestic quarrel. (University of Arizona. Directed by Peter Marroney).

A recent hit in London and New York, Whose Life Is It Anyway? by Brian Clark, deals with a paralytic's right to determine whether or not he shall live. The somber material was relieved by a good deal of comedy and the superb acting of Tom Conti in the leading role, and Jean Marsh as the Nurse. (Directed by Michael Lindsay-Hogg.)

Diction

The realists' interest in accurate observation and reporting prompted them to suggest the speech of everyday life. Dialogue frequently was ungrammatical, fragmentary, and disturbingly frank. Realists abandoned the theatrical devices of asides, soliloquies, unmotivated "purple passages," and the inflated bombast of "paper speeches." Even in scenes of strong emotional climax, the dramatist avoided rhetorical display, having learned the eloquence of a broken phrase, a small gesture, and silence. Stage dialogue became more utilitarian, serving to advance or delineate character, rather than to call attention to itself.

As Bernard Shaw pointed out, another benefit that resulted from realism was the opportunity to exploit discussion in drama. Dramatists became

Durrenmatt writes dark comedies in a realistic vein with a grotesque edge. He is concerned with moral questions and the corruption of power. One of his outstanding plays is The Physicists. *(College of the Desert. Directed by Frederick Thon.)*

concerned with ideas and they took pains to stimulate the audience's thinking about their ideas by expressing them on stage. Ibsen's and Shaw's characters not only act, they think—and they discuss their thoughts. Their dialogue becomes action—an investigation, an adventure, a verbal tug-of-war.

Critics of realism lamented that the speech of the new drama drove poetry out of the theater. It is true that the playwright turned his ear in another direction, and sacrificed the use of poetic speech—particularly the richness of imagery—but it is also true that much of the embellished dialogue of nineteenth-century romantic writers of melodrama was poor stuff—sentimental and pretentious. Moreover, in the hands of skillful playwrights, realistic speech had a clarity and intensity that went directly to the heart of the matter. Hamlin Garland found much to admire in Ibsen's dialogue:

> How true and unconventional his style. We hardly realize how false and stilted current stage conversation is, till we hear the real word spoken there. His words come to us at times like the thrusts of the naked fist. They shake the hearer with their weight of real passion. In one sense it is astoundingly direct, and then again it is subtly indirect—as in life.[3]

[3]Hamlin Garland, "Ibsen as a Dramatist," *Arena*, 2 (June 1890).

The realist's point of view toward diction was clearly expressed in a letter Ibsen wrote to Edmund Gosse, explaining why he did not use verse in writing *Emperor and Galilean*:

> You are of the opinion that the drama ought to have been written in verse, and that it would have gained by this. Here I must differ with you. The play is, as you will have observed, conceived in the most realistic style: the illusion I wished to produce is that of reality. I wished to produce the impression on the reader that what he was reading was something that really happened. If I had employed verse, I should have counteracted my own intention and prevented the accomplishment of the task I had set myself. The many ordinary insignificant characters whom I have intentionally introduced into the play would have become indistinct and indistinguishable from one another, if I had allowed all of them to speak in one and the same rhythmical measure. We are no longer living in the days of Shakespeare. . . . Speaking generally, the style must conform to the degree of ideality which pervades the representation. My new drama is no tragedy in the ancient acceptation; what I desired to depict was human beings, and therefore I would not let them talk "the language of the gods."[4]

Spectacle

Although realistic scenery had been employed in the theater in the past, its appeal was based on novelty and picturesqueness. The realist had quite a different purpose. It became important to show the environment in order to understand the character. Thus, realistic scenery is not a mere accompaniment of the action; it is a causal force of the action. It shapes and molds the characters and is an essential part of the symbolic configuration. In such plays as *Dead End, Street Scene,* and *Beyond the Horizon,* the setting is a major source of character motivation, with its sociological implication that to improve the man, it is necessary to improve his circumstances.

The realists' observation of actuality and concern with the commonplace prompted them to locate the action in a setting crammed with the domestic details of everyday life. The stage and action of their plays were filled with properties, but in the hands of the genuine realist these were not mere clutter for verisimilitude; they were selected because of their organic and symbolic relationship to the characters, such as Hedda's pistols, Nora's macaroons, and Oswald's pipe. The use of such props illustrated the notion of the significant trifle. Incidentally, the props were an enormous help to the actors in achieving naturalness in performance.

Just as the realists rejected the cardboard cut-out stock figures of the past, likewise they discarded the "painty" two-dimensional wing and groove, and backdrop setting. The box set (with three continuous walls, often capped with a ceiling) which had been introduced earlier in the nineteenth century now became a standard requirement for realistic drama. Practical doors and

[4]Henrik Ibsen, *The Correpondence of Henrik Ibsen,* trans. and ed. Mary Morrison (New York: Haskell House Publishers, Ltd., 1970).

Realistic staging in an arena theater of Ted Shine's Morning, Noon and Night, *directed by Owen Dodson, designed by Richard Baschky, at the University of California, Santa Barbara.*

windows, appropriate furniture, and genuine props were added to further the illusion of actuality. The actor was now surrounded by scenery, and played *within* a locale rather than in front of it. As a logical accompaniment of the new scenery came the convention of the "fourth wall"—a tacit agreement with the audience that the opening framed by the proscenium arch was the fourth wall of the set, thus giving the illusion of a solid room instead of a platform. The fourth wall defined the downstage limit of the acting area and confined the actor to the setting; he pretended not to see or communicate with the audience. Playwrights are no longer hemmed in by such conventions since, as we shall see in Chapter 10, the stage and scenery are now very flexible and free.

While realism was until recently the predominant mode of drama, it had, and still has, the seeds of revolt within itself. Later we will deal at length with modern experiments, but now we will consider two offshoots of realism in the past—naturalism and expressionism.

An interesting example of a contemporary realistic setting is this domestic exterior for Sunset/Sunrise *by Adele Edling Shank. (Directed by Theodore Shank. University of California, Davis).*

Naturalism

The term *naturalism* often used interchangeably with realism, is historically an independent movement that began in France in the 1870s under the messianic leadership of Émile Zola. Like the realist, the naturalist responded to the influence of science—especially to the notion of environmental conditioning of contemporary man. It was Zola who wrote the first naturalistic play and bombarded the senses of his contemporaries as he clamored for a dramatic method that would reflect the method of science:

> I am waiting for them to rid us of fictitious characters, of conventional symbols of vice and virtue which possess no value as human data. I am waiting for the surroundings to determine the characters, and for the characters to act according to the logic of the facts. . . . I am waiting until there is no more jugglery of any kind, no more strokes of the magical wand, changing in one minute persons and things. I am waiting, finally, until this evolution takes place on the stage; until they return the source of science to the study of nature, to the anatomy of man, to the painting of life in an exact reproduction, more original and powerful than anyone has so far dared to place upon the boards.[5]

[5]Émile Zola, *The Experimental Novel* (New York: Cassell, 1893).

Zola's play *Thérèse Raquin* (1873) dramatizes the story of Thérèse and her lover, who drown her unwanted husband, but are unable to live down their crime under the accusing eyes of the dumb and paralyzed mother of the victim. Zola's play was not a popular success, but his example led to similar attempts by others. Henri Becque, in *The Vultures* (1882), pictured the destruction of a family and its fortune as a result of the sudden demise of the father and the preying activities of the dead man's business associates. Gerhart Hauptmann, in *Before Sunrise* (1889), gave Berlin's independent stage, the Freie Bühne, a graphic view of the degradation of a Silesian coal-mining family suddenly grown rich, in a story of misery and death. His *Weavers* (1892) uses a rioting mob as the protagonist in one of the earliest and best plays of social conflict. Tolstoi, in *The Power of Darkness* (1886), tells a grim story of illicit love, drunkenness, and murder, although he tempers the gloom with spiritual overtones. Strindberg's *Miss Julie* (1888) is a story of lust and suicide. Shaw, who wrote two plays in the naturalistic style, *Widower's Houses* (1892) and *Mrs. Warren's Profession* (1898), indicated his motivation for writing as he did: "I felt the need for mentioning the forbidden subjects, not only because of their own importance, but for the sake of destroying taboo by giving it the most violent shocks."

The naturalists differed from the realists by concentrating on the squalid side of life, free from contrived situations, climaxes, and curtains. They introduced a new collection of characters to the stage—the dregs of society, the wayward and twisted victims of the lower depths. Their characters were bedeviled by doubts and frustrations, torn by inner conflicts, ridden by passions. As Strindberg said, "They are conglomerates made up of past and present stages of civilization, scraps of humanity, torn-off pieces of Sunday clothing turned into rags—all patched together as is the human soul itself."[6] The naturalist attempted to translate into concrete images what he had gained from the changing thought. The hard shell that protected the traditional views of love, authority, duty, honor, and morality was shattered when the playwright probed beneath the surfaces to investigate the innermost desires and passion of individuals in their relations with their mates, their families, and their society.

Although the rigid realism and naturalism of the first part of the twentieth century has given way to much more freedom and experimentation, many playwrights today aim at presenting the illusion of authentic daily life, especially in characterization, dialogue, and thought. The realists' and naturalists' penchant for forbidden or controversial material characterizes the theater of shock and cruelty that has emerged since World War II.

The naturalist's dialogue had a new texture and frankness as it reflected the speech of the lowborn and humble. Themes that had hitherto been considered too controversial or salacious for the theater-going public became the accepted norm. Although the new boldness aroused shocked protest in many places, the naturalists performed an important service in ridding the

[6]August Strindberg, "Preface to Miss Julie," in *Plays of Strindberg*, vol. 1, trans. Edith and Warner Oland (New York: Bruce Humphries, 1912).

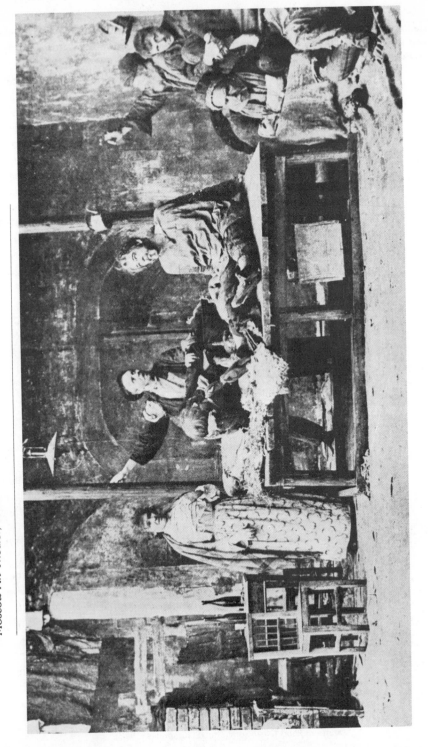

Naturalistic setting for Gorki's The Lower Depths, first produced at the Moscow Art Theater, 1902.

stage of bombast and sentimentality. They also made painstaking efforts to show the locale of their action as accurately as possible in order to emphasize how physical conditions may deform character. Sometimes the result was an excess of clutter and an obsession with the solidity and authenticity of material objects, which at its extreme led André Antoine of the Théâtre Libre to hang sides of beef on the stage.

As a literary style, naturalism gave way to the more moderate realism, which found ways of relieving the steady diet of misery, crime, and disintegration; but the naturalist did succeed in bringing to the stage new characters and themes with honesty and forthrightness. Although naturalism as a movement lost its impetus, echoes of its quality are seen in the present theater in such plays as Kenneth H. Brown's *The Brig*, an attack on the inhumane conditions in a Marine Corps prison; in LeRoi Jones's plays of racial discrimination, *The Dutchman* and *The Toilet*; in David Rabe's plays of the Vietnam war, *The Basic Training of Pavlo Hummel* and *Sticks and Bones*; David Mamet's *American Buffalo*, which shows a handful of sleazy characters in a junk shop trying to plan a crime; and in David Rudkin's *Ashes*, a parable of the turmoil in Northern Ireland about the unsuccessful attempt of a childless couple to preserve their heritage.

Expressionism

Another outgrowth of realism was expressionism. Actually the expressionist was a superrealist insisting that actuality is within. Beneath the social façade, there is a vast jungle where dwell man's secrets and often unconscious desires, aspirations, conflicts, frustrations, and hallucinations. It is this strange and confusing subjective reality that the expressionist wished to explore.

The Swedish playwright August Strindberg was the first to state the expressionist's approach to drama: "Anything may happen; everything is possible and probable. Time and space do not exist. On an insignificant background of reality, imagination designs and embroiders novel patterns; a medley of memories, experiences, free fantasies, absurdities, and improvisations."[7] A drama, he said, may have the "disconnected but seemingly logical form of a dream." He demonstrated his theory in two remarkable plays, *The Dream Play* (1902) and *The Ghost Sonata* (1907). For a time, Strindberg was an isolated innovator, but from 1912 to 1925 expressionism became an important theatrical style, especially in Germany for those who knew the traumatic experiences of World War I and its aftermath.

The expressionist rejected the ordered structure of the realist since he wished to center his attention on specific instances without being obliged to provide a chain of causes and effects. He presented the essential action—the

[7]Strindberg, "Preface to Miss Julie."

high points of an experience—without being bogged down by small talk or the machinery of plotting. The critical moments of a man's career were shown in a jagged series of explosive scenes. In Rice's *The Adding Machine* (1923), Mr. Zero's crime and punishment were shown in seven fragmentary scenes; O'Neill's *The Hairy Ape* (1922) dramatized the important steps in Yank's quest for status; Kaiser's *From Morn to Midnight* (1916) was a disconnected series of events that showed a bank clerk's theft, spending orgy, and death; in Toller's *Transfiguration* (1918) a kaleidoscope of dream pictures illustrated the horrors of war. Arthur Miller in *Death of a Salesman* effectively used expressionistic scenes combined with realistic ones to define Willy Loman's mental state. The expressionist flung open the windows of the mind and allowed the spectator to look in on the private, disordered associative processes of his character. He rejected the carefully shaped, logically organized structure of the realist and used a fragmentary system of actions because it created the effect he desired—a view of the chaotic inner reality.

Characters in expressionistic plays are often depersonalized. They are not individuals but types who are given such names as the Gentleman in Black, the Billionaire, the Young Woman in Taffeta, Mr. Zero, the Blues and the Yellows. They are not psychologically complex except perhaps for the protagonist through whose eyes all of the action may be seen. To reveal the inner state of the character, playwrights revived the technique of the soliloquy so the character could externalize his private thoughts. In witnessing the distortion that characterized the protagonist's subjective point of view, the spectator was often confused by bewildering symbols and actions, especially when the distortion was that of an abnormal psychic condition. Character itself was often handled symbolically and with great freedom as Strindberg indicates in *The Dream Play*: "The characters split, double, multiply, evaporate, solidify, diffuse, clarify. But one consciousness reigns above them all— that of the dreamer; it knows no secrets, no incongruities, no scruples, no law." Sometimes, the protagonist is the voice of the author, as in Ernst Toller's *Transfiguration* in which the hero, Friedrich, is the playwright protesting against militarism and nationalism. Friedrich is something of an individual with a specific background, but he is also an abstract symbol of man appearing in many guises as a soldier, professor, sculptor, judge, priest, and laborer.

In general, expressionists have had an axe to grind. Their plays have been linked to social causes, as for example in Germany where the frustrations and yearnings of a people tormented by guilt and despair found in expressionism not merely a theatrical style, but also a desperate and agonized plea for some kind of salvation. In Kaiser's *Coral* (1917) the Billionaire's son revolts against the injustice of capitalism: "We are rich, and these others who stifle in torment and misery are men like us." Again in *From Morn to Midnight*, Kaiser directly attacks materialism: "Not with all the money from all the banks of the world can one buy anything of value. . . . Money is the crowning deceit of all."

American expressionists worked over familiar social themes in a much milder vein. O'Neill's *The Hairy Ape* is a criticism of human disorientation in a materialistic society. His *The Emperor Jones* dramatizes man's inability to escape from his primitive past. Rice's *The Adding Machine* is a merciless satire on the plight of the little man trapped in a mechanistic world; and Kaufman and Connelly's *Beggar on Horseback* (1924) lampoons philistinism in America. The expressionists were not so notable for their advanced thinking as for their theatrical ability to give new shape and expression to familiar ideas.

One of these ways was a theatrical treatment of language to create effects and atmosphere. An interesting device was the use of short rhythmic bursts of staccato speech with a sharply marked tempo. The effect was to remove the speaker one step from reality, reinforcing the offbeat atmosphere and the dehumanized characterization. A typical example occurs in Kaiser's *Gas* (1918), part one:

> *(The door to left is flung open. A* Workman—*naked*—*stained by the explosion totters in.)*

Workman: Report from Shed Eight—Central—white cat burst—red eyes torn open—yellow mouth gaping—humps up crackling back—grows round—snaps

Setting by Lee Simonson for Elmer Rice's The Adding Machine, *produced at the Theatre Guild, New York, 1923.*

away girders—lifts up roof—bursts—sparks!—sparks! (*Sitting down in the middle of the floor and striking about him.*) Chase away the cat—Shoo! Shoo!—smash her jaws—Shoo! Shoo! bury her eyes—they flame—hammer down her back—hammer it down—thousands of fists! It's swelling, swelling—growing fat—fatter—Gas out of every crack—the tube![8]

Rice, in *The Adding Machine*, uses telegraphic speech to lampoon the inanities of social conversation. Toller, in *Masses and Man*, likewise uses fragmentary dialogue to show the characters of the bankers in the stock exchange. Kaufman and Connelly in *Beggar on Horseback* satirize the mechanized business world in this passage:

(*Four business men, all with hats and newspapers, and all looking just alike, enter one at a time and step into an imaginary elevator.*)

Cady: Good morning! Made it in twenty-eight minutes this morning!
First Business Man: Good morning! I got the eight-six this morning!
Second Business Man: Good morning! I missed the seven forty-three.
Third Business Man: Good morning! I always make the nine-two.
Fourth Business Man: Good morning! I thought you were on the eight-sixteen.[9]

The expressionists' free use of language in the theater anticipated most of the "innovations" of the absurdists and the present workers in the new theater.

An expressionistic play expanded theatricalism, by which we mean an approach to drama that rejects the pretense of copying actuality, and, instead, exploits the medium for itself. The purpose of dramatic production was to create theater—which was precisely what the expressionists did, often in their speech as we have just seen, in their episodic plots, and particularly in their use of spectacle. The realist stressed the appearance of actuality in setting to depict for the spectators real life; the expressionist used fragmentary, distorted images, skeletal settings, and odd lighting effects to reveal a disordered world. In so doing, the expressionist acknowledged the limitations of the stage and created a directly theatrical world. The phantasmagoria of weird landscapes, of dreams where images and symbols are projected in baffling and exaggerated shapes, colors, and patterns, made expressionism a designer's holiday. For example, in Oskar Kokoschka's fantastic play, *Hiob*, a parrot suddenly explodes and rises in the shape of a rosy cloud to heaven; in Kaiser's *From Morn to Midnight*, a tree struck by lightning becomes a human skeleton; and in Strindberg's *A Dream Play*, eerie landscapes appear, merge, and alter in the disconnected fragments of a nightmare.

The following excerpt from O'Neill's *The Hairy Ape* (1922) illustrates the distorted atmosphere of expressionism. Yank, an ignorant stoker emerging from the fireman's forecastle of a ship, finds himself among the social set on

---

[8]Georg Kaiser, *Gas*, I (Cologne: Verlag Kiepenheuer & Witsch, 1918).
[9]George Kaufman and Marc Connelly, *Beggar on Horseback* (New York: Liveright Publishing Corporation, 1924).

KAISER: VON MORGENS BIS MITTERNACHT — CESAR KLEIN

Stage design by Cesar Klein for Georg Kaiser's From Morn to
Midnight, *Berlin, 1923.*

Fifth Avenue, New York, on Easter Sunday, an environment where he is
completely alien:

> *(The crowd from church enter from the right, sauntering slowly and affectedly,
> their heads held stiffly up, looking neither to the right nor left, talking in toneless,
> simpering voices. The women are rouged, calcimined, dyed, overdressed to the
> nth degree. The men are in Prince Alberts, high hats, spats, canes, etc. A proces-
> sion of gaudy marionettes, yet with something of the relentless horror of Franken-
> steins in their detached, mechanical unawareness.)*

Voices: Dear Doctor Caiaphas! He is so sincere!
What was the sermon? I dozed off.
About the radicals, my dear—and the false doctrines that are being preached.
We must organize a hundred per cent American bazaar.
And let everyone contribute one one-hundredth per cent of their income tax.
What an original idea!
We can devote the proceeds to rehabilitating the veil of the temple.
But that has been done so many times.

> *(Yank after vainly trying to get the attention of the Easter Paraders)*

> *(He turns in a rage on the men, bumping viciously into them but not jarring them
> the least bit. Rather it is he who recoils after each collision. He keeps growling.)*
> Git off de oith! G'wan, yuh bum! Look where yuh're goin', can't yuh? Git outa

155

here! Fight, why don't yuh? Put up yer mitts! Don't be a dog! Fight or I'll knock yuh dead!

(*But without seeming to see him, they all answer with mechanical affected politeness:* I beg your pardon. *Then at a cry from one of the women, they all scurry to the furrier's window.*)

The Woman: (*ecstatically with a gasp of delight*) Monkey fur! (*The whole crowd of men and women chorus after her in the same tone of affected delight*) Monkey fur!

Yank: (*with a jerk of his head back on his shoulders, as if he had received a punch full in the face—raging*). I see yuh, all in white! I see yuh, yuh white-faced tart, yuh! Hairy ape, huh? I'll hairy ape yuh!

(*He bends down and grips at the street curbing as if to pluck it out and hurl it. Foiled in this, snarling with passion, he leaps to the lamp-post on the corner and tries to pull it up for a club. Just at that moment a bus is heard rumbling up. A fat, high-hatted, spatted gentleman runs out from the side street. He calls out plaintively:* Bus! Bus! Stop there! *and runs full tilt into the bending, straining YANK, who is bowled off his balance.*)

Yank: (*seeing a fight—with a roar of joy as he springs to his feet*). At last! Bus, huh? I'll bust yuh!

(*He lets drive a terrific swing, his fist landing full on the fat gentleman's face. But the gentleman stands unmoved as if nothing had happened.*)

Gentleman: I beg your pardon. (*Then irritably*) You have made me lose my bus.

(*He claps his hands and begins to scream:* Officer! Officer! *Many police whistles shrill out on the instant and a whole platoon of policemen rush in on YANK from all sides. He tries to fight, but is clubbed to the pavement and fallen upon. The crowd at the window have not moved or noticed this disturbance. The clanging gong of the patrol wagon approaches with a clamoring din.*)[10]

The expressionists' bold theatricalism demonstrated new and effective uses of the medium, it cleared the stage of the rigid three walls, and replaced the clutter with a few imaginative fragments, picked out by light on a relatively bare stage, which gave the actor the appropriate psychological setting for his performance. The creative influence of the expressionists was apparent in ballet, musical comedies, motion pictures, and in the simple settings of realistic plays. Every experimental venture in the twentieth century is in debt to the expressionists for their innovative theatricalism.

Naturalism and expressionism are passé and the revolt against realism is now going on. Actually, a revolt has gone on within the mode itself so that present-day realism bears little resemblance to Ibsen's. Our increased technical skills and facilities; the use of light, film, and sound; the arena and thrust stages give the playwright a previously unknown freedom. Moreover, today's audience, in its willingness to participate imaginatively in all kinds of new theatrical practices, has encouraged more creative and flexible playwriting and production.

The case against realism is couched in such terms as "narrow,"

---

[10]Eugene O'Neill, *The Hairy Ape* (New York: Random House, Inc., 1922).

"commonplace," "superficial," "contrived," "passive," and "illusionary." It is criticized as being a device for avoiding life rather than facing it—a process of hypnosis and delusion, deficient in spirit. In its selection of character and incident it is said to be too artificial. In its mechanically organized plots with their neat endings, it is charged with being too narrowly confined to a few unimportant people partitioned off from the real world, too much involved with psychological case studies rather than with the more significant issues of society. It is said to make a fetish of external appearance and factual data, and to be theatrically pedestrian and trivial in its restrictions of setting, vocabulary, plot situations, and style of performance.

Supporters of realism and its derivatives point out that historically it accomplished its initial objective of ridding the theater of much that was meretricious and false. Realistic playwrights returned the theater to a serious purpose and dealt with its fundamental theme—the dignity and integrity of the individual, and the vital interests of the common man. In their emphasis on the conditioning power of heredity and environment, the realists made the public aware for the first time of an important concept of human behavior. They created a respect for the objective observation of facts but they went beyond them to a concern with man's spiritual destiny in a changing and perplexing world. For example, some observers have criticized Ibsen's *Ghosts* because the ending is "bleak," without hope or elevation. This is precisely the point that Ibsen was making, that in the new world which was evolving, man was cut off from his spiritual heritage and that he was indeed alone.

The realists replaced inflated and artificial rhetoric with new means of communication in speech, action, and setting that encouraged more direct interaction. They were concerned with the problems that engage our foremost experimentalists today—self-realization and freedom from bourgeois conventionality. In their efforts to imitate men's action, the realists turned the theater in a new direction with their emphasis on the careful observation of human behavior. They sought to give pleasure through learning by means of their fresh perceptions of contemporary man and his world.

Bibliography

ANTOINE, ANDRE, *Memories of the Theater-Libre*. Coral Gables: University of Miami Press, 1964.

BENTLEY, ERIC, *The Playwright as Thinker*. New York: Meridian Books, 1957.

BOGARD, TRAVIS, and WILLIAM I. OLIVER, *Modern Drama: Essays in Criticism*. New York: Oxford University Press, 1965.

BROCKETT, OSCAR G., and ROBERT R. FINDLAY, *Century of Innovation*. Englewood Cliffs, N.J.: Prentice-Hall, Inc., 1973.

BRUSTEIN, ROBERT, *The Cultural Watch: Essays on Theater and Society*. New York: Alfred A. Knopf, Inc., 1975.

———., *The Theater in Revolt*. Boston: Little Brown & Company, 1962.

CLARK, BARRETT H., and GEORGE FREEDLEY, *A History of Modern Drama*. New York: Appleton-Century-Crofts, 1947.

MILLER, ANNA IRENE, *The Independent Theater in Europe, 1887 to the Present*. New York: Ray Long and Richard R. Smith, 1931.

SOKEL, WALTER, *The Writer in Extremis: Expressionism in Twentieth-Century German Literature*. Stanford, Calif.: Stanford University Press, 1959.

WAXMAN, S. M., *Antoine and the Théâtre Libre*, Cambridge, Mass.: Harvard University Press, 1926.

WILLIAMS, RAYMOND, *Drama from Ibsen to Brecht*. New York: Oxford University Press, 1969.

SEVEN
Theatricalism and the New Theater

When asked, "Why do we go to the theater?" Julian Beck, one of the founders of the highly controversial Living Theater, replied,

> To crack your head open and let in oxygen, to revivify the brain, inform the senses, awaken the body, consciousness physical and mental, to what's happening to you. To go beyond watching into action. To find its keys to salvation (a ceremony in which the actor serves as a guide). To find out how to enter the Theater of Life—to enter the Theater of Daily Bread.[1]

In these words Julian Beck suggests the point of view of the avant-garde theater of the late twentieth century. It is a rebellious spirit that expresses discontent not only with the theater, but with an entire culture. The world must change, and the theater with it. The linking of these two objectives is important, for the dissatisfaction is with the total human condition.

This contemporary age of anxiety had its roots in the scientific and technological revolutions of the nineteenth century. We have already seen how that disruption touched off a rebellion in the theater under the label of realism and its derivatives, as people tried to orient themselves to a materialistic and mechanical world. But this quest for meaning and identity was subverted by the holocaust of the First World War. The old faith in political institutions and the beneficence of scientific progress was shaken by the spectacle of toppling regimes, the barbarism of mechanized warfare, and the dehumanization of the individual. Those closest to the flames were infected by a deep sense of frustration and cynicism, which broke out in the savage distortions of the expressionists and in the dadaist's brash assault on everything. The Great Depression, the Second World War, the uneasy peace under a dangling bomb, the Vietnam disaster, the exposure of sordid political corruption, and the ruthless struggle for power turned pessimism and doubt into a general malaise instead of a localized infection confined to the defeated or the have-nots. The result has been a universal sense of concern, a gnawing doubt about the ability of the race to survive, and a search for something solid to hold on to.

Beginning with realism, as we have seen, some dramatists have raised questions about man's place in an increasingly perplexing and disordered universe, but the arts have not been at the center of our culture. And theater, a social institution usually tied by its purse strings to the status quo, has often lagged behind the others in revolutionary fervor. Dissidents have had a difficult time in attracting sympathetic audiences with the ability to pay. To many the popular function of the commercial theater is to provide relaxation, not friction nor serious investigation of the problems of society. Some questions one did not ask in public. The audience might lend an ear to the voice of protest if it were as witty as Bernard Shaw's, or tolerate political didacticism if it were as theatrical as Brecht's, but the main course of the drama was not obstructed by militant dispute. As the outside world became more precarious, however, the protest grew louder, and the walls could no longer keep out the clamor. Indeed, because those within began to bring their

[1]Toby Cole and Helen Krich Chinoy, eds., *Actors on Acting* (New York: Crown Publishers, Inc., 1970).

doubts with them, the theater could not remain aloof. The rebels found their way into song, film, and the visual arts; they turned coffeehouses into theaters, found audiences on the sidewalks and in the streets, and staged their own brand of events with such impressive numbers and raucous insistence that their message came through: The world must change and the theater with it.

The rebels oppose both form and content in drama. They would relegate the traditional, carefully structured system of action to the scrap heap, for to them system and order are suspect. Human experience, they say, is not tidily organized into a beginning, middle, and end. Life comes at us in spurts— without clear causes or predictable effects. Man is not a rational, logical creature. The protesters find support for their view of man in such statements as Freud's description of the id: "a chaos, a cauldron of seething excitement with no organization and no unified will, only an impulse to obtain satisfaction for the instinctual needs, in accordance with the pleasure principle." The form of art, the rebels insist, reflects the form of our lives—bewildering, confusing, illogical, incomprehensible.

After his early experience with El Teatro Campesino, Luis Valdez went on to write a mature, full-length play in epic style, dramatizing the plight of the Chicanos. Zoot Suit *premiered at the Mark Taper Forum before it opened on Broadway.*

As for the content of the drama, it must deal forthrightly with the larger issues of the human condition. It is not enough to dwell on the petty squabbles of little lives or probe into the personality problems of insignificant individuals. The visionaries asked for a theater that would rise up against all powers and institutions that belittle the individual, a theater that expands our levels of awareness—that challenges, stimulates, offends, and shocks.

Just as the cultural turbulence following World War II was mirrored by an assault on the conventional forms of the theater, the upheaval of the First World War was reflected in the arts. The poet Tristan Tzara led a group of European artists, writers, and thinkers in a nihilistic onslaught against nearly everything including the standards of conventional aesthetics. During a five-year period, Tzara and the dadaists expressed their disgust with social and artistic traditions as they "spat in the eye of the world." Their attack against the facade of the bourgeois ethic was motivated by a desire to clear the way for a better society. They rejected "art-art" in favor of anti-art. Instead of pure painting, they "engineered" new works. The dadaists exploited the "gratuitous act," the spontaneous, chance gesture which, by its rejection of preplanning, could convey the irrational and subconscious. Improvisation was at the center of their activities. Individual words on slips of paper were drawn out of a hat in a random fashion to become poems. Their often chaotic and accidental pranks and displays anticipated the "happenings" of the 1960s and the present "performances." (Tom Stoppard's *Travesties* (1975) deals with Tzara and some of the dadaists' activities in Zurich. pp. 127–28.)

Kurt Schwitters (1887–1948), one of the most prominent of the dadaists, developed his "Merz pictures"—collages made up of all kinds of found objects fastened together—as an attack on traditional bourgeois art. He explained his purpose in these words:

> Art is a primordial concept, exalted as the godhead, inexplicable as life, indefinable and without purpose. . . . The medium is unimportant. I take any material whatsoever if the picture demands it. When I adjust materials of different kinds to one another, I have taken a step in advance of mere oil painting, for in addition to playing off color against color, line against line, form against form, etc., I play off material against material.[2]

Another group of rebels were the surrealists who, like the dadaists, took the view that "man must escape from the control of reason," and that the artist should "surrender to the dark forces of the unconscious." They were interested in exploring the world of dreams and the imagination. They improvised games of "automatic writing and drawing"—creations entirely free from rational control, made up of strange and distorted images. André Breton, the chief spokesman, said that the surrealist "took pleasure in reuniting the sewing machine and the umbrella on the dissecting table." Their purpose was to bring about a kind of super or absolute reality—"surréalité."

The works of art growing out of dadaism and surrealism are characterized

---

[2]Kurt Schwitters, quoted in Robert Motherwell, *The Dada Painters and Poets* (New York: Wittenborn, Schultz, 1951).

Der Weihnachtsmann

K Schwitters 22

Kurt Schwitters' Merz: Santa Claus, 1922. A collage of papers and cloth.

by incongruous combinations of objects and figures, simultaneous action, fragmentation, and the distorted and seemingly irrational atmosphere of a dream. These characteristics of visual art objects are similar to those of much of the avant-garde drama, for they are rooted in a rejection of the strictures of conventional theater and an insistence on the need to be liberated and spontaneous.

Following the Russian Revolution (1917) the Soviet theater showed its dissatisfaction with the old regime by its rejection of the Stanislavski realism and illusionistic production. To show their hostility to the old order, the constructivists devised scenery that was deliberately antidecorative, emphasizing instead the stage as a machine—a playing area of steps, ramps, and platforms to serve the actors' functions. The leader of this revolt was Vsevolod Meyerhold, whose name is always associated with *theatricalism*.

Pablo Picasso's Guernica, 1937. A powerful combination of objects and figures, simultaneous action and fragmentation that projects the distorted quality of a nightmare.

164

Theatricalism is a catchall term for nonrealistic stylization of all types from symbolism to surrealism, from expressionism to epic theater. Theatricalism uses all aspects of theater, free from any attempt to create the illusion of actuality. The actor suggests or assumes a role, rather than becoming a character. The performer may step in and out of character, go from youth to old age in a single speech, play several roles, go in and out of emotional states, address the audience directly, and comment on the action. In staging, theatricalism employs scenery, lighting, costume, and sound for their own sakes, sometimes as the most important element and sometimes with no visual support at all. There is no illusion of the fourth wall. The visual and aural elements may be used as sensory stimuli, often at a high level of intensity. The total effect of the production may come from a series of signals in spurts, juxtaposed, overlapping, and simultaneous, projected in incongruous ways without obvious continuity or significance. Of course, theatricalism may also be used as a way of stylizing familiar plays and situations; but the important consideration is that the performance exists as a *theater piece*, not as dramatic literature. Theatricalism has a free and lively spirit. In the old theater, all elements were synthesized in support of the play; in the new theater all aspects celebrate a theatrical occasion.

Two examples from the Russian theater of the twenties show the nature of the theatricalism espoused by Vakhtangov and Meyerhold.

In 1922 Eugene Vakhtangov staged a highly theatricalized production of Carlo Gozzi's *Turandot* in Moscow. He told his cast, "Our work is senseless if there is no holiday mood, if there is nothing to carry the spectators away. Let us carry them away with our youth, laughter and improvisation." When the spectators came into the theater, the actors were already on stage wearing street clothes. They talked to the audience about the play and what they would see.

As a waltz played, the actors improvised costumes from pieces of cloth and fabric, turning rags into riches. Stagehands moved furniture and properties into place, while scenery appeared like magic from the flies and wings—window frames, doors, and pillars. And it was in this playful atmosphere that the play continued and became one of the notable Russian productions of the decade.

Our second example of theatricalism occurred in 1926 in Meyerhold's last great production—Gogol's nineteenth-century satire on greed and hypocrisy, *The Government Inspector*. The director transferred the locale from the provinces to Moscow and updated the text to make the comedy more relevant and biting. Gogol's plot deals with civic officials who learn of an impending visit of the government inspector. They mistake a ne'er-do-well young man, Kheslakov, and his companion for the inspector and his valet. Kheslakov, an opportunist, exploits the situation to the limit, accepting the officials' bribes and favors and pretending a romantic interest in the mayor's daughter. Before being exposed as an imposter, Kheslakov manages to escape with the loot just when the real inspector is about to arrive. Meyerhold's

Meierhold's celebrated production of Gogol's The Inspector General, *Moscow. 1926.*

theatricalism in this production made an enormous impression. Here is the bribery scene.

The setting is made up of fifteen highly polished mahogany doors. Following a public reception, Kheslakov returns to his quarters where he is besieged by fifteen petty officials who seek to curry favor with him by offering him bribes. Two guards stand at attention before the central doorway. Kheslakov staggers in through the wrong door, almost falls but regains his feet with acrobatic dexterity and drops into a chair. He confides in the audience that he is dead drunk. One of the officials hurries in to notify Kheslakov that others are coming to grease his palm. Suddenly all fifteen doors open at once and the politicians enter with the mechanical movements of a robot, chanting their lines in unison. Kheslakov responds in the same rhythmical manner, accepting each of the proffered gifts with clockwork precision. The image is of an immense bribe machine.

Meyerhold, originally associated with Stanislavski, became dissatisfied with conventional techniques and freely experimented with those he borrowed from the Oriental theater, the carnival, music hall and circus. He devised an acting style known as "biomechanics" aimed at training actors to perform as gymnasts or machines so as to convey their feelings through physical gestures. For example, an actor in order to express joy might turn a handspring or slide down a pole. Meyerhold's theory was that behavior is best expressed through theatricalism—not by words but by carefully controlled poses, movements, and gestures. Meyerhold's theories and methods were demonstrated in several remarkable productions, especially *The Magnificent Cuckold* in which he erected on a bare stage the skeletal suggestion of a hill, reached by stairs and ramps, with a bridge, trapeze, and other mechanical devices. The actors, dressed as workmen, gave an acrobatic performance accompanied by a jazz orchestra. In *Earth on Its Hindlegs*, the cast rode bicycles and motorbikes about the stage, and dragged on a heavy canvas followed by a regiment of marching soldiers.

Meyerhold's essential contribution was in his attitude toward the theater as a total vehicle to be exploited in all possible ways. By word and especially by example, he was the epitome of the theatricalism of the twentieth century.

Among contemporary directors, Peter Stein at the Hallenschen Schaubühne in West Berlin has earned a wide reputation for his theatricalism. Stein's Schaubühne since 1970 has become one of the finest performance ensembles in Europe. Based on the idea that art and politics cannot be separated, the Schaubühne took an active interest in the proletarian movement but has since shifted its emphasis to personal enlightenment. The company's first success was *The Mother* (1970), an antibourgeois production notable for its two styles of acting. The young revolutionaries were played simply and directly in contrast to the representatives of the bourgeoisie—the police chief, landlord, and teacher, who were played in a pompous, exaggerated manner. During the play, the mother demonstrated her enlightenment when she changed from a pompous character to a forthright one. Stein's purpose with his actors was to "make their own learning process available to spectators through the straightforward, friendly narrative manner in which they explored and demonstrated events on stage."

In *Peer Gynt*, Stein wanted to show how a human being was subverted from realizing his creative potential by his attempt to overreach himself. Since the Schaubühne produces just four plays a year, the company has time for thorough preparation. In connection with *Peer Gynt* the ensemble engaged in many seminar discussions of Ibsen's life, literature, and his brand of realism. It sought to understand the roots of nineteenth-century bourgeoisie life by investigating the art and culture of the period. The aim was to view the play from the outside. Ibsen's text was freely translated and interpreted to emphasize the theme of Peer's inability to fulfill himself because of his egocentric fixation rooted in bourgeois drives.

Instead of producing *Peer Gynt* in a theater, Stein elected to stage it in a large exhibition hall at the fairgrounds that could accommodate 700 people. The spectators sat in rows of seats at the side of a long rectangular playing area 25 meters long and 10 meters wide. This area was covered by a beige canvas with a hill at one end and a depression at the other. During the performance—which ran for nearly seven hours over two consecutive

Peter Stein of the West Berlin Schaubühne staged his free version of Ibsen's Peer Gynt *in an exhibition hall with spectators in banks of seats facing an enormous playing area. The theatricalism of the production illustrated Stein's view that* Peer Gynt *doesn't belong to the theater of illusion. "It describes an illusion."*

evenings—properties and set pieces were brought in either manually or mechanically to serve for the eight phases of Peer's life. The leading role was divided among six actors who played variations of a basic type—a bourgeois dreamer.

This production, like others in the new theater, interpreted Ibsen's play freely to suit the director's views, rejected illusionary scenery and acting, avoided psychological involvement, focused on ideas rather than entertainment, and created its excitement by its frank and imaginative theatricalism in a space outside the conventional playhouse.

Bertolt Brecht

One of the most influential playwrights and theoreticians of the twentieth century is Bertolt Brecht (1898–1956). In exile from Germany in 1933, he wrote most of his major plays while living abroad; he returned in 1947 to Berlin where he founded *The Berliner Ensemble*, one of the most remarkable acting companies of our time, which specializes in producing Brecht's plays. He was subject to varied influences such as dadaism, expressionism, as well as his association with Erwin Piscator and Max Reinhardt in Berlin. His first popular success was in 1928 with *The Threepenny Opera*.

Brecht links himself with theatricalism through his rejection of the illusionistic stage. "How long," Brecht asked, "are our souls going to have to leave our gross bodies under cover of darkness to penetrate into those dream figures up there on the rostrum in order to share their transports that would otherwise be denied us?" Brecht was a rebellious spirit who mixed his theatricalism with political propaganda, who explored, with incredible verve and gusto, this "ugly, brutal, dangerous" man in the seamy side of his existence. He was a brilliant inventor and a notorious borrower whose proclivity for criticism of man and all his institutions naturally included overthrow of the conventional theater, and led him to create his own imaginative "epic theater."

Traditionally, the epic form was sharply separated from drama, the latter being characterized by compact action that could be presented by living performers, and the epic, because of its freedom of time, place, and action, being confined to the written word. But Brecht looked on these two forms as no longer irreconcilable because technical advances enabled the modern theater to exploit the narrative through projections, films, lighting, and machinery for changing scenery more rapidly. Furthermore, Brecht felt that the most important human experiences were no longer personal stories of individuals but, rather, significant social events and the forces that caused them.

Since he was dealing with social content rather than emotions, Brecht sometimes described his stage as a "tribunal," in which he wanted "to teach the spectators to reach a verdict." The analogy is an apt one. Instead of presenting a tightly knit plot, Brecht used the stage as in a trial to present

Brecht's staging for his epic plays was theatrical rather than illusory. The wedding scene in The Caucasian Chalk Circle *is played in skeletonized fragments set on a revolving stage before an obviously painted landscape. Grusha, on the left, is preparing for her wedding, while the villagers gather around the priest on the right. Berliner Ensemble.*

evidence piece by piece, to introduce witnesses with conflicting testimony who are interrupted and cross-questioned. They testify by giving facts or relating events, rather than by impersonating. Evidence is presented in a variety of exhibits—weapons, drawings or photographs of where the action occurred, documents, letters, tape recordings, slides, models, and films. The intention is to put the event itself on trial.

As for the acting, Brecht was contemptuous of the Stanislavski method of character impersonation. His advice to the performer was that he should distance himself by playing the events as if they were historical, emphasizing their pastness. This distancing process Brecht called *Verfremdungseffekt* ("alienation effect") from the German word *verfremdungen* ("to make strange"). He intended that his actors should not impersonate their roles, but that they should demonstrate the action as if they stood outside their parts. Joseph Chaikin's explanation of the alienation effect clarifies the term: "The actor must come to a connection with the material as a person is connected with his environment. When he performs, he plays the material rather than

In his epic theater, Brecht attempted to develop an alienation style of acting—cool and distanced. Two characters from Caucasian Chalk Circle, *the Fat Prince and his Nephew. Berliner Ensemble.*

himself. He should be like a singer who sings the song rather than singing his voice, which one often hears."[3]

Brecht's alienation effect is not intended to antagonize the audience but rather to make it wary so that it will consider the action intellectually rather than allowing itself to be swept away by a tide of emotionalism.

What about the plot structure of the epic plays of Brecht? Kurt Schwitters made collages in which he pieced together all kinds of objects and colors and textures—"I play off material against material." In a similar manner, Brecht utilized the juxtaposition of disparate actions and moods to create the alienation effect.

Brecht's plots often startled and shocked the audiences, thus counteracting the tendency toward illusion. He made use of this practice by deliberately breaking the mood of a scene, by interrupting action with music, by playing irony against sentiment, comedy against seriousness, and by the constant use of inversion and reversal.

171   [3]Cole and Chinoy, *Actors on Acting.*

As a young man coming out of a bitter experience in the military as a medical orderly, and acutely aware of the social and economic calamities of postwar Germany, Brecht wrote savagely out of his view that "the meanest thing alive, and the weakest is man." His early plays are filled with depravity and crime and illustrate his cynical theme that virtue brings no reward; indeed, ethical behavior is really a sign of stupidity. He looked at all men with suspicion, for the poor are as cruel as the rich. As for justice—it is a delusion.

After he accepted Marxism, he came to believe that the evils of the world could be cured by revolution, and to that premise he devoted a number of his *Lehrstücke*, or learning pieces. In 1928 Brecht, along with Kurt Weill who wrote the music, staged his most commercially successful work, *The Three-penny Opera*. Brecht borrowed the plot of John Gay's *The Beggar's Opera*, a fashionable London hit of 1728. But where the original had been a lighthearted lampoon of the aristocracy, Brecht's play was a scathing satire of the bourgeoisie. He created a vivid collection of depraved characters, thieves, swindlers, prostitutes, and crooks who infest a human jungle—a jungle whose code is summed up in the pawnbroker Peachum's words: "What keeps a man alive—he lives on others by grinding, sweating, defeating, beating, cheating, eating some other man." But Brecht relieved the sting of the characters and situation through his considerable gifts as an entertainer, which he was never quite able to suppress despite his political purpose. He was fond of slapstick, vaudeville, sporting events, clowns, and beer-hall entertainers, and his theatricalism stems in part from the direct and earthy quality of these kinds of performers and performances.

Brecht's mature years are notable for his three "parables," which constitute his major contribution: *The Good Woman of Setzuan, Mother Courage and Her Children,* and *The Caucasian Chalk Circle.*

The good woman of Setzuan is a compassionate young prostitute, who is rewarded for her hospitality to three wandering gods when they set her up in a shop. Because she has no talent for money-making, others exploit her generous nature and bring her misery. In desperation, she assumes the role of a heartless male cousin. Only under the disguise of ruthlessness and avarice can she provide for herself and her unborn child. At the end, she is left unable to reconcile herself to the evil ways of the world. She says to the gods: "Something must be wrong in your world. Why is there reward for wickedness and why do the good receive such hard punishment?" The gods whom she has befriended give no answer.

Mother Courage, which Brecht wrote just before the outbreak of World War II, is a bitter attack on militarism as an aspect of capitalism. To Brecht, heroism invariably comes from human error and brutality. His attention is not centered on the military action, which is narrated with legends and slogans, but on Mother Courage, a camp peddler in Germany during the Thirty Years' War (1618–1648). She is a scheming, salty character who will use any means to serve her purpose. And her purpose is to survive by buying and selling life's necessaries and to protect her children from harm amid the shifting fortunes of princes and their marauding bands of soldiers. Her wagon symbolizes her view that war is "just the same as trading," and "you must get in with people. If you scratch my back, I'll scratch yours. Don't stick your neck out." It is while she is involved in bargaining that each of her children die. In a magnificently theatrical scene, Courage's good-hearted, mute daughter Kattrin climbs up on a rooftop and drums a tattoo to warn the villagers of the invading soldiers, until she is shot down. Like Miller's Willy Loman, Courage's absorption with profits causes her destruction, but she must go on—and at the end having learned nothing but with her spirit apparently unquenched, she finds it possible to go on dragging her load of misery behind her.

In his last work, *The Caucasian Chalk Circle*, written in 1944–1945, Brecht's tone mellowed and the political message was incidental. The story concerns a young girl, Grusha, who saves the despotic governor's infant son during rebellion. She makes her escape with the child, submits to a marriage of convenience, and is brought ultimately to trial; thanks to an eccentric judge she is allowed to keep the child because she has demonstrated true motherly spirit.

The "epic" qualities of the play are seen in the prologue and epilogue that frame the main story, the sharp break between Grusha's adventures and the trial scene, the extension of the social environment to include the military uprising and the comic marriage, and in the use of song and dance.

As we look at Brecht's plays, we are struck by the contradiction between his theory and practice. He speaks of scientific objectivity when one of the sources of his power is the towering indignation that gives his work such force and texture. His didactic purpose is deadly serious, but his lyrical gifts, his flair for the comic, and his talent for showmanship burst through the seams of his intent. He repudiates realism and the Stanislavski method of acting because they are based on emotional involvement, and Brecht speaks of his wish to keep the audience "cool" and estranged. Ironically, his plays offer some of the most irresistible acting roles in the theater which, time and time again in performance, arouse the emotions of their audiences profoundly. This contradiction brings us back to the playwright's problem of relating action and its effect.

Let us examine two widely quoted statements of Brechtian theory and attempt to square them with his practice.

In the chart below, Brecht compares the traditional stage and his own:

The dramatic theater	*The epic theater*
the stage embodies a sequence of events	the stage narrates the sequence
involves the spectator in an action and	makes him an observer but
uses up his energy, his will to action	awakes his energy
plot	narrative
implicates the spectator in a stage situation	turns the spectator into an observer, but

The dramatic theater	The epic theater
wears down his capacity for action	arouses his capacity for action
provides him with sensations	forces him to take decisions
experience	picture of the world
the spectator is involved in something	he is made to face something
suggestion	argument
instinctive feelings are preserved	brought to the point of recognition
the spectator is in the thick of it, shares the experience	the spectator stands outside, studies
the human being is taken for granted	the human being is the object of the inquiry
he is unalterable	he is alterable and able to alter
eyes on the finish	eyes on the course
one scene makes another	each scene for itself
growth	montage
linear development	in curves
evolutionary determinism	jumps
man as a fixed point	man as a process
thought determines being	social being determines thought
feeling	reason[4]

A second important statement, which Brecht included in "Little Organum" in 1948 after his plays were written, reads:

> Since the public is not invited to throw itself into the fable as though into a river, in order to let itself be tossed indeterminately back and forth, the individual events must be tied together in such a way that the knots are strikingly noticeable; the events must not follow upon one another imperceptibly, but rather one must be able to pass judgment in the midst of them. . . . The parts of the fable, therefore, are to be carefully set off against one another by giving them their own structure, that of a play within a play.[5]

Brecht is describing here his technique of alienating the audience by breaking up the structure into separate events in order that the spectator can "pass judgment in the midst of them"; the knots must be "strikingly noticeable." What is the basis for this theory of structured action? To encourage the spectator to think rather than to feel. But action has a way of speaking stronger than words.

[4]Bertolt Brecht, *Brecht on Theatre*, trans. John Willett (London: Methuen, 1964).
[5]Bertolt Brecht. "Little Organum for the Theater," trans. Beatrice Gottlieb, *Accent*, 11 (1951).

In his major works Brecht selected basic formulas for *stimulating feeling* by using the standardized patterns of melodrama and romanticism. In *The Threepenny Opera* he employed a dashing rebel with a price on his head, the enemy of a corrupt social system—a clichéd romantic hero. Brecht was able to accomplish his effect despite his central action by making Mack the Knife a corrupt character in a corrupt world. The atmosphere is mordant, not heroic. There is little humanity, no genuine suffering—and through inverted justice Mack is freed and rewarded at the end. When this work is produced in authentic Brechtian style as at the Berliner Ensemble or in Richard Foreman's version at Lincoln Center with an attitude of "serious playfulness," the author's purpose is achieved. On the other hand, *The Threepenny Opera* played for its quaint characters and picturesque situations completely distorts the play's impact. In *The Resistible Rise of Arturo Ui* (1941) Brecht again uses a potentially romantic central action—the rise of a little man to power—but the hero's evil ways and his obvious parallel to Hitler throws a chill over the action and keeps us at a distance, although we are captivated by the brilliant acting of the Ensemble. But the alienation works.

In Brecht's three parables, *The Good Woman of Setzuan* (1938–1940), *Mother Courage* (1937), and *The Caucasian Chalk Circle* (1944–1945), the action follows the most surefire melodramatic device of all: Women in distress try valiantly to protect their children against overwhelming forces of evil. In spite of Brecht's avowed purpose of interrupting the sequence to avoid empathic response, an audience has a way of holding on to the emotional momentum, just as an exciting football game on television holds the audience in suspense through the interruptions by commercials and the opening and closing of refrigerator doors. Despite the "noticeable knots" and Brecht's theory of keeping each event separate, his practice suggests that step by step his structure in these three parables intensifies the emotional response. We do care about the outcome. In a tribunal, the evidence and testimony form a structure leading suspensefully to a verdict that completes the action. If you put a woman on stage—even a sharp-tongued, grasping one—show her attachment and devotion to her children, place them in jeopardy, and give the audience concrete signs of her suffering, the effect is to gain audience sympathy. This engagement is especially true if the dramatist creates generous, well-intentioned characters like Shen Te, Grusha, and Kattrin. Dramatize an action showing a woman trying to save a child by crossing an abyss over a rickety bridge pursued by brutal soldiers, and the audience will root for her. Show a mother the bullet-riddled body of her child and force her to conceal her agony for fear of losing her own life, and the audience will be stirred.

Brecht was aware of the emotional consequences of the actions he placed on stage, and he took great pains to divert the normal response in another direction. Furthermore, the plays are not melodramas because at the end reward and punishment are not parceled out according to individual merits. Even in the case of Grusha, the ending is not personal but social. Nor is there an orderly world of good and evil. By showing with abrasive humor the futility

In Caucasian Chalk Circle, *Grusha's escape over the bridge generates suspense and involvement despite Brecht's wish to avoid emotional attachment. University of California, Santa Barbara. Directed by the author.*

of heroism and virtue, Brecht combats sentiment for justice. Instead of conceding to the audience's eagerness for wish fulfillment, he tramples on it. His frankly theatrical way of showing an action is intended to dilute the emotional content. In performance, however, what counts more than the degree of realism is the audience's *willingness to believe.* And an audience is quite capable of believing in actions in all kinds of styles, including the "epic."

Brecht is a very significant force in the contemporary theater not only because of his theories of a new kind of theater, but because of the theatricalism of his productions and plays. He gave the experimental theater of this century what it needed most—a first-rate playwright. He gave us a fresh insight into the uses of the theater and enlarged its scope, although the breath of fresh air was tinged with a chill that could cut to the bone.

Antonin Artaud

One of the most imaginative and influential figures between the great wars was Antonin Artaud (1896–1948). A tormented iconoclast, with scant success in actual production, he is, nevertheless, the fountainhead of much of

176

A production capitalizing on the theatricalism of epic staging for Kopit's Indians *at the University of Hawaii. Directed by Glenn Cannon; designed by Richard G. Mason.*

the experimental theatricalism on the contemporary stage. He began working in the theater in Paris in 1921 and opened his Theatre Alfred Jarry in 1927 (named in honor of another French innovator who wrote *Ubu Roi* in 1896 and is sometimes credited as the first absurdist because of his mockery of traditional values and conventional drama). Artaud spent two seasons with this theater, dedicated to the production of nonrealistic plays. Artaud's importance is not for his practical work in the theater, but for his astonishingly prolific imagination and his vision of theatricalism. His book *The Theater and Its Double* (1938) advanced many ideas that are the basis for the contemporary revolt in acting, playwrighting, design, directing, and architecture.

Artaud's criticism springs basically from his dissatisfaction with the shape of the world about him. He says, "I believe that our present social system is iniquitous and should be destroyed."[6] And again, "There are too many signs that everything that used to sustain our lives no longer does so, that we are all mad, desperate and sick."[7] The existing theater outrages Artaud because it fails to deal seriously with man's social and moral systems. The theater has lost its feeling for seriousness and laughter. It has "broken away from the spirit of profound anarchy which is the root of all poetry." He calls for a rejection of the idolatry of fixed masterpieces reserved for the self-styled elite and not understood by or appealing to the public. He rages against the falsehood and

[6]Antonin Artaud, *The Theater and Its Double*, trans. Mary C. Richards (New York: Grove Press, Inc., 1958).

[7]Artaud, *Theater and Its Double.*

illusion of popular distractions that serve as an outlet for our worst instincts. These descriptive and narrative distractions provide stories that satisfy only peeping Toms—a theater to decorate our leisure with intimate scenes from the lives of a few puppets. He repudiates well-made plots, which serve only to exploit the psychological aspects of human interest. He was enraged to see the theater offering stories about money, social careerism, the pangs of love, and sugar-coated sexuality—stories that fail to touch the public interest; stories that leave no scars.

Artaud was not merely an anarchist determined on a course of destruction; he was rather a true revolutionary dedicated to change. While his criticism of the modern theater is scathing, he is even more vehement when it comes to suggesting a cure. Extraordinarily creative about all aspects of the stage, technical as well as theoretical, he envisions a radically different kind of drama and production techniques to implement it. While he was never able to thoroughly realize his ideas in his own Theatre Alfred Jarry, the audacity and sweep of his imagination can scarcely be ignored by anyone involved in the contemporary theater.

The emphasis in his thinking was to create a theater that "stages events, not men," that deals with the metaphysical concerns of ancient rites—"an exorcism to make our demons flow." The theater must give us "crime, love, war, or madness, if it wants to cover its necessity." It must deal with "atrocious crimes" and "superhuman devotions" as the ancient myths do. His notion of a "theater of cruelty" stems from the mystical, magical forces of a "theater in which violent physical images crush and hypnotize the sensibility of the spectator seized by the theater as by a whirlwind of higher forces." His intention was to free the repressed unconscious in dramatic performance which resembles a plague because "it is the relevation, the bringing forth, the exteriorization of a depth of the latent cruelty by means of which all perverse possibilities of the mind . . . are localized."

The cruelty that Artaud called for is not physical, nor is the violence for its own sake. Rather it is a process of purification which "causes the mask to fall, reveals the lie, the slackness, baseness, and hypocrisy of our world." The theater is a means of ridding society of its institutionalized violence. For after experiencing the cruelty that he envisioned in the theater, Artaud said, "I defy the spectator to give himself up once outside the theater to ideas of war, riot and blatant murder."

Such a concept of the function of the theater reminds us, of course, of Freud's approach to psychoanalysis through the release of neurotic symptoms. Artaud's perspective also bears a striking resemblance to Aristotle's view of catharsis—the purgation of emotions, as we have seen in tragedy. In his *Politics*, speaking of the effect of music, Aristotle describes the so-called homeopathic theory of catharsis, which seems analogous to Artaud's purpose:

> In listening to the performances of others we may admit the modes of action and passion also. For feelings such as pity and fear, or, again, enthusiasm, exist very strongly in some souls, and have more or less influence over all. Some persons

fall into a religious frenzy, whom we see as the result of the sacred melodies—
when they have used the melodies that excite the soul to mystic frenzy—restored
as though they have found healing and purgation. Those who are influenced by
pity and fear, and every emotional nature, must have a like experience . . . and all
are in a manner purged and their souls lightened and delighted.[8]

The effect described by Aristotle is apparently close to the experience that
Artaud sought in his theater—incidentally, an experience not without parallels
in the rock festivals of our day.

Artaud conceived of theater as total spectacle that must have the
"ceremonial quality of a religious rite." Made up of violent and concentrated
action "pushed beyond all limits," it is addressed to the senses and to the
theatricality of the unconscious.

Artaud rebelled against the conventional use of language in the theater.
To understand his attack, one must remember his background; for the
French, more than any other people, have placed a high value on polished
diction, and the tradition of their theater is rich in rhetoric. Artaud found the
language of the theater "dead and fixed in forms that no longer respond to
the needs of the time." He objected to the "tyranny of the word" and the
dictatorship of the writer. Actually, his rebellion was against the conventionalized nature and form of drama, and in his call for a new theatricalism,
language was his first target. He wanted to get away from mere words
addressed to the mind. He proposed to use language in a "new, exceptional
and unaccustomed fashion." He wanted to replace the utilitarian spoken
word with an active language "beyond customary feelings and words," to
create a "subterranean current of impressions, correspondences and analo-
gies." Communication in his theater was not merely actors making speeches,
but the stage was to be a place filled with its own language to include sounds
used for their "vibratory quality," onomatopoeia, cries, and intonations. He
wanted words to have about the same importance "as they have in dreams."
Indeed, Artaud urged an extension of theatricalism so that everything that
occupied the stage would create an effect on the senses, even to the point of
physical shock.

Too much criticism of Artaud has been directed at his vivid rhetoric rather
than at the spirit of his ideas. He is not a pessimistic, destructive sensationalist.
At the core, his views are serious, humane, and positive. He invites us to take
the theater seriously, to cut through the sham and hypocrisy of society, to face
ourselves honestly, and to trap our deep, latent powers that will enable us to
take a "superior and heroic attitude." The process involves the cruel practice
of exposing society and *one's self* with complete honesty. Here is a voice of
one who sees ahead and links future to past:

Either we will be capable of returning by present-day means to this superior idea
of poetry and poetry-through-theater which underlies the myths told by the great

---

[8]Aristotle, *Politics*, in Aristotle's *Poetics*, trans. Leon Goldman, commentary by O. B.
Hardison, Jr. (Englewood Cliffs, N.J.: Prentice-Hall, Inc., 1968).

ancient tragedians, capable once more of entertaining a religious idea of the
theater (without meditation, useless contemplation, and vague dreams), capable
of attaining awareness and a possession of certain dominant forces, of certain
notions that control all others, and (since ideas, when they are effective, carry
their energy with them) capable of recovering within ourselves those energies
which ultimately create order and increase the value of life, or else we might as
well abandon ourselves now, without protest, and recognize that we are no
longer good for anything but disorder, famine, flood, war and epidemics.[9]

The Absurdists

The opening of Samuel Beckett's *Waiting for Godot* in 1953 focused attention
on a new dramatist and subsequently a new theatrical movement known as
"the theater of the absurd." When the curtain opened the first night, the
audience saw two bedraggled bums, Estragon and Vladimir, waiting in a
deserted place for a mysterious Godot. His identity is not clear and their
relationship to him is never made explicit. A master driving a heavily
burdened slave appears briefly, and later a boy enters to inform the tramps
that Godot will not arrive tonight. The play ends as it began with the two
waiting. While they wait, they talk, and their conversation explores such
themes as death and salvation, the need for affection, the perplexed state of
man, their personal biological problems, and the recurrent motif—waiting for
Godot. The dialogue is interlocked with a wealth of seriocomic business, and
the lines as well as the action provide an effective vehicle for the performers.

The audience greeted the play with mixed reactions. Some found it
bewildering and dull; others, provocative and fascinating. In any case, the
play made a remarkable impression throughout the theater world, and
Waiting for Godot became the prime example of absurdist theater. In addition
to Beckett, the most prominent absurdists are Eugène Ionesco, Arthur
Adamov, the English Harold Pinter, and the American Edward Albee. These
absurdists are not neatly compartmentalized and each of them works in a
variety of ways. What brings them together is the absurdist point of view,
foreshadowed by Camus in his celebrated statement in *The Myth of Sisyphus*:

> A world that can be explained by reasoning, however faulty, is a familiar world.
> But in a universe that is suddenly deprived of illusions and of light, man feels a
> stranger. His is an irremediable exile, because he is deprived of memories of a lost
> homeland as much as he lacks the hope of a promised land to come. This divorce
> between man and his life, the actor and his setting, truly constitutes the feeling of
> Absurdity.[10]

Earlier writers had foreshadowed the movement in several ways. Pirandello in his juxtaposition of the serious and the comic, his concern with illusion

[9]Artaud, *Theatre and Its Double.*
[10]Albert Camus, *The Myth of Sisyphus* (New York: Alfred A. Knopf, Inc., 1955).

Pozzo, a pompous task-master, demonstrates his control over the abject lacky, his slave, while Estragon and Vladimir watch with apprehension. Waiting for Godot, *Virginia Polytechnic Institute. Directed by Paul Antonie Distler.*

and reality, and with the difficulties of human communication, was an important forerunner. Kafka's stories and novels, and particularly Barrault's production of *The Trial* in 1947 with its nightmarish treatment of weird and puzzling actions, set an interesting example. And in the forthright theatricalism of the expressionists and Brecht, the absurdists found encouragement to strike out along new lines.

Another dramatist who was spiritually related to the absurdists was Alfred Jarry whose *Ubu Roi* caused a sensation when first produced in Paris in 1896 because of its blatant presentation of human grossness and sensuality.

Jarry's intentions were clear: "When the curtain rose, I wanted the stage to be before the audience like a mirror . . . in which the vicious one would see himself with the horns of a bull and the body of a dragon, according to the

Waiting for Godot *by Samuel Beckett is one of the most influential plays of the twentieth century by reason of its philosophical perspective and its style of writing and performance. Directed by the author at the Schiller Theater, Berlin.*

exaggeration of his vices; and it is not surprising that the public was stupefied at the sight of its ignoble reflection which had not yet been completely presented to it."[11]

Jarry's play dramatizes the career of King Ubu whose wife, like Lady Macbeth, drives him to murder the King of Poland in order to gain the crown for himself. His evil ways force him to hide in a cave where he is haunted by the spectres of his victims. The content of the play is not as important as Jarry's prophetic view of the world and his way of handling theatrical materials. The sacrilegious spirit of his attack, the naive directness of his characters and their speech, his sense of raillery—these are seeds that found root later on.

Jarry used the theater in a new way in order to produce a new effect. This was precisely the case with the absurdists who viewed the conventional drama

[11]Alfred Jarry, cited in Leonard Cabell Pronko, *Avant-Garde: The Experimental Theater in France* (Berkeley: University of California Press, 1962).

The London Royal Court Theatre production of Alfred Jarry's Ubu
Roi.

with contempt. They wanted to put it to new uses. In order to understand their
point of view, we must take into account the fact that those who led the
movement and gave it stature shared a similar experience: Beckett (born in
Ireland), Ionesco (born in Rumania), and Adamov (born in Russia) all lived in
Paris during World War II. At first hand they witnessed the military defeat of
France, and suffered through the occupation by the German forces. The
defeat meant the destruction of the political and social fabric and the ruin of
civilian morale, and the occupation resulted in an agonizing sense of
frustration in the face of overwhelming power. The existentialists—Sartre,
Anouilh, and Camus—responded to this experience by using conventional
literary forms to probe into such philosophic questions as the role of man in
the universe and the effect of materialism on the human spirit. Their answers
suggested that man was utterly alone and that he must create his own world,
his own set of values. The absurdists, who lived through the same era, asked
the same questions but did not arrive at the same answers. They generalized
from their experience. They felt that there were no answers—life was absurd.

Another production of Ubu Roi *captures the spirit of Jarry's bizarre characters. (Cameri Theater, Tel-Aviv. Directed by Shmuel Bunim.)*

And it was this attitude that they put into action in the theater. They were dramatizing a simple but terrifying idea: Man is lost.

Waiting for Godot begins with Estragon's line: "Nothing to be done." And the play ends:

Vladimir: Well, shall we go?
Estragon: Yes, let's go.

> *They do not move. Curtain.*[12]

Harold Clurman calls our attention to a parallel passage in Pinter's *The Birthday Party*:

Stanley: How would you like to go away with me?
Lulu: Where?
Stanley: Nowhere. Still we could go.

[12]Samuel Beckett, *Waiting for Godot* (New York: Grove Press, Inc., 1954).

Lulu:	But where would we go?
Stanley:	Nowhere. There's nowhere to go. So we could just go. It wouldn't matter.
Lulu:	We might as well stay here.
Stanley:	No. It's no good here.
Lulu:	Well, where else is there?
Stanley:	Nowhere.

Man doesn't go because there is no purpose to his going. As Camus said, man has no homeland to return to and no promised land before him. He has lost his identity in a dehumanized world; he has lost his perspective in a world without God or a fixed scale of values, and he has lost his reason for going because there is really no place where he can make a meaningful connection. From bitter experience he is wary of hollow ideas and men. He is trapped in the frustrations of an enigmatic universe.

A mild-mannered professor tutors a bright, confident girl student for her ''total doctorate.'' At first the characters seem involved in a normal situation of question and answer but a metamorphosis sets in. The professor's latent aggressiveness breaks out and the student, now nearly incoherent, is stabbed to death. She is the fortieth victim of the day. The corpse is removed and a new student arrives to begin the process over again. (Ionesco: *The Lesson*)

An elderly couple on a lonely island await the arrival of distinguished guests to hear the orator's important message. As the invisible guests arrive, the couple greet them and fill the stage with chairs. When the orator comes, the couple throw themselves out the window and his message is gibberish. (Ionesco: *The Chairs*)

Two professional killers hide in a basement kitchen waiting for their next job, but their hideaway is discovered. Footsteps are heard overhead, a note appears under the door, and the dumbwaiter begins to move bearing messages demanding more and more food. Finally a message comes that one man is to assassinate his partner. (Pinter: *The Dumbwaiter*)

A lonely, guilt-ridden pianist seeks sanctuary in a seaside rooming house. It is revealed that in the past he has offended someone with considerable power. Two sinister strangers appear and the fear-wracked Stanley realizes they are after him. A mock birthday party staged in his honor turns out to be a grotesque ritual when Stanley goes beserk. At the end the two men take the crushed Stanley away in a long black car. (Pinter: *The Birthday Party*)[13]

A family replaces an adopted child with a handsome physical specimen of American manhood, who turns out to be hollow inside. (Albee: *The American Dream*)

In such plays as these, the playwright abandons the notion of depicting psychologically complex characters. They are more apt to resemble puppets or marionettes because they are not personally responsible for their actions. They have been set in motion by an outside force. They cannot act rationally because there is no longer such a thing as logical behavior. They have no means for creating a complete identity, and since communication is virtually

[13]Harold Pinter, *The Birthday Party* (New York: Grove Press, 1959.)

Ionesco's Rhinoceros *is an absurdist play based on the transformation of human beings into rhinoceroses. Berenger is aghast when his friend, Jean turns into a rhinoceros before his very eyes. (University of California, Santa Barbara. Directed by the author.)*

impossible, they are not able to relate to one another with understanding and affection.

In a world devoid of meaning, language loses its value. Ionesco wrote his first play, *The Bald Soprano*, as the result of his efforts to learn a foreign language by memorizing standardized phrases. The play parodies the spoken word by exposing its banal vacuity. Here is its opening:

Scene: A middle class English interior, with English armchairs. Mr. Smith, an Englishman seated in his English armchair and wearing English slippers, is smoking his English pipe and reading an English newspaper, near an English fire. He is wearing English spectacles and a small gray English mustache. Beside him, in another English armchair, Mrs. Smith, an Englishwoman, is darning some English socks. A long moment of English silence. The English clock strikes seventeen English strokes.

Mrs. Smith: There it's nine o'clock. We've drunk the soup and eaten the fish and chips and the English salad. The children have drunk English water. We've eaten well this evening. That's because we live in the suburbs of London and because our name is Smith. (*Mr. Smith reads and clicks his tongue.*)

Mrs. Smith: Potatoes are very good fried in fat, the salad oil was not rancid. The oil from the grocer at the corner is better quality than the oil from the grocer across the street. It is even better than the oil from the grocer at the bottom of the street. However, I prefer not to tell them that their oil is bad.

(Mr. Smith continues to read, clicks his tongue.)

Mrs. Smith: However, the oil from the grocer at the corner is still the best.[14]

Ionesco has a special flair for satirizing language in his use of gibberish, nonsense words, and broken speech. On the other hand, Beckett and Pinter have a gift for the use of common language that in its diction and rhythm has almost the evocative power of poetry in its ability to suggest meanings beneath the surface. Albee has a good ear for the flavor of the American idiom plus an aptitude for parodying our colloquial speech. The dialogue in an absurdist's play is open to many interpretations and is remarkable for what it leaves to the imagination.

In an attempt to produce their desired effects, the absurdists have created their own arsenal of weapons: the use of shock effects by inverting behavior, by contemptuous mockery of sacrosanct ideas and institutions, by their candor and sometimes their bold frankness. Their comedy, often used ironically, crops out in unexpected places. They present the bizarre, the grotesque, and the unusual. They startle and astonish the audience by their wild flights of fancy and their sometimes incredible inventions. They keep an audience off balance by concealing their hands, making sudden shifts in direction. They bewilder the spectator and then lead him to a startling discovery. They use the theatrical tricks of the circus clown, the slapstick comedian, and the music hall entertainer, as this comic routine from *Waiting for Godot* indicates:

Lucky has left his hat behind. Vladimir finds it.

Vladimir: Must have been a very fine hat. *(He puts it on his head. Estragon puts on Vladimir's hat in place of his own which he hands to Vladimir. Vladimir takes Estragon's hat. Estragon adjusts Vladimir's hat on his head. Vladimir puts on Estragon's hat in place of Lucky's which he hands to Estragon. Estragon takes Lucky's hat. Vladimir adjusts Estragon's hat on his head. Estragon puts on Lucky's hat in place of Vladimir's which he hands to Vladimir. Vladimir takes his hat. Estragon adjusts Lucky's hat on his head. Vladimir puts on his hat in place of Estragon's which he hands to Estragon. Estragon takes his hat. Vladimir adjusts his hat on his head. Estragon puts his hat in place of Lucky's which he hands to Vladimir. Vladimir takes Lucky's hat. Estragon adjusts his hat on his head. Vladimir puts on Lucky's hat in place of his own which he hands to Estragon. Estragon takes Vladimir's hat. Vladimir adjusts Lucky's hat on his head. Estragon hands Vladimir's hat back to Vladimir who takes it and hands it back to Estragon who takes it and hands it back to Vladimir who takes it and throws it down.)* How does it fit?

Estragon: How would I know?

Vladimir: No, but how do I look in it?

[14]Eugène Ionesco, *The Bald Soprano,* from *Four Plays* by Eugène Ionesco, trans. Donald M. Allen (New York: Grove Press, Inc., 1958).

(He turns his head coquettishly to and fro, minces like a mannequin.)

Estragon: Hideous.
Vladimir: Yes, but not more so than usual?
Estragon: Neither more nor less.
Vladimir: Then I can keep it. Mine irked me. *(Pause.)* How shall I say? *(Pause.)* It itched me.[15]

The absurdist, antitheater in his approach to plot, makes no pretense of interesting the audience in story or character. The difference in the outcome from the traditional play is that the ending does not answer the questions raised, or else the ending is contrary to the expectations of the characters or the audience. The great leader has no head, the orator can only babble, the gorgeous young man is a hollow shell, the intellectual is really a barbarian, and Godot never comes. The playwright gives you a set of figures to add up, but your total is zero. An absurd play is characterized by an absurd ending because that is how the playwright feels about the world. In some plays he doesn't give us an answer at all, but brings the action back to the beginning of the circle, which is another way of saying that life is absurd because there are no answers.

The absurdist does not offer you a neatly organized, carefully selected set of signs, nor does he lead you by the hand so that you will know where you are all the time. You may get lost and return to your starting place. You may be the victim of a sudden ambush or a strange trap; you will be baffled by directional signs pointing every which way, or straight down. You may find yourself in a completely foreign place among strangers speaking in unknown tongues, behaving in odd ways. But the playwright has a map of the territory and he knows what he is about, although his method may baffle you. He may ask you to look at the stars, and then pour a bucket of water over your head; he may invite you to climb a tree to find your way, and then chop it down from under you. The absurdist offers you an absurd experience because he wants you to be aware that the world is absurd.

If the absurdist rejects a carefully organized chain of action, has no interest in story values, makes little effort to reveal the psychological aspects of characters, is uninterested in emotional involvement, refrains from specific identification of locale or character, what effects do his works achieve as theater?

Some spectators are bewildered and irritated because the action in an absurdist play seems nonsensical. Others enjoy it as a kind of intellectual game by trying to piece together the bits of experience offered to them. Their critical faculties are involved, and they enjoy the learning process of seeking a fresh perception imaginatively presented. They may delight in the playwright's skill of execution or in that of the performers. At a more profound level, the theatergoer becomes acutely aware of the universality suggested by the specific stimulus of the play, and from his awareness may come a strong sense of personal involvement in the playwright's statement.

[15]Beckett, *Waiting for Godot.*

Ionesco describes the creative process as "through an increasingly intense and revealing series of emotional states."

> Theater is for me the outward projection onto the stage of an inner world; it is in my dreams, in my anxieties, in my obscure desires, in my internal contradictions that I, for one, reserve for myself the right of finding my dramatic subject matter. As I am not alone in the world, as each of us, in the depth of his being, is at the same time part and parcel of all others, my dreams, my desires, my anxieties, my obsessions do not belong to me alone. They form part of an ancestral heritage, a very ancient storehouse, which is a portion of the common property of all mankind. It is this, which, transcending their outward diversity, reunites all human beings and constitutes our profound common patrimony, the universal language. . . .[16]

It is a cutting process—or perhaps more accurately, a probing one, a penetration, rather than a thin slice off the top layer. The absurdist does not invite you to pleasant escape into a make-believe world; instead he tears away the façade and says this irrational, absurd world is your world. Where do you go from here?

In this sense the action in an absurdist play is cumulative, a process of intensification that raises questions of importance so compelling that we carry them away with us from the theater.

Jean Genêt

A direct spiritual descendant of Artaud is another Frenchman, Jean Genêt (b. 1910), who conceives of the theater in terms of symbol and ritual. Just as the existentialists found it necessary to reorient themselves philosophically to a shattered world by creating their individual sets of values, likewise Genêt shaped his own existential view of the world from his strange, tormented childhood and early adult life. An illegitimate child, an unwanted orphan, he found out at age ten that he had no connection with the world, and from that discovery he developed his own inverted hierarchy of values. "I rejected a world which rejected me." Since he had no identity and no status, he turned to a life of crime and homosexuality. He attempted to find his life by losing it. While serving a prison sentence, he began to write and showed so much artistic promise that some leading French intellectuals secured his release. In his plays *The Balcony, The Blacks, The Maids,* and *The Screens,* he has gained recognition as one of the most provocative playwrights of our day, and in his works some of Artaud's ideas of a theater of cruelty have been most successfully realized.

Out of his personal anguish, he visualized dramatic works of myth and ceremony, but in a world of reversed values. Instead of climbing the heights and seeking salvation, man finds his spiritual identity by plunging into the depths of darkness and evil. The soul is redeemed only by death, and only the

[16]Eugène Ionesco, "Impromptu de l'alma," *Théâtre II* (London: Calder and Boyars, 1958).

criminal with the dedication of a saint can attain grace. Murder is the highest crime, and the act of betrayal is a sacrament.

A metaphor that Genêt finds appropriate to his purpose is a series of mirrors, some of them placed at odd angles, some that invert or distort the image, and some which, like Alice's looking glass, allow us to see into an oddly perverted wonderland. His metaphor suits his purpose well, for Genêt is concerned with the varied facets and layers of reality: the discrepancy between the genuine and the illusionary, and the loss or disguise of identity through assumed appearances and roles. In his plays, the spectator is often bewildered by the dazzling surfaces and the strange perspectives so that he is not sure if he is seeing an actual character in a genuine event, or a pretender in a masquerade.

Like Artaud, Genêt admired primitive rituals and the Oriental theater. He was enamored of the masks, the rich use of spectacle, and the communal act of participation in an event of primary significance enacted in mystery and symbols. He saw the playwright's purpose fulfilled as, in Artaud's phrase, "a master of sacred ceremonies." Ritual provided the opportunity for gaining status by assuming roles and participating in significant acts. In Genêt, these become reflections of the dark areas of the unconscious where primitive rites and sadomasochistic fantasies hold their strange spell—a many-faceted view through the myths of cruelty whose cathartic powers celebrate a collective ecstasy.

Peter Brook

Outstanding among present-day directors who demand a new theatricalism is Peter Brook. He came out of the traditional theater, serving as an associate director of the Royal Shakespeare Company where he staged several notable productions such as *King Lear* (1962), *Marat/Sade* (1964), and *Midsummer Night's Dream* (1970). Since then he has become the leader of the International Center for Theater Research in Paris. In 1971 he directed a memorable and controversial work, *Orghast*, in a natural outdoor setting in Iran, an extraordinary production for its use of Ted Hughes' invented language. Brook, like most theatricalists, is an eclectic, borrowing from a variety of styles and sources but with the ability to synthesize a production in his own unique way.

In his book, *The Empty Space* (1969) Brook criticizes the current theater and describes the theatricalism he envisions for the future.

He categorizes four kinds of theater:

1. The *deadly theater* is the sterile, conventional one that acts as a museum for the "classics," particularly Shakespeare, Molière, and opera.

2. The *rough theater* is close to the people, down-to-earth, natural and joyous, without style, antiauthority, and filled with noise, vulgarity, and boisterous action. Examples are the Elizabethans and Meyerhold's productions.

3. The *holy theater* is one of revelation and ceremony. Its rituals are the genuine ones that affect people's lives, not the pseudorituals injected in much of the contemporary theater. Artaud is the prophet of the holy theater and Grotowski its chief disciple for such productions as his *The Constant Prince*.

4. The *immediate theater* is an eclectic one, vigorous, restless, full of joy—a combination of the rough and holy. It is dynamic, not rigid.

Brook's productions demonstrate his preference for the immediate theater. In preparation for Peter Weiss's *Marat/Sade* by the Royal Shakespeare Company, Brook with Charles Marowitz in 1963 set up an experimental group, "the Theater of Cruelty," in which the performers attempted to capture the spirit of Artaudian theatricalism in exercises such as simultaneous playing, improvisations, "transformations" (going from one character or situation to another without transitions), and using forms of nonverbal expression. *Marat/Sade* (1964) was a particularly effective device for Brook's experiment with Artaudian technique because of its highly charged, bizarre atmosphere. The action takes place in an early nineteenth-century madhouse where the Marquis de Sade is confined as a patient. He has written a play to be presented by the inmates before an invited audience from Parisian society. Weiss uses the situation as a metaphor for the world, showing the chaos that results from the abuse of power. Brook's theatricalism made an enormous impact, although many spectators were confused and upset by the volatile nature of the acting and the apparent lack of focus or clarity of purpose (the same reaction expressed by many who first saw the work of Schwitters and the surrealists a generation before). Brook's analysis of *Marat/Sade* recalls the views of the dadaists and the surrealists in their approach to the arts:

> What's the difference between a poor play and a good one? I think there's a very simple way of comparing them. A play in performance is a series of impressions; little dabs, one after another, fragments of information or feeling in a sequence which stir the audience's perceptions. A good play sends many such messages, often several at a time, often crowding, jostling, overlapping one another. The intelligence, the feelings, the memory, the imagination are all stirred. In a poor play, the impressions are well spaced out, they lope along in single file, and in the gaps the heart can sleep while the mind wanders to the day's annoyances and thoughts of dinner.[17]

Jerzy Grotowski

One of the most vital forces in the contemporary theater was the Polish Laboratory Theater and its moving spirit, Jerzy Grotowski (b. 1933), whose seriousness of purpose and ability to create dramatic experiences with the

[17]Peter Brook, "Introduction to *Marat/Sade*" by Peter Weiss, (New York: Atheneum Publishers, 1965). From the introduction by Peter Brook to the play, *The Persecution and Assassination of Jean-Paul Marat as Performed by the Inmates of the Asylum of Charenton Under the Direction of the Marquis de Sade*, by Peter Weiss, Copyright © 1965 by John Calder Ltd. Reprinted by permission of Atheneum Publishers.

authenticity of myth linked him with Artaud and Genêt. His mark was made not on the basis of his contribution to drama but to performance, for he and his actors made an enormous impression through their talent and dedication. He achieved an intensity and excitement by a nearly literal return to the concept of theater as "bare boards and a passion," for in his "poor theater" he discarded the usual paraphernalia of scenery, properties, lighting effects, music, and even the stage itself. The playing area was sometimes among the spectators located in a variety of places in a hall or theater. His performances were aimed at a special kind of audience, small in number, who came to a production for a serious experience. Grotowski says, "We are concerned with the spectator who has genuine spiritual needs and who really wishes, through confrontation with the performance, to analyze himself." The seriousness of his purpose, as demanding as that of Artaud, was to attain a "secular holiness." And like Artaud, his theater was primarily performance-oriented but centered exclusively in the actor rather than in theatrical objects and effects. His performances suggested the evocative power of myth and religious rites, but without specific referents. The effect came through the force of the emotion rather than in literal terms. Grotowski's productions possessed

Grotowski's production of The Constant Prince *at the Polish Laboratory Theater. Drama returns to ritual.*

an aspect of cruelty in the overwhelming agony and suffering through which the characters received release.

Two of his best-known works, *The Constant Prince* and *Apocalypsis cum Figuris*, conveyed the quality of an authentic ritual. *The Constant Prince* was a free adaptation of Calderon's seventeenth-century Spanish play in which five characters acted out the hypocrisy and corruption of the world and caused the humiliation, anguish, and death of the Prince in an emotionally charged atmosphere that suggested the crucifixion. The *Apocalypsis cum Figuris* was a work assembled out of the experiments of the actors and directors in which the verbal aspects were improvised in rehearsal as needed. When the production took shape, quotations were substituted from well-known sources: Dostoyevski, the Book of Job, the New Testament, T. S. Eliot, and the Song of Solomon. Although the Bible was often a verbal source and the characters were named after biblical characters, the work did not make a precise religious statement, but the impact of the production is described as an exploration of the sources of myth—a fusion of religion and drama. The effect that Grotowski's theater achieved was chiefly the result of the shattering quality of the acting. His performers were remarkably trained in all aspects of their craft—speech, mime, and gesture—but in addition they conveyed the impression of a monastic zeal as if the body were the outward manifestation of the secrets of the soul.

The New Theater

In the United States the social upheaval of the sixties stemming from the cold war and disastrous entanglement in Vietnam were reflected in a "new theater" movement through which protesters vociferously expressed their discontent with nearly every facet of the establishment—including the theater itself. Just as many European artists and writers were dissatisfied with the political and social conditions that followed World War I, after World War II the American dissidents regarded the conventional commercial theater as a shallow and outdated institution. They were antitext, antiillusionistic production, and antitheater as a place for performing. On the creative side they were for new kinds of theatrical material—a mixture of action, words, sound, music, and theatrical effects. The new theater was not an organized, widespread, sharply defined movement, but the result of the efforts of several highly visible groups and individuals that demonstrated their talent for theatricalism.

These efforts came mostly from outside the commercial theater, from coffeehouses and off-off-Broadway groups or from actors' and dancers' workshops such as Ellen Stewart's La Mama Experimental Theater Club, and Joe Cino's Cafe Cino, which provided opportunities for an enormous outpouring of theatrical energy. In the early years, most of the participants received no pay and productions were put together on shoestring budgets. Hundreds of plays were tried out, providing invaluable opportunities for experimenting with new plays, techniques, and styles.

The Living Theater

One of the most visible groups in the new theater was the Living Theater founded by Judith Malina and Julian Beck. The company first attracted attention with its performance of Jack Gelber's *The Connection* in 1959. As a metaphor for everybody's compulsion or obsession, the plot deals with a number of drug addicts awaiting the arrival of Cowboy and his supply of drugs. The performance was two edged so that the audience was not quite sure what was real and what was pretense, even to the cast members who circulated among the audience during the intermission demanding a handout. The next production to achieve notoriety was Kenneth Brown's *The Brig* (1963). This is a violent, brutal depiction of the rigors of existence in a marine camp. The play was performed with searing directness underscoring the naked brutality of the situation.

Following the loss of its theater due to failure to pay taxes, the Living Theater went to Europe where it developed its own brand of theatricalism. The company returned from abroad and gained national attention, chiefly with its productions of *Frankenstein* (1965) and *Paradise Now* (1968). The Living Theater used its plays for Marxist political persuasion played with frenetic fervor. It was the aim of the actors to tear down the wall that separated them from the spectators. Beck instructed his company that its mission was "to help the audience to learn to take action." Performers moved aggressively to reach the spectators and, through insults and obscenities, attempted to goad the audience into responding, not just to the performance but to the corruption of the capitalistic, bourgeois society which the Living Theater projected as the enemy.

Actors were not interested in "the fine art of acting," or in interpreting a "fine" play, but in creating a real personal experience. Said Beck, it is on stage "the actor lives his most intense hours during the performance." He challenged his company to "act as if your life depended upon it. Acting is earnest communication of everything you are with people earnestly assembled to be guided through the mysteries." The Living Theater provided a dynamic example of theatricalism which, subordinating the script and characterization to secondary roles, created an assault on the senses. Its stock in trade was frenzied choreography, vigorous physical action, strident sound, shock techniques, vivid images, and a hyped-up atmosphere.

The Open Theater

Another group that developed its own kind of theatricalism was the Open Theater founded by Joseph Chaikin in 1963 for the purpose of exploring innovative approaches to acting—and to self-realization. Chaikin and his company were dissatisfied with the conventional theater because they felt it debased the actor to the status of a commercial product rather than a creative human being. In its reaction against the dehumanization of the performer, the Open Theater, during its decade of existence, found valid new ways of working with actors that were demonstrated in occasional public performances in *Viet Rock* (1966), *America Hurrah*, and *Terminal*. As a result of its disciplined explorations, the company was influential in acting, playwriting, and staging.

At the center of Chaikin's approach was the actor's need to establish "presence"—an awareness of his own body, a sensitivity to those about him, and an acute consciousness of the meeting of lives at a specific moment and space—a "visceral confrontation." The actor begins developing an awareness of himself, probing beneath the social conditioning that masks the real self. He must attempt to get beyond the usual "prepared responses" in order to *open up*. Said Chaikin: "We must open up to our deepest despair, to coldness around the heart, to the secret wishes about God."

As a part of the creative process, the actors of the company worked their way through personal and ensemble explorations to build their own plays from exercises, games, improvisations, and transactions. The final form of the text was shaped by writers and the director, but in the main the product was a group effort, so the actors were personally related to the material they played. The limitation of creating a play in this fashion is that the level of the group in dealing with dialogue and thought may not reach the same level as that of a gifted playwright. On the other hand, such productions subordinated the verbal content of the play to achieve dynamic, highly theatrical ensemble performances. Chaikin's method also gave the actor the freedom to perform in a way unknown to the illusionistic stage with its emphasis on psychological delineation of character.

The new theater of the last decade is no longer a strident voice of protest, but it continues to be a theater of experimentation with new forms of theatricalism. The carefully plotted play following a linear development has been replaced by all manner of handling materials. In some instances the original dialogue of "classics" may be replaced by the contemporary idiom, eliminated altogether, or improvised by the actors. In other instances, the plot is a loose amalgam of situations pieced together in workshops and made up of games, improvisations, and acting exercises as variations on a theme. In still others, plotting is rejected entirely in favor of performers in action with scenic effects, images, and music for the sake of the creative act itself. In place of a logical and continuous progression of incidents, emphasis is placed on fragments—moment-by-moment sensations, oftentimes simultaneously presented.

Robert Wilson is a highly regarded experimentalist whose theatricalism appeals primarily to the eye. He has been called a "seer genius" and a "feeler genius" because of his imaginative productions of striking visual displays in *The Life and Times of Sigmund Freud*, *Deafman Glance* (1971), *A Letter for Queen Victoria* (1975), *The Life and Times of Joseph Stalin*, *Einstein on the Beach* (1976), *I Was Sitting on My Patio This Guy Appeared I Thought I Was Hallucinating* (1977) and *Death, Destruction and Detroit* (1979). *Einstein on the Beach*, which was performed at the Metropolitan Opera House after highly successful productions in major European cities, combined all aspects of the theater but the emphasis was on the sensual imagery loosely tied to musical motifs.

Wilson's background as a painter explains his visual approach to theatrical production.

> I am always concerned with how the total stage picture looks at any given moment. The placement and design (shape, proportion, materials) of furniture, the color, or fabric and design of costumes, placement and content of film, paths and gestures of performers, and lighting were all major considerations, no less important than the dialogue or music.[18]

In *A Letter for Queen Victoria*, Wilson presented what one reviewer called a "phantasmagoric enigma" of striking and beautiful images. There is talk, some of it articulate, some gibberish, but with little apparent meaning. One sequence showed a group of masked aviators huddled up against a wall in fear. There were smoke and crocodiles and living monuments formed by the aviators watching crashing airplanes outside the window. In another scene a fragment of a cafe is set against a backcloth on which a repeated pattern of the words "Chitter" and "Chatter" appear. People in gray sit at tables with pink tulips, chattering away, at times interrupted by gunfire. One of the characters seems to be shot and slowly dies, only to revive nimbly and resume chattering.

And so Wilson leads the spectator from one beguiling moment to the next in a stunning collage of all elements of the theater.

In *Death, Destruction and Detroit*, which premiered in West Berlin (1979), Wilson made more extensive use of language than in his previous works. Some of it was fragmentary, oblique, precise, and lyrical but there was an ordered verbal sequence. Like the other elements—music, dance, and spectacle—the language was a way of stirring the imagination and expanding the awareness rather than a means of conveying factual information.

Death, Destruction and Detroit concerns the Nazi leader, Rudolf Hess, confined since 1945 in a prison in Berlin. One scene, particularly striking because of the evocative images that Wilson fashions, suggests Hess's prison cell. Dale Harris describes the action:

> . . . Hess, now an old man dressed in white tie and tails, dances by himself to the sound of a Keith Jarrett piano solo. He is preoccupied, self-absorbed, utterly content. Even when the stage begins to fill up—first with couples in evening dress, then with waiters carrying huge salvers and domed lids, all of them dancing with the same self-absorption and fixity of purpose—he stays in his own world, weaving in and out of the crowd as if they didn't exist. At the front of the stage, in the center, stands a little boy (who may or may not be Hess's son), wearing scarlet diplomat's dress, gleaming with gold frogging—a colorful note among the pervading shades of grey and black.
>
> Meanwhile, from one side of the stage a woman (who may or may not be Hess's wife) stares out at the audience during the course of the scene being

[18]Robert Wilson, "I Thought I Was Hallucinating," *Drama Review*, T76 (December 1977), p. 78.

Robert Wilson's theater emphasizes highly imaginative visual images.
His odd world-view is suggested in his Death, Destruction and Detroit in
its premiere production in Berlin at the Schaubühne.

transformed from a shabby looking *hausfrau* with a cotton scarf knotted under chin to a *grande dame* in magnificent black evening dress, her head crowned with feathers, her wrists and neck encircled with diamonds. It is hard to imagine a more telling comment on the economic rise and gradual historical amnesia of West Germany between 1945 and the present.[19]

Richard Foreman is another experimentalist who has received considerable attention through his Ontological-Hysteric Theater productions of *Dr. Selavy's Magic Circus, Elephant Steps, Angel Face,* and *Hotel for Criminals.* Like Wilson, his interest is in the presentation of a series of theatrical, provocative images, without a story line or continuity. He delights in the "act of making the thing we are looking at," which he regards as constantly changing directions. When asked what he would like an audience to experience from his productions, Foreman replied, "I would like them to feel refreshed, you know, energized."

Early in his career Foreman was attracted to Brecht's alienation theory of acting, but he now centers his attention on each particular image or instant as the source of enjoyment. He sums up his point of view:

It's enjoying moment by moment the choices that Stanley [Stanley Silver, composer] and I, as the creators of this particular piece, are making, and somehow delighting in the fact that we chose, very specifically, to have that combination at

[19]Dale Harris, "Berlin Report," *Performing Arts,* June 1979, p. 50.

that moment. It's seeing the seams, seeing the joints, seeing where we decided, okay, this is the next thing you should notice, rather than a kind of empathy following of the story and nothing but. They should be exhilarated by following all of our choices as artists and the joy of making art, as well as the art that is then made.[20]

Again like Wilson, Foreman as an experimentalist has earned recognition in the conventional theater for his striking production of Brecht's *Threepenny Opera* (1975) at the Vivian Beaumont Theater, Lincoln Center, New York. In this revival Foreman announced that he intended to "restore the original anguish to a piece meant to disturb, confound and thereby excite." Brecht's work has a definite story line and several clearly delineated characters so Foreman was not able to fragmentize the play as he does with his own creations. Nevertheless his actors achieved a cold, brittle "serious playfulness" that made the production a memorable one and enhanced Foreman's reputation for imaginative theatricalism.

Linked with Wilson and Foreman in its emphasis on a visual approach to production is Mabou Mines, an ensemble of seven performers and nine technicians who write, direct, perform, and stage their own work under the leadership of Lee Preuer. The company is best known for its "animations"— actions that are brought to life. *The Shaggy Dog* animation presents the life and loves of a dog named Rose who develops a fixation for her master and longs to take on human characteristics. Rose is played by a puppet about two-thirds human size manipulated by from one to four of the actors. The dog's past and her thoughts and feelings are projected over a sound track and accompanied by strange and evocative actions and images.

Beckett's *Come and Go* was a highly imaginative Mabou Mines production in which the three actors sat on a balcony behind the audience. They were made visible by a large mirror on stage. This play featured spectacular visual and sound effects—a bomb falls, splitting the stage floor and disintegrating the room amid fireworks, explosions, and vivid lighting.

Another innovator who has attained considerable prominence for his theatricalism is Andrei Serban, a Rumanian-born director who was associated with Brook in Paris and Iran before coming to the La Mama Company. Unlike Wilson and Foreman, Serban works with established texts, and his special interest is in sound. He probes beneath the surface of words in order to recapture the primal emotion behind them. For example, he says in everyday life we listen to words for information without really feeling the impact of the sound. When he directed Euripides' plays—*Medea, Electra*, and *The Trojan Women*—Serban worked vigorously with his cast on sound and rhythm which he felt were the key to the performance. The company for the trilogy worked on the sound not only in Greek but also in Elizabethan English, as well as two esoteric African languages. As a result, the aural aspect of the performance made a deep impression.

The new theater continues to be active on a wide front although less blatant

---

[20]Richard Foreman, "Ontological-Hysteric Theater," *Yale Theater*, 7 (1975), p. 28.

than before—the shock has worn off and many of the freedoms it fought for have been won. Indeed, the theatricalism that a short time ago seemed so novel has worked its way into the commercial theater. Musical comedy and dance, which have always been most responsive to innovation, readily absorbed the experimental theatricalism, especially in staging and lighting. Playwrights with an eye on the commercial theater imediately exploited the new permissiveness in handling language, behavior, nudity, and subject matter in ways hitherto considered unsuitable for the public stage. Writers now find much more latitude in shaping their material. The tight story line organized on a cause and effect pattern and the rigid confinement of a box set no longer dominate dramatic structure. Even plays written for the conventional stage are now conceived in terms of their theatricality—as for example in Peter Shaffer's *Equus*, in which a simple setting is transformed into a stunning theatrical experience by the imaginative use of lighting, sound, and acting. A generally realistic play like Stoppard's *Night and Day* begins with a theatricalized scene. The house lights dim; the curtain opens on a dark stage covered with mist. Suddenly the headlights of a jeep are seen coming directly toward the audience. Shots are fired and a character tumbles out of the jeep as it screeches to a halt . . . and the scene shifts to the exterior of a house.

One of the chief targets of the new theater was the tyranny of the word—the sanctity of the text. Traditionally, the play was the core of the production, and those who brought it to life on stage attempted to be faithful to the playwright's words and purpose. Now the play is regarded as one element of the performance, no more important than the acting or setting or music. Fragments of several plays may be pieced together in nearly haphazard fashion, or the language and images may be probed for a subtext to make the meaning relevant to the contemporary world. The Living Theater began its production of *Frankenstein* with a scene in which fifteen actors attempted to levitate a girl, but their efforts failed and she was caught in a net and placed in a coffin which was carried off in a procession. This interpolated action was a personal statement of the company about its faith overcome by frustration. In a production of *Oedipus the King* at the Kammerspiele Schauspielhaus in Munich, Director Ernst Wendt updated Sophocles' play to demonstrate that tragedy is the lack of communal rapport with the action of the individual. Wendt's modernized version replaced the original actions with contemporary ones. In the classic version of the play, the prologue shows a band of suppliants suffering from the plague, coming to Oedipus to ask for his help. Wendt showed the miserable condition of the citizens by individual actions: One character pounded on an electronic piano; a girl did a frenzied tap dance on top of a billiard table; a wandering man, mumbling incoherently, shuffled through the debris that littered the stage; and a woman stabbed herself again and again, screaming at the top of her voice. Later in the play, when Jocasta learns of her incestuous relationship to Oedipus, she goes silently into the house and hangs herself. Director Wendt updated this action by having Jocasta run up a moving escalator, collapse, and die.

In many cases, a company of actors creates its own version of a classic text or makes up a new one around a central theme through improvisation, rehearsal, and discussion. The text no longer dominates the performance.

Since the new theater is performance-oriented, a good deal of attention was placed on the acting, especially in such groups as the Living Theater, the Open Theater, Grotowski's laboratory, and Brook's Cruel Theater. They stressed ensemble play, and the intense discipline of the body and voice required by their theatricalism. Preparation for acting changed from method analysis with its concern for character identification and motivation to a cooler style suggested by Brecht or to a rigorous process of self-discovery and realization achieved through long periods of experiment and rehearsal.

In performances that are strongly visual in conception, such as those of Wilson, Foreman, and Mabou Mines, some of the participants may have little or no traditional training as actors; they appear as persons performing tasks rather than representing psychologically complex characters. They play the actions, not individuals.

Many of those in the new theater oppose the traditional playhouse because they view it as a fixed place of the privileged class—a museum for outmoded plays and performances. In order to make theater more accessible, "environmental productions" make use of existing "found spaces," such as basements, marketplaces, and warehouses. The site is regarded as a part of the production to be occupied by everyone. Richard Schechner, who popularized the term *environmental production*, said, "All space is used for performance; all space is used by the audience." Spectators are not passive onlookers but "scene watchers" and when they become involved in the action, "scene makers."

Schechner's own Performance Group, beginning in 1968, occupied an old garage fitted out with towers and platforms which were shared by audience and performer in his productions. In *Dionysus in 69* the audience sat on scaffolds or on the floor; the actors began their performance on the platforms and towers but soon moved among the spectators. In the "birth" ritual which was adapted from an ancient tribal rite, the performance became an ecstatic, frenzied communal event with members of the cast crawling beneath the audience's seats or leaping from the towers to the platforms. Schechner's production was an illustration of that brand of theatricalism that attempts to merge spectator, performer, and all aspects of production into a celebration.

Play production outside of the theater is older than the playhouse itself; we remember that the Greeks performed first on threshing floors and in marketplaces, that early medieval drama was played in churches and courtyards, Noh drama was originally given in shrines in river-beds, and Elizabethan drama made use of inn-yards, bear-baiting rings and banquet halls. So today, many directors find the use of "environmental" staging enormously stimulating. Much of the experimental theater work both here and abroad has first been played in improvised quarters, partly because budgetary limitations made it impossible to house the play in a traditional theater with the normal complement of scenery, and partly because in accommodating the performance to a nontheatrical environment the director and actors found a more invigorating environment for experimenting with audience-actor relationships. Even the theater itself has been used in untraditional ways to create a fresh approach to a production. For his *Timon of Athens* (1975) Brook gutted an old theater, made the stage into a deep pit, and played most of the action in the orchestra. Likewise, Serban pulled out rows of seats to make an acting area in the auditorium for his version of *Agamemnon.* In Basel, Switzerland, in a theater still under construction, the audience was placed in various sectors of the building, such as staircases and foyers, while a cast of 19 played several hundred roles in an eight-hour performance of an epic play. The new theater has made its point— theatricalism is not the result of the architecture; the spirit and imagination of those who make the performance create the atmosphere and environment.

Scenery as a supporting element of production is often gratuitous since time and place can be imaginatively induced without pictorial representation. Playing areas with ramps, platforms, and stairways picked out by light give the director, playwright, and actor an enormous amount of flexibility. But the visual element is not neglected. The use of film, slide projections, lighting, costuming, movement, and interesting use of space add immensely to the total effect.

One feature of the experimental production that breaks sharply with the past is the use of multifocus. Arguing that in our daily lives we often react to several stimuli at once and that we are able to shift our attention from one center of interest to another, spectators may be given alternative choices between competing simultaneous actions, or they may be overwhelmed by an assault of sensual stimuli to the saturation point. Hence, in some instances the audience is unable to see or hear what is going on elsewhere in the theater, and conversely they may at times be the observers or participants of some part of the performance not available to everyone.

In recent years the idea of a performance has been extended beyond the conventional play and playhouse in quasi-theatrical productions. They are often associated with the visual arts because they are given in galleries and museums and because they are many times created by painters or sculptors whose interest is in sensory perceptions. The makers of these "performances" break away from the controlled language and structured action in an effort to achieve a fresh experience of intuitive perception and heightened sensitivity not tied to formal themes or meanings.

For a time, a good deal of experimentation came under the catchall term of "happenings." More recently "performances" is the key word with such ramifications as "auto-performances," "activities," and "performance workshops."

A widow, Linda Montano, creates a public performance out of the act of mourning for her husband's suicide. She appears in gray makeup with a dozen accupuncture needles embedded in her face, and describes her former association with her husband in an attempt to achieve some measure of release from her grief.

Stuart Sherman sets up a TV tray on a street corner, or in a theater, or gallery, or the Staten Island ferry, opens up a battered suitcase and manipulates a variety of commonplace objects in a rapid series of brief "routines" that comprise his "spectacles." He makes no effort to involve the audience except to invite them to watch his actions.

Allan Kaprow gathered a group of interested people together, paired them off in couples and sent them out into the streets of Naples to find suitable doorways where each couple performed a "routine" consisting of a short passage of dialogue made up of simple phrases such as "after you," "excuse me," and "thank you." Their dialogue was to be accompanied by appropriate action. Each couple repeated the routine in four different doorways. There was no attempt to attract an audience—the pleasure was in the doing.

Those who work in performances usually reject the conventional forms of theater and art either because they are too limiting or because they are seeking new forms of expression that go beyond traditional means. They are concerned with investigations of signs, abstract ideas, sounds, space, and varied means of perception and communication. Performances make use of mime, dance, action, speech, and music, as well as films, videotapes, musical instruments, puppets, projections, recordings, images, and environments. A listing of "Performance/Nonstatic Art" events in an art journal reveals such intriguing titles as "What If . . . ?" "Pause Still," "Some Erts," "Tell Me," "Acute Mirage," "The Dog & Cat Dinner Party," and "Ghost Dances of Rosebud Hall." The performances are advertised as "a play," "film installation," "slide art works and music," "six-channel video installation," "multi-media dance concert," "performance using synthesizers, micro-computers, homemade electronic circuits and electric base," and a "wind, computer generated sound and sculpture."

The intended effect of such experiments is generally "perceptional enhancement." In our "mind-blowing" world we have become acutely aware of the rich lode of our inner resources and experiences. As Marshall McLuhan says, "Once more reality is concerned as being *within* one, and the search of truth has become an inward trip." Hence the efforts to break through the established patterns of fixed language and action to a fresh experience of intuitive perception and heightened sensitivity not tied to specific meanings.

Like so many other innovations in the arts, performances emphasize the creative process rather than the final product, and oftentimes technical skill yields to improvised inspiration. The act is its own excuse for being.

The future of the new theater will no doubt depend on the social climate of the times. The valid gains it has made in promoting a varied brand of theatricalism will be reflected in the main current of the theater while fresh attempts will be made to express the human experience. The door is wide open since there has never before been such a wide range of styles, technical facilities, or audience tastes. As always, with every form of theater, the future will depend mostly on the talent and imagination that is attracted to its service.

Bibliography

ARTAUD, ANTONIN, *The Theater and Its Double*, trans. Mary C. Richards. New York: Grove Press, Inc., 1958.

BROCKETT, OSCAR G., and ROBERT R. FINDLAY, *Century of Innovation.* Englewood Cliffs, N.J.: Prentice-Hall, Inc., 1973.

BROOK, PETER, *The Empty Space.* London: MacGibbon and Kee, 1968.

BRUSTEIN, ROBERT, *The Third Theater.* New York: Alfred A. Knopf, Inc., 1969.

ESSLIN, MARTIN, *The Theater of the Absurd.* New York: Doubleday & Co., Inc., 1961.

EVANS-ROOSE, JAMES, *The Experimental Theater.* New York: Universe Books, 1970.

GROTOWSKI, JERZY, *Towards a Poor Theater.* New York: Simon & Schuster, 1968.

IONESCO, EUGENE, *Notes and Counter-notes: Writings on the Theater.* New York: Grove Press, Inc., 1964.

KIRBY, E. T., *Total Theater.* New York: E. P. Dutton & Co., Inc., 1969.

KIRBY, MICHAEL, *The New Theater: Performance Documentation.* New York: New York University Press, 1978.

MARRANCA, BONNIE, *The Theater of Images.* New York: Drama Book Specialists, 1977.

PASOLI, ROBERT, *A Book on the Open Theater.* Indianapolis: The Bobbs-Merrill Co., Inc., 1970.

SCHECHNER, RICHARD, *Public Domain: Essays on the Theater.* Indianapolis: The Bobbs-Merrill Co., Inc., 1969.

SILVESTRO, CARLO, *The Living Book of the Living Theater.* New York: Graphic Society, 1971.

WELLWARTH, GEORGE, *The Theater of Protest and Paradox.* New York: New York University Press, 1967.

EIGHT
The Director

When Aeschylus produced his Greek tragedy, *The Suppliants* (c. 492 B.C.), he must have learned that directing a play is a complex and tricky business. Since he was the author, he did not have the usual problem of interpreting the meaning of his text, but like all directors he went through the intriguing and sometimes frustrating process of putting the words into action. Aeschylus had to make sure his lines were spoken or sung correctly, he had to work out all of the movement and choreography of actors and chorus members, and he supervised all aspects of production—costumes, casting, music, and dance.

Even a cursory glance at *The Suppliants* indicates the need for painstaking planning and rehearsal. Aeschylus dramatizes the story of the 50 daughters of Danaus who flee to Argos seeking sanctuary from the pursuing sons of Aegyptus. At the climax of the play the Herald and his attendants attempt to carry off the maidens by force, but they are saved by the king, who refuses to release them.

Perhaps the most difficult task Aeschylus faced in producing his play was training the chorus of fifty maidens, who recite and chant more than six hundred lines of poetry, sometimes combining words with dance, and sometimes engaging in vigorous action when they cling to the altar in terror, pleading for asylum. In addition to the careful preparation of speech and choreography of the chorus, it was necessary to provide them with appropriate costumes—striking Egyptian robes and linen veils fastened to their heads with gold bands. In the action of the other performers, two entrances required special care. In the first, the king and his retinue make a dramatic entrance, probably using horses and chariots. The second complicated entrance occurs when the Herald and his coterie appear and threaten to tear the suppliant maidens away from the altar. Although this play has a simple plot, its implicit demands for the movement of a large group of performers must have required arduous rehearsal. We may be sure that Aeschylus was grateful for his military experience when he prepared *The Suppliants* for performance.

Throughout the history of the theater, the manifold tasks of play production have been handled in a variety of ways. The assigned officials and Greek playwrights were in charge of the presentation of tragedies. In the medieval cycle plays, with their fragmentized episodes, many of them requiring realistic staging, an enormous amount of organization was necessary, much of which was parceled out to various participating groups. In the Elizabethan theater, with its permanent professional companies of actors and playwrights, the theater manager selected the plays and assigned the casts. Undoubtedly, the playwrights took considerable interest in seeing that their works were performed as they intended them to be. And just as Hamlet found it expedient to advise the players about their style of acting in the play-within-the-play, it requires little stretch of the imagination to believe that Shakespeare made a similar effort in the performance of his dramas at the Globe. Molière, in the seventeenth-century French theater, labored for twelve years with his troupe in the provinces, polishing and perfecting the performance of his plays before returning to Paris. That Molière not only set an example for his company but took care to improve the quality of his productions is suggested by his wry comment that "actors are strange creatures to drive."

In the eighteenth and nineteenth centuries, such stars as David Garrick and William Macready attempted to make play production less haphazard, but in general, many of the responsibilities of organization were delegated to underlings, or ignored altogether. Often, plays were patched together with "typed" characters assigned to roles with little or no genuine rehearsal, and almost no concern for ensemble acting. Stock sets were refurbished on a makeshift basis and little attention was paid to lighting. Costuming was mostly a matter of individual taste, and apparently no one worried about the resulting incongruities. There were, of course, a few notable exceptions to these practices. Charles Kean staged remarkable productions of Shakespeare in the 1850s, for which special scenery was designed and painted with accurate geological and botanical detail. In his productions of *A Midsummer Night's Dream* and *Henry VIII*, Kean was praised for the harmony of effect that resulted from music, scenery, and choreography especially created for the occasions. A decade later, the Bancrofts introduced rehearsal reforms which were in the direction of greater unity.

The Modern Director Appears

The Duke of Saxe-Meiningen in Germany performed an invaluable service for the theater through his exemplary staging of Shakespeare, Ibsen, and Schiller. All aspects of production were integrated into an artistic whole—acting, scenery, and costuming. His troupe emphasized ensemble playing, paying special attention to the use of crowds. The duke's company tour of the major theatrical centers of Europe (1874–1890) inspired theater workers elsewhere to emulate his synthesis of production and helped to establish the position of the director as the dominant force in theatrical production.

With the coming of naturalism and realism in the latter part of the nineteenth century, directors and actors became increasingly concerned with unifying all elements of the performance. The new plays representing authentic views of daily life based on firsthand observation demanded a new kind of scenery and acting. Since the conventional commercial theaters were not hospitable to innovation, it became necessary to set up "independent theaters"—places where a subscription audience could see the new kind of drama appropriately played. André Antoine led the way with his Théâtre Libre in Paris (1887), in which he directed all phases of production. He made a hall into an improvised theater, selected the plays and the casts, set the style of acting by directing and performing himself, and devised the scenery. He

Sketch by the Duke of Saxe-Meiningen for a production of Julius Caesar. *Note the careful blocking for the entire ensemble.*

207

even went out and rounded up an audience by hand-delivered letters and personal contacts. His efforts resulted in a unique integration of performance based on his ideal of achieving an honest representation of reality. In Berlin (1889) Otto Brahm followed Antoine's example at the Freie Bühne, another subscription theater that demonstrated realism, especially in the plays of Ibsen and Hauptmann. In Russia the Moscow Art Theater (1898) did similar work with the plays of Anton Chekhov under the direction of Constantin Stanislavski. The independent theater idea was also influential in England at the Independent Stage Society under J. T. Grein, and in America James A. Herne directed a production of his own *Margaret Fleming* (1890) in Boston. These efforts to achieve a style appropriate to the new playwriting were instrumental in defining the role of the director as the one responsible for aesthetic unity and the dominant one in the production hierarchy.

In addition to the independent theater pioneers, two visionaries championed the concept of unity in play production in a series of notable stage designs, as well as in their writings. These men were Gordon Craig and Adolphe Appia, whose contributions are discussed in chapter 10. At this juncture in our discussion of directing, we should emphasize that there were several forces at work in the late nineteenth-century theater which led to the guiding principle that all aspects of play production should grow from a central interpretation. The corollary of this idea was that to secure such unity, a single creative intelligence must be responsible for designing the whole production—namely, the director. This idea is widely accepted in the twentieth-century theater, and this dominating role has been assumed notably by Max Reinhardt, Alexander Tairov, Jacques Copeau, Constantin Stanislavski, Vsevolod Meyerhold, Leopold Jessner, Tyrone Guthrie, Erwin Piscator, Elia Kazan, Jean-Louis Barrault, Peter Brook, Peter Stein, and Victor Garcia.

Directors work under rehearsal conditions that vary depending on the type of theater they serve. A Broadway director may find it necessary to throw a play together in three weeks; in Russia, some plays have taken two years of rehearsal. Meyerhold, after two months of rehearsal, had not settled on the casting on any one of the three characters for a one-act play! Max Reinhardt preplanned his performances to the last detail so that the rehearsal period was one of teaching the actors what he wished them to do; Arthur Hopkins simply turned his actors loose with occasional stimulation and encouragement, his idea of direction being to "put on a play without anyone realizing how it was done." Some directors find that the law of diminishing returns sets in for rehearsals lasting longer than three hours; David Belasco was known to rehearse for twenty hours at a stretch. Meyerhold gave his actors every piece of business and read every line for them; Bertolt Brecht sat and waited for his actors to show him the meaning of his own plays, Eugene Vakhtangov conducted round-table discussions with his casts, trying to arrive at a common interpretation; and Peter Stein, through seminars and directed reading, leads his company in researching the period of the play in order to comprehend its cultural roots.

The Function of the Director

As the unifying force in the production of a play, the director has a number of specific assignments. From the time that the script is placed in his hands until the curtain rises on opening night, it is the director who initiates and controls all aspects of the presentation of the play. The director analyzes the script, auditions actors, casts the roles, sets the basic floor plan for the sets, supervises the design of costumes, scenery and lighting, instructs the cast in the meaning of the play, and conducts rehearsals during which he blocks out the action, assists the actor with interpretation of character and the reading of lines, and finally polishes, times, and unifies the play into a cohesive whole. Everything about the interpretation and performance of the play is the director's business.

The director's function may be indicated by quoting representative statements by four outstanding men of the theater. John Mason Brown said that the "director is a critic in action." Tyrone Guthrie, well known for his highly personalized productions, said: "The director, then, is partly an artist presiding over a group of other artists, excitable, unruly, childlike and intermittently 'inspired.' He is also the foreman of a factory, the abbot of a monastery, and a superintendent of an analytic laboratory. It will do no harm, if in addition to other weapons, he arms himself with the patience of a good nurse, together with the voice and vocabulary of an old-time sergeant-major."[1] Meyerhold describes his purpose in these terms: "A director builds a bridge from the spectator to the actor. Following the dictates of the author, and introducing on the stage friends, enemies, or lovers, the director with movements and postures must present a certain image which will aid the spectator not only to hear the words, but to guess the inner, concealed feelings." The eminent French director Louis Jouvet described his task in these words: "He must organize that area where the active players on the stage and the passive players in the auditorium meet each other, where the spectators penetrate and identify themselves with the action on stage."

The Director as an Interpreter

As we have indicated earlier, the function of the director as the interpreter of the play is a modern concept. When such playwrights as Aeschylus, Shakespeare, and Molière, experienced theater men, worked directly with the actors, the shape and meaning of the performance was undoubtedly determined by the writer. But where the dramatists were not trained in the ways of the theater, or not available (some of them being dead), the individual actors were left to their own devices, which usually meant that a star was concerned only with being

209

[1]Tyrone Guthrie, *In Various Directions* (New York: Macmillan, Inc., 1965).

seen in a favorable light, considering one's colleagues only insofar as they affected the star's performance. With the coming of contemporary drama, the director assumed the responsibility for integrating the production, and the most important influence of the director was that of interpretation.

Directors begin by working with the script. They must have a complete understanding of the play. This goes far beyond a mere acquaintance with the story line or even an intimate knowledge of the play's structure. Drama shows people in action—making decisions, reaching for objectives, attacking, withdrawing, resisting, yielding. In the course of the action there is talk—argument, pleading, persuasion, discussion. And all of this action and talk is about something. There is a residue of meaning beneath the surface—the subtext. Directors search the play for the essential core of meaning they choose to convey.

Let us consider some directors at work.

Norris Houghton in *Moscow Rehearsals*, a fascinating account of his visit to Russia in the 1930s, describes Meyerhold's approach to directing a play. He read it through a single time, trying to grasp the meaning of the author, noting his first impression of the script. When he produced a play, Meyerhold often changed the text to suit the interpretation he gained from his first reading. Once Meyerhold determined the motivating idea, he visualized a tentative plan for the scenery and lighting. He came to the first rehearsal without any notes or promptbook, but apparently with his head swarming with ideas, which he released spontaneously as he worked with the actors on their interpretation of the lines and their invention of movement and business. A staff of eight to twelve assistants recorded in detail every aspect of each rehearsal, so that by the time the play reached production there was a vast accumulation of material about the play and its performance.

Houghton describes Meyerhold's interpretation of Chekhov's *The Proposal*, which he gave to the actors at the first rehearsal: "Two things are essential for a play's production, as I have often told you," Meyerhold begins.

> First, we must find the thought of the author; then we must reveal that thought in a theatrical form. This form I call a *jeu de théâtre* and around it I shall build the performance. Molière was a master of *jeu de théâtre*: a central idea and the use of incidents, comments, mockery, jokes—anything to put it over. In this production I am going to use the technique of the traditional vaudeville as the *jeu*. Let me explain what it is to be. In these three plays of Chekhov I have found that there are thirty-eight times when characters either faint, say they are going to faint, turn pale, clutch their hearts, or call for a glass of water; so I am going to take this idea of fainting and use it as a sort of leit-motif for the performance. Everything will contribute to this *jeu*.[2]

After this introduction Meyerhold read the script to the cast and dismissed the rehearsal.

The noted German director Max Reinhardt, famous for his theatricalism, like Meyerhold, dictated every detail of the production. However, he did not

[2]Norris Houghton, *Moscow Rehearsals* (New York: Harcourt Brace Jovanovich, Inc., 1936).

depend on the inspiration of the moment. Reinhardt's presentations were the result of months of careful preparation during which time he developed a complete annotated account of the play. The purpose of his rehearsals was to teach his interpretation line by line to the actor. R. Ben-Ari, who worked with Reinhardt, describes his methods in this fashion:

> Reinhardt comes to work with his secretaries and his assistant directors all laden with books. They are volumes with interpretations and explanations, with various data, drawings and symbols relating to the production—the evidence of colossal artistic and technical work which was done in preparing the manuscript for the stage. In these books the working out of every scene, every phrase, is recorded exactly and in detail—precisely when this or that player, when this or that group has to move to another part of the stage; how many musical intervals they have before they move; how much space they have to move in; the exact moment when the light is to go on. All this put together gives birth to the Reinhardt production. Reinhardt, himself a wonderful actor, influences his actors in such a way that they are compelled to do everything that he shows them. Reinhardt's personality dominates one to such an extent that one must copy all his intonations, all his emphases. These are wonderful in themselves, and of the deepest and most convincing sort, but they come to life through Reinhardt and not through the actor.[3]

Two American directors who owe a good deal to Stanislavski in their method of approach to the directing of plays are Harold Clurman and Elia Kazan. Both make a careful study of the script in advance, searching for a basic interpretation, their interest centering on the psychological backgrounds of the characters. As they analyze the play, Clurman and Kazan make notes to guide their thinking during rehearsals. These personal notes are interesting for revealing the ways these directors arrive at their interpretations.

Here are a few sample notes from Clurman when he was preparing for a production of *The Member of the Wedding:*

> *The main action of the play:* to get "connected."
>
> It all happens in a hot summer atmosphere, the world is "dead"—the people suspended. Everything is slightly strange, not altogether real.
>
> A mighty loneliness emanates from this play. It is as if all the characters were separated from the world—as if the people were only a mirage in a vaporous space making wraiths of the people.
>
> More decisive than any of these notes is my line by line "breakdown" of script, which indicates the aim of each scene and what particular actions and adjustment (mood) moment by moment the actor must carry out and convey. These actions— what the character wants to do and why—together with any physical action (or "stage business") which might result from the character's purpose are duly noted by the director, or, in most cases in my own work, they may be left to the actor's nature and imagination—under the director's guidance— to accomplish.[4]

---

[3]R. Ben-Ari, "Four Directors and the Actor," *Theatre Workshop,* January–March 1937.
[4]Toby Cole and Helen Krich Chinoy, *Directing the Play* (Indianapolis: The Bobbs-Merrill Co., Inc., 1953).

These sample notes record Kazan's interpretation of the stage production of *A Streetcar Named Desire:*

> *Theme*—this is a message from the dark interior. This little twisted, pathetic, confused bit of light and culture puts out a cry. It is snuffed out by the crude forces of violence, insensibility and vulgarity which exist in our South—and this cry is in the play.
>
> *Style*—one reason a "style," a stylized production is necessary is a subjective factor— Blanche's memories, inner life, emotions are a real factor. We cannot understand her behavior unless we see the effect of her past on her present behavior.
>
> This play is a poetic tragedy. We are shown the final dissolution of a person of worth, who once had a great potential, and who, even as she goes down, has worth exceeding that of the "healthy," coarse-grained figures who kill her.[5]

To keep his interpretation of each scene clearly before him, Kazan broke the play down into its component parts and placed a label on each scene:

> *Scene 1:* Blanche comes to the last place at the end of the line.

[5]Cole and Chinoy, *Directing the Play.*

A Streetcar Named Desire *demands a style of acting that is completely convincing in characterization and in conveying intensity of feeling. (Directed by Glenn Cannon; designed by Richard G. Mason. University of Hawaii.)*

Scene 2: Blanche tries to make a place for herself.

Scene 3: Blanche breaks them apart, but when they come together, Blanche is more alone than ever. (etc.)[6]

Just as they searched for the core ideas of the plays as the basis for their interpretations of the total meaning, similarly Clurman and Kazan probed for the "spines" of action that determined the character's behavior.

These are some of the notations Clurman made about the character of Frankie, a twelve-year-old "ugly duckling" in *The Member of the Wedding:*

> Her main action—*to get out of herself.* Getting out of herself means *growth.* . . . She has "growing pains": she is both tortured and happy through them. . . . The juices of life are pouring through her. She is a fragile container of this strange elixir.
>
> Growth twists and turns her—as it does us—gives us new shapes. Frankie twists and turns. The play is the lyric drama of Frankie's growth. At the end of the play, she runs or twirls out—"to go around the world." She has achieved her aim—imaginatively. She is ready "to get out of herself."[7]

He continues detailing her chief qualities, each one suggesting clues to her actions and behavior on stage.

Kazan made similar notations, but he is even more explicit; his comments on the character of Blanche alone run more than five pages. These notes are extremely significant in revealing the way in which a director studies the play and the characters' motivations before he brings the play to life on stage. These are a few of Kazan's observations about Blanche:

> Blanche is a social type, an emblem of a dying civilization, making its last curlicued and romantic exit. All her behavior patterns are those of the dying civilization she represents. In other words her behavior is *social.* Therefore find the social modes! This is the source of the play's stylization and the production's style and color. Likewise Stanley's behavior is *social* too. It is the basic animal cynicism of today. "Get what's coming to you! Don't waste a day! Eat, drink, get yours!" This is the basis of his stylization, of the choice of his props. All props should be stylized: they should have a color, shape and weight that spell: style.
>
> *Her problem has to do with her tradition.* Her notion of what a woman should be. She is stuck with this "ideal." It is her ego. Unless she lives by it, she cannot live; in fact her whole life has been for nothing. Even the Alan Gray incident as she now tells it and believes it to have been, is a necessary piece of romanticism. Essentially, in outline, she tells what happened, but it also serves the demands of her notion of herself, to make her *special* and different, out of the tradition of the romantic ladies of the past: Swinburne, Wm. Morris, Pre-Raphaelites, etc. This way it serves as an excuse for a great deal of her behavior.
>
> Because this image of herself cannot be accomplished in reality, certainly not in the South of our day and time, it is her effort and practice *to accomplish it in fantasy.* Everything that she does in *reality* too is discolored by this necessity, this compulsion to be *special.* So, in fact, *reality becomes fantasy too.* She makes it so!
>
> *An effort to phrase Blanche's spine:* to find *protection,* to find something to hold onto, some strength in whose protection she can live, like a sucker shark or a

---

[6]Cole and Chinoy, *Directing the Play.*
[7]Cole and Chinoy, *Directing the Play.*

parasite. The tradition of *woman* (or all women) can only live through the strength of someone else. Blanche is entirely dependent. Finally the doctor![8]

Kazan and Clurman work from a close analysis of the text, probing into the psychological roots of the action. Tyrone Guthrie seems to work in an entirely different manner. In preparing a play he says:

> . . . I should like to discuss what to me is the most interesting part of the job, the blending of intuition with technique. If I may elaborate those terms, by intuition, I mean the expression of a creative idea that comes straight from the subconscious, that is not arrived at by a process of ratiocination at all. It is my experience that all the best ideas in art just arrive, and it is absolutely no good concentrating on them hoping for the best. The great thing is to relax and just trust that the Holy Ghost will arrive and the idea will appear.[9]

[8]Cole and Chinoy, *Directing the Play.*
[9]Tyrone Guthrie, "An Audience of One" in Toby Cole and Helen Krich Chinoy, eds., *Directors on Directing* (Indianapolis: The Bobbs-Merrill Co., Inc., 1964).

Tyrone Guthrie was noted for his innovative interpretations of Shakespearean drama. This scene is from his modern dress production of Hamlet *at the Guthrie Theater, Minneapolis, 1963. The action shows the entrance of the Players. Notice how the director has blocked the actors on the thrust stage so that one can clearly see the action despite the presence of more than a score of performers.*

He goes on to say that inspiration must be backed up by a very "cast-iron technique."

Directors vary not only in their methods of working with actors on their interpretations, but also in their approaches to the script itself. A play exists on many levels at the same time, and the director's interpretation may, therefore, stem from many sources. Craig based his interpretation on color, Reinhardt on spectacle, Stanislavski on characterization. A director may find justification for an analysis in the imagery of the poetry, in significant symbols, or in the atmosphere of the locale. Inspiration for a director's point of view may be found in music, movement, character, scenery, theme, archetypal patterns, or social milieu.

The director working with an established classic very often tries to give his production a fresh interpretation. A celebrated example was Akimov's *Hamlet* (1932) in Leningrad. He wanted to avoid the introspective, hesitant Hamlet and make him an active political strategist played with gusto and with a comic flair. Akimov wanted his audience to be entertained, so he cut some of the morbid lines and introduced considerable music, pageantry, and farcical touches. A particularly striking scene was the play within a play, which was played offstage. A huge stairway ran up the back wall. The king, queen and courtiers paraded up the steps above which were mounted guards in suits of armor. When the King revealed his guilt, he rushed down the stairway in panic trailing a large blood-red cloak. In another Russian production of *Hamlet* (1954), director Okhlopkov interpreted the central action to be Hamlet's efforts to escape from entrapment. The setting was made up of a series of compartments as a visual impression of the director's view of Elsinore as a prison. A more recent Russian *Hamlet* (1975) featured designer David Borovsky's setting whose main element was an enormous black curtain mounted on a center pivot and a track system so that it moved in all directions. The curtain was so flexible that it nearly looked alive, and symbolized the dark, driving force of a corrupt world.

Another celebrated example of a fresh interpretation of a Shakespearean play was Brook's *A Midsummer Night's Dream* (1970) by the Royal Shakespeare Company. In an attempt to avoid the traditional treatment of fairies in enchanted woodlands Brook used an enclosure of white walls with the forest suggested by a structure of coiled metal springs attached to fishing rods. Trapezes that could be adjusted to varying heights were used for flying the performers. Costumes resembled workmen's overalls with a sampling of circus and commedia dell'arte garb thrown in. In this setting, Brook's interpretation became an antiromantic exploration of love rather than the usual idyllic one.

Serban's version of *The Cherry Orchard* at Lincoln Center was a departure from the usually sad, bittersweet interpretations of Chekhov. Instead, the director treated much of the action as broad farce with such business as falls, chases, and adults playing at children's games. Serban also used choreographed groupings of peasants to create vivid images creating a multilayered reading of the text. In his production of *Agamemnon*, again at Lincoln Center, Serban rejected the notion of treating the play in a traditional way. He set the action in a wire cage inside of a pit at the front of the auditorium, and his performers were more concerned with evoking feelings by strong aural and visual signs of the subtext rather than a faithful rendition of an ancient drama. Serban's interpretation of his role as a creative artist was not to show the audience a play, but to involve the spectators in an experience that happened to be theatrical.

Some contemporary directors stress the theatricalized performance for its own sake without regard for the text. Tom O'Horgan, for example, who gained prominence for his productions of *Hair* and *Jesus Christ Superstar*, views theater as a celebration of color, movement, and sound combined in a sensory bombardment at high tension level in which "words are the weakest form of expression." Rather than the staging of a play loaded down with words, O'Horgan's goal is the production as a series of sensations.

Jean Gascon, in his memorable production of *Tartuffe* (1969) at the Stratford Festival in Ontario, Canada, describes his way of working:

> The style can only spring from the heart of a work. After patient spadework when director and actors clumsily try to define the precise sense of every word and thought; the subtlest rhythms of the text, the necessity of movement or gesture at any given moment; after offering themselves as receivers for all the vibrations and signals

Peter Brook's famous Royal Shakespeare Company's production of A Midsummer Night's Dream, *1970, designed by Sally Jacobs.*

Another scene from Brook's A Midsummer Night's Dream *showing the mechanicals rehearsing for "Pyramus and Thisbe." The performers with tangled wires represent trees. Royal Shakespeare Company.*

released on stage during long weeks of rehearsals, sometimes the sum total of all this collective effort results in a style of presentation. . . . At a particular stage of rehearsal, actors have to forget that Molière or Beckett has written the play. They must watch and listen, smell and search with no respite until they can speak and act and be precisely what is required at each and every moment.[10]

In *Tartuffe* Gascon wanted to achieve a fresh approach: "we wanted to strip *Tartuffe* from all the clichés which cluster, above all in the theater, around everything French in the seventeenth century. We hoped to remove the play's corset and free it to breathe and exist in a different setting and epoch.[11]

Sam Shepard, one of the most imaginative of the contemporary American playwrights, worked with an ensemble in San Francisco on *INACOMA*, a play depicting the struggle for survival of a girl who has been seriously injured in an

[10]Jean Gascon, quoted in *The Stratford Scene, 1958–1968*, ed. Peter Raby (Toronto: Clarke, Irwin & Co., 1968).

[11]Raby, *The Stratford Scene*

Tom O'Horgan's Hair *was one of the biggest box-office hits of the '60s. Originally produced at Joseph Papp's Public Theater, the director restaged it on Broadway, where its exuberant spirit caught the public's fancy.*

accident. Shepard in a program note, describes his open approach in shaping the production:

> I've tried to make use of every influence that has moved me. From vaudeville, circuses, the living theater, the open theater, and the whole world of jazz music, trance dances, faith healing ceremonies, musical comedy, Greek tragedy, medicine shows, etc. Our approach has been to include as much information as possible, coming from the material on every level we could find. To try to remain open to any new possibilities and at the same time discard what was unnecessary.[12]

Shepard's views echo the experimental theater's purpose of investigating the outer reaches of an expanding universe, searching for the new and unexpected beyond the prosaic formulas of "tasteless parlor drama." Andre Steiger, who attracted considerable attention with his free interpretation of *Measure for Measure*, says that it is the obligation of the director to take liberties with the text—to share the unmasking with the audience. "The actors must show the distortion between the words and actions of the characters."

[12]Sam Shepard, program note, *INACOMA*, 1977.

In today's theater, some directors are in complete charge, not only of all aspects of production, but sometimes of the company's way of life. They determine the actors' training and preparation, as well as the style and interpretation of a text. In situations in which the ensemble creates its own vehicle for playing through exploration and improvisation, the director can be the guiding hand in the creative process and the ultimate judge of what is to be performed. Grotowski controlled not only the actors' method of working, the material to be played, the place where his company performed, but also the number and location of the spectators. Serban, Garcia, and Brook made drastic changes in theater buildings to elicit new audience-actor relationships. Luca Ronconi decided to stage Kleist's *Kitchen von Heilliron* on barges on a lake in Switzerland.

The Director
as a Craftsman

The director begins as an interpreter of the play. Secondly, the director is a skilled craftsman capable of revealing the full meaning of the play to an audience in tangible theatrical terms.

Although this text is not a manual of play production, nor is it our intent to discuss in detail every phase of the director's function, it may be helpful in understanding the director's contribution to the presentation if we indicate the use of the tool of stage movement.

A play in the theater is dynamic. It is in a continual process of ebb and flow, action and reaction, adjustment and readjustment. Through its characters, changes take place: the frustrated boy finally gets the girl; a woman comes to understand herself through suffering; a hero falls from a high place to catastrophe; the downtrodden little man achieves status.

When Aristotle described the playwright's approach to writing a play, he suggested that the first step was to frame the central action. The director follows a similar process by searching first for the *main action* of the play, sometimes referred to by theater people as the "spine," or the "superobjective." In Clurman's analysis of *The Member of the Wedding*, he found that the main action was to get "connected." Franco Zefferelli in speaking of a production of *Hamlet* saw the hero as "living in a hard world—with no elasticity about it—a closed world, with high walls, no windows, lots of storms. Like a prisoner in a tower." Peter Brook found his approach to *Romeo and Juliet* in a single line: "These hot days is the mad blood stirring." Thus, the director works through the play, line by line and scene by scene, finding the most effective means of forming the action. Sometimes the director envisions almost all the action and gives it to the cast. Other directors set a general framework and then encourage the actor to work creatively within it. Joan Littlewood, the colorful English director, approaches the play through the actor as she did in Behan's *The Quare Fellow*, through improvisation to capture the feel of the play before tackling the script. The play is laid in a Dublin prison, so she had her cast begin by simulating aspects of prison life such as the dull marches in the "yard," and the bleak confinement of cell living.

The director oftentimes concentrates a good deal of attention on blocking out movement, inventing business, and grouping the characters. The playwright may provide directions for such essential plot actions as entrances and exits, duels, love scenes, death scenes, etc., and the context of the lines may provide clues for movement. For instance, it is clear in Act I, scene 1 of *Hamlet* that Horatio joins the soldiers in their vigil, that the ghost enters, and that the three watchers attempt unsuccessfully to restrain him. But the director must go far beyond this bare framework of action to devise movement and groupings which will bring out the full dramatic content of the scene. The director is concerned not only with *what* happens but also with *how* an action is performed. How does the ghost make his appearance? How does Horatio's expression of fear differ from that of the soldiers? How does Horatio attempt to stay the ghost?

Since a play is dynamic, the attention of the audience must be shifted constantly from one character to another. Unlike the motion-picture director who can concentrate the camera on a specific person or object at will, eliminating from the screen all extraneous matter, the stage director must find other means to evoke and sustain a steady flow of attention. One of the most important means for this purpose is the use of movement. For example, the opening scene of *Hamlet* is a rather simple one since it is short, relatively uncomplicated and requires only five characters; yet the movement and grouping need careful planning (see pages 5−7 and 16−17). The director's primary consideration probably will be to establish the audience's acceptance of the ghost. Most likely it will be kept remote from the audience, played in dim light and deep shadow, and perhaps elevated in position. The actor must be able to move freely and without noise so that entrances and exits create the illusion of an apparition in space. The attempts of Horatio and the soldiers to strike at the ghost must not destroy the feeling of majesty and dignity of the dead king. In the grouping of the three watchers, Horatio must be given the dominant position since the others look to him for counsel. Moreover, he carries the burden of the dialogue and has several long speeches, so that he must be placed in an advantageous position to project his lines to the audience.

The director uses blocking to create the appropriate emotional climate for the action. As we have seen with the opening of *Hamlet* the director may have to search the dialogue for clues. On the other hand, many modern dramatists provide very specific directions. As an example, John Osborne's *Look Back in Anger* which started the "new wave" of British drama, begins with a detailed description of a flat in a Victorian house followed by these stage directions:

> *At rise of curtain:* Jimmy and Cliff are seated in the two armchairs R and L, respectively. All that we can see of either of them is two pairs of legs, sprawled way out beyond the newspapers which hide the rest of them from sight. They are both reading. Beside them, and between them, is a jungle of newspapers and weeklies. When we do eventually see them, we find that Jimmy is a tall, thin young man about

twenty-five, wearing a very worn tweed jacket and flannels. Clouds of smoke fill the room from the pipe he is smoking. He is a disconcerting mixture of sincerity and cheerful malice, of tenderness and freebooting cruelty; restless, importunate, full of pride, a combination which alienates the sensitive and insensitive alike. Blistering honesty, or apparent honesty, like his, makes few friends. To many he may seem sensitive to the point of vulgarity. To others, he is simply a loudmouth. To be as vehement as he is, is to be almost non-committal. Cliff is the same age, short, dark, big-boned, wearing a pullover and gray, new, but very creased trousers. He is easy and relaxed, almost to lethargy, with the rather sad, natural intelligence of the self-taught. If Jimmy alienates love, Cliff seems to exact it—demonstrations of it, at least, even from the cautious. He is a soothing, natural counterpart to Jimmy. Standing L, below the food cupboard, is Alison. She is leaning over an ironing board. Beside her is a pile of clothes. Hers is the most elusive personality to catch in the uneasy polyphony of these three people. She is tuned in a different key, a key of well-bred malaise that is often drowned in the robust orchestration of the other two. Hanging over the grubby, but expensive, skirt she is wearing, is a cherry red shirt of Jimmy's, but she manages somehow to look quite elegant in it. She is roughly the same age as the men. Somehow, their combined physical oddity makes her beauty more striking than it really is. She is tall, slim, dark. The bones of her face are long and delicate. There is a surprising reservation about her eyes, which are so large and deep they should make equivocation impossible. The room is still, smoke-filled. The only sound is the occasional thud of Alison's iron on the board. It is one of those chilly spring evenings, all cloud and shadows. Presently, Jimmy throws his paper down.[13]

Few playwrights give such detailed assistance to the director and actor in establishing mood. Usually the directors, with the assistance of the actors, must rely on their own ingenuity to create atmosphere. Sometimes a director will invent an entirely new scene in order to provide the appropriate mood for an interpretation.

The Director at Work

The director blocks the action of the play to indicate character relationships. Congenial people draw together; enemies keep their distance until there is a showdown when they are brought face to face in open conflict. The director shows the moment-by-moment psychological interrelationships of the characters by graphic representation. Performers must be given opportunities to act out their emotions, to give pictorial evidence of the psychological climate of the social environment. A dominating figure may be given an elevated position, face front, emphasized by a bright light, a striking costume, visual focus, movement; a subservient character may grovel on the floor, in dim light, in a drab costume, closed in from the audience. The director composes a series of constantly changing pictures that present the emotional states of the characters. The director is concerned with all aspects of movement—its extent, speed, shape, direction, length, the position of the mover, manner of moving, and the

[13]John Osborne, *Look Back in Anger* (Chicago: The Dramatic Publishing Company, 1959).

relationship of the performer's action to the furniture, scenery, and other characters.

The first scene in *Hamlet* suggests that Bernardo, Marcellus, and Horatio are closely allied; they are friendly men sharing a common objective. The cold night and the atmosphere of foreboding draws them together. The ghost enters and they recoil in fear from the dreadful sight. Horatio recovers himself, bravely assumes command, and advances on the ghost pursuing him until he disappears in the darkness. Then the watchers are joined together again trying to find answers to the questions which the appearance of the ghost has raised. This opening scene with its homogeneity of grouping makes an interesting contrast to the one which follows in which Claudius and Gertrude are holding court. They make overtures to soothe the troubled and alienated Hamlet, but he spurns their efforts and isolates himself from the king and queen and those who seek royal favors.

Another function of the director closely allied to the blocking of movement is that of inventing and assisting the actor in creating "stage business," by which we mean the detailed actions of the individual characters, such as using a cane, opening a letter, pouring tea, smoking a pipe, etc. Stage business is similar to movement in its uses. In general, it is the director's and actor's way of giving life and verisimilitude to the acting of a play. Again, like movement, business may be inherent in the playwright's script, such as Hedda burning Lövberg's manuscript, Juliet drinking the potion, and Captain Boyle cooking his "sassige." However, much of the business that is not essential to the plot but is necessary for enriching the performance is imposed on the presentation by the inventiveness of the director and actor. This is especially true in comedy where one of the marks of the skilled performer is ingenuity in creating original business.

The following example records Stanislavski's preparation for a performance of *Othello* at the Moscow Art Theatre in 1929. This excerpt shows Stanislavski's way of interpreting the first few lines of the scene in Act III when Othello, his suspicions aroused, comes to Desdemona's bedchamber. The first line is spoken by Emilia, Desdemona's nurse.

Emilia: Look, where he comes.

(In the last pause Emilia hears steps below. She rushes to the stairs, sees Othello coming and then hurries to Desdemona so as not to be compelled to call out. Her movement shows alarm and excitement.)

Emilia thinks differently from Desdemona. She did not like Othello's behavior during the day. It does not seem the way to spend one's time during the first days of one's marriage.

Hearing that he is coming and thinking of last night's wonders, Desdemona wants to meet him suitably. She runs to the mirror to touch up her hair.

Emilia waits respectfully at the stairs to disappear at the first opportune moment and not to disturb the husband and wife.

Desdemona: I will not leave him now till Cassio
Be call'd to him.

She speaks these words while smartening herself up. Her hair done, she runs to the banisters to meet Othello.

(*Enter* Othello)

Pause. Othello's entry should be delayed to underline its significance. He enters trying to seem cheerful and cordial at all costs and not make Desdemona see how he feels inside.

> How is't with you, my lord?

She speaks, leaning over the banisters. Thus their meeting takes place as follows: flirting lightly, Desdemona at the banisters, looking at him questioningly and trying to find out how he is, while Othello stops on the stairs, having had not time to come up yet. Their heads are on a level.

Othello: Well, my good lady. O, hardness to dissemble! (*Aside*)

He tries to sound cheerful. Desdemona suddenly puts her arms around him over the banisters, leaving his head uncovered. His face is turned to the audience, she is showing the back of her head.

> How do you, Desdemona?

Desdemona stops dead still in the embrace. He starts at it. The embrace is intolerable, but he restrains himself. One can see by his arms how he would like to, but he cannot make himself, put them around her. His face shows suffering. The embrace over, however, he will try again to seem, if not gay, at least calm.

By the way—it would be better were the actor to make it his task to be cheerful; should he not succeed in being sincere about it, even better: this failure will accentuate the artificiality which Othello requires at the moment.

Pause. This scene of meeting and embrace must be played right through to the end; do not be afraid of prolonging the pause.[14]

Directors in the New Theater

The directors we have been discussing were mostly concerned with traditional drama and conventional practices. What of the director involved in the new forms of theater?

As we have seen, Brecht in his "epic theater" was attempting to find a new way of writing and producing plays. His situation was unique in that he was a playwright, and a theorist, and a producer. He was able to demonstrate his theories with his own plays at the Berliner Ensemble—and his effects were revolutionary.

When Brecht worked with actors on the production of his own plays, he constantly struggled against the old tendencies of empathic identification as he tried to establish the alienation effect. His purpose was to induce the spectators to evaluate critically the onstage events and to relate them to the social and

[14]Konstantin Sergeevich Alekseev, *Stanislavski Produces Othello,* trans. Helen Nowak (London: Bles, 1948).

Scene from Brecht's The Life of Galileo, *at the Berliner Ensemble.*

economic conditions of the real world, so that they might work for change. One of his favorite ways of explaining to his casts the quality of playing he wanted was to cite the example of a witness describing a traffic accident he had seen. The acting was "not to cast a spell over anyone, but to repeat something which had already occurred"; that is, "the incident *has* taken place, the repetition *is* taking place."

In the notes which he prepared for the production of *Mother Courage*, Brecht describes the business in detail for each of the characters involved. For example, in Kattrin's drumming scene he provided a complete scenario of action for the soldiers, peasants, and Kattrin, including the kind of actions and the attitudes of the participants.

Kattrin's action must "steer free of heroic cliché," Brecht said, and the scene must avoid "wild excitement." In order to counteract the temptation toward emotional involvement he suggested that the soldiers should appear apathetic, Kattrin's drumming should be interrupted, and the peasants' dialogue be spoken as though secondhand. For example, one peasant says, "The watchman will give us warning." Brecht was attempting to avoid the immediate impression of "unique, actual horror" in order to give the effect of repeated

Bertolt Brecht directing Mother Courage *at the Munich Kammerspiele, 1950.*

misfortune. "Fear must show through the ceremony in this scene." But despite these efforts to achieve objectivity Brecht had to admit: "Spectators may identify themselves with Dumb Kattrin in this scene; they may project their personality into this creature; and may happily feel that such forces are present in them, too."

At the end of the play when Mother Courage, completely alone in an unfriendly universe, drags her wagon into the gathering darkness, Brecht

225

In Mother Courage, *Kattrin drums on the roof to warn the village of the approaching enemy soldiers. Although Brecht wanted no excitement, the scene is so emotionally loaded that it is difficult to avoid involvement. (Prague National Theater. Designed by Josef Svoboda). [Compare with Berliner Ensemble production.]*

intended the audience to see her as an object lesson of one whose life and energies have been wasted in the traffic of war of which she is a willing part. But the solitary image was so loaded that the premiere in Zurich created a strong empathic response of compassion. Brecht is reported to have rewritten the part in an effort to make Courage less sympathetic.

Despite the fact that he was never able to reconcile his theories completely with the effects his plays created in the theater, Brecht gave the modern director a new and provocative way of using the actors and the stage.

Jerzy Grotowski's creative work as director of the Polish Laboratory Theater was unique since its orientation was spiritual rather than theatrical, and he served not merely as a stage director but as a secular priest providing a means of individual self-development directed toward "a search for the truth about himself and his mission in life." His actors underwent a demanding discipline and a rigorous program of training which made their performances before small, selected audiences an impressive exploration of the uses of theater. The heavy demands on the actor and the limited availability of Grotowski's theater to the public restricted his influence and few will attain his degree of commitment, but he has given us an authentic example of the dramatic potential of ritual and myth.

Peter Brook is a contemporary director who, although schooled in the traditional theater, is acutely aware of the drawbacks of what he calls the "deadly theater." He is responsive to and challenged by the new forces at work on the stage, and by word and example he points the way to the future. His approach is geared to answer his own question: "The whole problem of the theater today is just this: how can we make plays dense in experience?" As a partial answer, he seeks a theater which has the same freedom and "density" as that of Shakespeare. He says:

> Shakespeare seems better in performance that anyone else because he gives us more, moment for moment, for our money. This is due to his genius, but also to his technique. the possibilities of free verse on an open stage enabled him to cut the inessential detail and the irrelevant realistic action: in their place he could cram sounds and ideas, thoughts and images which make each instant into a stunning mobile.[15]

In his controversial production of Weiss's *Marat/Sade*, Brook fashioned a "total theater" out of a welter of sensory stimuli that resulted in the "density" he was talking about and that links him to Artaud. His production offered an emotional impact that recalls primitive ritual in its use of incantation, ensemble miming, discordant music, and the force of the acting, which seemed to be on several levels at once. The action of the play is set in a madhouse where the inmates act out their fantasies, giving the director unique opportunities for theatricality and macabre business, such as the mass guillotining to the accompaniment of raucous sound effects, and the pouring of red paint down the drains, as some of the inmates jump into a cavity so that only their heads show next to the guillotine.

Weiss uses the asylum metaphorically to suggest the state of the world outside. The play was influential not only for the devices of the "theater of cruelty" in production but also for the combination of social and political arguments with stunning theatricalism.

Peter Brook found much to admire in its theatrical richness.

> . . . It is above all in the jangle produced by the clash of styles. Everything is put in its place by its neighbour—the serious by the comic, the noble by the popular, the literary by the crude, the intellectual by the physical: the abstraction is vivified by the stage image, the violence illuminated by the cool flow of thought. The strands of meaning of the play pass to and fro through its structure and the result is a very complex form: as in Genêt, it is a hall of mirrors or a corridor of echoes—and one must keep looking front and back all the time to reach the author's sense.[16]

Preliminary to the production of *Marat/Sade*, Peter Brook and Charles Marowitz set up an experimental acting workshop affiliated with the Royal Shakespeare Company. Its purpose was to experiment with new kinds of acting—not the Stanislavski approach with its search for inner authenticity, but toward Artaud's vision of shaping the image of communication from a sequence of movements and gestures. The actors experimented with such exercises as one actor beginning to improvise a pantomime, a second actor recognizing the

[15]Peter Brook, Introduction to Peter Weiss's *Marat/Sade* (New York: Atheneum Publishers, 1965).
[16]Brook, Weiss's, *Marat/Sade*.

action and joining in with a related piece of business. A variation of this exercise was for the second, third, and subsequent actors to avoid relationships to preserve their own isolation. Other experiments involved disconnected incidents played as separate fragments without logical character or developmental relationships. The actors were stimulated to respond to change, to play games and scenes in which their attention would be on the subtext to merge actions with disparate moods and rhythms. It is apparent from the nature of these exercises that Brook was seeking the "density" of experiences he was speaking of earlier, and at least a partial realization of a theater of cruelty. It should also be clear that Brook's acknowledged admiration for Brecht's alienation concept was at work in the striking theatricality, the discontinuity, and the specific locale and characters distanced by the larger view.

An ensemble that has gained reputation for the excellence of its production through workshop techniques is Ariane Mnouchkine's Théâtre du Soleil in France. Three of its outstanding works are *1789 (The Revolution Must End with the Perfection of Happiness)* (1970) *1793 (The Revolutionary City Is of This World)* (1972), and *The Age of Gold* (1975). The Théâtre du Soleil began in 1964 as a workers' collective and attracted attention with compelling performances of Gorki's *The Courageous One* and Wesker's *The Kitchen*. But the company wanted to dramatize historical events from a popular point of view to show how "people might imagine, feel, live and suffer during the Revolution." *1789*, its most compelling effort, was created during rehearsals and workshops by the collective over long months of preparation in an attempt to retain the best material. The actors' performances were improvised to the extent that no one knew precisely what the other actor would do or say. As a part of its training, the company visited small villages where it tried out its material and acting on unsophisticated audiences. Mnouchkine's company achieved a highly theatrical acting style that was consciously coarse, free from psychological nuances. Although the Théâtre du Soleil rejected the playhouse, preferring to perform in an abandoned cartridge factory, the technical aspects of theater are considered very important, especially the lighting.

The basic changes in directing in recent years have been in new approaches to performance and the material. In the past the director aimed at bringing a text to life by giving the lines a careful reading, selecting and training the actors for accurate, credible characterization, and using the technical resources as support in presenting a dramatic work as a cohesive whole. Now the theatricalist often presents a series of sensations, which instead of showing characters involved in a story with a tidy plot line, creates an event—an occasion of songs, images, words, sensations, and effects that generate striking moments by their layered stimuli or compelling juxtapositions through incongruous relationships.

The modern director does not follow the conventional pattern suggested earlier. The interpretation of the material and the blocking of the action often comes out of ensemble experimentation in rehearsals and workshops. Indeed, the text itself may be a joint creation, or in performance actors may improvise dialogue and action. But still, the guiding hand of a director usually shapes the work.

Luca Ronconi's production of Orlando Furioso *that was first played in Italy, then elsewhere in Europe and America. The performance was staged on wheeled platforms in a large open space, among the audience which moved about to follow the action that was often multiplefocused and simultaneous.*

Some critics of the new theater resent the authority that directors wield over the production of a play, but the temper of our times suggests that the strong-minded individual with original ideas will continue to have a free hand. Innovations of recent years, particularly those in which directors emphasize performance over fidelity to the text, point toward even more stress on theatricalism—ritual, total theater, environmental theater, epic theater, open theater—even antitheater. While the traditionalist may be wary of some of the chances the daring director takes, it is from the inspiration of such leaders that much of the most exciting theater has come.

Bibliography

BROOK, PETER, *The Empty Space.* London: MacGibbon and Kee, 1968.
CARTER, HUNTLEY, *The Theater of Max Reinhardt.* London: F. and C. Palmer, 1914.
CLURMAN, HAROLD, *On Directing.* New York: Macmillan Publishing Co., Inc., 1972.

COHEN, ROBERT, and JOHN HARROP, *Creative Play Direction*. Englewood Cliffs, N.J.: Prentice-Hall, Inc., 1974.

COLE, TOBY, and H. K. CHINOY, eds., *Directors on Directing*. Indianapolis: The Bobbs-Merrill Co., Inc., 1964.

GUTHRIE, TYRONE, *In Various Directions*. New York: Macmillan, Inc., 1965.

HOUGHTON, NORRIS, *Moscow Rehearsals*, New York: Harcourt Brace Javanovich, Inc., 1936.

————, *Return Engagement*. New York: Holt, Rinehart and Winston, 1962.

JACOBS, SUSAN, *On Stage: The Making of a Broadway Play*. New York: Alfred A. Knopf, Inc., 1972.

KOTT, JAN, *Theater Notebook*, New York: Doubleday & Co., Inc., 1968

MORRISON, HUGH, *Directing in the Theater*. New York: Theatre Arts Books, 1973.

SAYLER, OLIVER M., *Max Reinhardt and His Theater*, New York: Brentano's, 1924.

STANISLAVSKI, CONSTANTIN, *My Life in Art*. New York: Theatre Arts Books, 1924.

TAIROV, ALEXANDER, *Notes of a Director*. Coral Gables: University of Miami Press, 1969.

NINE

The
Actor

The Actor's Contribution

The life force of the theater is the living actors playing before an audience. Our mechanical age may find ways to record their voices and movement on film and ship their likenesses from here to there in a small can, and their images may be projected in enormous colored enlargements on wide screens in immense drive-in lots, or their range of action may be reduced to a 21-inch frame within our living room, but genuine theater begins and ends with the actors' living presence. Their creations and interpretations give the theater its special quality. More than the stage settings or the director's skill in organization, sometimes more than the drama itself, it is the actors who give to the theater its reason for existence. It is their histrionic sensibility that induces the audience to live imaginatively in the characters and drama before them. It is the actors who ignite the spark and fan the flame that warms and illuminates the audience.

As we have seen earlier, the impulse to imitate, to impersonate, to act, is a very old one in the race and a very early one in our own lives. Because of the peculiarly subjective and intimate nature of acting, the creative processes of the actor are difficult to define and describe. Since acting is a private creation, actors may work through intuition and the unconscious, by means which they do not fully comprehend themselves. Actors, like other artists, vary widely in their methods of approach. Some actors insist that they must have complete emo-

Actresses Dressing in a Barn, *an engraving by William Hogarth, 1738, showing the vicissitudes of performers on the road.*

tional identification with the characters they are playing; others are equally adamant that acting is a matter of technique. Interestingly enough, exponents of both extremes can cite examples of brilliant actors in defense of their position.

Not only do the actors' approaches to their roles vary with individuals, but they are prisoners of their times, and especially of the kind of drama in which they appear. Although a modern actor like Laurence Olivier may play in many styles of drama from Sophocles to Shakespeare to Wilde, an Elizabethan actor like Richard Burbage was obliged to play according to the style of his own period. And no one approach serves all actors in all styles. An Athenian actor in the fifth century B.C. might have been called upon to play several roles in three different plays in a single day, speaking, dancing, and singing before an outdoor audience of thousands. Compare the Greek actor's task with that of a performer in Japanese Noh drama who plays in an intimate theater seating several hundred people at the most. He performs in an elaborate costume, speaking the archaic language of the old aristocracy, chanting, singing, and dancing within a six-meter-square stage, his every sound and gesture based on tradition, striving to give a performance worthy of his ancestors who played the same role six or seven generations before him. Consider the difference in demands on contemporary performers when they move from the stage to the screen. In a hit show on Broadway, their chief problem may be how to keep their performances as spontaneous and credible on the 300th night as on the first. The same actors working in motion pictures may satisfy the director if they can give a series of satisfactory performances of a few seconds' duration in two to six takes over a period of two weeks. There is no one approach that can be applied to all acting roles from Oedipus to Willy Loman, Scapin to Daddy Warbucks, Lady Macbeth to Blanche, Medea to Liza Doolittle, Mrs. Malaprop to Lady Bracknell. There is no one acting style suitable for the naturalism of Gorki, the stylized Kabuki drama of Japan, the neoclassicism of Racine, the romantic comedy of Shakespeare, the sophisticated comedy of Congreve, the expressionism of Strindberg, the epic parables of Brecht, the open theater of Chaikin, the sensual, frenetic style demanded by O'Horgan, or the impersonal puppets who become part of the scenery in Robert Wilson's visual displays. The actors' performances vary with the conditions under which they work, and while there is no rigid formula that can be applied for all plays and all theaters, there are certain basic qualities that obtain.

Requisites of the Actor

The first requisite concerns the actor's physical equipment. With the wide variety of roles available in drama, actors may be almost any size and shape, but whatever their physical endowments, they must have their bodies under as precise a control as violinists have over their fingers and instruments. The actor should move and gesture easily and in a variety of ways to fit the demands of different kinds of characters and plays. They should be as comfortable playing on a bare stage picked out in a cone of light as they are in a modern living room

Farce often required a great deal of physical activity. Expressive pantomimic movement is clearly evident in this production of Feydeau's Flea in Her Ear *at Wayne State Theater, directed by Richard Spear, designed by William Rowe.*

with chairs, cocktails, and cigarettes. They must have a feeling for movement that is expressive and meaningful, not only in their overt gestures but in a constant stream of subtle, nearly hidden images that reveal character and motivation to the audience. Their movements must not be mere posturing: The first law of stage deportment is that every movement should have a meaning and purpose. Actors should be imaginative in the invention of business by which they enrich the characters, indicate the mood, create atmosphere, or reveal emotions. They should be able to handle their props and costumes not only in authentic ways, but to use them in reinforcement of the meaning of their lines and characters. Stanislavski, who is generally thought of in terms of character motivation, was thoroughly insistent on the actors' training of their bodies so they possessed supple and expressive instruments. In a class session with his students he demonstrated his skill with a fan in order to convince them of the need for control over the "language of objects." Gorchakov, a visiting director in Moscow, describes Stanislavski's demonstration:

> Then he showed us how one should talk with a fan. The fan quivered in his hand like the wings of a wounded bird, revealing his excitement. Stanislavski's figure, face and half-closed eyes were seemingly calm. Only the movement of his hand and a slight

Stoppard's Jumpers *made extraordinary demands in physical movement. American Conservatory Theater production, San Francisco.*

trembling of the closed fan showed his inner excitement. Then the fan opened with a sharp impulsive movement, flying up and hiding his face for an instant, and just as suddenly it lowered and closed. We understood that in this brief moment the face hidden by the fan had time to give vent to feeling and time for a deep sigh or a short laugh. And it was possible that the hand lightly brushed away a tear with the aid of the fan. Then the fan, with scarcely a noticeable movement, ordered someone supposedly nearby to come closer and sit next to him. The fan stopped trembling. It opened calmly and began to sway softly in his hand as though listening attentively to the person sitting next to him. Then the fan smiled and even laughed. "We swore to him later that that's exactly what we heard." The fan closed again for a second and lightly struck the hand of the person next to him as though saying, "Oh, you are mean!"—and then suddenly covered the blushing face. Now his eyes entered the conversation. First they sparkled under the lace-edged fan; then they looked over the fan and half hid behind it. [1]

[1]Nikolai M. Gorchakov, *Stanislavski Directs*, trans. Miriam Goldina (New York: Funk & Wagnalls, Inc., 1958).

Another colorful collection of characters—peasant women and beggars in Ansky's The Dybbuk. *Mark Taper Forum. Directed by John Hirsch.*

A second requisite of the actor is clear and flexible speech. The performer's voice should be free from tension, monotony, and unpleasantness, and it should carry easily to all parts of the theater. Actors must be able to read a range of materials, from the verses of Shakespeare and Sophocles to the terse colloquialism of Pinter. They must communicate the full intellectual and emotional content of each line as it relates to their characters and the play as a whole. They must sustain long narrative passages and soliloquies or engage in the rapid repartee of smart comedy with precise timing that maintains the pace, without stepping on laughs. They must be part of an ensemble reading their lines in context with other players in the appropriate action and reaction.

The speaking skill of an excellent performer is apparent from critic Eliot Norton's description of Zoe Caldwell's performance as Cleopatra at the Ontario Stratford Festival production of Shakespeare's *Antony and Cleopatra.* Norton said:

> Miss Caldwell has an astonishing voice. She can purr like a lioness, hiss like an adder or, when anger shakes her Cleopatra, bellow out words with the power of a

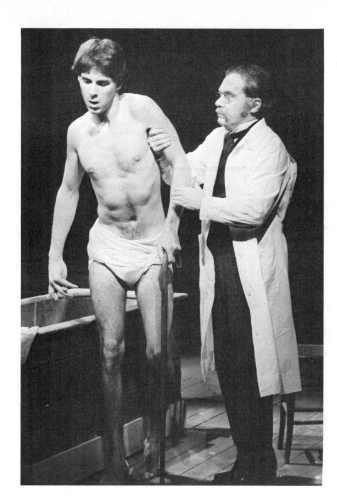

In Bernard Pomerance's The Elephant Man, *enormous physical demands are placed upon the actor when he must convey the impression of a grotesquely deformed character without the use of makeup. Phillip Anglim as John Merrick; Kevin Conway as Dr. Frederick Treves.*

boat whistle. . . . She did many remarkable things. Her Cleopatra, for example, spoke most of the time quite rapidly, which is fair and reasonable, for the woman's mind works rapidly and her eloquence is unlimited. Yet she was at all times easily and clearly audible. Whether brooding or bellowing her Cleopatra made her points with exquisite clarity and with the kind of music which is present in the verse.[2]

Finally, the actor must possess a quality difficult to define, which the great French actor Talma referred to as an "excess of sensibility." He meant by this a vivid imagination and an acute awareness which is indicated by the actor's insight into the role, an understanding of what the play and the character are all about, and in performance, a keen sense of the effect on the audience and the other members of the cast. One of the deadliest defects of actors is the inability to assess the effect of their performance, especially in comedy when, in striving too hard to "milk" laughs, insensitive actors unconsciously destroy themselves. The actors' sensibility enables them to perceive the response they are receiving

[2]Eliot Norton, quoted in *The Stratford Scene, 1958–1968,* ed. Peter Raby (Toronto: Clarke, Irwin & Co.), 1968.

and to project the playwright's full meaning in performances that are highly personal and unique, yet fitting and compelling, merging smoothly into the total effect of the production.

Beyond these three attributes, many people would suggest that the actor needs to possess a spark, a magnetism, a personality that projects out to the audience and woos and wins it. Many of our popular stars, especially in motion pictures, may have this as their sole talent.

Evolution of Modern Acting

Up until modern times, actors learned their trade mostly by observation and experience. In the past, the stagestruck youth watched the stars in action, became an apprentice, and worked his way up from a spear-carrier to a speaking part, assimilating what he could by his contact with the veterans. The beginner might be taken under the wing of an experienced actor or a sympathetic manager and be given pointers about acting, but, in general, newcomers were left pretty much to their own inspiration, imagination, and powers of observation. A number of published works appeared from time to time on elocution, oratory, rhetoric, and stage deportment, chiefly emphasizing oral interpretation and the use of the voice, and there were occasional attempts to define characteristic emotional states and to relate them to specific postures, gestures, vocal qualities, and facial expressions, but these were entirely subjective and mechanical. The great teacher was the theater itself, where through trial and error actors groped for interpretation and perfected their technique for achieving effects. Those who struck the public's fancy at their first attempt in the major theater centers were fortunate. Others, like Molière and Mrs. Siddons, two of the greatest performers of all time, met with initial failure and had to spend years in the outlying provincial theaters, mastering their craft before making triumphant returns to Paris and London.

In the latter half of the nineteenth century, as a part of the scientific revolution in which nearly everything was examined, classified, and catalogued, a Frenchman, Delsarte, devised an elaborate system of acting based on purely mechanical techniques. He found in each person a trinity consisting of the torso, the "vital zone"; the head, the "intellectual zone"; and the face, the "moral zone." Each zone and every part of the mechanisms were in turn divided into trinities, each producing its own specific expression. The student of Delsarte learned to act by memorizing and utilizing the appropriate gestures, vocal qualities, and inflections.

This artificial and external school of acting was opposed to another approach based on the inner life of the character being portrayed. In part this new method resulted from the contemporary interest in psychology, but the strongest impulse came from the new drama of realism and naturalism, in which playwrights took their cues from the scientist, attempting to record with strict fidelity the observed facts of human existence, even though they showed an individual in commonplace or sordid surroundings. Because the new science taught that a person was conditioned by environment, naturalistic playwrights depicted the physical surroundings in accurate detail as a causal force in their characters' motivation and behavior.

In 1877, Henri Becque, responding to the new influence, wrote a naturalistic play called *The Vultures*, a somber study of what happens to domestic life when the forces of the economic jungle prey on helpless and unsuspecting victims. In 1882, the Comédie Française was persuaded to give the play a production but, unfortunately, it was played in the traditional style of acting in which the performers declaimed with exaggerated gestures and inflections, rising from their chairs for their speeches and directing much of their dialogue to the audience, thus destroying the atmosphere of Becque's play. It was not until 1887, when Antoine gave *The Vultures* a sympathetic and effective performance at the Théâtre Libre, that the full impact of the drama was realized. Antoine recognized the need for a new way of acting in the new plays and demonstrated his ideas in performances in which he and his casts attempted to become completely absorbed in their roles, using such unconventional stage behavior as turning their backs on the audiences and speaking in a conversational manner with the fragmentary gestures of real life.

Antoine's ideas took root and a revolution occurred in the theater, driving out the old inflated bombastic acting with its pyrotechnic displays of the stars. The ground was ready for the modern style of acting, but it was not a one-sided victory. While the old exhibitionist school of acting had its faults in its wallowing emotionalism, it was also true that traditional actors could make verse sing, and they knew how to win and hold an audience in the palm of their hands. The virtues that Antoine brought to modern acting were a style that was simple, restrained, and uncluttered with mannerisms and posturing. But in relinquishing the old traditions, many contemporary actors lost much of their unique flair and flavor when they donned their blank mask. John Mason Brown aptly referred to the new style as the "transom school of acting," in which there are "teacup comedians and gas-jet tragedians."

The playwrights who wrote in a naturalistic or realistic manner introduced a new type of character to the theater audience. The protagonists were no longer picaresque heroes, romantic adventurers, or highbrow ladies and gentlemen in evening clothes. They might be middle or lower class protagonists—often the victims of their environments or their passions. Many of these characters were psychologically complex, because the primary purpose of the new dramatists might be the revelation of conflicting desires that resulted in aberrant conduct. Strindberg indicates the complex motivation of his protagonist in *Miss Julie:*

> And what will offend simple brains is that my action cannot be traced back to a single motive, that the viewpoint is not always the same. An event in real life—and this discovery is quite recent—springs generally from a whole series of more or less deep-lying motives, but of these the spectator chooses as a rule the one his reason can master most easily. A suicide is committed. Bad business, says the merchant. Unrequited love, say the ladies. Sickness says the invalid. Crushed hopes say the shipwrecked. Now it may be that the motive lay in all or none of these directions.[3]

[3]August Strindberg, "Preface to *Miss Julie*," in *Plays of Strindberg*, vol. 1, trans. Edith and Warner Oland (New York: Bruce Humphries, 1912).

The Stanislavski Method
of Acting

With the demands of this new kind of characterization, it was inevitable, as Antoine insisted, that new methods of acting should be devised. The most famous and most important innovator was Constantin Stanislavski, who not only wrote at length about his method of acting but also demonstrated his ideas through his teaching, his directing, and his own acting. The great Russian actor-director worked out his system at the Moscow Art Theater, of which he was one of the founders. As the result of years of experience in the theater, and of his self-analysis and the observation of others, he formulated his method of acting during the first decade of the twentieth century. His ideas were made known in his three books, *My Life in Art, An Actor Prepares,* and *Building the Character,* and through his work with his students and actors, a number of whom became teachers, spreading his gospel throughout the theatrical world.

The Stanislavski "method" is not an eccentric style of acting for psyched-up performers who are off on an emotional jag. It is not based on sheer raw feeling without consideration of the techniques and skills of movement and speech. These common misconceptions about the method are the result of the notoriety of some of the actors who have misunderstood, misapplied, or distorted the basic tenets that Stanislavski formulated.

Stanislavski's purpose was to devise an objective, regularized technique by which the actor could gain control of his body and emotions for the appropriate interpretation of his character and the play. Instead of depending on haphazard inspiration, Stanislavski searched for a system with basic principles by which the actor could discipline his art. Much of his emphasis was in *preparing to act* by means of a conscious technique for causing inspiration as a conditioned response. His books are full of examples by which he sought the practical application of his techniques as he worked with students and actors.

The following explanation of his thinking is in Stanislavski's own words. He is explaining his method to Gorchakov.

Now what are these basic principles of my method? First, my method gives no recipes for becoming a great actor or for playing a part. My method is the way to the actor's correct state of being on the stage. The correct state is the normal state of a human being in life. But it's very difficult for an actor to create this state on the stage. He must be physically free, must control his muscles, and must have limitless attention. He must be able to hear and see on the stage the same as he does in life. He must be able to communicate with his partner and to accept the given circumstances of the play completely.

I suggest a series of exercises to develop these qualities. You must do these every day, just as a singer or pianist does his scales and arpeggios.

My second principle concerns the correct state of being on stage. This calls for the correct actions in the progressive unfolding of the play: inner psychological actions and outer physical actions. I separate the actions in this manner intentionally. It makes it easier for us to understand each other during rehearsal. As a matter of fact, every physical action has an inner psychological action which gives rise to it. And in

240

every psychological inner action there is always a physical action which expresses its psychic nature; the unity between these two is organic on the stage. It is defined by the theme of the play, its idea, its characters, and the given circumstances. In order to make it easier for himself, an actor must put *himself* into the given circumstances. You must say to yourself, "What would I do *if* all that happens to this character happened to me?" I believe this *if* (I call it jokingly the magic *if*) helps an actor to begin to *do* on the stage. After you have learned to act from yourself, define the differences between your behavior and that of the character. Find all the reasons and justifications for the character's actions, and then go on from there without thinking where your personal actions end and the character's begin. His actions and yours will fuse automatically, if you have done the preceding work as I suggested.

The third principle of the method—the correct organic (inner plus outer)—will necessarily give rise to the correct feeling, especially if an actor finds a good basis for it. The sum of these three principles—correct state of being, actions and feelings—will give to your characters an organic life on the stage. This is the road which will bring you closest to what we call metamorphosis. Of course this takes for granted that you have understood the play correctly—its idea and its theme—and that you have analyzed the character accurately. And beyond all this, the actor must have a good appearance, clear and energetic diction, plastic movement, a sense of rhythm, temperament, taste and the infectious quality we often call charm.[4]

To develop the ability to control the state of being, Stanislavski prescribed a rigorous program of training, which, in addition to dance, fencing, movement, and voice and diction, included a series of exercises on concentration, observation, imagination, and improvisation. Considerable emphasis was also given to the analysis of plays and characters, seeking out the basic meanings and objectives as the so-called spine of interpretation.

A factor contributing to the misinterpretation of the Stanislavski method was that his *An Actor Prepares* appeared in English translation 13 years before *Building the Character* was available. The earlier book emphasizes an internal approach to acting and it was this aspect to which many actors and teachers gave their attention. Although *Building the Character* stresses much more the technique and training of the voice and body, it was not as widely read and followed as Stanislavski's earlier volume; therefore the method was often incomplete or distorted in practice.

Stanislavski in his early work developed the technique of "emotional memory" by which the actor is supposed to be able to draw upon personal experience in recreating its emotional content for performance. It was an intriguing idea, but the technique has its drawbacks—the actor's recall lacks spontaneity or the memory of the emotion may be faulty. Stanislavski himself abandoned the technique, but it was remarkably persistent and has its advocates to this day; they find in it a valid rehearsal technique for character analysis and sometimes for therapy. Another way of attacking problems, character motivation, and emotional states, popularized by Stanislavski, was the use of improvisations as a rehearsal procedure. Actors spontaneously created actions and conditions similar to those in the play under rehearsal. It was Stanislavski's

[4]Gorchakov, *Stanislavski Directs.*

way of extending the actors' background and understanding of the conditions in the play's environment.

While the central idea of the Stanislavski system is control, an admirable objective for any actor, the use of the method for all kinds of drama and all styles of production is doubtful. His approach to the production of realistic plays which permit long periods of rehearsal and experimentation may be eminently successful, but the method is quite inappropriate for the training of a Japanese Kabuki actor whose objectives at times may be to simulate the movement and gestures of a puppet. Nor was his system applicable to Meyerhold's acrobatic style of performance, nor does it seem suitable for farce or high comedy. Moreover, in the new theater of the twentieth century, emphasis on character identification is often replaced by a performance that is frankly theatrical or presentational in style. One of the most provocative innovators of a new approach to acting, Bertolt Brecht, flatly rejected the Stanislavski system in favor of nonillusionistic acting.

The value of Stanislavski's ideas has been discussed widely. Most of the criticism of the method centers about its abuse. Too many disciples and performers have exaggerated feeling and inspiration and paid too little attention to the originator's insistence on the importance of technique. Those who emphasize technical training point out that the actors must have complete mastery of their voices and bodies so that they are free to move and speak in a way that is expressive, projectile, and appropriate. It is not enough for Romeo to feel like fighting a duel; he must know how to fence. In reading a comic line, it is not enough to think that the dialogue is funny; the delivery requires skillful timing. Long before Stanislavski, generations of outstanding actors gave compelling performances based on their own intuitive approaches. All actors must find their own procedures. The value of the Stanislavski system is that it has helped many actors to regularize their way of working.

After Stanislavski, other avenues to realistic acting have focused on the action that accompanies the emotion, rather than the emotion itself. Jean-Louis Barrault suggested that the actor cannot really play emotional states but only actions that accompany them, and it is through his behavior that he expresses his feelings. Robert L. Benedetti echoes the James-Lange theory that emotions tend to follow the action—we are afraid because we run rather than the reverse. This approach recognizes the *gestalt* concept of the individual as a whole person whose mind and body are integrated. Feelings are, therefore, a part of a total configuration, not separate entities. So the actor centers on the actions and the feelings will follow.

An interesting and potentially profitable new approach to acting comes from Dr. Eric Berne, a Canadian psychiatrist who developed from his clinical research the technique of *transactional analysis*. His ideas were set forth in two books, *Transactions in Psychotherapy* (1961), followed by the widely read *Games People Play* (1964). His root idea is that because of each individual's basic need to interact with other human beings we develop systems of handling these transactions. In infancy, the child needs attention and communication, some of it through touch. As adults we continue to need contact with others for which we develop rather complex techniques. Berne identifies five kinds of transactions:

1 Rituals—stereotyped, repetitious social patterns

2 Pastimes—interrelationships in which characters have no ulterior motives

3 Activities—work, performing tasks

4 Intimacies—interactions for genuine exploration of feelings and attitudes

5 Games—an ongoing series of complementary, ulterior transactions that may be played on two levels at once. A salesman, on the social level, may take a client to lunch; on the psychological level, he is preparing the customer for a sale.

Berne defines three ego states of each individual—the Parent, the Adult, and the Child—and there are five levels of gain. Arthur Wagner in an informative article relates Berne's theories to drama and to his own work with actors.[5] An interesting use of this method of analysis is in the first scene of *King Lear* in which Lear sets up the game of "benevolent father and loving children" by asking his three daughters, "Which of you shall we say doth love us most?" Goneril and Regan play the game by their flattering answers in order to gain the reward, but Cordelia refuses to copy her sisters and her answer causes the king to break out into a fit of childish rage.

[5]Arthur Wagner, "Transactional Analysis and Acting," *Tulane Drama Review*, 11, no. 4 (Summer 1967).

The opening scene of King Lear, *Royal Shakespeare Theatre, 1968.*

Another use of the games approach to performance is Michael Langham's production of *Antony and Cleopatra* at the Canadian Stratford Shakespeare Festival. Langham's pre-rehearsal notes indicate this perspective:

> The play is full of games, of "putting on a scene," almost as if the author were saying that life, especially public life, were no more than an acted performance. Cleopatra has successfully wooed Antony by the scene she "puts on" in her barge on the river of Cydhus; the episode of the salted fish was "staged" like a charade; and early in the play she taunts Antony to "act" for her his outraged sense of Roman honour. It is all a game. Antony is continually conscious of the performance he is giving—privately and publicly: he "performs" in the Senate, ever mindful of the effect he is making, he "directs" the Bacchanalia, he "acts" to make his followers cry. . . .
>
> Finally, of course, there is the crowning "performance" of Cleopatra staging her death scene.[6]

In examining the conflicts that occur so often in drama, the actor may see them as products of crossed transactions or games. Berne's method is useful in clarifying interactions and making them more concrete than through the conventional Freudian analyses.

The Actors' Ways of Working

The actors' ways of working are highly personal since they are the result of their imagination, talent, and physical attributes; but whatever their procedure they face intriguing tasks, which Peter Brook describes:

> Acting is in many ways so unique in its difficulties because the artist has to use the treacherous, changeable and mysterious material of himself as his medium. He is called upon to be completely involved while distanced—detached without detachment. He must be sincere, he must be insincere; he must practice how to be insincere with sincerity and how to lie truthfully.[7]

The way in which an actor approaches a new play and builds a character has been the subject of endless conjecture and controversy. Actors themselves freely acknowledge their inability to describe what actually happens to them in performance. The literature of the art of acting is filled with conflicting statements indicating that the process is too personal for clear-cut intellectual analysis. To quote Brook again:

> Outstanding actors like all real artists have some mysterious psychic chemistry, half conscious, yet three-quarters hidden, that they themselves may only define as "instinct," "hunch," "my voices," that enables them to develop their vision and their art.[8]

The actor places faith in feelings. This point is made again and again in a series of interviews that Lillian Ross conducted with outstanding stage and

[6]Michael Langham, quoted in *The Stratford Scene, 1958–1968*, ed. Peter Raby (Toronto: Clarke, Irwin & Co., 1968).
[7]Peter Brook, *The Empty Space* (New York: Atheneum Publishers, 1969).
[8]Brook, *The Empty Space*.

motion-picture performers for *The New Yorker*[9] in which are found such statements as these:

> It's when you start to rehearse, with other people, that things begin to happen. What it is exactly I don't know, and even don't want to know. I'm all for mystery there. Most of what happens as you develop your part is unconscious. Most of it is underwater. (Kim Stanley)

> Once you set things you do and make them mean certain things, you then respond to the stimuli you yourself set up. Then you *feel*. (Maureen Stapleton)

> When I'm building a role, I start with a series of mental pictures and feel. (Hume Cronyn)

> Every actor has, as a gift from God, his own method. My particular method is to go first by the sense of taste. I actually have a physical taste for every part. Then I go to the other senses—hearing, seeing, touching. Thinking comes much later. (Vladimir Sokoloff)

[9]Lillian Ross, "Profiles: The Player," *The New Yorker*, October 21, 1961; October 28, 1961; and November 4, 1961. Reprinted by permission. Copyright © 1961 The New Yorker Magazine, Inc., October 28, 1961.

Hume Cronyn is one of the ablest and most hardworking modern actors. Here he is seen with Zoe Caldwell in Moliere's The Miser, trying to work out a suitable marriage with the matchmaker. (Guthrie Theater, Minneapolis. Directed by Douglas Campbell.)

In working on a new play, many actors testify to an initial period of trial and error before the image becomes clear. Geraldine Page, an outstanding American actress, sees her role developing like a jigsaw puzzle, a small piece at a time. Henry Fonda says, "I baby up on a part. I get the feeling gradually."[10] Apparently many actors go through a similar experience until all at once "a bell rings," or "there is a spark," or "suddenly there is a click." Henry Fonda describes the phenomenon in this way: "I always know when it feels real to me. . . . When my emotion takes over in a part, it's like a seaplane taking off on the water. I feel as if I were soaring. If five times out of eight a week the emotions take over, you've got magic."[11]

Geraldine Page makes an interesting observation concerning character identification:

> When you take the character over and use the character, you wreck the fabric of the play, but you can be in control of the character without taking the character over. When the character uses *you*, that's when you're really cooking. You know you're in complete control, yet you get the feeling you didn't do it. You have the beautiful feeling that you can't ruin it. You feel as if you were tagging along on an exciting journey. You don't completely understand it, and you don't have to. You're just grateful and curious.[12]

This statement suggests the interesting dichotomy of the actor who, while assuming the role of another character, still remains in complete control. Whether the actor's approach is emotional or sheerly technical, it must be recognized as a very personal and highly individualized process that defies complete definition or understanding. Nevertheless, there are certain general steps that may be followed.

Like the director, the actor's initial approach to a play is that of analysis— the search for the core idea, the spine. What does the play mean? What is the effect supposed to be on an audience? How is each role related to the complete play? Under the guidance and stimulation of the director, each performer analyzes the play to establish its basic interpretation.

The actor will want to know the style of the play and the production. By style is meant the *manner* of production—the *quality* of the actions and images. For example, it is obvious from the opening lines of *Hamlet* that the play is elevated in style, the language is dignified and poetic, the action controlled. There is nothing trivial or folksy about the guards and Horatio when they confront the ghost. Contrast *Hamlet* with the opening lines of *Death of a Salesman*—its ordinary characters, and colloquial language. Its style suggests a domestic environment with a man and wife in a commonplace situation.

The style of the particular production is usually determined by the director, who may elect to stage the play in a manner other than the original one—for example, *The Taming of the Shrew* might be set in a wild West in the nineteenth century, or a Molière comedy may be done in a style that suggests the com- media dell'arte. Even when a play is done "straight" the author may see the

---

[10]Ross, "Profiles." Reprinted by permission.
[11]Ross, "Profiles." Reprinted by permission.
[12]Ross, "Profiles." Reprinted by permission.

A deliberately theatricalized style of playing is evident in this shot from Ghelderode's Pantagleize *when the protagonist pays a visit on General Macboom to steal the national treasury. (Guthrie Theater. Directed by Stephen Kanee and sets by Jack Barla.)*

characters playing at different levels simultaneously in order to convey both text and subtext.

David Rabe's *Sticks and Bones* (1970) is a searing account of the return of a disabled Vietnam veteran whose family finds it impossible to adjust its life-style to reality. Rabe in an author's note to the published play describes the acting style in these terms:

> In any society there is an image of how the perfectly happy family should appear. It is this image that the people in this play wish to preserve above all else. Mom and Dad are not concerned that terrible events have occurred in the world, but rather that David has come home to behave in a manner that makes him no longer lovable. Thus he is keeping them from being the happy family they know they must be. He attacks those aspects of their self-image in which reside all their sense of value and sanity. But, curiously, one of the requisites of their self-image is that everything is fine, and, consequently, for a long time they must not even admit that David is attacking.
>
> Yet everything is being communicated. Often a full, long speech is used in this play where in another, more "realistic" play there would be only a silence during which something was communicated between two people. Here the communication is obvious, because it is directly spoken. Consequently the ignoring of that which is

David Rabe's Sticks and Bones *requires a many-layered style of performance over surface realism. (Miami University, Ohio Directed by Barry Whitham.)*

communicated must be equally obvious. David throws a yelling, screaming tantrum over his feelings of isolation and Harriet confidently, cheerfully offers Ezy Sleep sleeping pills in full faith that they will solve his problem. The actors must try to look at what they are ignoring. They must not physically ignore things—turn their backs, avert their eyes, be busy with something else. The point is not that they do not physically see or hear, but that they psychologically ignore. Though they look right at things, though they listen closely, they do not see or hear. The harder they physically focus and concentrate on an event, the clearer their psychological state and the point and nature of the play will be, when in their next moments and speeches they verbally and emotionally ignore or miss what they have clearly looked at. In addition, the actors should try not to take the play overly seriously. The characters (except David) do not take things seriously until they are forced to, and then they do it for as short a time as they can manage. Let the audience take seriously the jolly way the people go about the curious business of their lives.

Stylization, then, is the main production problem. The forms referred to during the time of writing *Sticks and Bones* were farce, horror movie, TV situation comedy. These should have their effect, though it must be remembered that they are where form was thought, not content. What is poetic in the writing must not be reinforced by deep feeling on the part of the actors, or the writing will hollow into pretension. In a more "realistic" play, where language is thinner, subtext must be supplied or there is no weight. Such deep support of *Sticks and Bones* will make the play ponderous. As a general rule, I think it is true that when an actor's first impulse (the impulse of all his training) is to make a heavy or serious adjustment in a scene, he should reverse

248

himself and head for a light-hearted adjustment. If his first impulse is toward light-heartedness, perhaps he should turn toward a serious tack. A major premise of the play is that stubbing your own big toe is a more disturbing event than hearing of a stranger's suicide.

At the start, the family is happy and orderly, and then David comes home and he is unhappy. As the play progresses, he becomes happier and they become unhappier. Then, at the end, they are happy. [13]

Another interesting view of acting style is suggested in an interview with Roger Planchon, the outstanding French director of Le Théâtre de la Cité in the suburbs of Lyons. He is primarily interested in bringing the experience of the theater to the common people. When asked by Planchon what kind of stories they would like to see, the factory workers suggested *The Three Musketeers*. A dramatization of Alexander Dumas' historical romance was made and proved to be an enormous hit. The play became a joyful vehicle for "demythologizing" a rigid view of French history. Played with great élan, the swashbuckling intrigue included movie techniques of westerns and slapstick comedies—incongruous homely touches such as Richelieu frying real eggs on stage, and menials interrupting a royal ceremony to change the candles in the chandeliers. Planchon described the acting style he was seeking in these terms:

I am trying to define a certain style, but it's very fine, very French, if you like, very . . . humorous to play the kind of theater I want. I need, as Brook has also said he needs for his kind of theater, *very intelligent actors*. The more intelligent they are, the more they can play what I want them to play. And another thing: my style is absolutely stripped bare of pathos. I think the Living Theater and others like them are fatally tempted by pathos. Not me, absolutely not. I've no taste for it at all, excess repels me. When I see an actor plunging into pathos, I always feel he is lying. In this I'm very Brechtian. I want someone to tell me a story I can watch smoking my pipe, and I don't want to have to ask myself questions about *feelings*. . . . I love relaxed performances. [14]

The analysis of the play should lead the actor to an understanding of the pervading atmosphere of the play. Does it suggest the hot, sensual quality of *A Streetcar Named Desire*? Is the mood one of menace, as if some alien force were trying to break in, as in many Pinter plays? Does the environment require the tempo and flavor of big city corruption as in some of Brecht's works? The dominating atmosphere of the play provides the actor with clues to interpretation and the method of playing—the tempo, the use of props, and business. From a study of the total play, the actor not only sees the relationship of one character to the action as a whole, as a part of a larger metaphor, but also finds many sources of inspiration for the interpretation of the spirit and quality of the playwright's creation.

After a performer has a clear comprehension of the play's structure, atmosphere, style, and basic interpretation, he or she studies the individual character,

[13]David Rabe, *The Basic Training of Pavlo Hummel* and *Sticks and Bones* (New York: The Viking Press, 1973), pp. 225–26.

[14]Roger Planchon, interviewed by Michael Kustow, "Creating a Theater of Real Life," *Theatre Quarterly*, 2, no. 5 (January–March 1972).

Acting in Pinter's plays is a challenge because so much is left to the imagination in pauses, ambiguities and often a complex subtext. In The Birthday Party, *the actors turn a child's game into a scene of terror. (Wayne State University. Directed by Richard P. Brown; designed by Norman Hamlin.)*

perhaps approaching the character from the outside, making an inventory of age, occupation, appearance, manner of speaking and moving, physical condition, posture, movement, carriage, and dress. Observations may be directly from life; if it is a period play, it will be profitable to study historical pictures showing the costume, architecture, and manners of the time. Peter Stein, working with his excellent ensemble at the Hallenschen Schaubühne in West Berlin, has found it worthwhile to spend considerable time getting acquainted with the cultural background of the play and the playwright through readings, seminars, and discussions.

The actor will find in the script four main sources of information about character. The modern playwright frequently provides a character description which includes some of the details listed above. Some playwrights, like Shaw, provide very complete portraits down to the color of the eyes and shape of the nostrils. Other contemporary playwrights may simply give the actor the barest

An interesting gallery of characters in Feydeau's Keep an Eye on
Amélie *is achieved by skillful costuming and makeup in this production
at California State University, Chico. Directed by Larry Wismer.*

hint, such as "a waiter," "a young man of twenty-four," or "a tramp." In period
plays, the dramatist usually gives no character description at all.

A second source of information comes from the lines the actor speaks. The
playwright has usually taken great pains to write dialogue that represents and
delineates the character. Lines, of course, are susceptible to a variety of interpretations and it is obvious that two actors playing the same role may find
marked differences in the reading of the dialogue. Indeed, the same actor may
give a variety of interpretations of lines in different performances. The skillful
playwright goes beyond the literal meaning of the words and uses dialogue as a
means of revealing characater as well as advancing the plot. The actor, therefore, must search the lines for their essential meaning, not only in reference to
the immediate context, but also to the revelation of the total character.

A third clue in the analysis of acting roles are the characters' actions. Is the
individual an active agent or is he or she acted upon? What change do they
undergo during the course of the play? What emotions are aroused? What are
their primary objectives and how do they go about reaching them? How much
of the inner life is revealed by what the performers do? To what extent do they
understand their own motives? What choices and decisions do they make and
how do these affect their fortunes? Do their actions make them sympathetic
characters? Playwrights must convey the inner lives of their characters in clear
and concise ways, and, very often, the actions are more revealing than their
251   words. The essential actions are usually created by the dramatist, but the

director and performers also invent stage business that is significant in interpreting the roles. In any case, all of the action in a performance should be relevant and essential to the meaning of the play. A pertinent example occurs in *Sly Fox,* a modern revision of Ben Jonson's *Volpone* based on the deceptive actions of Sly who pretends to be dying in order to elicit gifts from his greedy acquaintances hoping to become his beneficiary. The play opens with an action that is repeated throughout—Sly's feigned illness. He is heard groaning offstage, then he enters supported by his valet, Able, and three servants. Sly appears to be at death's door, but when the servants leave, he is miraculously "cured."

Sly *(Standing up on the bed):*   No one's better! No one's more fit! *(getting out of bed)* I've got enough health to start another man!

George C. Scott romped through the role of *Sly,* alternating his dying act with a vigorous contrast of ebullient life. His actions revealed his true character to the audience.

The actor's *way of acting* reveals character—not just what is done, but *how* it is done. Many accomplished performers bring to their roles a wealth of detailed actions—pieces of business that give dimension and sharpness to the portraits they create. A case in point occurred in a production of David Rabe's *The Basic Training of Pavlo Hummel,* a play about a misfit who hopes to find his manhood in the army going to Vietnam. (This is another part of Rabe's Viet-

The Basic Training of Pavlo Hummel *at the University of Hawaii.*
(Directed by Glenn Cannon; designed by Richard G. Mason.)

namese War trilogy.) Using the metaphor of basic training and military service, Rabe built up a vivid picture of a character who symbolized all of life's unnoticed young men. Critic Jack Kroll describes Al Pacino's way of playing the part:

> Like Ted Williams waiting for a pitch, Pacino builds potential energy out of a thousand jittery movements. He's one actor you want to film in slow motion. What you'd see would be a flow of behavioral hieroglyphics—jounce the pelvis, touch the hip, rub the face, swing the head, purse the mouth, shift the foot, paw the hair. Even the words come out reshaped by inner tension—the vowels mauled and flattened, the phrases syncopated with savage sensitivity.[15]

Finally, the actor learns a good deal about the role from the reactions of others—what they say and do. The actor must understand the character's dramatic purpose in the struggle, which is frequently revealed by the reaction of other characters. Shakespeare sometimes delineates his characters sharply in the lines of another character: "Yon Cassius hath a lean and hungry look." Coriolanus was captured in one sentence: "When he walks he moves like an engine, and the ground shrinks before his treading; he is able to pierce a corselet with his eyes, talks like a knell, and his hum is a battery." But it is mostly in the interactions of characters that the playwright indicates their motivations.

One of the sources of pleasure in the theater is fine acting, as critic Clive Barnes indicates in his review of George C. Scott's performance as Willy in *Death of a Salesman:*

> There is nothing on earth like the magic of great acting. An actor takes off—his words fly up, image and reality become one, the actor creates a patch of humanity on the quietly empty stage, a rustle runs through the theater, a breeze of awareness, a special alertness. One of the world's few renewing miracles flickers into life. Great acting. Not just good acting, or even magnificent acting. Great acting. The kind you can never forget. The kind you tell your grandchildren about. The kind that leaves you in a state of grace, enables you to jump beyond yourself, to see something that perhaps even the playwright himself only dimly perceived.[16]

Training for Performance in the New Theater

The new theater requires a fresh approach to training the actor, often through workshops. You will recall that Peter Brook's production of *Marat/Sade* was preceded by a workshop—the "theater of cruelty" to expose the actor to Artaudian techniques essential for Weiss's play. Similarly, Chaikin's Open Theater used an ensemble approach to performance through experimental exercises and rehearsal. Many of the groups that have achieved prominence have utilized workshop methods—the Living Theater, Mnouchkine's Théâtre du Soleil, Schechner's Performance Group, Grotowski's Polish Theater Laboratory, and the San Francisco Mime Theater, to mention a few.

[15]Jack Kroll, *Newsweek,* May 9, 1977.
[16]Clive Barnes, *New York Times,* June 27, 1975.

The performance of Group's Commune *showing the workshop quality of the production in the actor-spectator relationship. (Photo courtesy of Elizabeth Le Compte.)*

A workshop is usually composed of a dedicated group of people, working together over a period of time, under a leader, to explore ways of making theater. Sometimes the workshop is an extension of the rehearsal process searching for new means of expression demanded by a specific play. Sometimes it represents an effort to achieve a style appropriate to the group's overall perspective. For example, Mnouchkine's ensemble, in its commitment to productions with a historical slant, sought ways to get free of modern mannerisms. One method was to use masks so that the actors felt distanced from the present, and as Bari Rolfe says, "by blocking the path taken by the actor, you oblige him to look for another." Charles Ludlam's workshops for the Theater of the Ridiculous are geared toward developing commedia dell'arte techniques and a cinematic style of comic playing reminiscent of old movies.

The workshop method is also used to enrich the actors' creative processes without regard to a specific objective. The Théâtre du Soleil, for example, rehearsed *King Lear* for the stimulation it gave to the performers, with no thought of a public showing. Group playing and exercising may also be used as a means of self-exploration with no theatrical connection at all. For example, Ryszard Cieslak, the outstanding actor of Grotowski's Polish Laboratory Theater, in following his mentor's directive "to be as one is," leads groups in a "theater of roots" workshop, in which a handful of participants retreats from the world and lives together in isolation, joining in awareness exercises as individuals or as a group, attempting to find ways to break through the social ego and open up to life.

An example of a workshop aimed at developing a new manner of performing occurred in The Performance Group's production of *Commune* in 1970. The material for playing grew out of the players' personal backgrounds, their experiments in acting, and a study of American history—all joined together in a collage on the theme of investigating each individual's roots. William L. Trilby describes the kind of performance that evolved from the workshop.

> The performers begin with improvised singing and talking; they tell in overlapping speeches of their personal background in relation to the Performance Group; then the evening erupts into a rapid pattern of transformations that defies time and demands the spectator's engagement. As the performers reenact their personal beginnings, they discover archetypal beginnings; out of animal sounds and undefined movements, they become a boat and its inhabitants, as water is scooped and dripped from the tub; they sing revival songs, play cops and robbers, feed and become monkeys, act out scenes from *Lear, Richard III, The Tempest* and *Moby Dick.* All of these are discovered as part of their matrices; they are not cute memorabilia, but metaphors for finding meaning, performed by a people digging out their own roots.[17]

Since performers in the new theater reject most of the practices of the past, they search for a style that emphasizes theatricality—a search that goes on continually. Actors become agents of the action instead of individual characters or personalities. Their objective is not to play the role but the actions—like ball players or musicians. Their style may be cool, underplayed, or even flat—without emotional content. A distancing effect may be attempted by avoiding eye contact and physical proximity. Or their style may be frankly presentational when actors communicate directly with the audience. They may suggest several characters simultaneously, exchange parts with one another, go from youth to old age in a single speech, put on makeup and costumes before the audience, and set the stage and move the furniture. They may improvise their dialogue and actions, speak a synthetic language, use gibberish or animal sounds, speak simultaneously or not at all, fashion a wall of noise which is completely unintelligible to the audience. They may stress mime and dance and the use of space and rhythm, begin actions that are never completed, or make abrupt changes with no transition. They may appear as themselves or as ciphers without motivation or meaning. They often appear to be nondescript people performing tasks. In their urge to go beyond the literal word, beyond language itself to find a primitive base for performance that bypasses the conscious mind, the avant-garde performers may present a perplexing welter of sensory signals that many traditional theater-goers cannot or will not follow. One essential ties them to the theater of the past: the living presence of the performer.

[17]William L. Trilby, "Commune," *Educational Theater Journal,* May 1971.

Bibliography

BENEDETTI, ROBERT L., *The Actor at Work (3rd ed.)*. Englewood Cliffs, N.J.: Prentice-Hall, Inc., 1981.

BOLESLAVSKY, RICHARD, *Acting: The First Six Lessons*. New York: Theatre Arts Books, 1933

BRECHT, BERTOLT, *The Messingkauf Dialogues*. London: Methuen, 1971.

BURTON, HAL, *Great Acting*. New York: Hill & Wang, 1967.

CHAIKIN, JOSEPH, *The Presence of the Actor: Notes on the Open Theater*. New York: Atheneum Publishers, 1972.

FUNKE, GEORGE, and JOHN E. BOOTH, eds., *Actors Talk About Acting*. New York: Random House, Inc., 1961.

GLENN, STANLEY, *The Complete Actor*. Boston: Allyn & Bacon, Inc., 1977.

HETHMON, ROBERT, ed., *Strasberg at the Actor's Studio*. New York: The Viking Press, 1965.

SPOLIN, VIOLA, *Improvisation in the Theater*. Evanston, Ill.: Northwestern University Press, 1963.

STANISLAVSKI, CONSTANTIN, *An Actor Prepares*. New York: Theatre Arts Books, 1963.

———, *Creating a Role*, trans. E. R. Hapgood. New York: Theatre Arts Books, 1961.

TEN
Stage Design

We go to the theater to *see* a play—it is a *show*. Although the text is in words, at least part of the appeal of theatrical production comes from the scenery, lighting, and costuming. Indeed, in some cases the actors and the plays are subordinate to spectacular effects. In the past, producers like Charles Kean, Dion Boucicault, and David Belasco drew thousands of people to the box office mainly to see their lavish, eye-filling scenic displays. In England during the Restoration period and the eighteenth and nineteenth centuries, new scenery became a special event in the theater and admission prices were raised because of the sensational appeal. Although the motion picture has taken over the main burden of satisfying the public's craving for the spectacular, the live theater does not neglect eye appeal, as nearly any musical comedy attests—as for example, *Jesus Christ Superstar, Camelot, My Fair Lady, Pippin,* and *Evita.* Avant-garde experimentalists such as Robert Wilson, Richard Foreman, and Mabou Mines produce their own works which rely primarily on visual and spatial imagery. Others working in the new theater have a high regard for scenery, lighting, and color even though they use them as theatrical entities in themselves, rather than in the conventional manner as supports for the verbal text. Delighting the eye is still a basic theatrical ingredient.

As we have discussed elsewhere in connection with theater architecture (chapter 11), the scenic tradition of the proscenium arch came from the Italian Renaissance. For generations, many theaters used stock sets of painted canvas on a wood frame to serve as wings at the side of the stage, while at the rear

Painted scenery using wings and back drop for a production of Grillparzer's Bruderzwist Im Hause, *1909.*

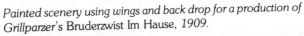

258

backdrops completed the picture. Since most of these scenic elements were two dimensional they were easily mounted and shifted. Occasionally, special and complicated scenery was created for productions, but, by and large, most drama in the eighteenth and nineteenth centuries was performed in stock sets of standardized units of wings and backdrops.

In the chapter on realism and naturalism we noted the nineteenth-century efforts to achieve appropriateness of environment not only as the visual background of the action but as a conditioning force on character. The naturalist went to great lengths to make his settings as credible as possible, but his excessive concern with imitating the surface aspects of life led to meaningless clutter as he attempted to implement the idea of the "significant trifle." The realist tempered the naturalist's approach with a degree of moderation and simplification. He performed a valuable service for the theater in clearing the stage of its flatness, its fake trim and unreal properties, it shoddy prettiness, and makeshift workmanship. Stage settings began to have a more substantial look, doors slammed, and windows could be opened and shut. The wings in the grooves were replaced by flats of canvas representing real walls which enclosed the acting area. Real properties were assembled, and the stage was filled with

A production of Dostoievski's The Idiot *designed by Josef Svoboda for a production at the Old Vic Theatre, London, directed by Anthony Quayle, 1970. Note how the atmosphere of the locale has been established by projections rather than by painted set pieces.*

casual objects of daily living. The painted perspective tradition was wiped out, and there was a new sense of the material rightness of things. But most importantly, the idea was advanced and accepted that the scenery should serve as the specific and appropriate environment for the action of the play.

Realism was no sooner the accepted way of staging drama than it was challenged by plays written in defiance of realistic practices, as in the works of Maeterlinck, Claudel, and Yeats. But even more significant was the appearance of two pioneering spirits, endowed with poetic fervor and imagination, who led the way toward the new stagecraft.

Gordon Craig

Although Gordon Craig was trained in the English legitimate theater, his contribution does not lie in the practical aspects of scene painting and construction but rather in his point of view, which was that of a visionary who crusaded for an ideal art of the theater. He castigated the contemporary stage for its shabbiness, its exaggeration of realistic detail, and most of all for its lack of artistic purpose and direction. Craig conceived of the theater as an aesthetic unity in which all aspects of production would be harmonized. Toward this end, he called for a director who would give this unified concept to the production of drama. Impatient with the actor, Craig even suggested replacing him with supermarionettes. His concept of design was based on the selection of a few simple, symbolic set pieces and properties, as his description of a designer illustrates:

> And remember he does not merely sit down and draw a pretty or historically accurate design, with enough doors and windows in picturesque places, but he first of all chooses certain colors which seem to him to be in harmony with the spirit of the play, rejecting other colors as out of tune. He then weaves into a pattern certain objects—an arch, a fountain, a balcony, a bed—using the chosen objects which are mentioned in the play, and which are necessary to be seen. [1]

Craig sought to replace imitation with suggestion, elaboration with simplicity. He insisted on the spiritual relationship between setting and action. He pointed out the emotional potentialities of figures moving in design, of shifting light and shadow, of the dramatic values of color. He emphasized that the theater was above all "a place for seeing." Craig illustrated his ideas with a series of provocative designs, and he sought to demonstrate his theories in production; sometimes these were doomed to failure because of impracticability, but sometimes they were brilliantly successful. Craig's contribution was not, however, in the utilitarian aspects of the theater; his real significance was in his dream, which he persuaded others to see by the compelling force of his enthusiasm and argument.

[1]Gordon Craig, *On the Art of the Theatre* (London: Heinemann, 1905).

Adolphe Appia

The other pioneer of modern staging was the Swiss Adolphe Appia, who in 1899 published his seminal work, *Die Musik und die Inscenierung,* in which he called for reforms in the theater. Appia began with the actor, and insisted that the design must be in harmony with the living presence of the performer. When a forest was required on stage, for example, it was not necessary to give an accurate representation, but to create the atmosphere of a man amidst the trees. The attention of the audience should be focused on the character, not distracted by detailed branches and leaves. Painted stage settings are incompatible with the actor because of the contrast between the actor's plasticity and the flatness of the scenic surroundings: "The human body does not seek to produce the illusion of reality *since it is in itself reality!* What it demands of the *décor* is simply to set in relief this reality. . . . We must free staging of everything that is in contradistinction with the actor's presence. . . . Scenic illusion is the living presence of the actor."

Appia suggested two tenets of good design: the lighting should emphasize the plasticity of the human form, rather than destroy, and a plastic scene should give the actor's movements all of their value. Implicit in Appia's theories is the fundamental unity of all phases of production, with the major emphasis on the

Drawing by Appia for a scene from Wagner's Die Walküre, *1892. Atmosphere is created by skillful use of light and the plastic quality of the setting.*

261

actor. Appia enforced his arguments by applying them to a series of designs for the production of Wagner's operas, fashioning uncluttered settings of simple forms in which skillful lighting created a remarkably appropriate and effective atmosphere. Appia's theories were well timed, since they coincided with the invention of the electric light, which gave theatrical production a marvelous dimension in design. Up until that time, stage lighting was an awkward and dangerous aspect of production, in which almost all effort went into merely getting enough light on the stage so that the audience could see. Now with electricity, lighting could be used for its evocative potential in creating and enhancing the mood of the play. Appia was the first to demonstrate this new force aesthetically.

The sparks kindled by Craig and Appia ignited and the "new stagecraft" made its appearance, based on the generally accepted point of view that scenery should augment and reinforce the atmosphere and meaning of the play, and that scenery should be utilitarian in providing the actor with a serviceable environment. This point of view is apparent from the following representative statements. John Gassner regards the function of the setting as a "psychological frame of reference"; Marc Blitzstein says that scenery "should be used to pull the play along its intended course"; and Harold Clurman stresses its practicability: "A set is a utensil which cannot be judged until its worth is proved in practice by the whole course of the play's development onstage."

Robert Edmond Jones, a moving force in the progress of scene design in America, reflects his debt to Craig in his concept of the purpose of stage scenery:

> Stage-designing should be addressed to this eye of the mind. There is an outer eye that observes, and there is an inner eye that sees. . . . The designer must always be on guard against being too explicit. A good scene, I repeat, is not a picture. It is something seen, but it is something conveyed as well; a feeling, an evocation. Plato says somewhere: It is beauty I seek, not beautiful things. That is what I mean. A setting is not just a beautiful thing, a collection of beautiful things. It is a presence, a mood, a symphonic accompaniment to the drama, a great wind fanning the drama to flame. It echoes, it enhances, it animates. It is an expectancy, a foreboding, a tension. It says nothing, but it gives everything.[2]

Meyerhold and Constructivism

Meyerhold (see pp. 209–10), although not a designer, is associated with the development of *constructivism* in Russia during the 1920s. Inspired by the machine and reacting against the ostentatious decor of the czarist regime, the constructivist created stage settings of skeletonized ramps, staircases, bridges, and similar structural forms. The spectator saw the bare bones of the setting against the backstage brick wall, unrelieved by any decorative or aesthetic intention. The set was based entirely on its practicability as a tool for action. Its

---

[2]Robert Edmond Jones, *The Dramatic Imagination* (New York: Duell, Sloan and Pearce, 1941).

advantages were that it was frankly theatrical, it gave the performer extraordinary opportunities for movement and the use of space, and it invited fluent and uninterrupted action. Meyerhold made full use of these advantages even to developing a style of acting, "biomechanics," suited to the machine age, a style that included training in acrobatics, circus movement, and ballet.

Epic Theater

One of the most interesting efforts in experimental drama was the "epic theater" that began in the 1920s as the result of the work of Erwin Piscator and Bertolt Brecht. As we have seen, the latter, in addition to being a director, was also a playwright who put his theories into practice—and like Meyerhold—even to inventing a new approach to acting. Epic theater workers revolted against the tradition of Ibsenian realism. They were not concerned with the domestic problems of a man and his wife in a home; epic drama called for a larger arena of action showing the dynamics of social forces at work. Hence, the epic theater playwright and designer demanded a stage that would serve for many fragments of action, some of them occurring simultaneously. In 1928, Piscator's production of *The Good Soldier Schweik* offered a brilliant and stimulating example of the new style. A dramatization of a novel, the play concerns the life of a private soldier ground down by the stupidity and brutality of war. His story is told in a kaleidoscopic arrangement of scenes, recitations, songs, and explanations. In addition to the usual facilities of the stage, Piscator used slides, posters, charts, maps, graphs, a treadmill for moving scenery and actors, and a motion-picture screen on which were projected cartoons, captions, and film sequences—all joined together in a welter of sights and sounds.

Gorelik describes the nature of Piscator's production:

> "I'll do my duty for the Emperor to the end," adds Schweik. On the screen a Russian soldier is swimming in a pond. A bush rolls on with the Russian's uniform hanging on it. "A souvenir," thinks Schweik. He puts it on. A shot rings out, and a Hungarian patrol rushes on and seizes him in loud Hungarian tones. "What do you mean, prisoner?" Schweik demands. "I'm on your side. . . . " A shell bursts. Schweik falls. From the upper corner of the screen a procession of crosses starts toward the audience. As the crosses, growing nearer in perspective, reach the lower edge of the screen, a muslin drop, lowered downstage, catches them once more, bringing them still closer to the spectators. A rain of crosses falls upon this wry comedy as the lights begin to go up.[3]

Brecht's *The Private Life of the Master Race,* another epic drama, dramatizes the experiences of a German panzer crew moving across Europe from the early stages of the war until it is defeated by the Russians. The play is really a series of one-acts depicting the effects of Nazism and warfare on the crew. The

[3]Gorelik, *New Theaters for Old.*

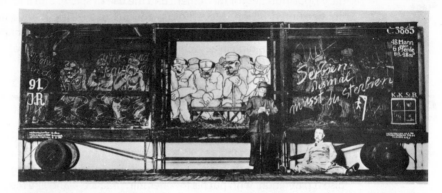

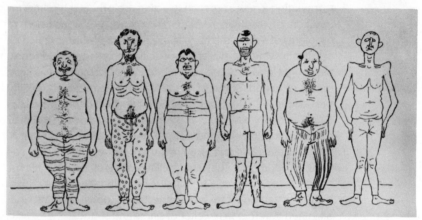

Erwin Piscator's "epic" staging of The Good Soldier Schweik. *Berlin, 1927. All elements of the theater were combined in this production.*

Scene from a "Living Newspaper" production of One Third of a
Nation, *1938. Set design by Howard Bay.*

various threads are knit together by lyrical passages. The play begins with this stage direction:

> *A band plays a barbaric march. Out of the darkness appears a big signpost:* TO POLAND *and near it a Panzer truck. Its wheels are turning. On it sit twelve to sixteen soldiers, steel helmeted, their faces white as chalk, their guns between their knees. They could be puppets. The soldiers sing to the tune of the Horst Wessel Song.*

There follows a series of scenes such as "The Betrayal," "The Jewish Wife," and "The Informer," dramatizing various phases of Nazi terrorism until the Panzer is bogged down in Russia. The sequences are bridged by voices out of the darkness and the roar of the armored car.

In America, epic theater techniques were used by the Federal Theater in production of the Living Newspaper series during the 1930s. The epic style is a deliberate attempt to break with tradition, to move away from the struggles of a single individual and consider instead the dynamics of social change. Since Brecht was a man with a message, he utilized all of the resources of the stage as visual aids to get his ideas across.

It is apparent that epic theater is not merely a matter of design, but a complete concept of dramatic writing and production whose techniques make use of the theater and scenery in a new and often startling way.

The "epic" style of production was captured in Kopit's Indians *at the University of Illinois. (Directed by Mary Arbenz; designed by Don Llewellyn.)*

The Architectural Stage

Still another revolt in the modern theater, but in quite a different direction, has been the rejection of scenery altogether. Recalling the simple playing area for acting of the Greek, Elizabethan, and Noh dramas, efforts have been made to devise a formal, unchanging "architectural" stage without a proscenium arch or any machinery of the theater except lighting. It is argued that such a stage provides a more functional and flexible place for the actors' performance. Dropping the pretense of picturing nature frees the spectator from visual distractions and the time lags between scenes, and focuses his attention on the play rather than on its surroundings. Moreover, the architectural stage offers exceptional freedom of movement, allowing the actor space in all directions rather than restricting him almost exclusively to lateral actions as he is in the proscenium arch theater.

The staging of Billy Budd *by the Trinity Square Repertory Company, Providence, brought the action to the audience. Eugene Lee's setting provided a remarkably flexible environment with its varied acting areas, as well as conveying a shipboard atmosphere. Directed by Adrian Hall.*

Jacques Copeau's Théâtre du Vieux Colombier in France provided the most notable experiment in architectural staging. With a few portable screens and properties and skillful use of lighting, Copeau's theater proved to be remarkably effective for the production of a wide variety of plays. Many other attempts have been made in recent years to use architectural stages, as we shall see in the next chapter.

The Scene Designer at Work

The designer begins work on a specific play by studying the script, perhaps recording initial impressions during or after a first reading, or thoroughly analyzing the script before arriving at a central dramatic image. The designer searches the play for answers to numerous questions: What is the mood of the play? What is germane to the play's meaning in its geographical location or historical period? What images continue throughout the play? How will the actor move? What are the most important scenes, and what areas will be used for them? Does the play have a unique flavor or style? The designer's preliminary study may provide some answers that will stimulate the imagination.

During this early preparation, the designer is not primarily concerned with the practical problems of construction, painting, and shifting, though of course the fact that eventually the design must be capable of being built and used cannot be ignored. Sometimes this poses interesting problems. Jo Mielziner, one of America's foremost designers, in his intriguing account "Designing a Play: *Death of a Salesman*," relates how the practical requirements of Miller's play influenced his work. It was an unusual challenge to Mielziner.

> It was not only that there were so many different scenic locations, [more than forty of them] but that the action demanded instantaneous time changes from the present to the past and back again.[4]

Mielziner describes how he approached Miller's play by reading the manuscript carefully, trying to see the play as if he were a member of the audience. Then he made a "breakdown" of the action to determine where he felt the most important scenes should be played. From that preparation, he arrived at his basic concept:

> One thought came to me: In the scene where the Salesman mentally goes back to the early years of his marriage, when his boys were young and the house was surrounded by trees and open country, I had to create something visually that would make these constant transitions in time immediately clear to the audience. My next thought was, that even if we ended up with a big stage, with plenty of stagehands, and I was able to design some mechanism for handling the large number of individual scenes, the most important visual symbol in the play—the real background of the story—was the Salesman's house. Therefore, why should that house not be the main set, with all the other scenes—the corner of a graveyard, a hotel room in Boston, the corner of a business office, a lawyer's consultation room, and so on—played on the forestage? If I designed these little scenes in segments and

[4]Jo Mielziner, *Designing for the Theater* (New York: Bramhall House, 1965).

fragments, with easily moved props and fluid lighting effects, I might be able, without ever lowering the curtain, to achieve the easy flow that the author clearly wanted.[5]

Mielziner went on from this preliminary approach to complete one of the most famous and effective settings in the American theater.

After an initial study of the play, the designer usually meets with the director, who may have very specific ideas of the areas of the stage to be emphasized—even to the extent of having a definite color scheme in mind, or a preliminary plan showing the arrangement of walls, entrances and exits, platforms, and stairways. Or the director's ideas may be nebulous, a general impression of the production without a clear-cut form. The designer mines the director for these ideas, looking for specific instructions on the practical aspects of the setting and for inspiration that will stimulate his imagination when he creates the visual image.

Ordinarily, the designer's next step is to make sketches of the impressions that occur in the search for the fundamental creative ideas growing out of the director's interpretation of the play. Gorelik produces numerous small sketches in which he strives to express the "poetic image of the scene." He pays no attention to the practicalities of the stage in these preliminary sketches. For example, in his designs for *Golden Boy,* Gorelik began with the concept of a prize ring, even though there was no scene using such a locale in the play, but this basic image influenced his design of each of the scenes. In his design for *Thunder Rock,* which the author set in the interior of a lighthouse, Gorelik's first impression was of an *exterior* view of a lighthouse against a stormy sky. Ultimately, he created the interior set, but his original concept persisted in the final design. Robert Edmond Jones apparently visualized his designs so clearly in his mind that he was able to set them down completely with little or no revision.

The creative scene designer is not merely concerned with reproducing a faithful copy of a piece of architecture. The scene designer is neither an interior decorator, nor simply a skilled draftsman who follows the director's orders in an arrangement of set pieces on the stage. Like the actor, the designer is also an interpreter who makes a unique contribution to the values of the play. Some directors give the designer a fairly free hand, since they find considerable inspiration in the designer's way of solving the visual problems of the scenic environment. At times, the designer has exerted such power that the set completely dominates the production. But in general, the designer's work is subservient to the total effect, attempting to reinforce the meaning of the play with the designs.

The manner in which the designer studies the script is interesting. For example, Gorelik looks for a basic motif:

As we study the script, we try to penetrate closer and closer to the deepest significance of the play. For myself, I usually work from the climactic scenes onward. That is, I try to visualize the most poignant or striking scenes. I try to understand the dramatic progression in intensity, or the change in quality, from one scene to another. When I

---

[5]Mielziner, *Designing for the Theater.*

know that I have provided for these essential scenes, I make the other scenes fit it. The climactic moments are like the piers of a bridge, on which the cables are afterward spun. I try, also, to fasten upon a *central motif* for each setting. Does the composition of the room revolve about a door? A table? A view from the window? A color? A texture? Just as the director must find a central action, so the designer must find a central scenic theme related to the action.[6]

An illuminating example of Gorelik's thinking is indicated in his approach to Chekhov's *The Three Sisters:*

It is the *dramatic metaphor,* probably, which sums up, for each setting, all the thoughts which the designer may have. Thus, the attic bedroom of the *Three Sisters* is not only an attic, not only a bedroom, not only a girl's room, not only a European room, not only a room of the period of 1901, not only a room belonging to the gentlefolk whom Chekhov wrote about. On top of all that, and including all that, it may be for the designer, the scene of a raging fever.[7]

Jo Mielziner describes his way of working, bearing in mind particularly the actor's use of the stage:

I used to begin working on a play by creating a visual picture of the *mise-en-scène.* I have since given that up, and nowadays, after reading the play through once, I go over it again, seeking this time to visualize in my own mind the actors in the important situations of the drama. This may give me an idea for a significant piece of furniture, a quality of light or shadow, a color combination; it may not be an entire setting at all—just something that is associated with the dramatic significance of the moment, but which may become a clue to, or indeed the cornerstone of, the whole setting.[8]

Still another example shows how the designer Donald Oenslager seeks to capture the atmosphere of the play:

Hamlet dwells in a dual world, the everyday world of external events which is the life of the Court, and the haunted, brooding world of the imagination which is the inner world of an avenging Prince, who drifts down endless corridors of dark, fir-bordered streams. . . . It is the conflict of these two worlds that unbalances his mind and goads him on to indecisive action and helpless frustration.

The way he distorts the external world through the eyes of his own inner world of the imagination must determine the nature and appearance of the scenes. Just as he sees the events of the Court in the curving mirror of his own brooding con-jectures, so the scenes which he inhabits must appear as indefinite embodiments of his own inner pre-occupations. The members of the Court must seem to be resolved into dewy shadows of this "too, too solid flesh" and cloaked in veiled fragments of reality. . . . For all the Castle scenes bare, chalky walls are pierced with tall tragic doors—always three, whose depth beyond is as black as Hamlet's sable suit. They must be high, very high, to admit his anguish and his spirit. Only flashes of red, the red of blood, livens the scenes—washed over walls, or splotched on characters' clothing.[9]

[6]Mordecai Gorelik, quoted in John Gassner, ed., *Producing the Play* (New York: Holt, Rinehart & Winston, 1953).

[7]John Gassner, *Producing the Play.*

[8]Jo Mielziner, "The Designer Sets the Stage," *Theatre Arts Anthology* (New York: Theater Arts Books, 1950).

[9]Donald Oenslager, *Scenery Then and Now* (New York: W. W. Norton & Co., Inc., 1936).

The sketches the designer creates should suggest the appearance of the setting as it will actually appear to the audience. It should be in proportion, and it must be reproducible within the limitations of the stage and theatrical materials. The sketch should also indicate the color schemes, and it may give some sense of the lighting.

These preliminary sketches are a basis for communication between director and designer. Once there is common agreement on the basic designs, the designer prepares a model set, which is a scaled replica constructed in three dimensions. It is usually rather rough in form since it is not intended for display, but for making the director aware of the plasticity of the set, the spatial relationships of the various parts, which are very useful to him in visualizing and planning movement. The model is also helpful to the designer in his preparation of the lighting, and it is extremely useful in solving difficulties of constructing and shifting scenery.

The next step in design is the preparation of working drawings through which the sketch and model are translated into actual scenery by the carpenters and painters. The working drawings usually include a scaled and dimensioned floor plan, elevations of the walls, a hanging chart of flying pieces, and detail drawings of special set pieces and properties. Complete specifications are a part of the drawings. In the professional theater, the designer may make only the sketches and the model, turning the preparation of the working drawings over to a draftsman, and the construction over to professional scene builders and painters. In the educational and community theater, the scene designer often works through all steps of the design from the preliminary sketches to the actual construction, painting, and mounting of the set.

Perhaps one of the most interesting ways of showing designers at work is to consider their efforts on the same play. The following are descriptive passages of three designers' approaches to *Macbeth*. The first is a celebrated statement of Gordon Craig, which illustrates his intuitive and aesthetic feeling for design:

Come now, we take *Macbeth*. We know the play well. In what kind of place is that play laid? How does it look, first of all to our mind's eye? Secondly to our eye?

I see two things. I see a lofty and steep rock, and I see the moist cloud which envelops the head of this rock. That is to say, a place for fierce and warlike men to inhabit, a place for phantoms to nest in. Ultimately this moisture will destroy the men. Now then, you are quick in your question as to what actually to create for the eye. I answer as swiftly—place there a rock! Let it mount up high. Swiftly I tell you, convey the idea of a mist which hugs the head of this rock. Now, have I departed at all for one-eighth of an inch from the vision which I saw in the mind's eye?

But you ask me what form this rock shall take and what color? What are the lines which are the lofty lines, and which are to be seen in any lofty cliff? Go to them, glance but a moment at them; now quickly set them down on your paper; *the lines and their directions*, never mind the cliff. Do not be afraid to let them go high; they cannot go high enough; and remember that on a sheet of paper which is but two inches square you can make a line which seems to tower miles in the air, and you can do the same on your stage, for it is all a matter of proportion and nothing to do with actuality.

You ask about the colors? What are the colors that Shakespeare has indicated

Gordon Craig's design for Macbeth.

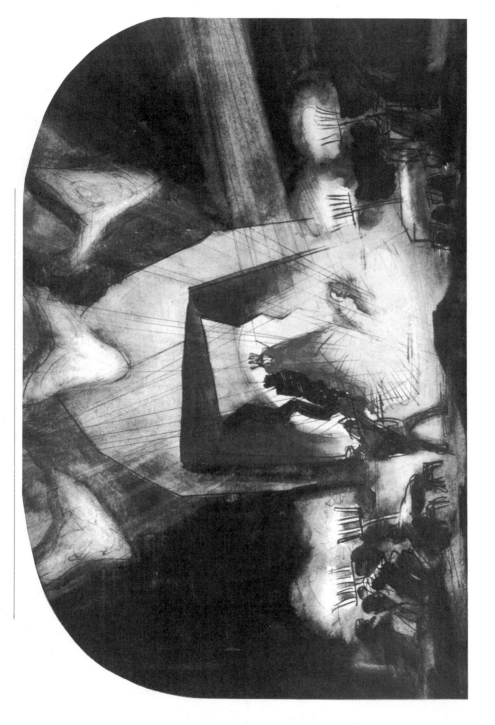

Set design by Robert Edmund Jones for the banquet scene in Macbeth.

273

for us? Do not first look at Nature, but look in the play of the poet. Two; one for the rock, the man; one for the mist, the spirit.[10]

The second description is of the banquet scene as it appeared in Max Reinhardt's production of *Macbeth*, designed by Ernest Stern. Lewisohn's account of the production emphasizes the overall severity:

> Take the scene of the banquet in *Macbeth*. Every line is a straight line, every angle a right angle. All form is reduced to a barbaric severity. But the two rectangular windows in the background through which the cold Northern stars glitter are narrow and tall—so unimaginably tall that they seem to touch that sky of doom. The torches turn the rough brown of the primitive walls to a tarnished bronze. Only on the rude table lie splashes of menacing yellow. There is something barren and gigantic about the scene—a sinister quiet, a dull presage.[11]

The eminent theater critic Stark Young described the celebrated designs of Robert Edmond Jones for a New York production in 1921.

> This design for *Macbeth* was the most profoundly creative decor that I have ever seen in the theater. There was a stage enclosed with a background of black, flat so that no light was caught to break the complete darkness of it. Drawings or photographs can give at least a suggestion, and only a suggestion of the gold frames, or sharp gold lines, or the forms like Gothic abstractions, or however we may define them, which, standing alone, against the black, defined the scenes. Three great tragic masks were hung to the front, high above the action, and from them vast daggers of light poured down, crossed, pierced, flooded the action below, as in the witches' scene or the banquet. The banquet hall with its gold and light figures moving, and above all else Lady Macbeth's robe, in which a hidden combination of many shades, an unheard-of-intensity of red was discovered, defied any conveyance in words.[12]

Each of these designs is valid in its own right. We see the designer's efforts to evoke the appropriate atmosphere of the play, to intensify its emotional content through judicious use of line, color, lighting, and texture, and to create the environment for the action. Each represents the approach of the designer in assisting in the interpretation of a play.

The Designer
in the New Theater

The cleavage between various *isms* in our theater today is largely a matter of academic argument, and while there is little profit in trying to separate various styles and modes into confining compartments, it may be helpful to distinguish between two points of view toward theatrical production. On the one hand, there are those in the Aristotelian tradition who look upon drama as an imitation

[10]Craig, *On the Art of the Theater.*
[11]Ludwig Lewisohn, *The Drama and the Stage* (New York: Harcourt Brace Jovanovich, 1922).
[12]Ralph Pendleton, ed., *The Theater of Robert Edmond Jones* (Middletown, Conn.: Wesleyan University Press, 1958).

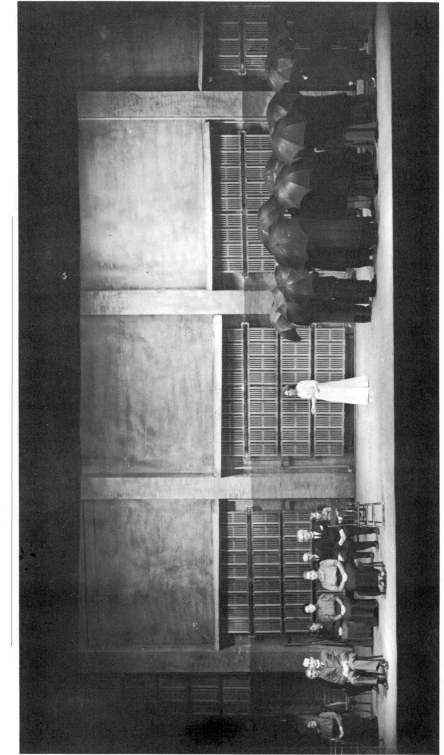

Scene from Thornton Wilder's Our Town, *1938, a production that used presentational staging.*

of life. This attitude, referred to as *representationalism* by Alexander Bakshy, endeavors to create the illusion of actuality. The characters and events on stage have, for the moment, the authenticity of real life. On the other hand, there is *presentationalism*, in which it is frankly admitted that the theater is make-believe and that the actors are only pretending. Although less familiar to Western audiences, presentational staging has a long tradition, notably in the Oriental theater where symbolic conventions are readily accepted. For example, two coolies carrying flags on which are painted wheels become a carriage; a stick becomes a horse when a rider mounts it; and a table may be a bridge, a bed, or a mountaintop.

The revolt in the theater since World War II has resulted in a much freer approach to all aspects of staging, although representationalism remains remarkably persistent, especially on the commercial stage. Two factors influence this preference. Most theaters are proscenium arch, picture-frame playhouses which were designed for productions using scenic background, and many nineteenth- and twentieth-century dramatists have written their plays in a

French farce is given the appearance of reality in Karl-Ernst Hermann's settings for Labiche's The Pot *at the Schaubühne in West Berlin. Directed by Peter Stein. Note the three-dimensional quality of the scenic elements and effective use of texture and lighting.*

Another set for Labiche's The Pot *at the Schaubühne in West Berlin.*

realistic mode. Additionally, many people accustomed to conventional scenery are more at ease with plays staged in a familiar manner. Hence, if you go to the Broadway theaters or those of West End London, most of the time you will see plays performed and mounted in a realistic manner, especially comedies, mystery-melodramas, and revivals of realistic playwrights such as Shaw, Ibsen, and Chekhov. The realism has become selective, and the playwright may make free use of time and place, but in general, there is an effort to achieve the illusion of reality— even when the box set is rejected. For example, in Brian Clark's *Whose Life Is It Anyway?* (1978)—a fascinating play about a paralytic who is unable to move his body (or *her* body—Mary Tyler Moore took over the leading role in New York), the protagonist manages to wage and win a battle for the right to die in the face of opposition from the medical profession. The action requires a hospital room and an adjoining doctor's office which are suggested by a skeletal framework and appropriate furniture. The illusion of reality is left to the audience's imagination. There is no need for a complete pictorial representation. This use of selective realism is quite familiar now and the suggestion of locale by props, costumes, and lighting is standard practice for period plays, musical comedies, and ballet. In the final analysis what is really needed to create the environment for the action is not a welter of physical detail, but a sense of aesthetic credibility that stems mostly from the actors' way of performing.

Another designer using multiple images to set the background for the environment is Rouban Ter-Arutunian for Arthur Schnitzler's Light of Love. *(Academy Theater, Vienna. Directed by Gerhard Klingenberg.)*

Stage designers explore the new theater in a variety of ways. They respond to the revolution and experimentation in the visual arts in expanding the areas of perception, in relating the external image to the unconscious, in the juxtaposition of disparate objects and experiences through the use of simultaneous viewing and the combination of media, and in showing the dynamic nature of creation through the use of mobile forms and kinetic objects. Again, taking their

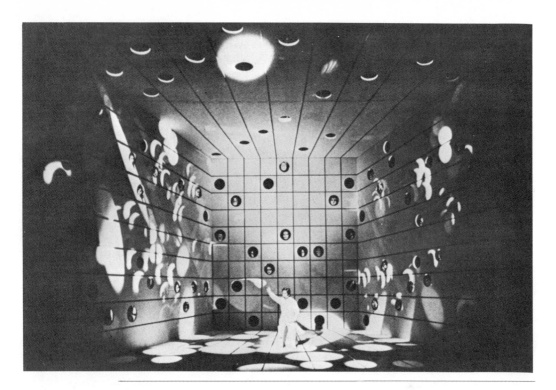

In this production of Hikarigoke *(Luminous Moss) by Ikuma Dan circular holes were cut in the ceiling and walls, through which the performers appeared and sang their parts. (Directed by Keita Asari; designed by Kaoru Kankmori at the Nissei Gekijo, Tokyo.)*

cue from contemporary painters and sculptors, designers have opened up a world of possibilities in new materials. As Saulo Benavente put it:

> I believe that contemporary dramatic art and its typical dramatists such as Brecht and Duerrenmatt are partly rooted in the world of plastics, anodized aluminum, steel tube scaffolding, gas-filled lamps, nylon, electronic controls, and polyethylenes, not to mention still and motion-picture projections and mobiles *à la* Calder. As, furthermore, I am convinced that the primordial condition of the existence of the theater is the contemporaneousness of its forms of expression, I do not think that the designer today can refuse to make use of new materials, new techniques and new methods to lend the imagination of true reality, conforming to the times in which we live. [13]

In the new materials, the designer has found fresh sources of visual impact through color and texture, and their structural quality has provided a freedom unknown to those who worked with wood and canvas. The new materials are strong yet lightweight, flexible, easy to manipulate, and ideally suited to the flow

[13]Rene Hainaux, ed., *Stage Design Throughout the World Since 1950* (New York: International Theater Institute, 1964).

Another use of varied images to create a theatrical environment was designed by Wilfred Minks for Wedekind's Castle Wetterstein. *(Directed by Armo Wustenhofer at Wuppertaler Theater in West Germany.) Note the incongruous juxtaposing of objects setting up tensions that echo the playwright's theme—the aggressive, disruptive force of sex in conventional society.*

that is so much a part of the changing forms of theater. Then, too, new potentials are opening up in stage lighting with the use of laser beams and holographs for expanding the use of projected scenery. But the most important ingredient in stage design is the imagination of the artist.

An example of ingenious scenography was David Boroyskij's design for Vassiliev's *Yet the Dawns Are Calm* (1975) in Moscow. A single, flexible setting was made up of an authentic-looking military truck. The parts are broken down during the performance and reassembled to suggest a variety of environments for a battalion of women who are sent to the front, where they all die. Combined with imaginative lighting and sound, the scenic elements represented a moving convoy, trenches, or a temporary shelter, boats, and a forest where a battle is staged.

Another Soviet designer, Edward Stepanovich Kochergin at the Gorki Theater in Leningrad, is famous for the "poor theater" quality of his settings in which he uses natural materials. From visits to the forests and countryside, he gathers rocks, branches, mosses, and old wood to inspire his use of color and

An interesting use of realism occurs in David Storey's The Contractor.
During the course of the play the performers go through the actual
process of erecting and dismantling the tent for a wedding ceremony.
(Directed by Martin J. Bennison; designed by Michael Griffith. Miami
University, Ohio.)

texture in his designs. Pushkin's *Boris Godunov* (1973) was constructed of a
framework made of tree limbs stripped of their bark. Over the frame Kochergin
stretched tattered burlap in patches that suggested leaves. The raked floor was
made of worn wood planking and the set was "decorated" by old church bells.
For Leo Tolstoi's *Tale of a Horse* (1976) the designer fashioned a courtyard
where horses are kept. Again he covered the walls with burlap with bulges that
opened like festered wounds showing red fabric in the gaps from which tiny
blossoms fell. During the climactic moments, red lights flashed with a pulse-like
beat to suggest the suffering of the horses. Kochergin is fond of the device of
breaking through the walls to let light pour in. His design for *Hamlet* was constructed of bleached wood that enclosed the acting area except for the audience
side. Cracks and fissures in the wooden shell allowed light to spill on the rough
floor. His set for *Monologue for Marriage* depicted the playwright's view of
matrimony as a precarious institution by surrounding the action with paper
walls, which through the play are torn away so that at the end the stage is a
shambles.

One of the most creative designers is the Czechoslovakian Josef Svoboda,
whose combination of aesthetic and technological talents has enabled him to

281

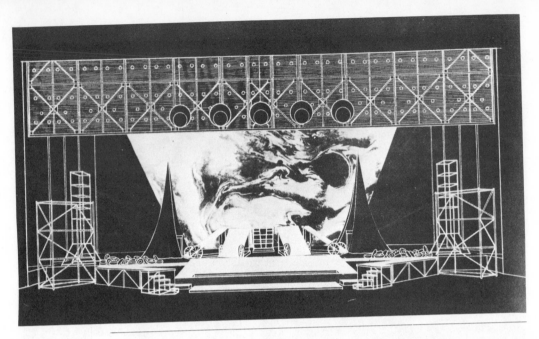

Spectacular set design for Tokyo production of Jesus Christ Superstar *by Kaoru Kanamori. (Directed by Keita Asari; lighting by Yuji Sawada. Nakano Sun Plaza Hall.)*

Designer Rene Allio provided a setting of extensive walkways that brought the action out into the audience for The Merchant of Venice. *(Directed by Peter Zadek, Schauspielhaus, Bochum, West Germany.)*

Ilmars Blumbergs designed a setting for Andris Oupite's Jeanna D'Arc *showing symbolically the increasing presence of evil through the encroachment of objects that transform the stage from white nothingness to black—and finally a pyre. (Directed by Arkady Katz at the Roussky Dramatitchesky Teatr, Riga, Latvia.)*

Josef Svoboda's setting for Rostand's Cyrano de Bergerac, *produced in Prague under the direction of Miroslav Machacek.*

provide stunning examples of the new uses of the stage. His view of the theater is to provide "a vivid sense of separate elements imaginatively combined to express new insights into reality." He considers that his purpose as a designer is not to provide substitutes for décor or delineation of locale, but to create new stage space. His designs exploit the theatrical possibilities of kinetic scenery and multiple images which can react to or against the live performer on stage.

For his production of *Hamlet* in Brussels (1965), director Ottomar Krejca based his interpretation on the idea that the ghost was a fiction of Hamlet—his alter ego—so that the play is concerned with this dual role. Svoboda's technical solution to the alter ego concept was to use a mirror whose reflections he could control to reveal not only the protagonist's state of mind but the disparity of his surrounding world as well. For a production of the Capek brothers' *The Insect Comedy* he used two mirrors, twenty-five feet square, which were placed at an angle so as to reflect the decorated area of the stage floor, which contained a turntable. No regular scenery was used and only the stage floor was lighted. Svoboda's set design for *Romeo and Juliet* at the National Theater in Prague (1963) was made up of architectural components that moved in a variety of ways—rising, sinking, sliding laterally or forward and back to accommodate the action.

284

Setting by Josef Svoboda for Gorki's The Last Ones, *Prague, 1966, showing the use of projected scenery in conjunction with live action.*

It is particularly in the use of projections that Svoboda has made such interesting contributions, for he is at once an artist and an engineer. One of his devices, the *diapolyekran*, is a complex screen on which simultaneous and synchronous slides and films can be shown and so controlled as to exploit the interplay between the images. His Laterna Magika is a multiscreen device designed for use onstage with the live actor. It enables the director to work with a visual collage of background or supporting material in a new way—as director Jan Grossman put it, to show "the multiplicity and contrariety of the world in which we live." Svoboda describes the use of projections in his designs for Gorki's *The Last Ones:*

We stacked things, people, scenes behind each other; for example, action around the wheelchair downstage, above that a girl in a tub being stroked by twigs, "in front" of her a boy being flogged on the screen; then suddenly, a drape covering part

285

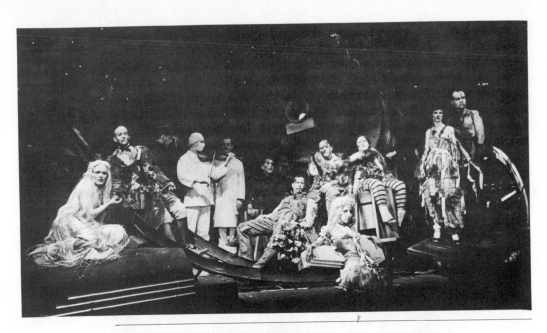

The Polish surrealistic playwright, Stanislaw Witkiewicz, viewed society as a train run by lunatics hurtling toward destruction in his The Crazy Locomotive. Chelsea Theater Center, New York. (Directed by Des McAnuff; designed by Douglas W. Schmidt). This shot shows the cast following the crash. Compare with the train wreck for The Whip (p. 83).

of the screen opens and we see a small, live orchestra playing a waltz, with pomp—an image of the regime. A space collage using a triptych principle, truly a dramatic poem—what I wanted to do. A clear spatial aesthetic is formed by the contrast of stage action, flat projection, and live orchestra behind the screen on which the images are projected. It's all structured like music, and a law is present. Break it and a new one is set up. This is what attracts me—leitmotifs and repetitions, then sudden contrast; plus tempo indications. Themes disappear only to crop up again later.[14]

Another production meshing live action with film occurred in the Chelsea Theater Center production of Stanislaw Witkiewicz's *The Crazy Locomotive*. The play, written between the two world wars, depicts modern society out of control, symbolized by a train hurtling toward destruction. The crash was highly theatricalized beginning with action on stage, then shifting to a film of an onrushing train, and back to the stage and the mangled train. The effect was heightened by a realistic soundtrack and glowing lights that swept through the auditorium.

As we have seen, one of the interesting developments of theatrical production comes from the fresh interpretation of an established play. We remember

[14]Jarka Burian, "Joseph Svoboda: Artist in an Age of Science," *Educational Theater Journal*, 22, no. 2 (May 1970).

One view of the monumental setting designed by Dan Nemteanu for
Brecht's St. Joan of the Stockyards *at the Helsinki City Theater. Directed*
by Eugen Terttula.

Brook's *Midsummer Night's Dream*, Stein's *Peer Gynt*, and Svoboda's *Hamlet* and *Romeo and Juliet*. At the Bayreuth Festival Theater in Germany, the designer for Wagner's *Ring* cycle created a sensation with his opening *Rheingold* set. Instead of the traditional great stone setting at the bottom of the Rhine River, a huge dam was built across the stage, complete with practical metal walkways and ladders which were used by the maiden attendants. An elevated cylinder was placed horizontally at the center that revolved as the water passed over it and flowed down the sluices and through metal grills in the forestage.

Antoine Vitez's production of Brecht's *Mother Courage* presented a highly personal and innovative approach to the play. Instead of the peddler's wagon specified in the script, Vitez substituted a baby carriage to shift the image of the title role to suggest perpetual maternalism. And instead of the usual revolving stage, the designer represented the acting area as a long road, endlessly traversed by Courage with her carriage.

Earlier on, we described Foreman's novel approach to production, in which he rejects most of the traditional practices in favor of a theater of images. For the past several years he has worked in a Soho loft. The audience sits on seven rows of raked bleacher seats facing a large, rectangular acting area. Foreman's innovations aim at discovery rather than illusions of reality. He works with spaces inside of spaces, using frames, pillars, runways, and sliding walls that are changed manually before the audience. He plays with perceptions of proportions, scale and perspective, creating elaborate images with rapid changes full of

287

Mother Courage, *staged in the round by Antoine Vitez, at the Theatre des Quartiers d'Ivry, Nanterre, France. The rectangular acting area represents a road that Courage travels with her vehicle—a baby-carriage rather than a huge peddler's cart. Designed by Yannis Kokkos.*

Designer Eugene Lee placed the final scene of King Lear *in this barn-like environment when Lear grieves over the body of Cordelia. The setting is interesting for the grubby texture of the materials. (Directed by Adrian Hall. Trinity Square Repertory Company, Providence.)*

289

*Setting by Josef Svoboda for
Duerrenmatt's* The Anabaptists *at
the National Theater, Prague,
directed by M. Machacek.*

exotic and fascinating details. In productions like *Phedra in Potatoland* (1976), *Book of Splendors* (1977), and *Blvd. de Paris* or *Torture on a Train* (1977) Foreman manipulates set pieces and movable walls of alternate opaque and transparent materials to hide and reveal discoveries, while setting up varied planes through railings or low walls combined with framing devices. The visual material is orchestrated with tape recordings of dialogue and sounds to elicit an oddly evocative sensory response.

In his concern with productions that discard the usual plot and character pattern, and instead produce a flow of images, Foreman joins with Robert Wilson and the Mabou Mines in making theater in a fresh and original way.

It is apparent that the trend to make the theater more theatrical will encourage the elimination of the gaps between performer and spectator, playing space and auditorium. With a more open climate for playwriting, designers will be more and more concerned with the total environment. With the availability of new materials and facilities, the only limitation will be the sweep of designers' imaginations.

Bibliography

APPIA, ADOLPHE, *The Work of Living Art*, trans. H. D. Albright. Coral Gables: University of Miami Press, 1961.

BAY, HOWARD, *Stage Design*. New York: Drama Book Specialists, 1974.

BURDICK, ELIZABETH B., PEGGY C. HANSEN, and BRENDA ZANGER, *Contemporary Stage Design, U.S.A.* Englewood Cliffs, N.J.: Prentice-Hall, Inc., 1974.

BURIAN, JARKA, *The Scenography of Josef Svoboda.* Middletown, Conn.: Wesleyan University Press, 1971.

CRAIG, EDWARD GORDON, *Theater Advancing.* Little, Brown & Company, 1963.

GILLETTE, A. S., *Stage Scenery.* New York: Harper & Row, Publishers, Inc., 1972.

HAINAUX, RENE, ed., *Stage Design Throughout the World, 1970–1975.* New York: Theater Arts Books, 1976.

JONES, ROBERT EDMOND, *The Dramatic Imagination.* Middletown, Conn.: Wesleyan University Press, 1941.

OENSLAGER, DONALD, *The Theater of Donald Oenslager.* Middletown, Conn.: Wesleyan University Press, 1978.

PARKER, OREN W., *Scene Design and Stage Lighting.* New York: Holt, Rinehart and Winston, 1979.

PILBROW, RICHARD, *Stage Lighting.* London: Studio Vista, 1970.

SIMONSON, LEE, *The Art of Scenic Design.* New York: Harper & Row, Publishers, Inc., 1950.

ELEVEN
Theater
Architecture

The physical environment for performance exerts a considerable influence on those who use it. The shape, the arrangement of the parts, the relation of performers to the audience, and the size of the structure affect the conventions of staging, the style of production, and the nature of the drama. For example, the Kabuki theater, with its raised passageways leading from the stage to the back of the auditorium, capitalizes on striking entrances and exits in a manner unknown in Western drama except in the Greek theater. The large unlocalized platform jutting out into the center of the pit of the Elizabethan theater gave to Shakespeare and his contemporaries a stage of exceptional versatility for putting most of the action of a complicated plot before the eyes of a spectator. A modern arena stage with the playing area enclosed by a few rows of spectators in a small hall with little or no scenic support, dictates an intimate style of performance free from exaggeration. A renovated warehouse adapted for performance not only conditions the physical relationship of spectator and actor, but imposes a psychological climate unknown in the traditional playhouse. To understand the drama of any period, it is helpful to know something of the characteristics of the theater which housed it.

When drama began with the Greeks it made use of existing structures such as a threshing floor or a marketplace. Before the Theater was built in London in 1576, performances were given in inn-yards, banquet halls, churches, and city squares. But as drama became more mature and complex, it was necessary to design and construct a theater specifically suited to dramatic production. And as a corollary, once the theater found a satisfactory form, the architecture affected the playwright's way of writing.

A theater must be appropriate to the kind of drama it serves. We have had to learn this lesson though trial and error, such as the efforts to produce Shakespeare in the pictorial tradition of the proscenium arch theater with the resultant loss of fluency so essential to playing Elizabethan plays. Likewise, the production of Greek tragedy in the cramped playing area of a modern playhouse is awkward, not only because our taste for illusion is at odds with the conventions of the Greek theater but also because there is the problem of the handling of the chorus. In most Greek plays it remains visible throughout the performance. In the ancient theater it was possible to position the chorus at the outside edge of the orchestra because the audience was seated high enough to see over it. In a proscenium theater or thrust stage, there is no place to put the chorus. Most of those who work in the educational theater today feel that student audiences should be offered a wide variety of dramatic productions of all periods and all styles, but in an effort to achieve flexibility in an all-purpose building we risk the danger of constructing a theater that does not serve any drama very well.

While over the years there has been a good deal of variety in theater architecture, two basic requisites have obtained. The audience must be able to see and hear, and the actors must have an area where they can perform. The comfort and convenience of the audience has often been a requisite so that the spectator is free from distractions. (In recent experimental situations none of these imperatives have been considered important!) In order to get some notion of various solutions to the staging of plays, let us briefly examine four representative theaters.

The Greek Theater

The first Greek theater was built on the slopes of the Acropolis in Athens at the beginning of the fifth century B.C. It consisted of three parts: (1) the *theatron* for the audience, (2) the *orchestra*, or dancing circle for the performer, and (3) the *skene*, or stagehouse for the background õf the action. The theatron, at first with wooden seats and later replaced by stone, seated about 16,000 spectators, and it was comprised of 80 rows of seats arranged in a semicircular pattern around the orchestra. Although the theatron was large, the absence of barriers between players and spectators gave the effect of close relationship between them. Most authorities agree that all of the performers—actors as well as chorus—played in

A reconstruction of a Greek theater based on the ruins at Epidaurus, which date from the fourth century B.C.

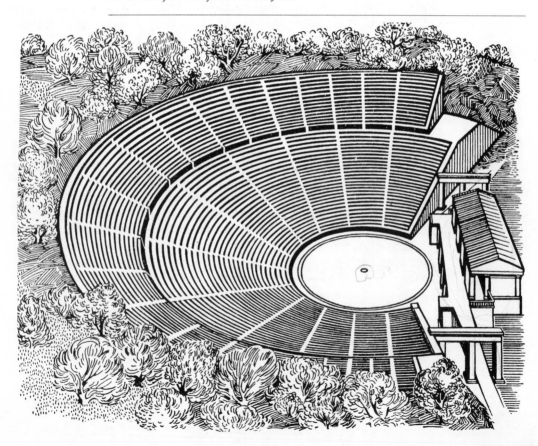

the orchestra, a large, earthen circle about twenty meters across with an altar in the center. Passageways at either side of the orchestra called *parodoi* made possible spectacular and lively entrances and exits. Actors could also enter from three openings in the skene. There was no stage, as such, although the actors would have been well served by a platform with steps in front of the skene as a place for speeches, debates, and entrances and exits. In the orchestra circle were three acoustical centers at which the actors could most easily be heard. One center was at the very middle where an altar was placed, and the other two are about five meters at either side. In festival productions at Epidaurus these centers affected the blocking of the action, because directors and actors had learned to capitalize on them during many of the most telling moments of the play. The style of acting in the Greek theater demanded broad gestures because of the immense size of the theater, but because of the excellent acoustics, the actors' speeches did not require extensive volume. As a result the acting style in the Greek theater was probably neither stagey nor bombastic.

Two mechanical devices are of interest in the Greek theater. The *deus ex machina* or "god of the machine" was a cranelike device for raising and lowering a god into the scene. Another mechanical contrivance was the *eccyclema*, some sort of portable platform which could be moved out into the audience's view for an interior scene, and for exhibiting dead bodies, as in *Agamemnon* and *Medea*. Aristophanes also used these devices when he was spoofing tragedies. Although the Greeks used scene painting, it is a mistake to think of elaborate settings as enclosing the action. There was probably simple iconographic suggestion of locale mounted on the skene wall to suggest place,

A mechanical flying device was used in the Greek theater, especially in the plays of Euripides. Aristophanes was fond of satirizing Euripides, even in his use of the flying device. In Thesmophoriazusae, *Euripides flies away in an attempt to rescue Mnesilochus, held hostage by the women's assembly.*

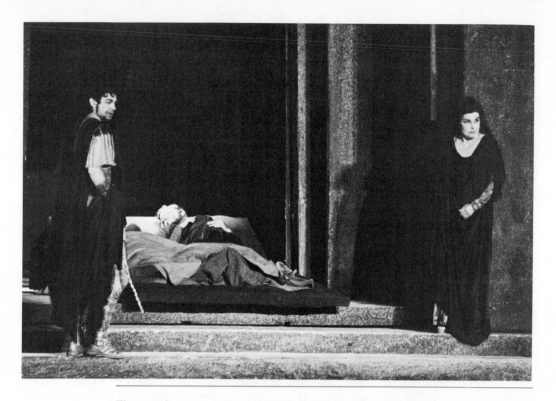

The eccyclema was a low, movable platform that could be positioned in the central doorway for displaying corpses. In this shot, the bodies of Agamemnon and Cassandra are shown along with their slayers, Aegisthus and Clytemnestra. Greek National Theater, Epidaurus.

but no doubt the actors played a good deal of the time well out in the orchestra, often in close rapport with the chorus. The fact that the spectator could look over the chorus into the center of the orchestra opened up the potential for a great deal of movement and an enormous number of blocking arrangements. Despite the minimal use of scenery, the Greek theater was not lacking in spectacle. The theater itself was a handsome structure, and in addition the eye was delighted by the costumes and masks of the participants and the movement and dancing of the chorus. No performer or spectator in history ever enjoyed a more felicitous theater.

Medieval Dramatic Production

The revival of theatrical activity after the dark ages is usually associated with the church, when the liturgy was expanded by using elements of drama until they became entire plays. The favorite material depicted the events surrounding Easter, Christmas, the miracles, and the lives of saints. As religious drama became more popular various stations of the church were utilized for each segment of a story until productions became so complex and the material so secular that they moved outside to churchyards or marketplaces.

Staging conventions evolved, centering on two elements, the *mansions* and the *platea*. Mansions were small scenic representations of caves, inns, palaces, ships, or most importantly Heaven and Hell. They were sometimes arranged in a straight line, at other times in a square or circle, behind a raised platform; the platea was an unlocalized acting area where most of the performance took place. The mansions set the locale and provided entrances and exits but they were usually too small for playing a scene; the bulk of the action took place on the platea that served as any place the actors required. The combination of mansions and platea provided a versatile kind of staging eminently suited to the playing of a series of incidents.

By the early thirteenth century, plays were being given outside the church, although liturgical drama continued to be performed inside as well for the next three centuries. The reasons behind the increasing scope of drama outside the church may have been the introduction of the Corpus Christi festival by Pope Urban IV in 1264, which was designed to center attention on the redemptive power of the sacrament of communion, making symbolic use of the bread and wine. This festival was widely celebrated and among other things it was a theme that encouraged display and action. It is thought by some to have been one of the influences leading to the development of cycle plays by the middle of the fourteenth century. As drama moved from the liturgical it used the vernacular, so the cycle plays are not in Latin, but in the vernacular.

Although in England more than a hundred towns are known to have performed plays when medieval drama was most popular (1350–1550), not many of the texts survive. The four principal extant mystery cycle plays are from York, Chester, Wakefield (Towneley), and Lincoln. Each cycle was actually a series of plays based on stories from the Bible. In France a larger number of plays survive, ranging from short playlets to extensive cycles requiring 25 days to perform. In addition to the texts, there also remain records of productions, plans for staging and costuming, and many fascinating details of production. The plays were performed by laymen from religious guilds or confraternities on the continent and by craftsmen's guilds under the watchful eye of the church, and often of town councils as well. Plays were assigned according to the work done by the guild. For example, in Lincoln, the popular *Harrowing of Hell* was assigned to the cooks because they were used to boiling, baking, and working with fire. Another popular episode was Noah and the ark played by shipwrights, featuring a lively domestic quarrel when a cantankerous Mrs. Noah refused to go in the ark, and was dragged inside, clawing and scratching, by her husband and sons. Many such familiar and local touches enlivened the plays which were performed in the vernacular and included a good deal of secular and comic material.

Another kind of drama appeared which did not come from a biblical background—these were morality plays whose purpose was to teach moral and religious duties. Its characters were allegorical figures representing virtues and vices such as Covetousness, Pride, Lust, Gluttony, Fellowship, and Good Deeds, along with God, the Devil, and Mankind. In writing these moral interludes, playwrights developed the ability to sustain a conflict and to organize a plot with considerable detail. The most famous morality play is *Everyman*.

Since medieval drama sought maximum identification with the spectator, great efforts were made to achieve realistic and sensational effects, especially in harrowing scenes of torture, legerdemain, and spectacle. With considerable ingenuity and zeal, ways were devised for showing miracles such as changing water into wine, walking on the water, or feeding the 5000. A favorite special effect was "flying" through the use of ropes, pulleys, and winches that enabled angels to float in the sky and saints to soar toward Heaven. Likewise, trap doors in the stage floor made possible startling discoveries and appearances. Scenes of torture were staged with careful attention to detail. For instance, in the enactment of the hanging of Judas, an effigy was stuffed with animal entrails so that when the body burst open, a realistic and gruesome effect was achieved. In one production that depicted the martyrdom of St. Paul, his head was severed and bounced three times, and at each spot the head touched a well flowed with milk, blood, and water.

The scope and complexity of vernacular theatrical production demanded considerable preparation and organization, since there were many people involved in setting up, crewing, and performing the plays. The overall supervision was given at times to a "pageant master" who was paid for his services, as were many of the craftsmen. Some men developed such expertise that they traveled from town to town organizing the staging and directing the actors. Many of the performers were local laymen who were paid for performing. There were also local veteran performers who were probably assigned roles. Discipline was maintained by the guilds; performers were sometimes fined for failing to learn their roles or for missing rehearsals.

Vernacular drama was produced with either a fixed or movable stage. Although both were in wide use throughout Europe, the movable or "pageant" version was most prevalent in England and Spain. The pageant stage was drawn through the streets in a procession so that each episode could be performed at stopping places along the way. The best notion we have of the pageant comes from a description by David Rogers in his *Some Few Recollections of the City of Chester* from about the beginning of the seventeenth century. He says the pageant wagons "were a big scaffold with two rooms, a higher and a lower, upon four wheels. In the lower they apparelled themselves, and in the higher room they played."[1] The accuracy of this description is questioned on the basis that the wagon would be too cumbersome a vehicle for easy hauling and would offer too restricted a playing area. However, it does not take much imagination to suggest that the upper level could have served for locating the episode and, following the convention of liturgical drama staging, the action could have included the ground level around the wagon. Moreover, the curtained lower level of the wagon might very well have been used for entrances, exits, and for such business as hiding.

[1]David Rogers, *Some Few Recollections of the City of Chester.*

Glynne Wickham suggests another version of the pageant in *Early English Stages.* He argues for a single-storied wagon occupied by mansions and used for dressing rooms and scenic background. For the acting area, he envisions a scaffold cart placed alongside the pageant wagon.[2] Wickham's reconstruction approximates a common practice in Spain in which playing platforms were available at each site and were used in connection with movable wagons.

The more common fixed stages were set up in marketplaces, courtyards, public squares, or churchyards; sometimes they made use of existing structures such as Roman amphitheaters and old forts. Usually the staging utilized a long, rectangular platform backed by permanent buildings. At Mons in 1501 *The Mystery of the Passion* employed 67 mansions. At Valenciennes (1547) a stage was erected over forty meters long with Heaven at one end and Hell-mouth at the other. In between were a variety of other stations, including a Temple, the House of the High Priest, and a marketplace. At Lucerne, more than 30 stations were placed about the sides of the Wine Market for the Passion Play (1583).

The conventions of staging liturgical drama were continued, using the mansions for representing the locales and the platea, the neutral stage space, for the action. Two mansions received the most attention, Heaven and Hell. Every effort was made to make Heaven as resplendent as possible with rich ornamentation and even flying angels. But the dominating mansion was Hell, made as terrifying as possible to frighten the sinful into salvation. Very often the mansion was a huge monster's head with billowing smoke and fire from which devils emerged to capture the sinners and drive them into the great mouth which swallowed them up as they screamed in terror.

Medieval staging had several important consequences. The audience was closely related to the performer. There was no architectural separation, no spatial detachment. Furthermore, the introduction of comic material into serious drama and the use of lowly characters encouraged intercommunication and rapport between performer and spectator. The playing area allowed for unrestricted freedom of movement, which meant that all of the action could be performed rather than talked about. The physical characteristics of the medieval stage encouraged the use of episodic or loose-knit plot structure, the mixture of comic and serious material and characters, and stories filled with vigorous action.

The graphic representation of specific locale, combined with the neutral playing area of the platea, had two interesting effects on subsequent dramatic development. In France, the pictorial tradition continued, but when drama went indoors again, the size of the theater made it impossible to show more than a few mansions at one time. This, coupled with the misinterpretation of Aristotle by classical scholars in insisting on the unities, led to the imposition of a rigid structure on French playwrights which profoundly affected the future of their drama. In England, the reverse was true. The Elizabethan theater capitalized on the freedom of the platea as the main acting area, and virtually ignored the need for representational background. This flexible physical theater gave to Shake-

[2]Glynne Wickham, *Early English Stages, 1300–1660* (New York: Columbia University Press, 1959–1963).

A medieval mansion stage at Valenciennes, France, 1547. Note various "mansions" or stations with Heaven at one side and Hell-mouth at the other.

300

speare and his contemporaries the opportunity to continue the medieval tradition of using a complicated plot, and putting much of the essential action of their stories on stage before the eyes of their audience.

During the six centuries in which medieval drama grew from simple liturgical playlets to complex vernacular cycle plays produced with considerable care and expense, the theater was a communal affair associated with the localities where it was performed. Furthermore, it enjoyed the patronage of religious and civic institutions who supervised and sponsored its activities. But by the end of the sixteenth century religious theatrical performances, outside of Spain, were gone, victims of the Reformation and the withdrawal of the church from dramatic production. The way was left open for the development of the professional actor, secular plays, and commercial and aristocratic patronage.

The Elizabethan Stage

The first professional playhouse in London was the Theater, built by James Burbage in 1576 in Shoreditch, on the bankside south of the Thames. This area was outside the jurisdiction of the civic authorities who viewed theatrical productions as a threat to public morality. The Curtain was built the next year, followed by the Rose in 1592, the Swan (1594), the Globe (1598), the Red Bull (1599), and the Fortune Theater (1600).

Before these theaters, actors performed wherever they could improvise a place to play, most frequently in inn-yards, which were fairly well suited for production since they were enclosed on all sides forming a place for the audience with room for a temporary trestle stage—a common device widely known for centuries on the continent.

The lack of evidence about the physical theater in Elizabethan times has invited a great deal of conjecture and controversy leading to a number of hypothetical reconstructions. The most important pieces of primary evidence available are a sketch of the Swan Theater drawn by Johannes de Witt from a description of a visit to London, and the contract for the construction of the Fortune Theater. In addition two sketches of London show distant views of theater exteriors. Other kinds of evidence are the texts of the plays and accounts and diaries that indicate the building materials, financial records, and considerable information about the theater companies and the plays they performed.

The de Witt sketch of the Swan shows a three-galleried, circular frame with a large projecting raised platform, partially covered by the "heavens" supported by two pillars. The tiring-house (reserved for the actors for dressing and preparation), which the sketch shows as being included within the framing structure, has two double doors and at the second story level appears to be a balcony in which it is suggested there are spectators. One explanation offered is that the sketch may represent a rehearsal situation. If it is meant to show the theater during a public performance, it is strange indeed because no other spectators are shown, and those in the balcony have a very poor view of the actors on stage, who are "opened out" toward the pit and not the tiring-house.

This is a copy of Johannes de Witt's sketch of the interior of the Swan Theater, 1596. The accuracy of the original drawing is a subject of considerable controversy among scholars, especially concerning the area at the back of the stage.

The contract for the Fortune Theater gives us some specific dimensions. It was unique in that it was square—80 feet at the exterior, and 55 feet inside. The first story was 12 feet high, the second, 11 feet and the third, 9 feet, each being 12 feet wide. The contract provides for a stage and a tiring-house with "a shadow or cover over the said stage." The stage was 43 feet wide and extended to the middle of the pit. In some other respects the Fortune was to be "like the Globe."

From these pieces of evidence we can envision a roofed, wood framed, three-storied structure, round, octagonal, or square in shape. The open pit or yard was enclosed by the galleries, which were equipped with benches. A large raised platform projected into the pit and the stage was usually partially covered by "the heavens" as protection in inclement weather and for the installation of stage machinery for special effects—such as for flying objects or people—as well as for housing sound effects. In most instances the roof was supported by large pillars, although in others it was known to be cantilevered from the main structure behind the stage.

The area behind the stage is the subject of most controversy. All agree that it contained at least a two-storied façade, although some argue that the galleries for the audience completely surrounded the yard including backstage. There is

302

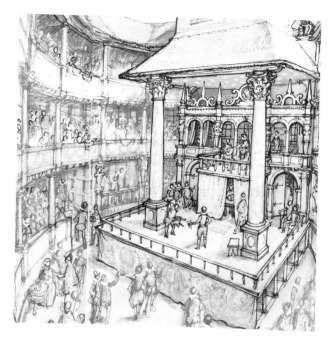

C. Walter Hodges' reconstruction in his *Shakespeare's* Theater *shows the interior of the Globe with its large platform stage backed by a two-storied facade to the tiring house that included two large doors and a second story gallery. For a production of* The Merchant of Venice *Hodges imagines a temporary structure projecting from the rear wall that could be used for entrances and properties at the floor level and by the musicians above.*

general agreement that there were two large doors, one at either side, which served as entrances and exits, usually unlocalized although they could be used for specific sites such as gates and entrances to various kinds of buildings. In between the doors, some scholars reconstruct an "inner below" alcove, covered by a curtain, and large enough for holding cumbersome properties (for "discoveries") and even for some action. But this latter conjecture seems dubious, because most of the audience would not have been able to see inside such a structural arrangement. Another version of an inner below is suggested by C. Walter Hodges, who envisions a temporary pavilion projecting out from the back wall. This too would have involved sightline problems except for "discoveries" when the person or object was immediately brought forward into the spectator's line of vision. Still others insist that there was no opening in the center since the doors filled the need for entrances, establishing locale, and for bringing properties (and bodies) on and off stage.

Likewise, there are conflicting theories about the "inner above" at the second-story level, which might have been used for scenes requiring elevation. Those who argue for an upper alcove base part of their case on the notion that Shakespearean production involved the use of multiple areas so that the action could proceed from place to place without interruption. Opponents agree on the need for continuous action but suggest that this can be accomplished entirely on the large stage. Due to the paucity of primary evidence, the controversy will probably never be resolved. Actually, the Elizabethan practice may have been as diverse as the scholarly conjectures.

In any case, the Elizabethan theater was a fortunate architectural creation for the drama it served. Working with a playhouse that may have held as many

Shakespeare Festival Theater at Ashland, Oregon, with a platform stage, during a production of Hamlet.

as 2000 spectators in close proximity to the performers, the playwright was able to exploit the possibilities of the language to the full, and the unlocalized stage allowed enormous flexibility for filling the stage with the action of a complex plot. It also provided an intimacy that made possible close rapport between spectator and performer.

The Renaissance
Proscenium Arch Stage

In Italy during the latter part of the fifteenth century, interest in the revival of classical drama led academies and wealthy noblemen to the performance of ancient plays. The court at Ferrara presented plays as early as 1471 and it is alleged that a theater was erected there half a century later. Part of the interest in revival of drama came from the Roman architect, Vitruvius (first century B.C.) whose work *De Architectura* was discovered in 1414 and published in 1486. Vitruvius' version of the Roman stage included descriptions of settings for three kinds of plays: tragedy, comedy, and pastoral. Interest in Vitruvius was coupled with the Italian fascination for perspective painting, especially as demonstrated in the painting of Brunelleschi (1377–1446). This Florentine artist showed how it was possible to suggest spatial relationships on a flat surface from a fixed point of view. Efforts were made to capitalize on perspective scenery but it was not until Serlio (1475–1554) that the idea gained popular attention. Serlio's *Architettura* (1545) included his celebrated drawings of the three settings described by Vitruvius. His book was widely read throughout Europe and his sketches became models for scene design. Serlio's settings for tragedy, comedy, and pastoral are perspective scenery with a central vanishing point. They are made up of four sets of wings at the sides, slightly raked except for the rear ones. Behind the wings he completed the scene with a painted backdrop. Serlio's settings were fixed in place on a temporary stage at the end of a great hall. The front of the stage was used by the performers, while the back half was sloped to add to the illusion of depth.

Plays were customarily given in connection with various social celebrations. Architects were commissioned to adapt large halls or other commodious buildings for dramatic performances, often using sets modeled on Serlio's drawings.

Three important Renaissance theaters were constructed in "antique" style to satisfy the vogue of reviving things classical. The oldest of these extant theaters was the Olympic Theater at Vicenza built by the Olympic Academy, which was founded in mid-sixteenth century to foster interest in classical literature. It was designed by Palladio (1518–1580) who attempted to follow Vitruvius in his plans. However, the Olympic Theater has semielliptical tiered-up seating constructed around an orchestra, also a semiellipse. It is a roofed-over theater seating about 3000, with a colonnade at the rear. The most interesting feature is the stage—a long, narrow platform backed by a decorative

Olympic Theater interior. Note the perspective vistas.

façade in the Roman tradition of pillars, niches, arches, and statuary. The central arch is at least five meters high. There are four other openings in the façade in which Scamozzi (1552–1616), after the untimely death of Palladio, placed permanent perspective street scenes creating the illusion that the stage is a city square from which five streets disappear into the distance. The Olympic Theater opened in 1585 with Sophocles' *Oedipus Rex*, which was sung before a gala crowd. Scamozzi also built another smaller theater at Sabbionetta (1588) with semicircular seating before a stage with angled wings for background.

The Farnese Theater at Parma was designed by Aleotti and completed in 1618, but was not used for performance until a decade later. The Farnese is important because it is the oldest extant theater with a proscenium arch. There is considerable dispute over this feature since some scholars believe the framing arch to have evolved from the visual arts, others from triumphal arches, still others as an expansion of the center doorway of the ancient Roman theater as anticipated at the Olympic Theater. In any case, the proscenium arch served an important function: the frame made it possible to use changeable scenery. During the seventeenth century, the proscenium arch became a standard theatrical feature that continues to this day.

Although the proscenium arch of the Farnese Theater was a model that was followed during the next three centuries, its other features were quite atypical. The auditorium was U-shaped with an amphitheatrical bank of seats high above a flat floor. It is obvious from the size of the entrances that the theater was often used for tournament-style performances that included players on horseback. The Farnese Theater is the forerunner of the stage with a proscenium arch, but the development of the auditorium came from the opera house.

In the early part of the seventeenth century, Italian opera's enormous popularity profoundly affected architecture; many of the theaters erected on the continent for the next century and a half were intended for the production of elaborate musical spectacles. These were often public structures so the auditoriums were large, usually accommodating from 2000 to 3000 spectators. The auditorium assumed a narrow horseshoe shape so that spectators could see the stage area behind the arch. Architects soon learned that tiers of galleries along the walls of the auditorium would enlarge the seating capacity. From three to seven galleries were built, supported by posts which separated the galleries into boxes. Up until this time, in court celebrations members of royalty occupied seats on the floor level directly in front of the stage, but several meters back. No one could sit in front of these seats for fear of obstructing the view. In the new auditorium of the Renaissance, a royal box was placed in the center of the first gallery, allowing a clear view of the stage, and making it possible to increase the capacity of the auditorium by adding seats to the floor level which was sloped to improve the angle of vision.

The stagehouse became gigantic in size and complex in organization when the scene designers and playwrights required increasingly spectacular sets and effects. For example, the Salle des Machines erected in Paris in 1660 had a stage more than 40 meters deep. Ingenious equipment was devised for producing all manner of sensational visual displays. The basic settings were made up of side

Farnese Theater (1618–1619). Parma, Italy. A conventional court theater but with the stage framed by an arch, the prototype of the Renaissance proscenium-arch theater.

307

The eighteenth-century opera house at Bayreuth designed by Giuseppe Galli-Bibiena. Typical Renaissance taste for ornamentation and display.

wings, backdrops or shutters, and overhead borders. At first scenery was changed manually but Torelli (1608 – 1678) developed the "chariot-and-pole" system in Venice in the 1640s. At the stage level scenery was attached to poles which were inserted in slots cut in the stage floor. Underneath the stage the poles were fastened to pulleys on tracks. When the chariots were rolled toward the center, the scenery moved onstage. The scenery was removed from view by moving the chariot toward offstage. The chariots and poles were rigged by a series of ropes and pulleys to a single winch, enabling a stagehand to change all of the scenery simultaneously. Torelli's system became the standard method of handling scenery in the major theaters until well into the nineteenth century. Another mechanical innovation was the use of machinery for flying to create all kinds of spectacular effects, especially for the magnificent entrances of performers or patrons on clouds, chariots, or fantastic elements. The single vanishing point perspective gave way to multiple perspective vistas, especially in the lavish scenery of the Bibiena family. All kinds of visual displays were created in an attempt to satisfy the audience's craving for novelties—fires, earthquakes, storms, and disasters. By the end of the eighteenth century, Italian-style theaters and scenery extended over the continent and England.

The audience which was attracted to these public theaters was made up of the upper and middle classes. Their taste in theater fare was not so much for spoken drama as it was for opera, ballet, and spectacular exhibitions. Moreover, the play was not always the thing, since the theater was considered a social center. Boxes became private drawing rooms for gossip and entertainment, flirtation, and ostentatious show. In attempting to make the theater décor as impressive as possible, extravagant ornamentation was used. Walls were covered with baroque contortions of entablatures, wreaths, cornucopias, statues of nymphs and cupids, and fat rolls of swirling, gilded plaster.

When the public theaters of the late eighteenth century became too crowded with irksome hoi polloi, there was a resurgence of smaller private theaters, more suitable for tasteful performances given to the genteel people of quality. However, the general characteristics of the European theater up through the nineteenth century followed the pattern of the Italian Renaissance opera house.

The general effect of the picture-frame Renaissance theater was to encourage spectacle and music. The dramatist was compelled to create plays in which there was ample opportunity for lavish pageantry and show. Drama was often grandiose in style. As a consequence of the size of the auditorium and of the competition of the scenery, the actor faced a difficult task in making himself seen and heard. Such a theater was not conducive to the development of spoken drama. It was the smaller, private court theaters that gave the playwright a more congenial atmosphere in which to work.

From our brief description of four representative theaters it is clearly evident that the architecture imposes a strong formative pressure on the drama and its performance. Conversely, the physical theater reflects the needs and tastes of the dramatist, actor, and audience. Since this interaction is constantly at work, it is necessary to visualize a play in terms of the theater for which it was written.

Architects in the nineteenth century protested about the traditionalism that dominated the theater. It was Gottfried Semper (1803–1879) and his associates who made a major breakthrough in his design for Wagner's Bayreuth Festival Theater (1876). Most of the innovations were in the auditorium, in which Wagner wanted to have a "classless" audience. So there were no side boxes and no gallery. Instead there was a single bank of thirty rows of seats arranged like a fan to enable every spectator to get a good view of the stage. The rows of seats were widely spaced in what has since been known as "continental seating." This arrangement eliminated the need for a center aisle because spectators could reach their seats without disturbing those already seated. Other features of this theater were an orchestra pit that was partially under the apron and deep enough to conceal the musicians. A double proscenium arch framed the illusionary scenery and created a "mystic gulf" between audience and performer.

The deep, straight slant of the seats did not completely solve the sightline problem, so other innovations were tried—the most successful being a "dished" floor, which greatly improved the visibility.

During the nineteenth century the impact of science was felt on architecture as well as on dramatic material. A most important technical advance growing out of the scientific revolution was made possible by the use of steel: Theater architects could design large cantilevered balconies extending at the rear and sides and over the lower level amphitheater like half-opened drawers. Because of the strength of the material, the balconies needed few or no supporting pillars. Thus it became possible to jam a great many people into a limited area—a fundamental consideration in New York and London where the cost of real estate was astronomical.

Another major technical advance was made in lighting. For centuries, theaters were inadequately (and dangerously) lit by oil lamps, mostly as chandeliers over the stage and the auditorium. In 1817 gas was used for the first time in the Drury Lane Theater in England and it was quickly installed in most theaters not only because it gave better illumination but also because it could be controlled from a central position, often by the prompter, who could run a series of valves and stopcocks. Such gas systems became quite complicated. In a French opera house in 1880 no less than 28 miles of gas piping were used with 88 valves controlling 960 gas jets.

The major breakthrough in lighting came with Edison's invention of the incandescent lamp in 1879. That same year, the California Theater in San Francisco became the first to use electricity for stage lighting. Within a decade electricity was installed in most theaters throughout the world. Adolphe Appia, (see pp. 261–62) was the first to envision the possibilities of electric lighting and his ideas and designs have been the basis for most lighting design since. His aesthetic theory reflected his view that since the actor was a three-dimensional agent, it was incongruous for him to play before flat, painted scenery. Artistic use of lighting could achieve the plasticity desired. Not only was Appia a theoretical visionary but he was also a practitioner who showed how stage lighting could enhance the performance by creating atmosphere, emphasizing the actor, and following the shifting patterns of meaning. He demonstrated the means for breaking up the light and diversifying its direction, intensity, and color. During the twentieth century vast improvements have been made in the quality and control of stage lighting and it is universally recognized as a most important element of theatrical design.

Many of the changes in theater design during the first part of this century were possible because of the availability of electrical power. For generations, scenery consisted mostly of two dimensional painted drops and wings, which could be readily shifted. A system of ropes and pulleys enabled stagehands to raise and lower the units, most of which were lightweight in construction because the emphasis was on illusionistic painting. But when scenery became three dimensional and solid, some other means had to be devised for moving sets quickly, noiselessly, and economically. Steele MacKaye demonstrated his elevator stage at the Madison Square Theater in New York in 1880. He developed a large double deck elevator about 7 meters by 10 meters. While one deck was being used for performance in view of the audience, the other platform could be set at the basement level. The entire elevator was counterbalanced and was moved by electricity, permitting a change of scenery within 40 seconds. MacKaye's ingenuity was widely admired but its cost was prohibitive for most theaters. The use of mechanical facilities was more prevalent in Europe, especially where government support enabled many cities to build permanent plants for residential companies with generous work and rehearsal spaces, as well as bars, restaurants, and lobbies for the public. In Germany, especially, theaters were equipped with hydraulic lifts, turntables, winches, and lighting equipment—all electrically controlled so that the scene technician nearly needed to be a trained engineer.

Cutaway drawing of the National Theater, Munich, 1896, showing an electrically operated revolving stage used in conjunction with sky cyclorama. Such mechanical devices simplified the use of rapid changes of scenery.

During much of the twentieth century, commercial theaters in New York and London produced plays in inadequate buildings crammed into parcels of expensive land whose cost usually dictated the size and arrangement of the structure. Since playhouses are frequently rented for single productions, and there is limited work space, scenery is very often built elsewhere and trucked in and many rehearsals are held outside the theater. These theaters are usually proscenium arch buildings with the traditional separation of performer and spectator, although the trend is to bring the two together as much as possible.

Despite a great deal of criticism of the proscenium, most twentieth-century plays have been produced within the frame. The development of stage lighting enabled designers to selectively control all areas of the stage and to obliterate the frame. Thus they are able to focus on the actors who play in a void or before suggestive set pieces. The simulated walls of canvas that formerly confined the performer were replaced by scenic fragments or projections on the *cyclorama* (a large curtain hung horizontally from a U-shaped frame enclosing the rear and sides of the playing areas—often used as a sky drop).

A production designed in this manner is known as a "space stage" which is eminently suitable for multiple scene plays (such as those by Elizabethans) because no bulky scenery needs to be changed. Indeed, the action can be continued without interruption with the playing areas controlled with light. Restoration comedies and those of Molière can be set with a few pieces of furniture, and perhaps a few screens—and of course the lighting. Although the space may seem bare, well-chosen properties and colorful costumes supported by an orchestrated light plot that follows the action and constantly changes to fit the play's atmosphere provide an entirely satisfactory visual experience.

As for realistic plays originally intended to be played in authentic-looking rooms with complete walls and ceiling and with a full complement of furniture, as well as practical doors and windows, experience has demonstrated the efficacy of staging with almost no scenic support except for a few pieces of furniture, the minimal suggestion of locale, but most importantly, the light. The space stage has the great virtue of focusing the audience's attention where it usually belongs—on the actor.

Another innovation within the traditional theater and its end (proscenium) staging was made by Brecht with his Berliner Ensemble. Although working in an old structure, the Theater-am-Schiffbauerdamm, with its end staging in a proscenium arch, Brecht gave his productions a novel look by emphasizing theatricality instead of illusion. Scenery was simplified by skeletal pieces, lighting equipment was exposed to the audience's view, the arch was ignored, and the stage action was combined in a presentational way with film clips, slides, soundtracks, banners, diagrams, and projections.

The contemporary playwright, given an open theater, writes without tight restrictions on time and place, as we have seen with Miller's *Death of a Salesman*, which requires forty-odd scenes. The change in direction in staging within proscenium theaters is mostly a matter of attitude. The frame no longer controls the style; rather the staging frequently achieves theatricalism in spite of the frame. Robert Wilson's *Einstein on the Beach* was a remarkably innovative production despite the fact that it was presented on the conventional proscenium stage of the Met.

Another trend in architecture has been to break through the proscenium arch. Sean O'Casey, the Irish playwright, put it this way: "Sculpture, architecture, literature, poetry and the domestic art are actively walking about in new ways, and the drama isn't going to stay quietly in her picture frame gazing coyly out at changing life about her, like a languid invalid woman looking pensively out of a window in the fourth wall." William Poel in the late nineteenth century and early twentieth century demonstrated how effectively a bare platform stage served in playing Elizabethan drama.

Max Reinhardt in Berlin also proved it was theatrically sound for the performers and the spectators to share the same space. His circus style struc-

These elevations and plans show how the Memorial Theater at Stratford-on-Avon was changed from a proscenium arch theater to a thrust stage. A & B show the 1932 version of the conventional proscenium arch structure and C & D show how the thrust stage was added and new gallery arrangements made it possible to seat an additional 576 people.

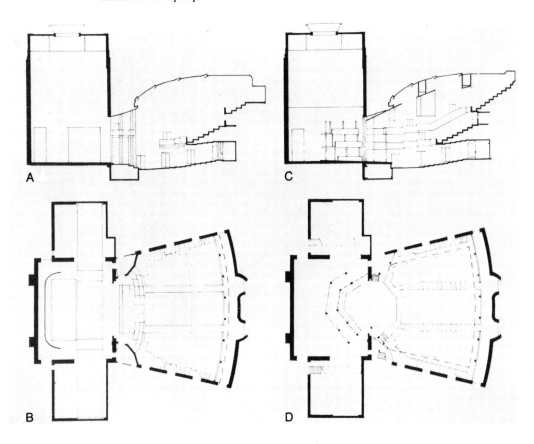

ture, the Grosses Schauspielhaus (1919), also known as the Theater-of-Five-Thousand, featured a vast U-shaped auditorium around a large orchestra equipped with elevator stages. At the rear a large proscenium arch stage was equipped with a turntable and backed by a sky dome. Reinhardt attempted to place most of the action in the orchestra after the fashion of the Greeks. Unfortunately, a house of such scale demanded a large staff as well as capacity audiences and ultimately the venture had to be abandoned. But Reinhardt had demonstrated the desirability of putting the performer and the spectator in the same room to achieve a sense of participation and immediacy unknown in traditional end staging.

Other innovators in removing the arch were Jacques Copeau at the Vieux Colombier in Paris (1919–1924), Norman Bel Geddes' projects for open stages, and Walter Gropius' "total theater" (1927). Copeau relied mostly on a main platform backed by a permanent structure that included an arch at the back and a stairway that led over it. The front of the platform also included a

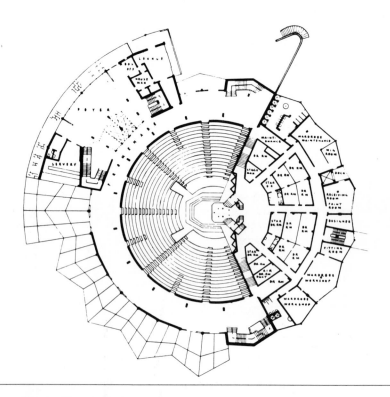

*Tyrone Guthrie was responsible for the design of the very influential
Stratford Festival Theater, Ontario, Canada, 1957. (Capacity 2,258.)
The main features are tiered up seats after the Greek theater and the
open platform stage of the Elizabethans.*

series of steps and the center and smaller ones at the side. On this stage, broken up by several levels, Copeau used screens, props, and furniture to suggest locale.

Since World War II, the thrust stage has found considerable acceptance. In 1953 an English director, Tyrone Guthrie, designed a thrust stage theater that proved to be such a successful arrangement for staging Shakespeare and other playwrights that it has been widely influential. The thrust stage is a bare platform with the spectators on three sides. The stage, which often has steps leading to the audience level, is reached by entrances from the sides, the rear, and below, making for great variety in movement. Because of the sightline problems, scenery is often fragmented or eliminated altogether, so the actor is no longer confined by canvas walls. A good example is the Crucible Theater thrust stage at Sheffield, England, which has the same dimensions as the Shakespeare Festival Theater at Stratford, Ontario. It is 18 feet wide, 28 feet deep, 2 feet 6 inches above the moat, and 2 feet 9 inches below the audience's eyeline. The latter dimension is critical because at the Mark Taper Forum in Los Angeles the eyeline is too high. As a result no armchairs can be used onstage because they would block the audience's view of part of the acting area. As it is, a seated actor's knee may block out his face.

The Mark Taper has other limitations because it was designed not for theatrical production so much as for chamber music and lectures; but the auditorium and thrust stage have proven to be exemplary for an intimate style of production, so directors and designers have learned to live with the limited backstage space. One of the directors with considerable experience at the Mark Taper described the use of the stage:

> The most difficult plays to stage are realistic, naturalistic, etc. . . . . Chekhov can and has worked on this stage, but it is not easy, particularly with scene changes. We have severely limited backstage space and almost no storage space for one thing. Then too, sets must be changed in full view of the audience. . . . In a production of *Major Barbara* I directed, I changed time periods as part of the production concept, and I staged the changing of the sets. It worked. And with Shaw, all the talk works very well on the thrust stage; it is rather like a platform for debate, discussion, speeches, and pronouncements. The problem then is to get everybody else out of the way.
>
> The Greeks and Shakespeare of course are a minimum of trouble.
>
> The truly exciting challenge of the thrust stage is that it *looks its best with nothing on it*. Nothing, that is, except the actor and the words of the play. Whatever looks sculptural, simple and three-dimensional acquires a richness and purity that, with the right play, can be breathtaking.[3]

Another director with extensive experience with the thrust stage is Michael Langham at the Stratford Theater, Ontario. He shows his preference for this kind of architecture.

> I am convinced that one can achieve a greater imaginative bond between actor and audience with a thrust stage theater. In a picture-frame theater, I think the tendency is for the actor to pretend to play to his colleagues where in fact he is playing to the

[3]Edward Parone, *Theater Quarterly*, 3, no. 11 (July–September 1973).

The thrust stage of the Shakespeare Festival Theatre at Stratford. Ontario, Canada.

The thrust stage at the Tyrone Guthrie Theatre, Minneapolis.

audience. This is an impossibility on a thrust stage—the actor is forced to play to the actor and consequently the relationships that develop between characters are deeper and draw the audience more fully into the experience.[4]

A widespread form of theater architecture particularly among campus and civic organizations is the arena stage, also referred to as "theater in the round" or "central staging." Glenn Hughes at the University of Washington led the way in this venture with his Penthouse Theater. He simply placed a few rows of seats around an acting area in a large room. Locale was defined by props, furniture, and costumes, and the only separation between performer and spectator was an attempt to keep the latter in the dark, although it was difficult to keep the light from spilling on to the audience from the playing area. The advantages of arena staging were immediately apparent—it was more economical without scenery, it gave the audience a fresh kind of theatrical experience, and it was excellent training for the actor in concentration and ensemble play.

At first central staging was considered suitable only for drawing room plays, but Margo Jones in her Dallas theater in the fifties demonstrated that many

[4]Michael Langham, *Theater Quarterly*, 3, no. 11 (July–September 1973).

The Mark Taper Forum, Los Angeles.

The Mark Taper Forum thrust stage with a complicated set designed by Ming Cho Lee for Shakespeare's Henry IV, Part I; directed by Gordon Davidson. The setting is actually mostly a background with the acting areas picked out by light.

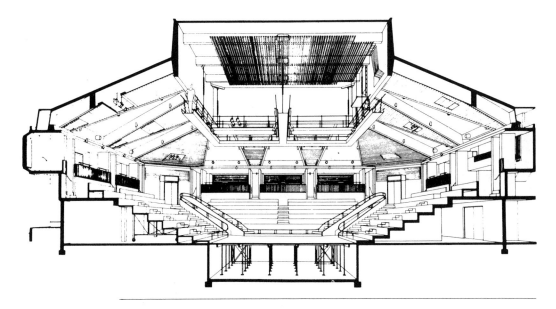

Arena Stage, Washington, D.C. The rectangular playing area is
surrounded by tiers of seats for 752 spectators. One section of seats is
movable for a three-quarter arrangement. A cat-walk lighting grid
overhead and the trapped floor of the acting area give added flexibility.

other kinds of drama could be performed successfully—except for those with too much violent action. The original Arena Stage in Washington, D.C. demonstrated that theater in the round could be used for professional productions in a theater that seated 750 people, and that nearly any kind of play was possible. The idea spread, especially to tent and music theaters. Now most college and university campuses work with some version of arena staging, although various arrangements are tried, such as placing the audience on two or three sides and including a considerable amount of scenery.

In the United States a unique development in the twentieth century was the rise of college and university theaters. Since these buildings generally grew out of the needs of dramatic art or theater arts departments, and were designed as an extension of the academic program, a distinctive kind of architecture emerged. Freed from the pressure to make box office appeal the primary target, the academic theater was able to construct buildings that had auditoriums well suited for spoken drama, and excellent facilities for production in terms of space and equipment.

One of the first university theaters in this country was built at the University of Iowa in 1935. It included an auditorium with continental seating for 500 spectators, a double proscenium, and, most importantly, a great deal of offstage space for shops and storage. The University of Iowa theater thus set the standards which scores of other academic institutions have emulated.

A persistent problem of theater buildings occupied by residential and repertory companies on a permanent basis is providing suitable staging for plays

In Bucharest Liviu Ciulei transformed the Lucia Sturdza Bulandra Theater's Studio into a highly flexible arrangement for his production of Popovivi's Power and Truth. *All elements of the theater are movable thus permitting the director a wide variety of options for the use of space for the performers and the audience.*

intended for varied playing conditions—from the Greek orchestra to Shakespearean thrust, to nineteenth-century proscenium arch to contemporary avant-garde. In general, attempts to serve all needs result in serving none well. In 1927 Walter Gropius, a German architect noted for his leadership of the Bauhaus School, designed a "total theater" for Piscator, an experimental director who, you will remember, worked with Brecht in developing epic theater. Although Gropius' plan was never built, his design provoked a great deal of thought. He attempted to include in one structure three stage forms—proscenium, thrust, and arena. By means of mechanical equipment, the components of the building could be arranged to make any of the three stages. The thrust stage was mounted on a large circular platform that could be revolved, placing the stage in the center of the auditorium. An open platform ran around the auditorium that could be used by the actors, and behind it a series of screens provided places for projections. A wide stage house that could accommodate wagons was backed by a translucent screen for rear projections.

The Malmo Municipal Theater built in 1941 in Sweden was a fairly successful attempt to design a multipurpose structure. The front of the orchestra was provided with elevators that made possible use of the area for a thrust stage, for an orchestra pit, or for audience seating. Another interesting feature was the flexible auditorium that could be varied in size by the use of large, movable panels—so that the building was suitable for large concerts and musical productions; when reduced in size, it is an effective house for spoken drama. As a civic structure it is an exemplary one by virtue of its spacious lobbies, working and rehearsal areas, an experimental theater, and its park-like setting.

Another, much more satisfactory solution to providing for various kinds of production conditions is the development of plans that include several theaters—proscenium, thrust, and/or arena as experimental stages. Many American universities and regional theaters have found this a satisfactory solution.

An excellent example of the multitheater solution is the National Theater in London. After 125 years of planning, it was finally opened in 1976. It includes three kinds of theater. The Olivier has a thrust stage in the corner of a two-tiered, fan-shaped auditorium that holds 1160. The Lyttelton is an adjustable prosce-

*The National theater, Mannheim, Germany, during a production of
Schiller's* The Robbers. *Note the acting area with the spectators on
both sides.*

nium theater with continental seating for 895. Experimental productions are
given in the Cottsloe, a flexible studio space with galleries around three of the
four walls that range in capacity from 200 to 400, depending on the arrangement of the playing space. A most attractive feature of this plant are the
supporting facilities for audience convenience and comfort—terraces, foyers,
exhibition spaces, bars, restaurants, and parking facilities.

We have seen how Artaud's ideas affected playwriting and acting; he also
had an enormous influence on staging as well. His views are worth quoting at
length because in them are the seeds that have since reached fruition in the
experimental theater:

> The Stage—The Auditorium: We abolish the stage and the auditorium and replace
> them by a single site, without partition or barrier of any kind, which will become the
> theater of action. A direct communication will be reestablished between the
> spectator and the spectacle, between the actor and the spectator, from the fact that
> the spectator, placed in the middle of the action, is engulfed and physically affected
> by it. This envelopment results, in part, from the very configuration of the room itself.
>
> Thus, abandoning the architecture of present-day theaters, we shall take some
> hangar or barn, which we shall have reconstructed according to processes which
> have culminated in the architecture of certain churches or holy places, and of certain
> temples in Tibet.
>
> In the interior of this construction special proportions of height and depth will
> prevail. The hall will be enclosed by four walls, without any kind of ornament, and
> the public will be seated in the middle of the room, on the ground floor, on mobile

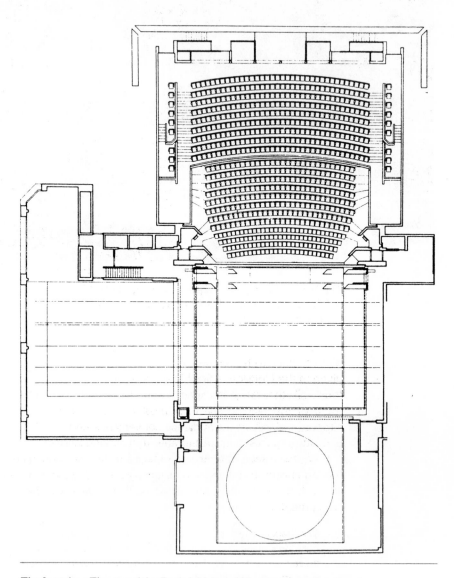

The Lyttelton Theater of the English National Theater is a conventional proscenium arch structure that seats 895 people in two tiers. Spacious areas in the wings and backstage, separated from the auditorium area by soundproof doors, are equipped with motorized scenery wagons. Scenery can also be flown by the use of equipment overhead in the stage house.

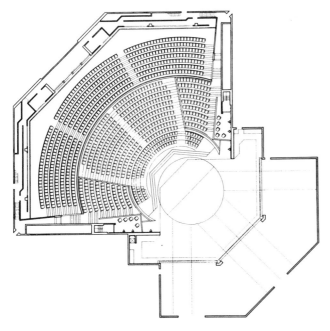

Ground plan of the Olivier Theater of the new National Theater in London. The large platform stage projects into the fan-shaped auditorium that seats 1160 people. In the center of the stage is an 11.5 meter revolve and overhead a large fly tower is equipped with power-operated spot lines. The back of the stage can be opened or closed off to suit the scale of the various productions.

View of the auditorium of the Olivier Theater from the performers' perspective. Note the variety of positions for lighting instruments and the adjustable panels for acoustical control. Although the theater has a capacity of 1160, the feeling of the spectator is one of a close communion with the performer.

chairs which will allow them to follow the spectacle which will take place all around them. In effect, the absence of a stage in the usual sense of the word will provide for the deployment of the action in the four corners of the room. Particular positions will be reserved for actors and action at the four cardinal points of the room. The scenes will be played in front of whitewashed, wall-backgrounds designed to absorb the light. In addition, galleries overhead will run around the periphery of the hall as in certain primitive paintings. These galleries will permit the actors, whenever the action makes it necessary, to be pursued from one point in the room to another, and the action to be deployed on all levels and in all perspectives of height and depth. A cry uttered at one end of the room can be transmitted from mouth to mouth with amplifications and successive modulations all the way to the other. The action will unfold, will extend its trajectory from level to level, point to point, paroxysms will suddenly burst forth, will flare up like fires in different spots. And to speak of the spectacle's character as true illusion or of the direct and immediate influence of the action on the spectator will not be hollow words. For this diffusion of action over an immense space will oblige the lighting of a scene and the varied lighting of a performance to fall upon the public as much as upon the actors—and to the several simultaneous actions or several phases of an identical action in which the characters, swarming over each other like bees, will endure all the onslaughts of the situations and the external assaults of the tempestuous elements, will correspond the physical means of lighting, of producing thunder or wind, whose repercussions the spectator will undergo.

However, a central position will be reserved which, without serving, properly speaking, as a stage, will permit the bulk of the action to be concentrated and brought to a climax whenever necessary.[5]

Now, avant-garde directors often have no use for scenic illusion and like Artaud they are interested in the total environment that includes audience and actors. In some cases directors working in conventional playhouses have found ways to change the customary actor-audience relationship.

At the Chelsea Center Theater in New York, a double-decked framework of a ship was designed by Eugene Lee and erected in the middle of the auditorium for Le Roi Jones' *Slaveship*. In Brazil, Victoria Garcia gutted the inside of a theater, tearing out the seats and erecting a large circular metal tower complete with elevators and transparent spirals for Genêt's *The Balcony* (1970). Peter Brook reconstructed Théâtre des Bouffes du Nord for his production of Shakespeare's *Timon of Athens* (1975). The old Italianate proscenium arch theater was gutted and revised for production. Brook took up the seats of the orchestra and put in a concrete slab floor which became the primary playing area. The raised stage was removed and replaced by a pit six meters deep reached by a wide set of steps. The orchestra pit was covered by a wooden platform, part of which was removed to serve as Timon's cave. Spectators sat on rows of seats under the balcony at the sides of the playing area. The decaying walls of the old theater remained unchanged and unpainted to suggest Timon's decaying universe.

Another aspect of the search for greater freedom was the experimentalists' rejection of the playhouse altogether. They wanted to get away from a theater of

[5]Antonin Artaud, *The Theater and Its Double*, trans. Mary Caroline Richards (New York: Grove Press, Inc., 1958).

Peter Brook reconstructed an old Parisian proscenium arch theater for his production of Shakespeare's Timon of Athens. *This view from the balcony looks down on the acting area that was formerly the orchestra floor, now cemented over. The orchestra pit was covered with wood, except for a section that opened up to provide an entranceway for the actors. Inside the proscenium arch, the raised stage was replaced by a deep pit reached by a large staircase.*

illusion, of painted scenery and actors on display like commercial products. They believed that all aspects of production should make their own statements—not merely support the words of a dead text. The quest for new environments led to making performance areas out of "found spaces," adapting productions to existing structures, or performing in the open air.

Schechner's Performance Group adapted an old garage by moving scaffolding and platforms around the interior. Mnouchkine's Théâtre du Soleil occupies an abandoned cartridge factory. Peter Stein moved from his theater in Berlin to an exhibition hall for *Peer Gynt*; Peter Schumann's Bread and Puppet Theater plays in the streets, or in the Coney Island concession hall formerly occupied by a freak show; Serban, Garcia, and Brook have staged productions in an ancient Persian monument.

In part this exodus from the theater stems from the necessity of experimental groups to put on their shows with a limited budget. (We remember how Antoine began the Théâtre Libre in Paris in a room over a billiard parlor, and O'Neill's early one-acts were tried out in a Provincetown living room before they were shifted to a warehouse on the wharf.)

One of the most innovative European directors is Luca Ronconi. In his quest to reinvent ways of communicating he experiments with new uses of

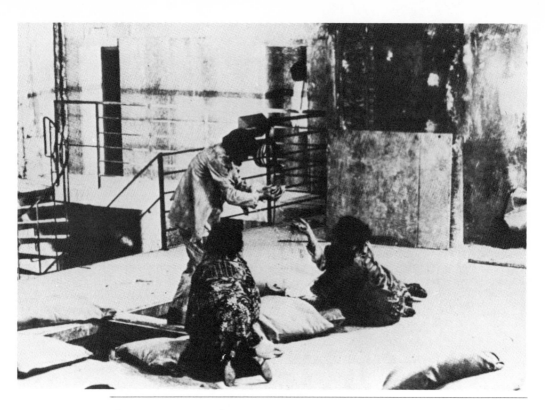

This action from Brook's Timon of Athens *is played on top of the former orchestra pit, now partially covered by wood. In the background steep steps lead to the pit, which used to be the raised stage.*

actors, language, and spaces. He is especially noted for his multifocus staging and simultaneity. His staging of XX at the Odeon in Paris took place in a set representing a two-story house with twenty rooms in which several actors performed for about twenty spectators who could not see into the other nineteen rooms. At times the performers changed spaces and presented another segment of the action. Finally, the partitions between the compartments began to disappear and the actors interacted from space to space until all the walls were gone.

For Kleist's *Kathchen von Heilbroun* Ronconi put the audience and the actors on barges out on a lake. His celebrated production of *Orlando Furioso*, based on Ariosto's sixteenth-century poem, was first given in 1969 in Milan and then toured throughout the continent. Ronconi described the work as an "environmental spectacle." It was a loose conglomerate of events and characters well suited for the director's penchant for lively simultaneous action.

Franco Quadri describes the staging of the Milan production:

Ronconi designed the performance for a large space, measuring at least 120 feet by 45 feet, having two open portable stages (with projecting platforms) on the space's

The audience is seated on three sides of an environment, suggesting a farmer's house by the use of rough planking on the floor, few sticks of furniture, and piled up sacks of grain. Kroetz's Stallerhof *at the Deutsches Schauspielhaus in Hamburg.*

two shorter sides. The central space is occupied at the same time by the audience and by the actors, who for the most part act, speak, gallop, and duel on wooden floats which are either bare or embellished with metal constructions: sheet-metal horses, an enormous monster which looks like the skeleton of a prehistoric animal, a hippogriff with great wings which a wooden machine raises in the air above the spectators' heads, many transparent plastic cubes forming the castle of Atlanti, and cages of gauze and plywood which at the end of the spectacle come together and enclose the audience in a labyrinth. The floats, propelled by actors who for a moment are not participating in the action, pass through the whole stage area. Their continuous movement—endangering the spectators and forcing them to move away suddenly—is a means of attack and a means of communication.[6]

Since 1966 plays have been performed deep in the desert and among the ruins of the tomb of Arta Xerxes (409–359 B.C.) near Persepolis, Iran. Outstanding directors such as Brook, Serban, and Garcia have adapted their productions to the skeletal structures of ancient columns, sculptured entranceways, and broken walls. Various sites have been tried among the ruins, which imparts to the performances an air of mystery. The most noteworthy work to be staged here was Brook's *Orghast*.

And so we have come full circle. Long ago Thespis made theater of a bare space by the act of performing. So today, in many places, actors and directors,

[6]Franco Quadri, ''Orlando Furioso,'' trans. Helen R. Lane, *Drama Review*, T47, 1970.

Peter Brook and Ted Hughes in Orghast *experimented with relation between the verbal and nonverbal world in a production at an ancient tomb in Iran.*

in their efforts to reduce their art to its basic essentials, emphasize the act of playing—and in the process remind us that theater is not architecture or set design, but performers in action before an audience.

Bibliography

BECKERMAN, BERNARD, *Shakespeare at the Globe, 1599–1609.* New York: Macmillan Publishing Co., Inc., 1962.

BIEBER, MARGARETE, *The History of the Greek and Roman Theater,* Princeton: Princeton University Press, 1961

BURRIS-MEYER, HAROLD, and EDWARD COLE, *Theaters and Auditoriums* (2nd ed.). New York: Van Nostrand Reinhold Company, 1964.

GASCOIGNE, BAMBER, *World Theater: An Illustrated History.* Boston: Little, Brown & Company, 1968.

HODGES, C. WALTER, *The Globe Restored.* New York: Coward, McCann & Geoghegan, Inc., 1968.

IZENOUR, GEORGE C., *Theater Design.* New York: McGraw-Hill Book Company, 1977.

328

MOLNARI, CESARE, *Theater Through the Ages*. New York: McGraw-Hill Book Company, 1975.

MULLIN, DONALD C., *The Development of the Playhouse*. Berkeley: University of California Press, 1970.

NICOLL, ALLARDYCE, *The Development of the Theater* (5th ed.). New York: Harcourt Brace Jovanovich, Inc., 1966.

SILVERMAN, MAX, and NED A. BOWMAN, *Contemporary Theater Architecture*. New York: New York Public Library, 1965.

WICKHAM, GLYNNE, *Early English Stages, 1300–1660*. New York: Columbia University Press, 1959–1963.

TWELVE
The Audience

You may not have your name in lights on a Broadway marquee, nor know the thrill and frustration of seeing your work put on stage, but nevertheless you play an important role in the theater—as a member of the audience. It is for you that the theater is built, the play written, the actors rehearsed, and the performance given. While they labor to find the precise words for their characters to speak on stage, dramatists try to anticipate your response. All too frequently you bedevil them with your fickleness, because sometimes you give them the response they hope for, and sometimes you sit on your hands, or stay away from the theater in droves.

While the physical environment affects the way a play is staged, it is the audience that dictates the kind of material that can be used. As Samuel Johnson observed:

The drama's laws the patrons give,
And we who live to please, must please to live.

A painting may be viewed by a solitary viewer, and a novel may be enjoyed as you sit alone on a cold night before a fire, but the play is a social event. Its full effect must be experienced as a group response to a live performance. Drama is a dynamic communal celebration that requires the union of all aspects of the theater—a coming together.

Most plays are written for immediate consumption; the obvious way of measuring success is at the box office. This influences the playwright who is aware that he usually must create a work that will elicit a ready response from a sufficient number of patrons to pay the bills and perhaps even show a profit. (In these days of astronomical production costs on Broadway, the play must pack the house every night for months in order to break even.) Most dramatists are aware of the economics of producing a winner, and they know that the popular hits are mostly musicals and lightweight comedies with little intellectual stimulation. The list of long-run hits on Broadway in recent years indicates that approximately 50 productions have run over 1000 performances. Of these, half were musicals, 13 were light comedies, and only 1 serious play by a major playwright—Peter Shaffer's *Equus*, which ranked forty-third.

The list of off-Broadway long runs showed a larger selection from more substantial playwrights. Among the top 40 were 2 plays from Miller, 2 of Genêt, and single works of Pirandello, Ionesco, Behan, Brecht, Pinter, Euripides, and Albee.

In the past generation there is evidence of the development of an increasingly mature and discriminating following in the theater, and of a new openness to experimentation; this means the present-day dramatist and producer are able to find an audience for works of more than momentary interest. It should be remembered that many masters of drama in the past transcended the problems of catering to the lowest common denominator of the audience. Sophocles, Aristophanes, Shakespeare, Molière, Jonson, Lessing, Schiller, and Sheridan satisfied public taste while creating landmarks of dramatic literature. But popularity itself is no criterion of lasting value; many plays of enormous popularity are

331

The theater has a strong appeal for audiences of all ages. Elementary school children watching Marie Starr's production of Old Silent Movie.

very thin, and conversely some of the masterpieces of the theater are not major attractions to most of the public. As educational, civic, and regional theaters continue to grow, they are developing audiences for all kinds of theatrical experiences, including that of literary, provocative, and experimental plays.

The Nature of Attention

To create a play and a performance that will evoke an appropriate response, it is essential for the playwright and the theater worker to know something about the nature of attention. Attention comes in short spurts. Concentration requires constant renewal, because it is impossible for us to fix our attention on a single object and hold it there as we might a spotlight. Ordinarily, a theater audience comes with the expectation of giving its attention freely to the play, but if the drama is dull and the performance monotonous, if attention is not captured and sustained, the spectator makes his escape into a world of his own imagining.

There are two kinds of attention—voluntary and involuntary. Voluntary attention implies that spectators look and listen by an act of the will. They make an effort to pay attention. Involuntary attention, on the other hand, requires no conscious effort; it results from responding to stimuli—we hear a scream in the night, a fascinating story, or our name spoken aloud by another. Theater workers are interested in securing our involuntary attention. They employ such devices as bright lights and colors, movement, emotional stimulation, the use of space and elevations, sound, and visual focus. Directors combat monotony by varying the groupings of characters, by changes of pace, by making sure that actors do not imitate one another's pitch patterns, by inventing business and action—in short, by every possible way of renewing attention. They aim to control and direct every instant of our attention throughout the course of the play. This is one of the director's most difficult tasks, since the play, by its very nature, is a stream of complex visual and auditory stimuli; attention constantly flits from one character to another and back again. Motion-picture directors have far greater control of the spectator's attention because of their ability to focus the camera on one object, one person, one face at a time, eliminating all extraneous elements, and by the opportunity to edit a film after it has been shot and to order retakes if desirable. But stage directors must find other means of achieving much the same effect.

A part of the problem of controlling attention is avoiding the distractions that plague a theatrical performance, such as late arrivals, program rustling, foot shuffling, coughs and wheezes, and the vicissitudes of production that may occur onstage—missed cues, long waits, poor costumes, obvious makeup, scenery that shakes when the door is slammed, a crooked picture, light-reflecting surfaces. Some aspects of the production itself may destroy the audience's concentration, such as an unexpected novelty that arouses surprise and comment in the audience, scene shifts that take too long or involve too much noise, special spectacular effects, or an unexpected laugh. In a well-managed theater, every effort is made to focus and control the audience's interest so that their voluntary attention becomes involuntary as they become thoroughly engrossed in the action and the play.

The Audience as a Crowd

Although an audience comes together as individuals, the theater is a group effort. Through mutual stimulation in the release of emotions, the group may become a crowd. This has important psychological implications, because as individuals merge themselves into a crowd, marked changes take place. They lose their identity, becoming more susceptible to emotional appeals and more easily swayed than the single person in isolation. They relax their discrimination and become more gullible. The social psychologist Emory Bogardus states: "A heightened state of suggestibility is characteristic of a crowd. The preponderance of feelings over reason heightens suggestibility. The excitement that frequently prevails in a crowd throws persons off their guard. The force of numbers is overwhelming."[1]

Thus, a theater audience loses some of its sense of personal responsibility. There is a temporary release from restraint with the result that, in a crowd,

[1] Emory Bogardus, *Sociology* (New York: Macmillan, Inc., 1949).

The audience participates in the action during the "Old Price" Riots at the Covent Garden Theatre. London. 1763.

334

people may respond to stimuli that would leave them untouched as isolated individuals. For example, they may laugh in the theater at salacious humor they would consider vulgar in their own living room. There is the pressure to conform, the contagion to join in. These psychological phenomena of audience behavior are at least a partial explanation of how the effectiveness of a play may be enhanced by a responsive audience, which willingly suspends its disbelief and succumbs to the emotions of the play.

Types of Audiences

Anyone experienced in theatrical production can testify to the fact that audiences vary from performance to performance. A Saturday night crowd will almost invariably outlaugh a Monday night one. A matinee audience with a preponderance of shoppers or tourists reacts quite differently from one dominated by business travelers. Audiences likewise differ from place to place. A performer meets a different reception in Las Vegas than he does in Boston. University campus theater-goers are a marked contrast to those in a community theater. Spectators may find their responses to a play varying according to the stimulation they receive from others, the way they feel, the temperature of the auditorium, and the location of their seats. They will also notice that their reactions to a motion picture in a crowded theater are not the same as their response to a film seen in the seclusion of their own home.

Different kinds of plays attract different kinds of audiences. Compare an audience that attends an opera with that of a musical comedy, or note the difference between the spectators attending a farce and a tragedy. A striking example of audience variation may be seen in Japan where the archaic, restrained Noh drama is met with dignified, nearly reverent attention, while the popular Kabuki audience may give the performance a noisy and enthusiastic demonstration. Spectators at an experimental or far-out production are often a strange mixture; some are sympathetic to any kind of provocation while others may remain aloof—baffled, shocked, or offended by what is going on.

As a social institution, the theater has at times served as a tribunal, a propaganda agency, a house of the devil, a temple of worship, a meeting place for disreputable characters, a showcase for ostentatious display, and a place for intellectual stimulation. Its status and function have depended on the audience that patronized it. Consider, for example, three representative audiences.

The Greek Audience

The theater of Greece was a religious institution, which every free male attended during the two main festivals—the Lenaia, primarily a local celebration since the seas were rough for travel in winter, was especially important for comedy. Since most of the audience were Athenians, Aristophanes took great delight in satirizing local situations and prominent people, and even the audience itself. The City Dionysia, which offered competition in tragedies, satyr

The Greek theater unified the audience, because there were no architectural barriers separating the spectators from one another or from the actors. A performance was a communal celebration.

plays, and choral singing was a more serious occasion, though still a celebration. They came to share in the great searching problems of mankind—problems which elevated the human spirit through suffering.

The Athenian audience was remarkable because of their great zest for living and thinking. Art, literature, philosophy, and logic were not mere subjects of contemplation for them. They were an active, inquiring people with an unquenchable thirst for learning. Their interests and tastes ranged widely, so that their infrequent dramatic productions could accommodate the tragic grandeur of Aeschylus and the comic irreverence of Aristophanes—whose uninhibited shafts of ridicule are a commentary on the amazing tolerance of Greek society.

The Greeks were a knowledgeable audience, steeped in their literary heritage, with keen ears for the rhythm and texture of language, and so thoroughly familiar with the plays of their time that they could identify specific passages of Euripidean and Aeschylean dialogue in Aristophanes' comedy, *The Frogs.* Such an audience invited dramas of great ideas and magnificent language. The culture that produced the idea of the golden mean—moderation in all things—led to a drama that was clear and logically organized, usually free from the excesses of pathos and sentiment. Their search for truth in life resulted in drama that was unflinchingly and relentlessly honest in confronting evil, suffering, and catastrophe. Their intellectual tolerance and sense of balance enabled them to see the sense and nonsense of the Aristophanic satire that scathingly attacked the follies of the time. The Athenians of the fifth century B.C. were astonishingly civilized human beings and their level of culture is nowhere reflected so admirably as in the dramas that were created for their pleasure and edification.

The Elizabethan Audience

Like the Greeks, the Elizabethans had an enormous enthusiasm for life. Shakespeare's time was one of remarkable intellectual ferment, with great interest in language, literature, music, and politics. The Elizabethans viewed human be-

The audience at the Globe Theater as visualized by C. Walter Hodges in Shakespeare's Theater. *This view looking toward the stage shows spectators standing in the pit, while others occupy the galleries. The drawing conveys the feeling of intimacy that characterized the Elizabethan playhouse even though it may have seated as many as 2,500 spectators.*

ings as creatures of great potential. The spirit of the times was positive, dynamic, tumultuous.

The theater reflected the climate of the age. It was a professional theater to which more than 30,000 customers a week flocked to see half a dozen competing companies in London offer the richest concentration of dramatic fare that the world has ever known. The theater appealed to the public's taste for pageantry and action, which elsewhere manifested itself in masques, processionals, and bear-baiting. The plays capitalized on the audience's interest in language, and the Elizabethan playwright enthusiastically followed the practice of medieval drama in putting as much vigorous and vivid action on stage as possible. Such a combination of words and action enlarged the appeal of drama so that all the motley audience could find something to suit its pleasure in the play. For the groundlings, there was exciting and violent action and raucous comedy. For the discriminating, there was delight in the magnificent language and food for thought in the elevated ideas. The Elizabethan audience's interests and tastes covered a wide range, and for it the playwright wrote both serious and comic dramas, which were full-bodied, exuberant images of a turbulent and heady age.

The Restoration Audience

The Restoration audience offers a sharp contrast to the Elizabethan. When Charles II returned to the throne, the theater became the preoccupation of the court. The audience was made up of fashionable wits, fops, beaux, parasites, and women of easy virtue. So limited was the audience that only two theaters were active in London, despite the fact that the population had doubled since Elizabethan times. For twelve years one theater was sufficient to accommodate this narrow following. It was a plaything for fashionable people. Such patronage resulted in drama that was artificial and deliberately unconcerned with the stern realities of life. When the Restoration playwright attempted to write serious heroic dramas, the result was exaggerated and false pseudoclassic plays full of excessive emotion. The special achievement of the period was high comedy, which dealt with the foibles of social conduct rather than ethics. Puritan morality was satirized. Comedies dealt with the complications of intrigue and defects of manners. The level of the playwrights' subject matter was offset by their brilliant use of language. They achieved a high polish in their repartee and their eloquence of style. The limited audience allowed the playwright to capitalize on personal invective and local and timely allusions. Thus, Restoration comedy is a particularly explicit example of the effect of an audience on the drama.

Perhaps these three historical examples are enough to make the point that people come to the theater for a variety of purposes, and that they constitute a vital force on the writing and production of plays.

The Modern Audience

In Europe and England, the professional theater is an established cultural institution; nearly every major city boasts of at least one or more permanent residential companies offering a continuous repertory of classical and new plays. In West Germany there are over 200 professional theaters and in England more than 50 residential repertory companies enjoy government subsidies. Such support makes possible a permanent audience, knowledgeable in the ways of the theater, which enables the producing group to work out a varied and continuous program of plays with some sense of security not directly related to immediate box office appeal.

In this country we have been without a permanent dramatic tradition. We have no national theater and no American classical repertory, but we have had a long background of professional production, especially before the coming of the film. The development of television following World War II had a pronounced effect on both motion pictures and live theater. The film has been forced to search for new ways to attract an audience. The availability of so much free entertainment came at a time of rising production costs and higher ticket prices. One of the reactions to this was to expand the off-Broadway theater where costs could be cut and new plays and different kinds of theater could be experimented with. By the mid-fifties nearly 100 such theaters were in operation in out-of-the-way auditoriums, churches, and halls. But they often became "farm clubs" for the main theaters, which picked off the most promising new talent and opened their doors to the experiments that had proved most appealing. The next development was the off-off-Broadway theater, which began in coffeehouses, cafes, and clubs and offered an opportunity for scores of new playwrights to show their works with minimum production facilities to audiences that had little or no contact with the main commercial attractions. From these experimental groups have come some of our freshest ideas and most promising talent in acting, directing, designing, and playwriting. They also created a more tolerant, open audience for all kinds of theater.

Meanwhile the regional theater has become a potent force with more than 60 permanent companies that are not only developing their own audiences and corps of production talent, but also staging new plays that find their way to Broadway and other theaters. There are now more actors making a living in the theaters outside of New York than on Broadway. In addition college and university theaters, community and children's theaters are developing audiences for the future. The National Endowment for the Arts, an agency established by federal legislation, has given a modicum of support to more than 50 residential and experimental groups. Three dozen university resident companies now augment the American theater scene. Outside of the mainstream, performers are finding and creating their own audiences in such ventures as Peter Schumann's Bread and Puppet Theater, guerrilla theaters, "performances," happenings, and mime troupes performing in the streets, at shopping centers, rallies, parades, and demonstrations, taking theater back to the people.

Few playwrights have been more concerned with the nature of audience response than Brecht, who wanted to radically change it. He contrasts the traditional reaction with his own:

> The audience in the dramatic theater says: Yes, I have felt that way too.—That's how I am.—That is only natural.—That will always be so.—This person's suffering shocks me because he has no way out. This is great art: everything in it is self-evident.—I weep with the weeping, I laugh with the laughing.
>
> The audience in the epic theater says: I wouldn't have thought that.—People shouldn't do things like that.—That's extremely odd, almost unbelievable.—This has to stop.—This person's suffering shocks me, because there might be a way out for him —This is great art: nothing in it is self-evident.—I laugh over the weeping, and I weep over the laughing.[2]

Artaud, on the other hand, seeks the complete absorption of the audience:

> It is a question then of making the theater, in the proper sense of the word, a function; something as localized and as precise as the circulation of the blood in the arteries or the apparently chaotic development of dream images in the brain, and this is to be accomplished through involvement, a genuine enslavement of the attention.[3]

Grotowski, like Artaud, seeks a special kind of involvement:

> We do not cater to the man who goes to the theater to satisfy a social need for contact with culture: in other words, to have something to talk about to his friends and be able to say that he has seen this or that play and that it was interesting. We are concerned with the spectator who has genuine spiritual needs and who really wishes, through confrontation with the performance, to analyze himself . . . toward a search for the truth about himself and his mission in life.[4]

Grotowski was keenly interested in controlling the audience as well as the players and he often specified the performance place and the number of spectators to be admitted. An example of how he included the audience in his production design for the *Acropolis* is described by James Roose-Evans:

> The production is set on a large rectangular stage standing in the middle of the audience. The platform is piled high with scrap metal. A ragged violinist appears and summons the rest of the cast, who hobble on in sacks and wooden boots. The action takes the form of daydreams in the breaks, between work. The seven actors attack the mound of rusting metal, hammering in unison, and fixing twisted pipes to struts over the audience's heads. The audience, however, is not involved. They represent the dead. . . . At the end of *Acropolis* there is an ecstatic procession following the image of the Saviour (a headless corpse) into a paradise which is also the extermination chamber.[5]

It is clear that no one kind of audience will satisfy these theorists. They agree

---

[2]Bertolt Brecht, "Theater for Learning or Theater for Pleasure," trans. Edith Anderson, *Mainstream*, 11 (June 1958).

[3]Antonin Artaud, *The Theater and Its Double* (New York: Grove Press, Inc., 1958).

[4]Jerzy Grotowski, quoted in *Time*, October 29, 1969.

[5]James Roose-Evans, *The Experimental Theater* (New York: Universe Books, 1970).

The Constant Prince *at the Polish Laboratory Theater, directed by
Jerzy Grotowski, setting by Jerzy Gurawski. The playing area is
surrounded by a fence over which the spectators view the performance.*

only on a seriousness of purpose in the uses of the theater to achieve their
various responses.

Another kind of audience is sought for by groups concerned with a
"people's theater." A number of dedicated people have labored to make live
drama available to the culturally impoverished.

In France in recent years efforts were made to eradicate the image of the
theater as an after-dinner diversion for the elite by taking plays to people
unfamiliar with the theater, especially workers in factories and young people in
school.

Roger Planchon, an outstanding director in Lyons, described his ambition
to expand the influence of significant drama.

Among theater people, there's a desire to save the theater by going beyond it—into
revolution, experiment for its own sake, the science of the actor. In this respect Peter

Brook and Ariane Mnouchkine, and agit-prop theater communes are all on the same track. They want to make theater more than it is, they want to reform the theater by putting it at the service of other ends. It's a very Christian idea—redemption.[6]

Pierre Debauche, aware of the vast minority of people who never attended the theater, describes an approach made to reach audiences in the suburbs of Paris:

We began with the idea that we should work to serve the inhabitants of a town rather than the spectators of a theater. . . . We are trying, outside the theater and in the town as a whole, to educate the imagination. Our task is to try to build bridges between all the ghettos of the town. Universities, primary schools, shanty towns are all ghettos of one kind or another and we wish to link them up to each other so that things will begin to happen, if possible independently of us. All we will need for that is standards, a building, decent heating and the keys to get in.[7]

In trying to reach a theatrically unsophisticated audience, many of whom were factory workers, Planchon realized that his audience was more familiar with film, so he adapted cinematic technique to his performances and made his material more relevant to the spectators. For example, in doing old plays he centered attention on the servants rather than the leading characters. He poked fun at *The Cid* and used *Hellzapoppin* vaudeville techniques in historical pieces. He asked his audiences what stories they would like to see, and when they requested *The Three Musketeers*, he worked up a dramatic version that won wide popularity everywhere. Planchon was following the influence of Jean Vilar who, during his leadership of the Théâtre National Populaire, did much to "demystify" the drama in updating productions of such classics as *The Trojan Women* and Aristophanes' *Peace*. The popular movement also turned up an interesting playwright, Armand Gattis, whose *13 Sons of Blaise* appealed to the laboring class audience with its depiction of the dreams of 13 workers living in an area scheduled for demolition.

Germany has a record of Volksbühnen theater productions dating back to the 1890s. Now there are scores of fine theaters and productions resulting from the folk movement. In England there has been considerable support in recent years for touring companies such as The Young Vic Company and Ed Berman's Fun Art Bus, playing to rural and suburban audiences in schoolrooms, factories, or out in the open—wherever a crowd gathers. In Italy, Dario Fo has spent years in staging agit-prop plays satirizing capitalism, the Church, and the government—playing under all sorts of circumstances—often just one step ahead of the police.

The United States is teeming with all sorts of theater groups working out their versions of what theater should be—often in makeshift conditions—in black ghettoes, inner cities, vineyards, schoolhouses, and parks. With astonishing vitality they attract and touch all kinds of audiences.

[6]Roger Planchon, "The Theatre National Populaire," *Performance*, no. 4, (September–October 1972).
[7]Pierre Debauche, *Theater Quarterly*, 6, (Autumn 1976), p. 69.

The rebellion in the theater in the sixties here and abroad aimed at giving audiences a new kind of theatrical experience. Experimental groups in direct opposition to the "canned entertainment" of television and movies tried to capitalize on *live* theater that could jolt the spectators out of their seats and give them a fresh experience. Tom O'Horgan, whose stock in trade is a high level of energy, said: "You have to keep nudging the audience; to say, 'You're alive. You do exist, right now!' You try to make the audience feel that it's not something that's nailed to a chair." O'Horgan demonstrated his theatricalism in his famous production of the rock musical *Hair*.

The audience in the new theater very often sees a different kind of drama than the theater-goer in the commercial playhouse. The story line gives way to sensory experience oftentimes multilayered, with multifocus and simultaneous action. Instead of following clearly defined characters involved in a plot, spectators respond to the moment-by-moment stimuli that impinge on them. They are interested in what is happening now, rather than what will happen next. Lighting, scenic effects, film, projections, and sound are often used as separate entities as well as for support. The theater worker operates in a world of permissiveness since there are almost no barriers on subject matter, nudity, obscenity, and behavior. Anything goes. As a result, there is a good deal of straining for effect and an exaggerated use of novelty and sensational effect, often without control or taste. Once upon a time theater-goers took seats in the theater, settled back in the darkness, and drifted off to a never-never land released from mundane cares. Now they may sit on the floor or in bleachers, with no assurance that they will be aloof from the show. They may be invited to participate—to dance, to come on stage, to argue, to ask questions. They are teased, insulted, fondled, whispered to, offended. Experimental production seeks a new immediacy, intensity, and exuberance in an effort to reach all levels of audience consciousness. The rebellion is directed against a narrow concept of drama as amusement and toward making theater a means of enlightenment and release, a place of wonder, celebration, fulfillment, and release.

Bibliography

BLAU, HERBERT, *The Impossible Theater: A Manifesto*. New York: Macmillian Publishing Co., Inc., 1964.

LEE, VERA G., *Quest for a Public, French Popular Theater Since 1945*. Cambridge, Mass.: Schenckman Publishing Co., Inc., 1970.

MCLUHAN, MARSHALL, *Understanding Media*. New York: McGraw-Hill Book Company, 1964.

SONTAG, SUSAN, *Against Interpretation*. New York: Farrar, Straus & Giroux, Inc., 1966.

STYAN, J. L., *Drama, Stage and Audience*. Cambridge: Cambridge University Press, 1975.

YURKA, BLANCHE, *Dear Audience: A Guide to the Enjoyment of the Theater*. Englewood Cliffs, N.J.: Prentice-Hall, Inc., 1959.

Glossary

(The reader should also refer to the Index, since many terms are given extended treatment in the text.)

Acting Area.   Traditionally, that part of the theater occupied by the performers. Usually the stage, but in experimental productions it may be any area used by the actor.

Aesthetic Distance.   The physical and psychological detachment between a work of art and those who respond to it. Experimentalists are now trying to eliminate this area of separation.

Alienation.   A technique used by Bertolt Brecht in his "epic dramas" to negate the emotional involvement of his audience in order to make an intellectual appeal for his message.

Antagonist.   The character of force in opposition to the protagonist or hero.

Apron.   The forestage extending beyond the proscenium arch.

Arena Stage.   An arrangement for "central staging" of plays with the acting area in the middle of the room, surrounded by the audience.

Aside.   A dramatic convention in which the actor speaks private thoughts aloud, unnoticed by the other actors.

Automatism.   A comic theory based on mechanical repetition. *See* Bergson in Index.

Backing.   Stage scenery used to mask the openings so as to prevent the audience from seeing the offstage areas.

Beat.   A basic unit for rehearsal.

Blocking.   The director's organization of the stage movements of his cast.

Bourgeois Drama.   Pseudoserious plays involving middle-class society, with the general emphasis on pathos and morality.

Business.   The individual actions of the characters in a play; for example, taking a drink, smoking a pipe, writing a letter.

Catharsis.   The act of purging, cleansing, or purifying; usually associated with tragedy.

Chorus.   In Greek drama a group, varying in size from 12 to 50, that recited lines in unison. As the first element to develop in Greek drama, it provided information and, in its most elaborate state, commentary on past actions and forebodings about future ones. With the invention of the second and third actors, the chorus gradually became less important.

344

Classical Drama. Usually refers to the dramas of ancient Greece and Rome. *See also* Neoclassicism.

Climax. The strongest point of emotional tension. Most plays have a series of climaxes culminating in a major climax.

Comedy. Drama designed to amuse the audience, often showing human frailities and foibles. Usually ends happily.

Comedy of Humours. Comedy of character based on a dominant trait, such as greed or jealousy. Popularized by the Elizabethan playwright Ben Jonson.

Comedy of Manners. Social comedy wittily satirizing characters in terms of their shortcomings as measured against a specific code of conduct; for example, *The School for Scandal*.

Commedia dell'Arte. Improvised Italian comedy of the sixteenth, seventeenth, and eighteenth centuries put together out of stock roles in formula situations. Performed by small companies of professional actors who were very popular all over Europe.

Confidant(e). A minor character paired with a major one, who shares the latter's confidences, usually for expository purposes.

Constructivism. An approach to staging developed by the Russians in the 1920s which was anti-decorative, anti-illusionistic. The setting was a framework for action.

Conventions. Common agreements between theater worker and spectator concerning the manner of production, that is, certain "ground rules" that determine how the game is played; for example, the physical separation of actor and spectator.

Crisis. A time of decision; a turning point.

Cycle Plays. Medieval plays dealing with scriptural stories from Creation to the Last Judgment.

Cyclorama. Drapery or canvas usually hung in a half circle to mask the wings and backstage areas. It often represents the sky, or it may be a simple drapery.

Denouement. The resolution or unraveling of a plot so that an equilibrium is usually restored.

Deus ex Machina. In the Greek theater, a "god from a machine." A mechanical device used for the intervention of some outside agent to resolve the plot. As a general term, it refers to the intervention of any outside force to bring about a desired end.

Diction. Aristotle's fourth element—the language of the play; the words that the actors speak.

Discovery. The revelation of important information about the characters, their motivations, feelings, and relationships. Discovery is often accompanied by recognition (*anagnorisis*), when a character learns the truth about himself.

Doubling. One actor playing more than one character in a single play. In the ancient Greek theater, the actor usually doubled.

Downstage. The area of the stage closest to the audience.

Drame. Any play that deals seriously with themes, characters, and ideas of the present day.

Dress Rehearsal. A rehearsal conducted under complete performance conditions, including all technical aspects.

Eccyclema. A movable platform in the Greek theater, thought to have been positioned in the central opening of the *skene*, usually to show corpses.

Empathy. Literally, "feeling into"; the imitative motor response of the spectator.

Environmental Theater. The performers play around, above, behind, and among the spectators. Any environment can be used as a theater that has enough space for performing and viewing. Often takes place in "found spaces."

Epic Theater. The nonillusionistic theater of Piscator and Brecht, dealing with broad themes, with loosely organized plots presented in a frankly theatrical style.

Exposition. Dramatic techniques for acquainting the audience with antecedent information and background material.

Expressionism. A style of drama which attempts to present "inner reality," the man beneath the skin. Often distorts the normal to present symbolic action in dreamlike sequences.

Farce. Low comedy, written for amusement, usually emphasizing physical action.

Flat. The most useful element of stage scenery, consisting of a wooden frame generally covered with muslin or canvas to represent walls.

High Comedy. A general term referring to comedy that evokes thoughtful laughter through its concern with character, ideas, and dialogue.

Histrionic Sensibility. The spectator's ability to perceive and discriminate actions and visual symbols, just as in music the trained ear discriminates sounds.

Illusionistic Theater. Any theater that attempts to create the effect of an actual experience—authentic places, real people, and genuine situations.

Imagery. Communication by means of concrete and particular meanings through the use of language devices such as metaphors, similes, and clusters of related words.

Improvisation. Spontaneous invention by the performers of actions, dialogue, and characters usually around a basic idea, situation, or theme. Although widely used for actors' rehearsal and training, it is now employed in happenings, performances, and other experimental forms of theater.

Incongruity. A comic theory based on the use of contrast.

Irony. A discrepancy between what a character plans or anticipates and what actually occurs.

Linear Plot. A plot that follows a carefully articulated sequence of action generally organized in chronological order.

Magnitude. The elevation that Aristotle says should characterize tragedy. May refer to character, thought, diction, and spectacle.

Mask. To conceal the backstage, wings, or flies from the spectator's view.

Melodrama. Pseudoserious drama that is played at the game level, employing exciting action aimed at audience involvement. Usually ends with poetic justice. Popular in nineteenth century but still stageworthy in present-day mystery and suspense plays.

Method Acting. Stanislavski attempted to devise a systematic approach that enabled the actor to gain more control over himself and his performance. Involves control of the voice and body, the "correct state of being" on stage, and inner psychological response as the basis for outer physical actions.

Mise-en-Scene. All of the visual aspects of the staged production.

Mixed Media Performances. Experiments that may involve a combination of the arts and technical equipment such as tapes, slides, and films.

Motivation. Logical justification, or the giving of plausible reasons, for the behavior of the characters in a play.

Myth. Archetypal stories that suggest widespread cultural beliefs, events, and feelings.

Naturalism. An exaggerated form of realism that emphasizes a sordid and deterministic view of life. First appeared in France in the late nineteenth century as a response to the scientific revolution.

Neoclassicism. An attempt in the sixteenth, seventeenth, and eighteenth centuries to "regularize" dramatic techniques by following scrupulously what were thought to be practices of the ancients, e.g., adherence to the "unities," use of a chorus, preservation of "decorum" in language and action, avoiding acts of violence on stage, and use of only royal or noble characters.

Objective. A dramatic character's goal.

Open Stage. Sometimes an attempt to break away from the proscenium-arch theater so as to play as close as possible to the audience. Also, experimental productions freed from the strictures of a prepared script.

Orchestra. In the fifth century B.C. Greek theater, the large circle (approximately 22 meters across) that served as the playing area. Located between the *theatron* and the *skene*.

Pathos. The "suffering" aspect of drama, especially that quality which evokes pity.

Peripetia. In ancient Greek tragedy a reversal, usually in the protagonist's fortunes.

Pity and Fear. The emotions aroused and purged in tragedy. Pity goes beyond pathos to include compassion and shared grief; fear goes beyond fright to include awe and wonder.

Plot. The structure of the incidents; the formative agent of drama; dramatic composition.

Point of Attack. The moment in a play when a precipitating force sets the mechanism in motion and disrupts the equilibrium; the first complication.

Practical. Functional, utilitarian; for example, doors and windows that are workable, not simply decorative.

Presentational Staging. Production that is frankly theatrical, free from the illusion of reality. The performer confronts the audience directly.

Probability. An attempt by the playwright to establish credibility or, as Aristotle says, to make the action of a play seem "necessary and probable."

Project. Vocally, increasing the volume so as to be heard by the entire audience. Technically, showing enlarged slides or films on backgrounds as a part of the scenery.

Prologue. The introduction to a play, sometimes a monologue delivered by an actor directly to the audience. In classical drama, that part of the play preceding the chorus's entrance.

Properties (Props). Includes objects used by the actors in the production of a play, such as letters, weapons, food.

Proscenium Arch. The architectural frame through which the spectator views the stage.

Protagonist.   The chief character in a play.

Purgation.   *See* Catharsis.

Rake.   To slant the stage floor so that it is higher away from the audience in order to aid in the perspective illusion. Also, the slant of the auditorium floor, designed to give all of the audience a good view.

Realism.   Drama that attempts to establish authenticity through the use of the observed facts of daily existence.

Recognition.   *See* Discovery.

Representational Staging.   Production that imitates experience, that seeks to create the illusion of reality.

Reversal.   An Aristotelian critical term *(peripetia)* referring to a sudden change in the fortunes of the protagonist.

Ritual.   Social customs, events, and ceremonies whose repeated actions are directed toward specific goals.

Romanticism.   Concerns itself with adventurous, emotionally loaded characters in remote and exotic circumstances; in contrast to classical drama.

Satire Comedy.   Uses wit as a weapon to correct antisocial behavior.

Scenario.   The skeletal outline of the plot.

Setting.   The scenic environment of the action.

Skene.   Originally a small hut at the back of the orchestra in the Greek theater, which later became the stage-house.

"Slice-of Life."   Attempt to give the impression of unorganized actuality without an apparent beginning, middle, or end. Used principally in naturalistic drama.

Soliloquy.   A "solo" speech of a single character, which is usually taken to be introspective analysis; a character's internal thoughts.

Spectacle.   The visual aspects of a produced play.

Spine.   Stanislavski's idea of "line of through-action" of an acting role. A means of connecting motivations and objectives of all parts of a play.

Stage Left or Right.   Left or right side of the stage from the actor's point of view facing the audience.

Stylization.   Theatrical production that usually emphasizes the visual aspects and the manner of performing.

Subtext.   Interaction beneath the surface of the spoken language of a play.

Surrealism.   A literary movement that began in France in the 1920s, exploiting the irrational and unconscious with emphasis on dreams.

Sympathetic Magic.   Primitive ceremonies used in an attempt to enlist the help of the gods by enacting the desired objectives.

Theatricalism.   The direct use of all aspects of the theater to exploit the play as a staged work.

Theatron.   The seating area in the Greek theater.

Theme.   The general subject of the playwright's concern; his interpretation of the meaning of his action.

Thought.   Aristotle's third element. The reasoning aspect of drama—the argument, the theme, the meaning.

Thrust Stage. A platform or "open stage" projecting into the auditorium, bringing the performer in close proximity to the audience.

Tracking. An approach to performance in which several elements develop simultaneously in parallel tracks, such as music, images, and mime. The elements may remain separate from one another.

Tragic Flaw. An Aristotelian concept of an "error in judgment," or missing the mark. A frailty in an otherwise good and prominent character that accounts for his or her downfall.

Tragic Hero. The central figure in a tragedy. Aristotle described the hero as a prominent person "not pre-eminently virtuous and just, whose misfortune is brought upon him not by vice and depravity but by some error of judgment."

Tragicomedy. That form of drama that is serious and evokes apprehension for the fate of the protagonist but ends happily.

Transactions. An approach to action through the "games theory" of Eric Berne that analyzes behavior in terms of the social, or overt, level and the psychological, or concealed, level.

Unity of Action. Aristotle stipulated that all parts of a plot should be essential and organic to make a complete whole, free from digressions or subplots.

Unity of Place. All action occurs in a single locale. By convention, the Greeks usually observed this unity.

Unity of Time. The action of a play takes place, as Aristotle suggested, "within the single revolution of the sun." Covers a short span of time.

Upstage. The acting area farthest from the audience.

"Well-made Play." Dramatic technique associated with French playwrights Scribe and Sardou in which all aspects of plot are carefully worked out in a logical cause-and-effect relationship.

Wings. The area offstage of the acting area.

General Bibliography

BENTLEY, ERIC, *The Life of the Drama*. New York: Barnes & Noble Books, 1967.

BROCKETT, OSCAR G., *History of the Theater*. Boston: Allyn & Bacon, Inc., 1974.

BRUSTEIN, ROBERT SANFORD, *The Culture Watch: Essays on Theater and Society*. New York: Alfred A. Knopf, Inc., 1975.

CORRIGAN, ROBERT, *The World of the Theater*. Glenview, Ill.: Scott, Foresman & Company, 1979.

ESSLIN, MARTIN, ed., *The Encyclopedia of World Theater*, New York: Charles Scribner's Sons, 1977.

GUERNSEY, OTIS L., *Directory of the American Theater, 1894–1971*. New York: Dodd, Mead & Company, 1972.

HARTNOLL, PHYLLIS, *The Oxford Companion to the Theatre* (3rd ed.). New York: Oxford University Press, 1967.

HEWITT, BERNARD WOLCOTT, *Theater U.S.A., 1668–1957*. New York: McGraw-Hill Book Company, 1959.

HUGHES, LANGSTON, and MILTON MELTZER, *Black Magic: A Pictorial History of the Negro in American Entertainment*. Englewood Cliffs, N.J.: Prentice-Hall, Inc., 1967.

MITCHELL, LOFTEN, *Black Drama: The Story of the American Negro in the Theater*. New York: Hawthorne Books, Inc., 1967.

———, *Voices of the Black Theater*. Clifton, N.J.: James T. White & Company, 1975.

NICOLL, ALLARDYCE, *The Development of the Theater*. London: Harrap, 1966.

TAYLOR, J. R., *The Penguin Dictionary of the Theater*. London: Penguin Books, 1966.

VINSON, JAMES, ed., *Contemporary Dramatists*. New York: St. Martin's Press, 1977.

Text Acknowledgments

Page 9: *Death of a Salesman* by Arthur Miller (New York: Viking Press, 1949).

Pages 10–11: *The Lower Depths* by Maxim Gorky, translated by Dorcas Hatlen.

Page 12: *Desire Under the Elms* by Eugene O'Neill (New York: Random House, 1924).

Pages 13–14: Reprinted by permission of S. G. Phillips, Inc., from *Look Back in Anger*, by John Osbourne. Copyright ©1957 by S. G. Phillips, Inc.

Pages 50–51: From *The Birthday Party*. Copyright ©1959 by Harold Pinter, pp. 87–88. Reprinted by permission of Grove Press, Inc.

Pages 71–72: From *Oedipus The King* and *Antigone* by Sophocles. Translated by Peter D. Arnott. Copyright ©1960. Reprinted by permission of Appleton-Century-Crofts, Educational Division, Meredith Corporation.

Pages 155–56: Eugene O'Neill, *The Hairy Ape*. Copyright 1922 by Random House. Reprinted by permission of the publishers.

Pages 184–85 and 187–88: Samuel Beckett, *Waiting for Godot*. Copyright ©1954 by Grove Press, Inc. Published by Grove Press, Inc.

Pages 186–87: Eugène Ionesco, *The Bald Soprano*, from Four Plays by Eugène Ionesco, trans. by Donald M. Allen. Copyright ©1958 by Grove Press, Inc. Published by Grove Press, Inc.

Pages 222–23: K. S. Alekseev, *Stanislavsky Produces Othello*, trans. by Helen Nowak. Reprinted by permission of Geoffrey Bles, Ltd., London, 1948.

Page 227: Peter Brook, "Introduction to *Marat/Sade*" by Peter Weiss (New York: Atheneum, 1965). From the introduction by Peter Brook to the play, *The Persecution and Assassination of Jean-Paul Marat as Performed by the Inmates of the Assylum of Charenton Under the Direction of the Marquis de Sade*, by Peter Weiss. Copyright ©1965 by John Calder Ltd. Reprinted by permission of Atheneum Publishers.

Pages 240–41: from Stanislavsky Directs by Nikolai M. Gorchakov, trans. by Miriam Goldina, copyright 1954 by Funk & Wagnalls. Reprinted by permission of the publisher.

Page 245–46: Lillian Ross, "Profiles: The Player," *The New Yorker*, October 21, 1961, October 28, 1961, and November 4, 1961. Reprinted by permission. Copyright ©1961 by The New Yorker Magazine, Inc., October 28, 1961.

Page 263: Mordecai Gorelik, *New Theatres for Old*. Copyright, 1940, 1962, by Mordecai Gorelik. Reprinted by special arrangement with Samuel French, Inc.

Pages 321–24 and 340: Antonin Artaud, *The Theater and Its Double*. Copyright ©1958 by Grove Press. Translated by Mary Caroline Richards, pp. 96–97. Reprinted by permission of the publisher.

Photograph Acknowledgments

Chapter 1:
Page 1, D. A. Harissiadis. Page 2, D. A. Harissiadis. Page 4, Conard, McCann, and Geoghegan, Inc., from C. Walter Hodges' *Shakespeare's Theater*, ©1964. Page 6, Peter Smith, courtesy of Stratford Shakespeare Festival, Ontario. Page 9, Page 11,

Theatermuseum, Munich. Page 13, left, Royal Shakespeare Co.; right, courtesy of Alley Theater, Houston. Page 14, Percy Paukschta, courtesy of Berliner Ensemble. Page 18, Martha Swope. Page 20, Albert F. C. Wehlburg, University of Florida. Page 22, D. A. Harissiadis.

Chapter 2:

Page 24, University of Missouri, Columbia. Page 29, Portland State University. Page 30, University of Missouri. Page 31, D. A. Harissiadis. Page 34, American Conservatory Theater. Page 37, Will Swalling, UCSB. Page 38, Steven Keull, courtesy of Mark Taper Forum, Los Angeles. Page 39, courtesy of Lincoln Center Repertory Theater, New York. Page 41, courtesy of North Carolina Playmakers Repertory Company. Page 42, courtesy of the University of Houston. Page 44, Mark Taper Forum. Page 46, Martha Swope. Page 51, courtesy of Wayne State University Theater. Page 53, Martha Swope. Page 56, courtesy of Victoria and Albert Museum. Page 57, courtesy Wayne State University.

Chapter 3:

Page 58, courtesy of American Shakespeare Festival in Connecticut. Page 62, courtesy of Prague National Theater. Page 63, D. A. Harissiadis. Page 66, D. A. Harissiadis. Page 67, courtesy of Berliner Ensemble. Page 68, D. A. Harissiadis. Page 69, Joe Cocks. Page 74, Keith Hardisty, courtesy of Indiana University. Page 75, courtesy of Wayne State University.

Chapter 4:

Page 77, Harvard Theater Collection. Page 81, courtesy of Victoria and Albert Museum. Page 82, Martha Swope. Page 83, courtesy of Victoria and Albert Museum. Page 84, Harvard Theater Collection. Page 88, Harvard Theater Collection. Page 90, Martha Swope. Page 91, Harvard Theater Collection. Page 93, courtesy of University of Minnesota. Page 94, Martha Swope. Page 95, courtesy of Wayne State University. Page 96, Jay Thompson, courtesy of Mark Taper Forum. Page 97, courtesy of The University of Illinois.

Chapter 5:

Page 99, courtesy of West Virginia University. Page 101, Will Swalling, University of California, Santa Barbara. Page 103, D. A. Harissiadis. Page 105, Tom Casella, courtesy Indiana University. Page 106, courtesy of University of Missouri. Page 107, courtesy of Cincinnati Playhouse in the Park. Page 108, Henry Waitt, courtesy of Asolo State Theater. Page 110, D. A. Harissiadis. Page 111, D. A. Harissiadis. Page 114, courtesy of Wayne State University. Page 118, courtesy of American Conservatory Theater. Page 119, Patti Russotti, courtesy of Indiana University. Page 121, courtesy American Conservatory Theater, San Francisco. Page 123, courtesy of Miami University, Ohio. Page 127, courtesy of Wayne State University. Page 129, courtesy of University of Arizona.

Chapter 6:

Page 137, courtesy of Asolo State Theater, Florida. Page 140, Steven Keull, courtesy of Mark Taper Forum. Page 141, Al MacKenzie, courtesy of Asolo State Theater, Florida. Page 142, courtesy of Dave Flaten. Page 143, Peter Balestrero, courtesy of University of Arizona. Page 144, Martha Swope. Page 145, Dennis Holmes, courtesy of Frederick Thon. Page 148, Richard Rose, courtesy of University of California, Davis. Page 147, Will Swalling, University of California, Santa Barbara. Page 150, Munich Theatermuseum. Page 153, courtesy New York City Museum. Page 155, Munich Theatermuseum.

Chapter 7:

Page 161, Jay Thompson, courtesy Mark Taper Forum. Page 163, courtesy Museum of Modern Art, Lillie P. Bliss. Page 164, courtesy Museum of Modern Art. Page 166,

355

Acknowledgments

The Munich Theatermuseum. Page 168, Ilse Buhs. Page 170, courtesy of Berliner Ensemble. Page 171, courtesy of Berliner Ensemble. Page 176, Will Swalling, University of California, Santa Barbara. Page 177, Francis Haar, courtesy University of Hawaii. Page 181, courtesy of Virginia Polytechnic Institute. Page 182, courtesy of Schiller Theater, Berlin. Page 183, courtesy of Royal Court Theater, London. Page 184, Mula-Haramaty, courtesy Cameri Theater, Tel-Aviv. Page 186, Will Swalling, courtesy of University of California, Santa Barbara. Page 192, courtesy Polish Laboratory Theater. Page 197, Ilse Buhs.

Chapter 8:

Page 207, courtesy Victoria and Albert Museum. Page 212, Francis Haar, courtesy University of Hawaii. Page 214, Marty Nordstrom, courtesy Guthrie Theater. Page 216, Joe Cocks. Page 217, Joe Cocks. Page 218, Martha Swope. Page 224, Peray Pavkschta, courtesy of Berliner Ensemble. Page 225, Hildegard Steinmetz, courtesy of Kammerspiele, Munich. Page 226, Dr. Jaromir Svoboda, courtesy of Prague National Theater. Page 229, Martha Swope.

Chapter 9:

Page 232, courtesy of Victoria and Albert Museum. Page 234, courtesy of Wayne State University. Page 235, courtesy of American Conservatory Theater. Page 236, Steven Keull, courtesy of Mark Taper Forum. Page 237, Martha Swope. Page 243, I. F. Holte, by permission of Royal Shakespeare Theater. Page 245, courtesy of Guthrie Theater. Page 247, Robert Ashley Wilson, courtesy of Guthrie Theater. Page 248, courtesy of Miami University, Ohio. Page 250, courtesy of Wayne State University. Page 251, courtesy of California State University, Chico. Page 252, Francis Haar, courtesy of University of Hawaii. Page 254, courtesy of Elizabeth Le Compte.

Chapter 10:

Page 258, Munich Theatermuseum. Page 259, courtesy of Prague National Theater. Page 261, Munich Theatermuseum. Page 264, Munich Theatermuseum. Page 265, courtesy of The New York Public Library, Astor, Lenox, and Tilden Foundations. Page 266, courtesy of University of Illinois. Page 267, Trinity Square Repertory Company, Providence. Page 272, courtesy of Lee Simonson Collection, New York Public Library. Page 273, courtesy of New York Public Library, Astor, Lenox, and Tilden Foundations. Page 275, courtesy of New York Public Library, Astor, Lenox, and Tilden Foundations. Pages 276 and 277, Ilse Buhs. Page 278, Ilse Buhs. Page 279, courtesy of Keita Asari. Page 280, Ilse Buhs. Page 281, courtesy of Miami University, Ohio. Page 282 top, Shigeko Higuchi, courtesy of Keita Asari; bottom, Ilse Buhs. Page 283, Karl Hakli, courtesy of Eugen Terttula. Page 284, Dr. Jaromir Svoboda, courtesy of Prague National Theater. Page 285, Dr. Jaromir Svoboda, courtesy of Prague National Theater. Page 286, Martha Swope. Page 287, Karl Hakli, courtesy of Eugen Terttula. Page 288, drawing by permission of Antoine Vitez. Page 289, courtesy of Trinity Square Repertory Co., Providence. Page 290, Dr. Jaromir Svoboda.

Chapter 11:

Page 294, drawing by Gerda Becker With; from *The Living Stage*, courtesy of William Melnitz. Page 295, D. A. Harissiadis. Page 296, D. A. Harissiadis. Page 300, drawing by Gerda Becker With, from *The Living Stage*, courtesy of William Melnitz. Page 302, courtesy of Victoria and Albert Museum. Page 303, from Walter Hodges' *Shakespear's Theater*, Coward, McCann, and Geoglegan. Page 304, Dwaine Smith, courtesy of Oregon Shakespeare Festival. Page 305, drawing by Gerda Becker With, from *The Living Stage*, courtesy of William Melnitz. Page 307, courtesy of Rockefeller Collection, Yale University. Page 308, courtesy of Munich Teater. Page 311, courtesy of Munich Teatermuseum. Page 313, Architectural Press, Ltd., London. Page 314, courtesy of the Tyrone Guthrie Theater. Page 316, courtesy of Stratford Festival Theater. Page 317, courtesy of Tyrone Guthrie Theater. Page 318, courtesy of Mark Taper Forum. Page 319, courtesy of Arena Theater. Page 320, courtesy of Lucia

Sturdza Bulandra Theater. Page 321, courtesy of Mannheim National Theater. Page 322, Architectural Press Ltd., London. Page 323, Architectural Press, Ltd., London. Page 325, by permission of Peter Brook. Page 326, by permission of Peter Brook. Page 327, courtesy of Deutsches Schauspielhaus, Hamburg. Page 328, by permission of Peter Brook.

Chapter 12:

Page 332, courtesy of Marie Starr. Page 334, courtesy of Victoria and Albert Museum. Page 336, D. A. Harissiadis. Page 337, from *Shakespeare's Theater*, by C. Walter Hodges, Coward, McCann, Geogegan. Page 341, courtesy of Jerzy Grotowski and the Polish Laboratory Theater.

Index